SHOW BUSINESS KILLS

Other novels by Iris Rainer Dart

THE BOYS IN THE MAIL ROOM

BEACHES

'TIL THE REAL THING COMES ALONG

I'LL BE THERE

THE STORK CLUB

Show Business Kills

A NOVEL BY

Iris Rainer Dart

LITTLE, BROWN AND COMPANY
BOSTON   NEW YORK   TORONTO   LONDON

First Edition

This book is a work of fiction. Names, characters, places, and incidents
are either products of the author's imagination or used fictitiously. Any
resemblance to actual events, locales, or persons, living or dead, is entirely coincidental. The names of some real celebrities appear as characters in the book to give a sense of time and place. However, their actions
and motivations are entirely fictitious, and should not in any way be considered real or factual.

Excerpt from "I'm Still Here" by Stephen Sondheim. Copyright © 1971
by Range Road Music Inc., Quartet Music Inc., Ritling Music,
Inc., and Burthen Music Co., Inc. Used by permission.

Library of Congress Cataloging-in-Publication Data

Dart, Iris Rainer.
    Show business kills: a novel / by Iris Rainer Dart.—1st ed.
        p.   cm.
    ISBN 0-316-17334-7
    1. Motion picture industry—California—Los Angeles—Fiction.
2. Middle-aged women—California—Los Angeles—Fiction.
3. Friendship—California—Los Angeles—Fiction. 4. Murder—
California—Los Angeles—Fiction. 5. Hollywood (Los Angeles,
Calif.)—Fiction. I. Title.
PS3554.A78S56 1995
813'.54—dc20   94-22947

10 9 8 7 6 5 4 3 2

MV-NV

Published simultaneously in Canada
by Little, Brown & Company (Canada) Limited

Printed in the United States of America

This book is dedicated to my extraordinary women friends, who have carried me, taught me, supported me, propped me up during my worst times, and cheered me on during my best. I love you all and am so grateful for the love you give me in return.

First you're another
Sloe-eyed vamp.
Then someone's mother
Then you're camp.
Then you career from career to career.
I'm almost through my memoirs
And I'm here.

Stephen Sondheim, *Follies*

ACKNOWLEDGMENTS

The author wishes to thank Jeff Galpin, M.D., Dorothy Sivitz Jenkins, M.D., Joyce Brotman, Wendy Riche, Judith McConnell, M. E. Loree Fishmann, Shelly Glaser, Barry Adelman, Dr. Melanie Allen, Susan Schwartz, Wendy Duffy, Karen Fell, Joe Gunn, Sharleen Cooper-Cohen, the cast and crew of "General Hospital," Elaine Markson, and Fredrica Friedman. And of course there would never be a book without Rachel, Greg, and Steve.

SHOW BUSINESS KILLS

ONE

"LOOK UP, sweetheart, look up. That's it. Now I'll just add a little more concealer under your eyes and you'll be all set." Bert, the makeup man, was wearing too much Royal Lyme cologne, and Jan didn't have the heart to tell him that, at this hour of the morning, the thick, tangy scent made her nauseous.

"As soon as I finish this, I'll whisk a little mascara on your lashes, and then you can take the rollers out and get your hair combed." Bert's face was so close to hers that while he patted the creamy cover-up under her lower lashes she could smell the Tic Tac he held in his mouth as an antidote to coffee breath, sometimes even while he was still drinking the coffee. But it was Bert's constant barrage of chatter, always in the form of well-meant advice, that got to her.

"If you'd like the benefit of my personal and my professional opinion . . . ," he said, while he moved his hand down to Jan's chin, raised her face up into the light, and squinted so he could get a better look at his work.

His opinion, professional or otherwise, was the last thing she wanted. In fact she'd been so lost in her own thoughts, she wasn't even sure where his latest story had drifted. All she wanted was for him to hurry up and finish her face, so she could get back to reading the new script pages for Friday's show. But Bert took her silence for interest and kept talking.

"As far as I'm concerned, and I know a little bit about this subject, to say the least, Frank Kamer is 'the man,' " Bert announced. "He is a star in the plastic surgery firmament. When that genius gets through with you, you can't even see a tiny scar.

He did Goldie Hawn and Streisand, who both deny it, and Dolly Parton, who flaunts it, and all three of them are flawless."

The last was punctuated with a few fast dabs of the sponge, after which Bert stepped back and sighed with satisfaction at the good job he'd done on Jan. Then he put the sponge down, picked up a mug with the words BERT WESTON GIVES GREAT FACE on the side, took a long swig, and winced from the taste of the sludgy backstage coffee.

"Of course, Steve Hoeflin's very big these days, too," he said, his mouth still puckered from the bad taste. "But I always think he makes the customers look like someone other than themselves. You know what I mean? He did Ivana, and if you look at her old head shots and her new ones, she looks like two different women."

Jan smiled to signify agreement and polite dismissal, and picked up the pages for Friday's show, hoping Bert would stop talking. But he didn't.

"Now quite a few knowledgeable people swear by Norman Leaf, who I've known since he was in medical school. He's a gem of a guy, and he did Jane Fonda and Shirley MacLaine, and I have to tell you, I've seen both of their faces up close and personal, and they ain't bad, for a couple of old broads," he said, laughing to excuse the dumb remark, and moving around behind Jan's makeup chair to take a longer look in the mirror at his handiwork.

Jan put the pages back on her lap and her stomach ached. Bert's sledgehammer of a hint was his way of trying to tell her she'd better go out and throw herself at the feet of some Beverly Hills plastic surgeon and invest twenty thousand dollars in a face-lift.

Of course she'd considered it. What woman her age, what actress at least, hadn't stood in front of a mirror when no one else was around and gently pulled the skin on the side of her face up toward the tops of her ears, just to see how it would be if that little bit of extra flesh was gone? And those fatty little pads below the eyes. While she was under, he could take those, too. But then she'd think it over and decide it wasn't for her.

Too many friends had come out of those surgeries with their skin so tight against their bones they looked as if they were standing in front of a jet plane about to take off. She even knew an on-camera news reporter who kept her recently removed turkey wattle in a jar of formaldehyde on her mantel and told everyone it was the "Pullet Surprise."

And then there were those scare-the-pants-off-you articles in magazines about how it was done! That they peeled the skin away from the skull the way the Indians used to scalp people. After reading a few of those, she vowed to grow old gracefully. One article said that after the surgery they put staples directly into your skull! Office supplies to keep your face from falling into your soup. Hah! The idea made a nervous giggle rise in her chest.

Besides, she couldn't imagine when the hell she'd have the luxury of the time it took to recover from something like that. Her schedule on this show was so brutal, she couldn't even make an appointment to have her teeth cleaned, because she never knew when she'd have a day off.

"Not for this girl, honey," she said to Bert. "When they start taking you apart and sewing you back together, it smacks a little too much of taxidermy to me. I didn't even like when they did it to Trigger and put him in that Western museum." She laughed, putting her hand up to feel the prongs of the plastic rollers to see if they were cool. She hoped that now that Bert was almost through with her makeup, the discussion would be over. She had a costume fitting to squeeze in before she went out on the floor to shoot today's scenes.

"You know what, doll?" Bert said. And when Jan looked into the mirror at him, her dark-with-too-much-liner eyes caught his gentle warning expression. "If I were you . . . I'd at least check it out."

Jan stopped laughing and was stabbed with panic. He could be warning her that she was about to lose her job.

"Bert," she said, turning to touch the sleeve of his long-sleeved striped shirt. Bert had been doing the makeup on "My Brightest Day" for twenty years. He'd started on the show long before she did. Every morning he saw the actors at an hour when their brains were still in a pre-coffee, partially awake state, when their tongues were still sleepily loose. He knew the gossip, the juice of what was happening on the show. If there was some plan to dump Jan because she was looking too old, Bert probably would've heard rumblings about it, and now he was trying to get her to do something to save herself.

"Good morning, you two." Shannon Michaels, the twenty-two-year-old actress who played Julia, slid into the next chair sleepily, and with a slim pink-nailed hand brushed her thick flaming red hair away from her perfect face. Hair the same color Jan's used to be naturally. A color no artificial mixture, designed to disguise gray, could ever reproduce.

"Mornin', gorgeous," Bert said. Then he took the mascara out of his case, opened it, and applied it to Jan at the same time he was gazing at Shannon, so the tip of the wand hit Jan's cornea, making her flinch and her eyes water. "Sorry, doll," Bert said to her, then he twisted the mascara closed, took another long sip of coffee, and moved on to do Shannon's makeup.

Jan looked in the mirror at her own thickly made-up face, with one red watery eye, her head surrounded by the spiny electric rollers with their wiry clips sticking into her scalp, and it was no mystery to her why Bert thought she was a candidate for the knife. Her cheeks were taking a slow but unmistakable slide down, just like the hill behind her Hollywood Hills house did every time it rained.

She'd rationalized it away before by telling herself that she wasn't out on the street competing with young actresses for jobs. She was one of the leads on a soap, where it was supposed to be okay for actors to age with their characters. To become the senior generation of the show's family. But Jan's character, Maggie Flynn, had always been a glamorous seductress, and now she was afraid there was a chance the producers figured aging might not look so great on her.

Recently, as an experiment, she'd tried wearing a pair of those little stick-in-the-hairline gizmos she bought at a beauty supply store on Laurel Canyon near Riverside. Little V's that hold your face in the "up" position. And two weeks ago, after she begged Ellen to take her along to an "A list" movie-business cocktail party, while she was in the middle of a conversation with Alec Baldwin, the left one fell into her drink. The story about how she tried to ignore it floating in her glass of wine would get a few laughs at Girls' Night.

Thank God for the girls, she thought. On Friday night she'd get together with her three best friends and collapse. They'd all howl with laughter in that free-at-last way they did when it was just the familiar four of them. And boy did Jan need to be able to fall apart with people who had loved her long before she got the part of Maggie Flynn.

Poor Maggie. Now there was a woman who'd really been through the ringer. A travesty of womanhood who'd survived murders, mayhem, runaway lovers, vengeful children, vengeful lovers, and runaway children. "And that was just on last Thursday's show," Jan liked to joke. But Jan the actress was starting to show the strain of Maggie the character's struggles. Five days a week, fifty-two weeks a year, she'd tiptoe out of her house at six A.M. and drive in the dark, chilly morning to the studio, feeling lucky if her workday was over at seven or eight at night, when it was dark again.

And on Saturdays and Sundays, when she wasn't at a children's birthday party or Coldwater Park with her angelic son Joey, she'd be staring at a script, memorizing what could sometimes be forty or fifty pages of dialogue. There was never time to let down, to have a cold, to look bad, to just flake out and not think about the show or what she was going to wear in the publicity shots for *Soap Opera Weekly*.

You'd think after fifteen years of landing on her mark no matter how hysterical the scene, of spewing all the exposition no matter how badly it was written or how emotional the monologue or how real the slap she had just taken, she'd feel secure, confident, and assured of her status in the business. But the truth was that most people in the industry thought daytime acting was schlocky. A joke. Hammy, facile, overdone. In fact at a recent network affiliates luncheon the producers insisted Jan attend, a reporter from an entertainment magazine came over and asked her, "Excuse me, but do you know when the *real* actors are getting here?"

This morning while Shannon and Bert gabbed away, Jan pulled the spray-encrusted rollers out of her hair with her left hand, and with her right she turned the pages of the script. She already had her lines down for today and Thursday, but she wanted to read ahead to the scenes Maggie had on Friday.

MAGGIE'S OFFICE.
There she was, good old Maggie, who had kept her in food and shelter for the last fifteen years. What havoc was the nasty bitch wreaking now?
MAGGIE IS ON THE PHONE; SHE'S ANXIOUS AND TREM-
BLING.

> MAGGIE
> (QUIETLY INTO PHONE) But I must
> speak to Doctor Cartright immedi-
> ately. I don't care if he's with a
> patient. You go in there and tell
> him it's Maggie Flynn. This is an
> emergency.

THE DOOR BANGS OPEN AND LYDIA ENTERS, FOLLOWED
BY SAMANTHA. MAGGIE GASPS.

> SAMANTHA
> (APOLOGETICALLY) I'm sorry, Mrs.
> Flynn. I tried to stop her.

> LYDIA
> Hang up that phone and tell me where
> my husband is.

> MAGGIE
> (HANGING UP THE PHONE) Get out or
> I'll have security remove you.

Ooh, now this is a good scene, Jan thought. Maggie and Lydia are finally having it out. But more important, it could be a great trend in the show. If there was a big Maggie-versus-Lydia story line coming up, it could go on for ages. Jan's current contract expired in eight weeks, so she needed a story like that. She sighed and leaned back in the big, comfortable makeup chair, thanking heaven for this good news.

She had to keep this job. She had to hang in. Forty-nine was a lousy age to be in Hollywood. Last month Marly called her, laughing so hard on the phone she could hardly get the story out about the part she just read for in a commercial. Marly Bennet, who had starred in two situation comedies and a zillion commercials beginning in the sixties when she ran down the beach in a bikini as the symbol of "The Pepsi Generation," was up for a part in a commercial where her only line was, "My doctor told me . . . Mylanta."

That one put them all away. They belly-laughed themselves stupid over it. It was the kind of story the friends swapped all the time. An incident that made them marvel over the distance they'd come together, the absurdity of the kind of work they did, the importance, as Ellen said, of "taking the business with a shit-load of salt."

The business which had beaten them up, made them stronger, enhanced their collective sense of humor, and brought them closer even than they'd been in college, when they all lived on the same floor in the dormitory.

"We're witnesses to one another's history," Rose said recently, liked the thought, took out a notebook and jotted it down.

"She thinks she said something profound." Ellen laughed. "Tomorrow she'll try to sell it to me as a movie."

"Not at all," Rose said. "I'll try to sell it to someone classy."

They loved getting together to exchange their stories, the old ones that were now part of the legend of the four of them, tales of their history revisited and revamped. And the new stories, too, that caught them up with the current insanity about their men, their kids, their bodies, their careers. Funny ones, terrible ones, stories of their tragedies and triumphs. Stories about the lousy things that happened to them at work.

Last week when Marly called to invite Jan to Girls' Night, she reminded her that next week it would be twenty-seven years since they all arrived in Hollywood and, Jesus, could it possibly be thirty-one years since they met in the drama department at Carnegie Tech. The first official Girls' Night after they all moved west was in Jan's tiny studio apartment, where they all smoked dope for the first time together.

Jan remembered the way Marly, the most adept at everything, figured out how to get the Zigzag paper into the rolling machine, and just the right amount of the little leaves to shake into it to make a respectable joint. "An oxymoron if ever I heard one," Marly said when she laughed about that night. And after she lit it, inhaled, then took in a few fast little sucks and held her breath, the strange pungent odor hung in the air and the others sat glassy-eyed.

"Wow," Ellen said. "I can understand why people get the munchies with this stuff. It really makes you famished. Hand me that bag of cookies, will you?"

All three of them looked over at her quizzically.

"Um, Ellen," Rose said, taking off her glasses and breathing on the lenses, then wiping them off on her pajama-top hem. "I think you're supposed to smoke it first." It was a line she would sometimes say now when Ellen jumped to conclusions, and it still made them laugh.

"Look what's happened to us," Marly said last month. "Our drug of choice has become estrogen."

"Not me," Rose said. "Anyone who wants to ingest the urine of a pregnant mare, say 'Aye,' and anyone who doesn't, say 'Neeeigh'!"

That one got a chuckle from all of them. But these days the laughter they shared was a very different brand from the stoned giggle of the sixties. This was the laughter of survivors, a victorious "We're-still-here" laugh that buoyed the four of them much higher than the marijuana of long ago. They also laughed about the idea that the jokes that made them laugh the loudest were usually about aging.

"Let's sing that song from *South Pacific*," Marly said when they were all gathered around her piano the last time. "The one about plastic surgery."

"There's a song in *South Pacific* about plastic surgery?" Ellen asked. "I don't think so."

"There is!" Marly insisted. "It's called 'You Have to Be Taut.'"

"Two old Jewish men are sitting on a park bench," Rose told them. "One says, 'So I think my wife is dead.' The other says, 'You *think* your wife is dead? Whaddya mean? How come you don't know?' And the first old man says, 'Well, the sex is still the same, but the dishes are piling up!'"

Jan loved the way she made them laugh with the stories she told about her jackass producer, Ed Powell. A man she described as hating women so much he made Clarence Thomas seem like Alan Alda. But it was the old ones about her days as a sexy little starlet that were by far their all-time favorites. Particularly the one they made her tell a million times, about the one-night stand she had in the sixties with Maximilian Schell.

"Tell us again about you and Max." It was usually Rose who would urge her, when they were about three glasses of wine into the evening. The story might have been apocryphal — Jan had a way of making things up — but they didn't care, because true or not, it was still funny to them, all these years later.

"Max Schell?" Jan would ask, her face actually flushing when she thought about it. "Ohhh, no. Do you really want to hear that one again?" Then she'd sigh, an "If-you-insist" kind of sigh, and she was back there. Lost in a reverie of being an aspiring twenty-one-year-old actress who went to New York when they were seniors at Tech to audition for summer stock and met and was seduced by Maximilian Schell, a dashing, sexy movie star.

Every time she told it, she'd embellish it a little, adding a nuance or a new detail, throwing in a moment she'd somehow forgotten to mention before. How intimidated she was by his stardom, how brusque he was with her, and how sure of himself. How after he got young Jan to his hotel suite, she went into the bathroom to undress and looked at herself despairingly in the mirror that reflected the elegant fixtures in the expensive hotel bathroom and Max's monogrammed robe hanging on a brass hook and her own frightened face as she thought, What could he possibly want with me?

They still giggled like teenagers when she talked, in her breathy voice, remembering the night that marked the downfall of her innocence. About the zealous way she'd over-gelled the diaphragm she'd "just happened" to have with her. So that when she squeezed it together to insert it, it got away from her and flew across the room "like a leaping frog" and landed with the gooey rim splat on the floor, sticking stubbornly to the bathroom tile.

Then she described the way after Max fell asleep, she stared at him all night long, enthralled by his snore. And always when she got to that part, she imitated the sounds of a specifically Maximilian Schell snore.

But the unequivocally best moment in the story was how, at the break of dawn, the trembling Jan, who hadn't slept a wink, dragged herself from under Max and pulled herself back into the fuschia cocktail dress she'd worn the night before, and the matching spike-heeled shoes and bag, mortified to have to wear them outside in the light of the New York day.

And just as she was about to tiptoe away, Max opened one eye, looked at her accusingly, and said "Yessss?" as if he thought she was the hotel maid intruding on his sleep. And Jan, standing in the open doorway, with as much savoir faire as a terrified, guilty, star-struck twenty-one-year-old could muster, said, by way of bidding him good-bye, "Thanks a million, Maximilian."

That was the part that always slayed the others, made them laugh that out-of-control, over-the-top, hysterical kind of laugh Ellen always described as Sammy Davis laughter. The way Sammy Davis used to laugh when Johnny Carson said something funny. Pounding with appreciation on the side of the hot tub, kicking their feet in the water. "Thanks a million, Maximilian." Those four words had become a standard phrase among them after that. Part of their group language. The way they'd express their gratitude to one another, forever afterward.

Thanks a million, Maximilian. Jan laughed to herself now, thinking that one good evening with her women friends could keep her going for months afterward. Then she looked over at Shannon Michaels, in the next makeup chair, jabbering away so confidently. Noticed the way the young woman tossed her hair and joked with Bert about her date last night, and she was reminded of herself at that age. The way all beautiful young ingenues behave, never imagining the day will come when they'll be the leading lady in the next chair so desperately worried about the future.

MAGGIE STANDS ANGRILY.

                    MAGGIE
          Did you hear me, Lydia? I don't know
          how you got in here, but I want you
          gone.

                    LYDIA
          I don't care what you want. Just
          tell me where Phillip is so I can go
          to him.

LYDIA PULLS OUT A GUN.

                    MAGGIE
          Put that away, Lydia. Don't be in-
          sane. Phillip means nothing to me.
          I swear to you . . .

LYDIA SMIRKS AND COCKS THE GUN.
ON MAGGIE'S FACE. WE CUT TO:

Wow, great opening scene, Jan thought as she turned the pages looking for more scenes for Maggie, but there weren't any more in Friday's show. They were ending the week with Maggie's life in jeopardy. They were going to play that scene on Friday, so she had to go home for the weekend not knowing until her pages arrived, and maybe not even then, if she was going to live or die. The paranoia crept into her mind and lodged there.

She had to get herself upstairs to Ed Powell's office and talk about it right now.

Her hands were damp and she wiped them on the protective Kleenex Bert had stuffed in her collar. "Fight for yourself," Ellen would say. "No agent will do it for you." Shannon and Bert were laughing a yuck-it-up kind of laugh while Jan took the last of the now-cool rollers out of her hair, ran a brush through the stiff curls, and walked out of the makeup room and down the hall to the elevator. As it rose to the fifth floor, she thought nervously about what she ought to say when she got to the producer's office.

The fifth-floor hallway was a gallery of black-and-white eleven-by-fourteen portraits of the cast. She stopped to look at the one of herself taken in the seventies, when she'd joined the show to play "the evil vixen, Maggie." She was thirty-four that year. God, I was a vision, she thought with a mixture of pride and wonder. And when she took a step back, the light from above made the protective glass on the photo reflect her tired, nearly fifty-year-old face, over her glamorous young one.

She sighed and turned and walked down the lushly carpeted hall, still not sure what she'd say to the producer, and feeling even less confident than she had in the elevator. Ed Powell's secretary, Maxine, must have gone to the ladies' room, because no one was in the reception area. Perfect, Jan thought, and she walked right past Maxine's desk into Powell's office. Jan had survived four producers in her fifteen years on this show. They had all either quit or been fired, and the new ones seemed to be getting younger each time.

Last month Ed Powell celebrated a birthday which he kept referring to with dismay as "the big four-oh," as if that number made him ancient. Ed looked up, surprised at first to see her, but then he smiled a very forced smile. "Janny Bear," he said. The big welcome was completely phony. In his eyes she could see he was wondering, "How the fuck did she get past that pit bull Maxine?"

"I came up so you could tell me what Lydia is going to do with the gun, Ed," Jan said, holding up the script, knowing she sounded a little too hysterical, thinking too late that maybe it was the progesterone she was taking that was talking for her. It made her moody and blue and she always thought of it as her "bitch pill," because it also sometimes made her paranoid and panicky. Maybe Ed would tell her what she wanted to know about Monday's script and everything would be fine. That Lydia would never shoot Maggie.

But Ed Powell had a suspiciously flustered look on his face that confirmed her fears. "Janny, chill out. Maggie Flynn's a linchpin in 'The Brighter Day' family. She's not going anywhere. Starting next week she'll be in the hospital for a while and you can have a vacation. You always say you never get a chance to be with your little boy. So this little break'll give you some time off."

"I'll be delighted to stay home, but I need to know you're telling me the truth, Ed. I was able to adopt a child as a single woman, and buy a house, because you always tell me I'm here to stay."

"Darling girl, you are."

"I told you my sister in Pennsylvania lost her job, so I have to support her now," Jan said, suddenly afraid that she might cry.

"Right," Ed said. "I know all about your sister, and I sympathize." Then he laughed and asked her, "What's the name of that place again where you told me she lives? That funny name?"

"Beaver Falls," Jan said, and Ed's face broke into a grin followed by a big toothy laugh. His face was so shiny it looked as if someone had just polished it.

"I always laugh at that," he said, "because it sounds as if it should be the name of a disease women get when they're old." He was still laughing at his own joke as Jan left his office in a more urgent panic than the one that had brought her there, and went downstairs to wardrobe.

TWO

LINCHPIN, my ass," Gladyce Colby said, talking the way she always did, with her teeth clenched around a line of straight pins. "Ed Powell told Elwin Martin that *his* character was a linchpin, too." Gladyce was fitting a dark green wool-crepe suit on Jan for tomorrow's taping. Gladyce had been doing wardrobe on the show for twenty years, and Jan trusted her. "Then Ed fucked him over royally. Last year they used to joke about Elwin in the booth. Any time he flubbed a line, Ed would turn off the mike and say, 'Elwin, baby, you're not dead yet . . . but Doctor Kevorkian is starting the car.' "

Jan laughed in spite of the ugliness of the joke.

"This suit is great on you, hon," Gladyce said. She had watched Jan's body "matronize," the breasts sag, the waist thicken, and though in Jan's early days on the show, Gladyce would dress her in clingy little silk dresses, these days she dressed her in suits with long jackets. And never with any criticism or comment.

She was choosing shoes with lower heels to bring in for Jan, too. Not just because they were more seemly for a character of Maggie's age, but because Jan's feet were too tired to wear the high heels all day, the way she used to.

"And you remember what happened to Elwin," Gladyce said with eyebrows raised.

Jan remembered. Elwin Martin was the actor who played Aubrey Flynn, Maggie's husband, for ten years. Until one day, the producers decided Elwin was too dull, but they still loved the character of Aubrey. So they had the writers write Aubrey into a serious auto accident that took his Rolls-Royce into a crash-and-burn over a cliff in northern California. There was no sign of his remains.

Six months later they had Maggie walk onto a set that was supposed to be a bar in the Virgin Islands, and suddenly, while a steel band played their song in the background, there was the new, improved Aubrey. Now he was played by Tom Patterson, a handsomer, younger-looking actor. And the truth was maybe Tom Patterson was too handsome and too young, and by comparison Jan looked too old to be Maggie.

She worried about it while she sat on the set of Maggie's office and ran over the lines for today's taping with Tom. In the scene today, Aubrey confronted Maggie about his nemesis, Phillip Jenkins, a brilliant biologist who worked for Flynn Laboratories. Sitting on the plush set of Maggie's office, Jan and Tom chatted casually while they waited for lights to be set and the boom microphones to be moved and for the prop man to fill the coffee cups they were using in the scene.

"I saw the script for tomorrow's show," Tom said. "Great scene for Maggie and Lydia." Tom was a hardworking actor, with a square jaw and a leading-man look, who had made a career of daytime TV, appearing on a few other soaps before he got to this one. He was easy to work with because he was comfortable with himself, happily married, and almost apologetic about putting his predecessor, Elwin Martin, out of a job.

"It is a great scene," Jan said, searching Tom's eyes to see if he knew anything. They were speaking in the hushed tones they always used, while the prop man straightened a flower in a vase and plumped a pillow and a hairdresser was spraying and patting down a stray hair on Jan. "Unfortunately, the great scene with Lydia may turn out to be my last."

"I don't think so," Tom said. "It's just a scare tactic from the boys upstairs. Do you have a new deal pending?" Tom asked.

She nodded.

"Well, there you go," he said reassuringly. "You say no to their deal, Lydia shoots Maggie. You say yes to their deal, Maggie calms her down." He shrugged. "You know the drill. Producers have all the options, actors are garbage. Besides, there's always that buddy of yours who helped you get a spot on one of his networks' prime-time series. Maybe if you leave the soap, he'll give you a lead."

There was envy in his voice, envy from all the actors on the show, because two months ago when Maggie was having such bad headaches that she had to lie down for ten days, Jan had begged her way into a small but meaty part on one of Jack Solomon's hot prime-time network shows. She'd had a horrible experience doing it, but everyone in the soap was impressed that she'd gone to college with the president of a network. Last month, at least six people asked her if she'd seen Jack's picture on the cover of the *New York Times Magazine* and the article about how he was changing the face of network TV.

"Okay, folks, let's shoot this." The director's voice came over the PA from the booth, interrupting their conversation. Jan did a last-minute run-through in her mind of Maggie's lines for this scene and what Maggie wanted from Aubrey. The lights were all on now, and one of the hairdressers was smoothing down a flyaway hair of Tom's.

"Aubrey." The director's voice came over the box, addressing the actor by the character's name, the way he always did. "Remember that the goal is to get Maggie to reassure you that she loves you. And Maggie, don't move until he says the line, 'All those late meetings you two were having. It made me worry.' Then do the turn away. Okay?"

Jan nodded and took a breath, and Hal, the potbellied, Hawaiian-shirt-clad stage manager, said, "Okay, people, quiet on the set." He was relaying the countdown from the booth. "Here we go in five, four, three, two . . ."

"You can imagine how—"

A piercing scream from off camera interrupted Tom's first line. Jan spun around in terror and heard someone off camera shout, "Hold it, pal! Don't move or we'll hurt you." But the bright lights were in her eyes, and the space beyond the cameras was black to her.

She could see everyone on the office set standing frozen in fear. There was some loud scuffling, and shouts, and then she heard an eerie plaintive cry, "Maggeeeee, I love you." She was shocked when the stage manager suddenly grabbed her hard by the arms and pulled her out of the chair and through the open doorway of the office set. Running with her past the jail-cell set, past the Flynn living-room set, and onto the intensive care unit set, which was the farthest away from the cameras. There was terror in Hal's eyes and he was gasping for breath as he leaned against the bed in the mock hospital room.

"My God! What is it?" Jan asked him. But before he could answer, she heard one of the grips holler, "It's okay. Not to worry, folks. We got him. He's outta here." Hal was heaving hysterical breaths that made Jan afraid he was going to have a heart attack. Finally he fell on her in a sweaty hug.

"It's okay. They got him. It was that guy again, hon," Hal said, trying to catch his breath. "That fan. I just caught sight of him lurking back there by the coffeemaker. He must have gotten past the Pinkerton security boys downstairs and wanted to say hello to you. That's all."

That's all, he said, but he looked more afraid than she was. It was the man, that fan of hers who sat across the street from the studio every night so he could wave to her when her car drove out. And today he'd managed to get all the way onto the lot, and the sound stage, and the set, and Hal, who now pulled a hand-kerchief out of his pocket and mopped the sweat from his own face, kept repeating the words "That's all."

Chilled with dread, Jan sat on the bed on the ICU set and tried to calm herself. Soap-opera fans were notorious for believing the characters on the shows they watched were real, so every day there were weird letters and phone calls and threats to the producer's offices from fans who obsessed about their favorite character's fate. AUBREY FLYNN IS A DEAD MAN IF HE DOESN'T GIVE HIS SON THAT MONEY HE ASKED FOR. WHO DOES THAT BITCH MAGGIE THINK SHE IS? FLIRTING WITH EVERY MAN THAT GOES BY, IF I EVER GET MY HANDS ON HER . . .

"Jan, you okay down there?" she heard the director ask from the booth as she and Hal made their way back onto the office set. Hal was so shaky she felt as if she was holding him up.

"I'm fine," she said, even trying to force a smile, but her face was twitching. "What did they do with the man?" she asked, hoping someone would assure her that they'd taken him to jail.

"Nothing much they can do. They threw him off the lot," came the voice.

"That's all?" Jan asked. Bert was touching up the concealer under her eyes. A few pats with the sponge, his Royal Lyme engulfing her. "Look up, sweetheart. That's it. Look up."

"He didn't do anything," the disembodied voice from the booth told her dismissively.

Jan tried to make her breathing normal as Bert left the set, and she looked around at all the people who were uncomfortably looking anywhere but into her eyes. They were afraid for her, and probably for themselves. Last year, at Universal Studios, some nut stood outside the executive office building and let go with an automatic rifle. And everyone knew about the fan who tracked down and murdered that poor young actress Rebecca Schaeffer.

She sat down at the desk in Maggie's office and tried to regain her composure. "Is he going to have to kill me before they arrest him?" she said to nobody in particular. No one answered. Tom Patterson patted her hand as if to tell her he understood. But he didn't understand. She was panicked. What if that man waited outside the lot and then followed her home? What if he hurt Joey? She wanted to stand up and scream, "Somebody help me," but she knew none of them could or would.

"Can we go on?" the director's voice asked, as if he'd been inconvenienced by Jan's popularity. There were three directors who alternated shooting the episodes of this show, and there was always competition among them about coming in on time and under budget. If someone had called the police, their intrusion on the set would have slowed things up significantly. This little incident could have thrown off the whole day. They had to keep moving.

"Let's make this one, people," Hal called out, his voice still quivering. "Places, please. Here we go in five, four, three, two . . ."

"You can imagine how worried I've been," Tom Patterson said as Aubrey to Maggie. "I mean, there's no mistaking the look in Phillip's eyes when you walk into a room. I thought perhaps you felt . . ."

It was Jan's cue. "Darling, don't be silly." She managed to say Maggie's words, but inside she was trembling, worrying about driving home alone and wondering if that fan had any idea where she lived.

"All those late meetings you two were having. It made me worry."

Jan turned away, as Maggie had been directed. It was all by rote. Years of technique taking over. Thank heaven she could rely on the automatic system she'd developed after playing this part for so long, because her heart and her brain were not there, and her insides were rumbling with fear. "Darling, don't be absurd," she said, afraid she might lose it any second. Nobody had spotted that man today, and he'd made it all the way onto the set. Only a few yards away from her. No one mentioned whether or not he was carrying a gun.

"You aren't in love with Phillip Jenkins, are you, Maggie?"

"Oh, Aubrey. Don't be absurd," she said, as the camera moved in for her close-up. Later everyone commented when they watched that episode that Maggie really looked as if she was afraid Aubrey had finally caught her cheating on him. And how ironic it all was, in light of what happened later.

Today was a block-and-tape day, which meant that the actors taped each scene immediately after they blocked it, so after the scene in Maggie's office, and one more in the reception area of Flynn Laboratories, Jan's shooting day was over. She spent a quiet time in her dressing room, removing her makeup, changing into leggings and a long sweater. When she opened the big, heavy studio door, she squinted, surprised to see the sun. It was the first time in weeks she'd actually left work while it was still daylight.

As she drove off the lot in her silent black Lexus, she looked both ways to see if she could spot anyone suspicious pulling away after her car, but in the early afternoon the streets were quiet and surprisingly traffic free. She put her hand on her car phone and considered calling The Prince of Power. Just to tell him what happened and hear him say, "Oh sweetheart, I'm so sorry."

Sometimes she could get through the first and second assistants to his executive secretary, who had worked for him at that studio and the one before it, long enough to remember the way in the old days he had a phone on his desk with a private number just for her calls. Sometimes Isobel would still hustle her call through so she could hear his husky voice say, "My angel face . . . how awful you must feel. I've got Barry Diller holding. I'll ring you back."

No, she wouldn't call him. It didn't matter. In a few minutes she'd be hugging Joey, and that would make the insanity of the day disappear. It amused her that hurrying home to be with her son excited her more than anything she'd ever felt when she was on her way to a tryst with The Prince. This little boy was magical for her. And every day she thanked heaven for the day she'd finally had the guts to adopt him, finally admitted to herself after too many difficult romances that waiting for some man to someday make a family with her was a vain hope.

Everyone thought she was crazy to start raising a child at this stage of her life. The other actors on her show, her sister, and of course The Prince all advised her to forget it. But Marly, Rosie, and Ellen urged her to go for it. Ellen had recommended the adoption lawyer, who found Jan a birth mother willing to turn over a baby to a single working woman. Marly found Jan a therapist who specialized in adoptions to prepare her for the experience. Rose found a good obstetrician for the birth mother.

All three of them managed to have careers and children, but to a woman they reported that nothing in their work lives, no matter how big a part, how hot a deal, "not even my Oscar nomination," Rose said, could compete with the love of their children.

Jan had envied them for so long, watched their joy while she played Aunt Jan to all of their kids.

Joey's adoption ceremony was an emotional event from start to finish. Jan dressed him in a sailor suit, and no one could get over the way he laughed and smiled through the entire ceremony. And none of them would ever forget the tender moment when Marly, Ellen, and Rose all stood in a circle, and as they passed the infant boy to one another's arms, each made an eloquent and loving promise to him, like the fairies did in *Sleeping Beauty*, to guard him with their lives.

Today as Jan drove up the long, winding driveway and pulled into the carport of her house, she congratulated herself again for buying it. It wasn't grand, just a little two-story, built-on-stilts Laurel Canyon house. Stucco with the fifties' sliding-glass-door style. But what had sold her on it, the minute the broker walked her in, was the panoramic view from every room. On days when the air wasn't too thick with smog, she could see the mountains that were miles away.

And at night, the lights below twinkled and made the view look just the way she remembered it in the opening of a TV show she used to watch as a kid, where the searchlights spanned the night sky and the announcer's voice said, "Lux . . . presents Hollywood."

"Mommmeeee," Joey shrieked happily, running to Jan. She crouched so her arms would receive her four-year-old, whose wispy blond hair and round blue eyes ironically made him look just like the baby pictures she had of herself.

"Hello, my lovely boy," she said, inhaling the dear little-boy scent of him. It was unusual for her to be home in time to be the one who made Joey dinner instead of arriving just in time to tuck him in. Hurrying in to give him a few pre-sleep kisses and then watching him drift off. It was an incredible luxury to have hours of daylight left to play with him. Jan nursed a glass of wine while they sat on the floor and put together a jigsaw puzzle. Then they each colored a page in the "Beauty and the Beast" coloring book, Jan carefully shading a blue dress on Belle, and Joey scrawling with bright red all over the Beast.

"Some children are natural nurturers," a child psychologist told her. "From the start they feel that they're here to take care of you." Ellen told Jan that her son, Roger, had always been a caretaker. Joey was like that, too, with Jan. When her mind wandered to the man breaking in onto the set today, he climbed into her lap and gently patted her face.

"It's okay, Mommy," he said. "It's okay."

The day was getting just a little gray, and the sky over the valley was orange and magenta when she stood at the stove, tasting the DynoMac pasta to see if it was ready for the sauce. She promised herself that one of these days she'd stop giving Joey such junk food, but she kept breaking the promise because he seemed to love it so much. She was getting the milk out of the refrigerator when the phone rang.

"They're fucking you, babe." It was her lawyer.

"Ooh, Bernie, I hope so," she kidded, while she mixed the cheese and the milk into the pasta. "I also hope like hell they're using protection." Bernie had his serious voice on. He was bringing what he thought was grim news from Ed Powell and the other producers of "My Brightest Day."

The scene between Maggie and Lydia for Friday was leading to a shooting followed by a prolonged hospitalization for Maggie, as a warning to Jan that she was dispensable. To make sure that she'd accept the meager raise they were offering for a new three-year contract. An offer Bernie was telling her was "a real up-yours."

"But, Bern," she said, "I'm happy they want me back. I was starting to think Maggie Flynn was going to have soap opera reincarnation as a younger actress. Thank God at least I can get some more time out of this deal. I have a child to feed, sweetie."

"If I were you, I'd threaten to walk," Bernie said. "Otherwise they'll shit all over you. That new girl? The twenty-two-year-old with the headlights out to Kishnev. She started on the show with a higher salary than they're offering you after fifteen years. So I don't want you to be a schmuck. I mean, you can be a schmuck if you want, but I wouldn't cave at this point. I'd say no to the offer and let them come back to us."

"Yeah? And what if they say, 'Okay. Thanks for the fifteen years, and ciao, baby?' " she asked, spooning the minidinosaurs smothered in the gooey orange cheese sauce onto a "Ninja Turtle" plate.

"Well, that's the chance we have to take, isn't it?" Bernie said.

"Bernie, I've watched them get rid of other actors on this show with great ease. I did a guest shot on a high-rated prime-time show because my old college chum gave me a handout. The producer of the show probably resented it so much that he'll never use me again. No one is exactly beating my door down to beg me to do anything else. I'm a forty-nine-year-old actress, and a long-running soap is asking me back. I appreciate you wanting to get me some fancy raise, but I am unable to authorize you to tell them I'm walking if they don't give me what I want. If I don't send my sister a monthly check, she'll be moving into her car. Close the deal," she said.

"Janny, let's take a day or two or three to get back to them," Bernie said. "Maybe you'll change your mind and give me some leeway."

"We can take a few days, Bern," she said. "But I'm not going to turn my back on a real live job."

"Call me next week when you're a little more rested," Bernie said.

"Fine," Jan said, and she caught the telephone receiver just before it fell from under her ear into the DynoMacs.

She put the dish in front of Joey at the table, and Maria poured some apple juice into a plastic glass for Joey and put that on the table, too. "I tell my hosban I stay here Friday night so you can be with Misses Marly and Ellen and Rose," Maria said. "I stay the night to watch Joey, and you go have fun with your friends."

"Thank you, Maria," Jan said. "I can't wait!"

THREE

OVER THE LAST TEN YEARS, *she'd moved from one piece-of-shit apartment to another so often that by the time some of her mail actually found her, it had two or three forwarding stickers slapped one on top of the other. Most of the junk shoved in her mailbox wasn't worth the tree they had to kill to get the paper. A few catalogues, with a lot of fancy items in them that she couldn't afford. A bill there was no way she could pay, so with a flick of her wrist she tossed that one right in the wastebasket.*

Let them come and get me, she thought. As it was, she could barely make the rent for this rathole apartment, in a neighborhood so bad she had to keep a gun in the kitchen drawer just in case one of those spics who lived across the way got any ideas.

Wasn't it great, she thought, that the one slick, good-looking upscale magazine that found its way to her every time was the alumni news? She didn't have to pay for it, and she always made sure to supply that office with her new address so they'd know where to send it. Of course when she wrote to them, she never told them any info about what she was really doing, like they asked. Oh please. With all the big-time players they listed in there from her class alone?

Every few months when the magazine was there in her mailbox at the end of a long day's work, she'd drop everything to sit and read it. Not the articles about homecoming and the new student computer center. She skipped over those, right to the part where they listed the goings-on about the people from her department and her year.

```
DRAMA—Class of '66
Albertson, Sherry. Sherry writes in, "I am
```

still teaching acting technique at the La Jolla Playhouse and loving it."

Teaching. Big deal. She knew the frustration of teaching when what you really wanted to do was act. She'd done it herself for a while. Taught speech to a bunch of airheads at an acting school. Forget that shit! Skip Sherry Albertson. Who else?

Bradford, Freeman. Freeman is scene designer for the Seattle Repertory Company.

Nice going, Freeman, she thought, remembering he had been a nerd.

Bass, Ellen. Ellen Bass was Ellen Feinberg and is now the vice president in charge of feature films at Hemisphere Studios in Hollywood. Recent films under her aegis starred Jodie Foster, Julia Roberts, Richard Gere, and Michelle Pfeiffer.

That one made her close the magazine for a minute and sit staring around her dingy dive of an apartment. She had written her first letter to Ellen Bass when she read that she was in some production job at 20th Century-Fox a few years ago, but she never got an answer. Then she actually got up the nerve to call her when she saw that she got that big job at Hemisphere Studios, and some male secretary with an attitude problem asked, "Will she know what this is regarding?" It was so condescending, she hung up. Then last year she sent her the tape, the brilliant tape, and Ellen fucking Bass never so much as sent a thank-you note. Why was it so hard to just scribble a few lines saying, 'Thank you. I got the tape.' But not one word.

Feldman, Sanford. Composer Sandy Feld has scored five Broadway musicals. He lives with his wife and children in Connecticut, and this year he generously gave his time to come and speak to the music majors about how to break into the theater.

Her stomach acid surged up into her esophagus. That little musical genius Sandy Feldman had gotten her stoned one night at a party dur-

ing their senior year and tried to score her. *Cut me a break, she thought. Five Broadway musicals? She hadn't even seen five Broadway musicals. Only one. That glorious time a bunch of them piled into a car and drove from Pittsburgh to New York City.*

It was before seat belts, and there were too many of them for Sandy Feldman's little Chevy, so most of the way she sat on Jack Solomon's lap. Best time he ever had in his whole life, he kept joking. And then they got to New York. What a city. It was all lit up and it was snowing, and they all stood in line together waiting to buy twofers for How To Succeed, *singing Christmas carols and laughing.*

The musical made her feet leave the ground. Robert Morse, Michelle Lee, and Charles Nelson Reilly, and every song was a gem. Afterward they all walked, with their arms around one another, all over the theater district, Shubert Alley, and Sardi's, singing that song "Brotherhood of Man," and swearing that someday they'd all be working there. Together. All of them were so sure then that working in the theater was their destiny.

She was one of them then. Young and pretty, with her carrot-colored hair down to her waist. The best actress in the class. Jack Solomon called her that for the first time right after freshman year, during a re-hearsal of The Cherry Orchard. *He told her it was her great, deep, sexy bedroom voice that filled the theater and made her impossible to ignore on stage. And he wasn't even looking to get laid when he said it. No, Jack was always hot for Jan O'Malley. Besides, he was such a little jerko in those days, no one would have dreamt of him as a boyfriend. And now he was big-time Jack Solomon, who wasn't even on this list, probably because he was too famous now to take the time to write in and tell the alumni magazine what he was doing.*

In some newspaper article she read a while back, it said that Jack Solomon gave two million dollars to some museum in New York. Imagine having a spare couple of million you could just give away. That was something. Her eyes moved down the page and stopped to read a little piece of juicy gossip.

Mann, Marly Bennet. Marly was a key player on a long-running situation comedy, "Keeping Up with the Joneses." You've also seen her in many movies of the week and miniseries. Also since her arrival in Hollywood, Marly has acted in over one hundred and fifty commercials. Marly writes whimsically to this office, "Am happy to report that I'm legally separated from Billy Mann, so all college sweethearts can contact me through the alumni association." Marly and ex-husband, late-night-TV-star Billy Mann, have twin daughters, Jennifer and Sarah.

Oooh, separated. Maybe that's why Marly didn't get her letters. She'd mailed them to Marly in care of "The Billy Mann Show," think-ing Billy would bring them home. But the big TV star dumped her. Tough break, Marly, she thought. But you'll survive. Someone with my simple tastes could probably live for a year on one month of the child support you'll get for the twins. Now she skipped down the list, looking only at the names of the people she used to know well.

Morris, Rose. The film *Faces*, which starred Meryl Streep and Al Pacino, brought screen-writer Rose Morris Schiffman an Oscar nomina-tion for best original screenplay. Rose was widowed in 1982 by the death of department-of-architecture graduate ('66) Allan Bayliss. Rose and her second husband, physician Andrew Schiffman, have a ten-year-old daughter, Molly.

She thought about the day Rose Morris and Allan Bayliss got pinned in a fraternity-pinning ceremony held outside in front of the dorm. Those two loved one another big time, in an almost mystical way. They were the couple she always thought about when she heard the term soul mates. They even looked alike.

She could still picture that funny little four-eyes Rose Morris ner-vously running down the stairs to untie Allan from the tree where the Sigma Nu's had tied him as part of the ritual. She had to kiss him in front of everyone and she was mortified, didn't want to go out there alone, but none of her buddies would go with her. Brave it, or some shit like that, they told her. You can do it.

Rose was terrified. She was on her way up to her room after a dance class, and when Rose spotted her, she grabbed her. "Please just walk me out there," she said. "I'm too afraid to do this alone." It was no big deal to her, those fraternity jerks didn't intimidate her. So she walked Rose down the steps and out to the tree. Stood next to her while she kissed Allan and untied him and the Sigma Nu's sang the goopy sweetheart song, with Rose blushing flame red.

So naturally when she was sitting with her daughter in the State Theater, and Rose's name came on the screen, she let out a yelp and embarrassed the shit out of Polly. "I know her," she said, really loud, "I saved her ass one time," and Polly covered her face with her hands and someone a few rows back yelled, "Shut up, lady!"

All the way home from Rose's movie that night, she kept thinking, I could have played the part in Faces *better than Meryl Streep did. I could have at least played the sister. She tried to call Rose the day after she saw her movie. She was going to remind her about the pinning. She was going to say she remembered how much she and Allan loved one another. Rose would appreciate that.*

She was going to ask her for help in the business, but the information operator in Los Angeles told her, "Sorry, but that phone is unlisted." Unlisted! Who do these people think they are? Who are they hiding from, when they don't list their goddamn phone numbers?

```
Norell, Betty. Betty Norell spends summers
with her family in California, but through an
exchange with British Equity, she winters in
repertory at Chichester, the theater started by
Lawrence Olivier. Writes Betty: "It's theater
just as we'd all once hoped it would be. And
many of our glorious productions move on to the
West End."
```

She read that one over three times. Looks like good old Betty was the only one who was living up to the vow. Doing the kind of thing they all swore they'd do some day. Making the rest of them seem as if they'd gone the way of the glitz. Sold themselves down the old L.A. river. Well, Betty always was the best actress in the class, and the most serious one about her work, she'd give her that.

O'Malley, Jan. Jan is now in her fifteenth
year of playing the part of Maggie Flynn on the
daytime drama "My Brightest Day." In 1991, Jan,
still single, adopted a baby son, Joey, and
tells us in her letters, "As a result, I am finally alive."

That one made her close the magazine and fling it across the room. A baby. They gave Jan O'Malley a baby. See what being a star can get you? I lose custody of my kids, and she gets to buy a baby! Look at these women's lives! Look at mine! I graduated from that same school! I was the best one, and now I have nothing to show for it. And they have it all. Money, babies, their pictures in TV Guide *and the paper. And the clothes. That sequined dress Jan O'Malley wore on the Daytime Emmys had to cost at least five thousand dollars.*

She got up and walked over to the window of her apartment, the window with the view of the back alley and the trash cans from the building next door. I'm forty-nine years old, she thought. When do I get mine? When do I get to have a decent life? And why don't they help me? The tears of jealousy that had been burning behind her eyes finally came and rolled down her unhappy face.

I have to get them to help me. I know they will, she thought. If only I can get them on the phone.

FOUR

ELLEN'S Donna Karan control-top panty hose were a little too controlling, and the waistband was cutting into that bulging place around her middle where her waistline used to be before she ate all those power lunches at Le Dome. She always got so pumped up at those meetings, brainstorming new projects, courting the talent, hearing their ideas, that most of the time she gobbled her lunch without thinking about what she was eating. Lost her head and devoured all the bread, ordered too much food and then ate it too fast.

Once in the middle of a story pitch, over lunch at the Ivy, she noticed the writer was frowning uncomfortably at her, and when she looked down she realized it was because her fork was spearing a roasted red potato she'd been about to remove from his plate. Usually by the time the valet brought her BMW to the curb of those restaurants, after the big good-byes and hyped-up promises everyone made to one another, she couldn't wait to drive away alone so she could reach back, unbutton the back of her skirt, and breathe.

Today's meeting in the conference room had been going on for four hours, and it threatened to keep going on for a few more. She had to pee, but she didn't dare get up and go to the bathroom again, since she'd already excused herself twice, and not one of the men had left the room once.

As usual, there was more testosterone in the air than at a fraternity party on a Saturday night, and the late-adolescent arbiters of America's taste in film were really going at it.

"Even Shakespeare couldn't polish this turd of a script," Bibberman said.

"He could," Schatzman said. "But Ovitz told me he's not available 'til July." A blast of a laugh from Richardson.

"He's doing Last Action Hero Two," he said, which got an even bigger laugh from the boys, and Ellen thought how lucky it was for her that she'd once been the room mother for the second grade, so she understood their behavior.

Why did it still amaze her what yo-yos the three of them turned into the minute the door to the conference room was closed? Why did it gall her how ruled by their maleness they became? All day long they all kissed the asses of the talent and made nice with the agents and spoke in conciliatory, unctuous tones to the lawyers. So when they finally got into the room to talk among themselves about the deals and the projects, the rage they'd been holding inside finally blew, and it wasn't a pretty sight.

After so many years in this town, during which she'd somehow managed to work for some of the legendary pigs in the business, Ellen was sure she'd seen and heard it all. And yet now and then she still found herself embarrassed by the behavior of these three. Just that morning, Randy McVey, a gifted British director, was in a meeting with all of them, discussing a project, and he brought up his background in classical theater.

"Of course," he said, "my first love is to work in the summer season at Chichester. If only they played all year long, I'd never leave the place."

And behind the very elegant man's back, for the entertainment of the others, Bibberman actually made that open fisted moving-in-and-out, jerking-off gesture the boys used to make, back when she was in elementary school. Ellen wanted to grab him by his Armani lapels and shake some sense into him. Later when the director left, Bibberman imitated McVey's dialect and his passion for theater, thinking he was being terribly funny. Now they were talking about one of the writers.

"How much does he want?" Bibberman asked.

"Two hundred thousand."

"Pass," Bibberman said. "I could shit on the page and it would be better than his first draft."

Ellen had her usual wave of wishing she could afford to quit this job. Give up the perks and the pricks and go open a bookstore in a beach town somewhere. Or at least work at a company that was run by grown-ups. This was getting to be too much, watching the boys sitting there all day, wagging their dicks at one another.

Each of them believing with the hubris that their excessive salaries gave them that they were going to be in these heady positions of power forever. And worse yet, claiming that they actually knew how to predict what the audiences wanted to see, what would make money. All Ellen knew was that even Nostrafuckingdamus couldn't tell how a movie would do until the popcorn was popped and the audience was either cheering, laughing, crying, or walking out in the middle.

But she chose to shut up and do what Rose told her, which was not to "rock the yacht." Not let the "boys" win their battle to get her out of the locker room, since they were the only real downside of the job for her. Otherwise it had a lot to recommend it.

She'd grown accustomed pretty damn quick to the expense-account life, including the high-priced car that the studio transportation department not only provided, but had serviced, detailed, washed, gassed, and waiting in her personal parking spot for her every day. And since day one of the announcement in the trades that she had this job, she always got the great tables everywhere in town. At Morton's and at Wolfgang Puck's restaurant Granita in Malibu, with Barbara Lazaroff fawning over her.

But what stoked her more than the trappings, what kept her awake at night with excitement, was the charge she got putting together the deals to make the movies. There was something incredibly heady about the alchemy of matching just the right script with a director no one else would have dreamed of using for that genre, and watching the project take off. It was a spike, the part of the job that made her as giddy as the studio secretaries got when Daniel Day-Lewis walked into the commissary. That was what made it all worthwhile for her. Spending her days locked in a room from early morning to midnight, shepherding a film from its conception to its premiere.

Nothing could beat those hours of being part of the process, when the director and the writer worked to make a product that was bigger, broader, grander than the sum of its parts. To watch each idea bring forth the next one, to see the product metamorphose.

And then to be the one who could make words on a page come to life by finding the right stars, to give it what Ellen jokingly called Tina Turners, meaning not just legs, but the greatest legs in the business. That part of the job meant so much to her that she could put up with the "boys club" to have it.

Now the fucking panty hose were rolling over and sliding down her belly, goddamn it. She promised herself to have her secretary call Neiman Marcus to order a dozen pairs of panty hose without the control top. Then she could be comfortable and not care if her stomach stuck out.

Schatzman was droning on about casting the male and female leads for *Out There,* a hot action-adventure film the studio was eager to make. Ellen knew these casting discussions could go on forever. Each of the men had his personal favorite actors, and hated the other's favorites, so they could fight about casting for days on end.

Names of stars were flying, careers were hanging in the balance. First they talked about the women. "You'd like to fuck her, wouldn't you?" "Only with your cock, in case there's something wrong with her." "Hey, believe me, when I visit the set, I'll bring my good dick."

Ellen was sure they sometimes overdid the childish male shit just to fry her. To see how bad they could make it before she fell apart and said, "I quit, you infantile assholes." Probably they were wishing she'd walk, so they wouldn't have to have a broad around, and more important, if she left on her own, they wouldn't have to pay her off.

Now they'd moved on to talk about casting the men, so what

Bibberman called the "pussy factor" was being weighed, because they needed to lure the women audiences into the theaters.
They were all ripping apart the available actors. One male star
was a "wimp," another a "wuss."

Ellen made what she thought was a great suggestion for the
role.

"No chance." Bibberman sneered when he heard it. "He's too
high-maintenance."

"Meaning?"

"Meaning I'm not interested in being the one who goes to the
emergency room to pull the gerbils out of his ass." Big laugh.

"Why gerbils?" one of them said. "Why not hamsters or mice,
or maybe white rats?"

"White rats would show the dirt!"

Screams of laughter.

"White rats never ask, 'Was it good for you?' " More screams.

Ellen sighed. Let them play, she thought. When they get serious, I'll jump in. Her mind was wandering as she doodled with
her Mont Blanc pen on the legal pad in front of her. She knew if
she didn't stand soon and start packing up her briefcase, she'd
never get out of there. And she wasn't going to disappoint
Roger. It was his birthday, and she was meeting him at
Adriano's for dinner.

Rogie, her gorgeous son, whose father left him and Ellen and
Los Angeles when Roger was less than a year old. Today her di-
vine boy turned twenty-four, and they would celebrate and reminisce. And for a few hours she'd forget about the scripts that
were stacked on her night table, piled in her briefcase, sitting on
the passenger seat of her car, and being delivered in a steady
stream to her office every time the mail room gofer came by her
studio bungalow.

"Ellen?"

When she looked up from her doodling, she realized that all
of the men were not only looking at her, they were waiting for
the answer to some question Bibberman must have just directed
at her, which she'd been too preoccupied to hear. All of their
eyes glistened with glee. He had to have guessed she hadn't

heard the first time, because now he repeated it. "I asked, which one of the men on this list makes your snatch get juicy?"

Heat burned her face. Typical Bibberman, putting her in a spot where she ought to tell him to rephrase his juvenile question or she'd go get a job somewhere where men were men, not spoiled brats trying out the provocative words on the girls in the class. Her mind ran through the possible answers, but before she could speak, Bibberman added, gleeful at his own cuteness, "Or at your age, does your snatch still *get* juicy?"

This wasn't sexual harassment, this was just plain harassment. Get nasty and see if you can make the girl fall apart, lose it, be sorry she ever came into the locker room. Ellen fought to keep her stoic expression, took a deep breath, and said, "I'd go with Kevin Costner and some K-Y jelly."

Her joke got a tepid laugh from Richardson and Schatzman as she stood. She had to get out of here.

"Gentlemen," she said, "and I use the term loosely, I have to go now. I have a pressing engagement."

"Get out the K-Y jelly," Bibberman said. "Sounds like a hot date. Forget 'women who run with the wolves,' we have 'woman who sleeps with cats.' "

"It's my son's birthday," Ellen said, and she realized she'd stopped herself from saying which birthday, since they all had young children.

"Again?" Richardson joked. "Didn't your son just have a birthday last year?"

"My kids have all their birthday parties in a screening room downstairs," Schatzman said.

"See you tomorrow," Ellen said, walking out the door of the conference room and down the hall, where she could hear Bibberman's laughter at Schatzman's comments about being so devoted to the job that he never left the studio, so his family had to move their lives there in order to see him. Wait until she told them she was leaving early on Friday night, too, because it was Girls' Night.

She had to go to the bathroom so badly she knew she'd never make it out of the building and over to the bungalow to her own office, so she stopped in the employees ladies' room near the elevator. "At your age." Bibberman's pointed words, the amusement dancing in his beady little eyes. Yes, she was getting to be what was perceived as old to have her job in this town, and she knew it. Most of the other women in top studio jobs, with the exception of Sherry Lansing, were in their thirties.

"Now who could this harridan be?" Ellen thought, wondering if it was the fluorescent lights that were making her face look yellow in the mirror, or the new shade of auburn, the hair color Lizanne tried on her last month. God bless Lizanne, who always fit her in when those telltale gray hairs started sneaking in. Gray hair, tired eyes. I've got those just-looked-in-the-mirror-and-thought-I-saw-my-mother blues, Ellen thought, looking wearily at herself.

Sometimes the young hairdresser at José Ebert would stay in the salon until ten, long after the others were gone, just to fit Ellen in. Too bad she didn't do pubic hair, too, Ellen thought, and then laughed a why-bother laugh at herself in the mirror at how dumb that thought was. No one saw her pubes anyway but the cats, and this coming Friday night in the hot tub, her buddies.

Once at a Girls' Night last year, while they were on God-knows-what glass of champagne, someone, probably Rose, had asked "What's the most narcissistic thing any of you have ever done?" Ellen remembered how Janny piped right up with a giggle, and then when she could get her words out, after the stream of laughter at herself, she confessed, "Put a mirror between my legs and tweezed out all the grays."

"How about the time after a good mammogram," Marly said, "when I was so relieved that after the radiologist left the room, I kissed my own breasts."

"If I could only reach my breasts to kiss them," Rose said, "I never would have remarried."

Ellen sighed, thinking how ready she was for Friday night. Jan, who was always so elegant on "My Brightest Day," with her great red hair and her green eyes and those gorgeous high cheekbones, would be the first one to holler, "Let's get naked," drop her clothes, and head for the hot tub.

Then she'd probably have some new stories about all the shit she took from the people who worked on her show, the backstage plots, all of which were tons more interesting than the ones on that dopey daytime show. And Marly would have the latest chapter on her ex-husband Billy's awesome ego, and Rosie would be half there and the other half of her brain would be in her current screenplay. They'd sit naked in the hot tub, where their aging bodies felt healed and light, and so did their world-weary souls.

Christ, they'd been close for so long, they each knew who had taken the others' virginity and the stories that accompanied the deflowering. They each knew what the others wore or didn't wear to sleep, and what each of their bodies looked like when they were young and effortlessly hard, before gravity took its toll, in spite of the Stairmasters they'd all climbed so fervently that if they were really ascending, by now they'd all be in heaven.

Ellen even knew their scents by heart, probably because it was their custom every year to exchange cologne, soap, body lotion, some product of their favorite scent for Christmas. Marly wore Joy, she had since the sixties. Rose liked Opium, Jan still loved sultry Jungle Gardenia, and every year each of them gave Ellen some product from her own favorite scent, Norell. Last year she announced at their private Christmas dinner that maybe it was time to switch to another kind of gift, since she had enough Norell to last until she was a hundred.

Tonight Ellen hurried across the quiet lot to make a quick stop at her own bungalow office, just to see if there were any last-minute calls she needed to return from her car while she was on her way to meet Roger.

"Greens?"

"In here," her secretary called. Ellen walked through her own spacious, high-ceilinged office, furnished with chrome and glass, and into the pretty Italian-tiled bathroom, where Greenie was washing out coffee cups.

"You're out of Dodge already?" he asked. Greenie never left the building until Ellen did, even though she told him that once she went into a meeting, only "the deal gods" knew when she'd come out. He was loyal and true and he used the quiet time while Ellen was in meetings to cover each script she'd be taking home with a typed-up synopsis, which was always astute and thoughtful.

"It's Roger's birthday," she told him. She was still smarting from Bibberman's treatment of her, and she knew if she mentioned it to Greenie, he'd get on that kick again about how that shithead Bibberman wanted her out of there, and now the jealous little mongrel was going to try anything he could to get her to quit, so the studio wouldn't have to pay her off. He'd also remind her that the way Bibberman treated her in meetings was nothing compared to the things he said about her behind her back.

Ronald Greenberg was gay and as gorgeous as a runway model, and this was the third studio to which he'd followed Ellen. He was, Ellen always told close friends, her "secret weapon." He had no desire to be an executive himself because, he said, he didn't want the pressure, but he was Hollywood wise, understood the politics, and somehow managed to know where every body in the industry was buried.

"Want me to walk you to the car?" he asked Ellen now, taking her briefcase out of her hand, removing obsolete drafts of scripts and changing them for the current ones with his notes clipped to them, then handing the case back to her.

"Nahh," she said. "I'll be okay. I can't imagine any mugger who could want to hurt me worse than Bibberman does."

"He's looking to get you crazy. So don't you cave, my love," Greenie said sympathetically, then added, "because I can't afford to be out of a gig."

"I'm hanging in tooth and nail, Greens," she told him. "Even if, in my case, it *is* bonded tooth and acrylic nail."

Greenie laughed. "That reminds me, you need a manicure," he said. "I'll get someone to come to your house late Saturday afternoon so you can read at the same time."

"Thanks, Greens," she told him, and in a minute she was out the door and out of the building into the dark, full-moon night.

FIVE

SHE LOVED the leather smell inside her black 735i BMW, and after she slid behind the wheel, she heaved a sigh of relief and sat back against the soft tan seat. In that room upstairs she knew the others were probably giving Bibberman "high five" for humiliating her, and she hated the poor schmucks and pitied them at the same time. All three of them had stories flying around about them that even if they were partly true made them really sad cases.

Like the one that Richardson's model marriage was a front for his real sexual pleasure, adolescent boys. That Schatzman hadn't had an erection in his life, and his two beautiful blond children were the result of his wife's donor insemination. And that Bibberman's wife of fifteen years had left him once for a woman in New York, but the woman dumped her, so Bibberman took her back.

Who cared if they sat there trashing everyone in town, using the late meeting as an excuse not to go home to their bad marriages, she'd be having dinner with Roger. The guard in the kiosk waved as she drove through. "Eat my dust," Ellen said quietly through a smile and a wave.

Making movies for audiences made up of what H. L. Mencken called the "booboisie," was not exactly the career Ellen Feinberg Bass had intended for herself. Once she planned to produce plays, or work in production for a repertory company, and Marly used every opportunity to remind her that she'd fallen off her course. In fact, tonight as she drove up Beverly Glen she remembered that at the last Girls' Night the argument that had ended the party too early was about that very subject.

These women had known one another so long and so well they could really push one another's buttons, and turn an evening that started out with a great dinner and a lot of good wine and a million laughs into a battle. So that within minutes everyone would be marching off to bed huffy and testy and insulted, or sometimes just slamming out of the party to go home.

It was amazing to Ellen the way four grown women could still fight like kids. Over the years the four of them had whoppers, about things which in retrospect seemed so dumb. Like the night Marly came back from New York and told them she'd had dinner with Diane Sawyer and Mike Nichols and Jan called her a star-fucker. And the night Rose told Marly she thought her problems with Billy were a result of her parents not being affectionate enough, and Marly called her a condescending Jew.

But the last fight had been Ellen's fault. It started right after Jan told the Maximilian Schell story for the millionth time. They were still in the hot tub, hooting with laughter about Thanks a million, Maximilian. Rose was wearing her owlish glasses, which were too steamed up for her to be able to see out of them, but the tears of laughter came streaming down under the frames, onto her cheeks and into the water. And Marly's laugh was her usual outraged gasp that had inherent in it the words "It's a good thing my mother's not listening to this."

"You know, I think that story about Max is a great germ of an idea for the beginning of a film," Rose said that night, and she ran her fingers across the lenses of her glasses as if the glasses were windshields and her fingers were the windshield wipers, until they could all see the serious expression in her big brown eyes. "About a young woman whose life is changed because of one night with a pompous movie star. It's wonderful and poignant. A little low-budget piece, like *Garbo Talks*. It could be all about the way one night with a man like that affects her feelings about men forever."

"Yeah, great artsy-fartsy idea," Ellen said re-pinning a fallen lock of her abundant auburn hair. She loved her friends, but they didn't have a clue about the realities of how the business worked. "Except for two small things. No studio would make it, and nobody would pay to go and see it. Other than that . . . a classic!"

Rose pursed her lips and then frowned. She looked as if she were deciding whether or not to speak her mind while she took her glasses off and laid them next to the hot tub. "You've been working at a studio too long, El," Rose said, blinking rapidly. "You're starting to sound like one of the 'suits.' You *are* one of the 'suits.' I can't believe a woman I'm close to is on *their* side. It's like *Invasion of the Body Snatchers*."

Ellen had lost it. She hated herself when she flew off the handle the way she did that night, but it was a rap she didn't want to take. Especially from any of these three. "It's my fucking job, Rosie," she said, flaring. "So let's not confuse it with some manifestation of my inner core or my aesthetic sensibilities. I like art as much as you do, but it doesn't sell tickets. Christ, where do you all get off copping to the artistic sensibility bullshit? You wrote for TV, and Jan's on fucking daytime," and then she turned to Marly and said, "and peddling Mylanta isn't exactly playing Medea!"

"I think Rose is right," Marly said, turning her pretty face away from Ellen's tirade, the way they all were sure her very proper mother must have with her any time she behaved inappropriately. She had that look in her eyes that always glimmered there when she was ready to battle to the death for a cause, a challenge. "Because, unlike the rest of us who are scavenging around for jobs, you're in a power position, so you can make a difference. You're the one who can push for quality and taste in this trash-filled industry. I think the story of Jan and Max could be the beginning of an important concept. And if it was well told, it could be turned into a feminist statement. A beautiful little piece of art."

"The problem with a little piece of art," Ellen said, and she tried to control the tone in her voice that meant *you stupid dipshit*, "is that the only person who goes to see it is a little guy *named* Art. That's one ticket sold. Who's going to buy the rest of them? Get real. *You* know what people go to see. The head of production at my studio has what he calls a kaboom chart on his wall. If someone or something doesn't blow up every ten minutes in your script, he already has a deal negotiated with a new writer to come in and fix it, and you're toast."

There was a tsk, and a patronizing shaking of their heads that made Ellen's blood pressure rise. She had an overwhelming childish urge to splash the hot water right into all of their faces.

"Then I think that job is toxic and you ought to quit," Marly said, her eyes flashing angrily and her white-blond hair glistening in the moonlight.

"It may be," Ellen said, and now she was really steamed. "But at the moment it's feeding me, my unemployed son, my aging mother, and two very hungry Persian cats."

"And is it worth it?"

"Unlike you, Mrs. Billy Mann," Ellen said, her voice rising defensively, "I'm not divorcing a big star, so I can't afford to quit that toxic job. But I promise if I ever do marry someone that rich, I'll divorce him and get the kind of money you have, so I can have an organic job with no pesticides, and make art the whole fucking day long. In fact, it'll be so noncommercial that I'll even be able to use people with no names to star in it, like you and Jan." She regretted the outburst instantly but was still enraged that not one of them, people so close to her heart, got the point. That she had to make decisions that were based on the bottom line because that was how she kept her job. That many times she wished like hell she hadn't trapped herself in a lifestyle that was jacked up so high that she had to keep the job to afford herself and her family.

It was painfully quiet then, and one at a time they each found reasons to get out of the hot tub and make their way to their individual guest rooms in Marly's giant house, and it wasn't even midnight.

At dawn when they all stood in Marly's kitchen having their morning coffee, all of them looking as rumpled as the beds they'd just left, Ellen felt awful about saying all the mean things she'd said.

"I'm sorry," she told Marly. "I love you, and I'll still come and bail you out if they ever throw you in a Turkish prison." That

had been their promise to one another since the night they all
went to see *Midnight Express,* about a young American trapped
in a jail in Turkey. They swore over coffee at Ships in Westwood
that they would never be the kiss-the-air-next-to-your-face
bunch, but the real, be-there-asking-the doctors-if-they're-doing-
everything-they-can kind of friends.

"I love you, too," Marly said. "And I promise I'll still ride in
the back of the ambulance when you keel over from working too
hard at that poisonous job." They had all laughed at that, ending
the morning with warm feelings. The girls, Ellen thought, pulling the Beamer up to the valet parker at Adriano's. She would
have a blast with them on Friday night.

In Adriano's she waved at the hostess and headed for her
usual table, where Roger was already seated, and when he stood
to greet her, his astonishing good looks overwhelmed her. She
still thought of him as her baby, the son she'd raised alone after
her divorce from Herb Bass the podiatrist. Herbie, as his frat
brothers called him, was a spoiled brat she'd made the mistake
of marrying when he was in podiatry school at UCLA and had
the good sense to divorce by his graduation. He'd never given
her or Roger a dime since he moved back east.

"Hi, Mom," Roger said.

There was always an instant of needing to do a reality check
when she saw the man that he was now. Over six feet tall, with
shoulder-length black hair and huge hazel eyes that danced with
his sweet sense of humor.

"Sorry to be late, honey," she said, hugging him and sitting in
the chair he'd pulled out for her.

"Mom, for you fifteen minutes late is early," he said, grinning
at her.

"Happy birthday," she said. "I'm giving you cash."

"Thank you. It's just what I always wanted." He gestured for
the waiter to bring his mother a San Pellegrino, which was what
he was drinking.

Ellen studied his handsome face. A face she knew so well she
could tell a story about every funny little scar on it. The one on
his chin that he got when his dirt bike hit a bump and he went

flying over the handlebars. The one near his right eyebrow that happened one day at Little League when instead of catching a baseball in his glove, it hit him in the face. Ellen had a fast slide show in her head of all the emergency rooms they'd sat in playing "Go Fish."

Somehow they'd survived a life with no husband for her and a deadbeat father for him, a million different nutty jobs for her, and assorted homes, rented and owned, depending on her financial status at the moment. Now things were good, now she was where she'd fought to be. Now she could afford to give Roger the moon, and no Bibberman was going to get that good feeling away from her.

"So how's life at the top?" Roger asked.

"Believe me, baby, if I knew how to do something else, I'd do it," she said, working to keep it light. She'd never trouble Roger with her fears about her job. "But I'm too old to have babies and too anal retentive to get married, so what's left? Limos, lunches, deals. Right? That reminds me," she said, pulling her electronic organizer out of her purse and pushing a few buttons, "I have to input the alarm to remind me to call an agent at nine in the morning about an auction for a screenplay." While she typed a note into the minicomputer, adding a note to herself about the exact wording she wanted to use with the agent, she heard Roger say, "Mom, I'm gay."

She dropped the screen tapping pen and looked at him.

"Oh, honey . . ."

"I'm lying," he said, "but I figured I'd get your attention, and now what I have to tell you will be a relief by comparison. I want to go to USC film school."

Ellen looked closely at him, hoping she'd misheard.

"There's no contest. I'd much rather have gay," she said, taking his hand. "I mean, Rogie, you really do?" she asked, her brow furrowing as he nodded. "I'm amazed. How can you want to go to film school and be in this business after all you know about all the awful parts of it."

"How can I not? I'm a tinsel diaper baby," he said, grinning. It was a grin that had cost her thousands of dollars in braces. It was true. His whole life had been spent in show business. He'd gone everywhere with her, sat under directors' chairs playing with his Matchbox cars, spent weeks on locations all over the world. At four, he discussed divorce with Cher. At seven, he "did lunch" with John Travolta. When he was nine, Michael Keaton was directing a short film with a part in it for a young boy, and he'd asked Ellen if he could "borrow" Roger to star in it.

"Rogie, the business really stinks," she tried, already knowing it was a lost cause. "It's mean and ugly and shitty. They lie, they cheat, they steal, they're phony and immoral. They'll screw you six ways till Sunday and then hug you and say, 'We're family.' "

"Mom," he said, squeezing a lime into his mineral water. "I don't know how to break it to you, but to a lot of people in the business, you're the 'they' in that story."

She put the organizer back in her purse and watched the fizzy mineral water as the bubbles rose in her glass. "Besides," Roger said, "what else do I know? I grew up in the business. I understand grosses better than geography. Once I was in the library and I saw a copy of *Sophie's Choice* and I said, 'Oh, wow! The novelization.' All my life I thought when kids played doctor, the doctor was supposed to be a plastic surgeon."

Ellen laughed. "Okay, enough with the Hollywood jokes," she said. "I can see your mind is made up. Just when I thought I was finished paying tuition. Why couldn't you have gone into your father's business instead of mine?" she joked.

"Podiatry?" he laughed, knowing she was kidding. "Somehow it doesn't send the same excitement through my body."

Ellen sighed, and her only child put his hand over hers and looked into her eyes. "Hey, Mom, look at it this way. Maybe I'll be among the exceptions. The one honest, uncompromising director. The one who cares more about the product than the bottom line." It choked her with emotion to hear words she remembered saying herself somewhere a long ago time. But that was before she moved to Hollywood and her first job was as a gofer on "The Monkees," and the idealism started slipping away.

"Sure, honey," she said now, "maybe you will."

Roger had a late date with a new girlfriend, so Ellen was home by nine-thirty. While she fed the cats, she played back her answering machine. She had calls from Richard Gere, Mike Ovitz, Meryl Streep, and Marly Bennet. Marly's call was reminding her that Girls' Night was on Friday and that she'd better be there.

The wine she had with dinner was making her a little woozy, and she thought she'd fall asleep immediately, but after she took off her makeup, flossed and brushed her teeth, and shooed the cats away so she could slide into her bed, she picked up the stack of scripts from her night table and sorted through them.

One of them was an action-adventure piece that interested her because she saw on the title page that it was written by two women. Maybe that would mean there would be some heart in it. Maybe if it had emotions along with the explosions and she really liked it, she could bring in a woman to direct it, too. Wouldn't those kaboom films benefit by a human touch that made the characters more accessible, so that the audience actually felt something for the people involved?

Yes, maybe she'd just look this one over. Even though she felt worn out, she kept reading. Good opening, she thought, after the first four pages. And after a few more pages the story was starting to intrigue her. By the time she was on page forty, she had grabbed a pen and a pad and was feverishly making notes. Hurriedly writing down what she knew were wonderful ideas to make this project work. People she could put together. The people who would make it happen. She could even imagine the kind of musical background it should have.

When she'd finished the script, she put it and her pad of notes on the table next to the bed and turned off the light. Ah, Bibberman, you son of a bitch, she thought. There's life in this old girl yet, and I am not going to let you get to me. I'll hang in and get some good work done, even if I have to be known as the menopausal mogul. Then she slid into sleep with a smile on her tired face.

SIX

SHE WASN'T EVEN SURE if her rattletrap clunker of a car would make it all the way to L.A. She couldn't afford to have it serviced. Couldn't afford to do anything. She had one credit card that wasn't maxed out, so she'd use that to fill the tank and get the oil checked. Of course once she got down there and one of them gave her a job, things would be different.

After she decided on the plan, it was so easy she wondered why she hadn't thought of it before. Well, not easy, it took some nerve, but hell, she was an actress. She could sound as if she were somebody important. She took a deep breath and dialed the alumni office in Pittsburgh.

"CMU Alumni Office. This is Dee Dee. How may I help you?"

"Oh, hi, Dee Dee. This is Rose Schiffman. I was Rose Morris when I was at school there," she said, and then she took a beat to hear if Dee Dee would make some remark to let her know she didn't sound like Rose Schiffman, or if Dee Dee knew Rose Schiffman, but she didn't seem to notice that anything was weird. It was a great idea because since Rose Schiffman was a writer, most people didn't know what her voice sounded like.

She said she was part of the West Coast Drama Alumni Clan, and she wanted to do some personal solicitations for the new building fund, to write a personal letter reminding all of the entertainment-business alums that the drama department had been responsible for their success and that now it was time for them to "give back." Boy was that the right thing to say. The very friendly Dee Dee flipped.

She said, "Oh, Mrs. Schiffman, I loved the movie you wrote, Faces. I cried so much when I watched it. My husband and I just rented the video again the other night, and I cried again as if I'd never seen it *before. I know a personal letter from you to some of the alums would mean so much. I mean there's such a lot of money in the entertainment industry, and who better to give it to than us. Right?''*

"My sentiments exactly,'' she said, thinking what idiots people made of themselves over celebs.

"Why don't I fax you a list of the people we're trying to get involved in the new fund-raising campaign?'' the girl asked her.

"Great,'' she said. "Home phones and addresses, too, Dee Dee. And I'll get right on the case. But I'm out of town, so if you don't mind, I'll give you a local fax number where you can reach me.''

"No problem,'' said Dee Dee.

She gave her the fax number of a drugstore outside of town, and by the time she got there, the pages were waiting for her. Names and phone numbers and home addresses of the big-time West Coast drama department alums. Yes! That night she sat and read the fawning cover letter that came from the alumni office to Rose Schiffman. Then she went over and over the list of names and home addresses, trying to picture the houses that went with those addresses.

She circled the names of the people who would remember her and who would be nice to her. Trying to decide which of them might have a job for her. Then next to their names she wrote ideas for what the jobs might be. That way when she went to see them, she wouldn't be wasting their time. She could go right in and ask for what she wanted. That night in bed she copied all the addresses into her own little address book by hand. Put them in their alphabetical locations, as if they'd been in there all these years. They should have been. She should have stayed in touch. That's what she'd tell them when she saw them.

Early in the morning, she packed a few things in her little duffel bag, the only piece of luggage she owned. Then she called in to her boss and told him, in a voice she knew would be convincing, that she was deathly ill. "You sound awful,'' he said. Hah! She thought, at least all those years of acting training didn't go totally to waste.

When she was ready to leave, she checked her purse to be sure she had the little remote control for her answering machine with her in case she needed to call home for messages from L.A. Then she went into the kitchen to turn on the answering machine she'd had for a million years.

When she caught sight of her face in the oven door of her murky little kitchen, she laughed a pained laugh.

It was the face of Marterio looking back at her, the character she played in The House of Bernarda Alba *at Tech. She had coveted the part of the beautiful young Adela, the starring role, but when the casting went up on the call board, the part of Adela had gone to Jan O'Malley. And instead she had been cast as Marterio, the dried-up, jealous sister.*

Poor Marterio, she thought, looking critically at herself, and poor me. She remembered sitting in the dressing room in 1966, putting mauve shadows under her eyes and lines across her forehead, drawing more lines from her nose to her mouth. Then pulling her long orange silky hair back and spraying it with a black-colored spray, except for the temples, which she powdered gray. And when she heard her cue, she'd charged out on that stage and given the best performance the school had ever seen.

The little theater shook when Marterio said to Adela, "I have a heart full of a force so evil that, without my wanting to be, I'm drowned by it." Now the not-so-funny joke was that she looked like Marterio without the makeup. The lines and bags and gray hair were there on their own. Pushing fifty. How did it all go by so fast?

Of course, not one of the others probably looked this bad. In fact on the rare days when she was home from work, she watched Jan on "My Brightest Day" and couldn't get over how gorgeous she still looked. Once when she was still married to Lou, he came home for lunch one day while she was watching Jan in a scene and said, "You went to school with that woman? She looks twenty years younger than you do." Even though she thought so, too, it hurt to hear the derision in his voice when he said it.

She should have told him, "Of course she does. Because she never had the pleasure of being married to you." And the truth was that the good life made a big difference in how you held it together. Money didn't just talk. It sang and danced and paid for fancy skin products with secret ingredients from Switzerland. Not to mention little nips and tucks in the face, and boob jobs that made your knockers stand straight up, even when you were pushing fifty.

Every one of those people on that alumni list probably had a job they could give her. Rose Schiffman was a writer. A writer must need a proofreader or something like that, she thought, noting that on the list. And Ellen Bass. She probably wanted to get rid of that jerk who answered her phones and get someone in there who would say, "Ellen Bass's office," in a deep, rich voice, and then be nice to the people who called, instead of rude the way her overprotective male secretary was. Receptionist would be a great foot-in-the-door job for her.

And how about Jan O'Malley, who had her plate full with a full-time job on that soap opera and a little boy. She probably needed someone who was good with kids to help her with him. I'd be great with that little boy Jan adopted, she thought. He'd be better off with me, his mother's old college friend, than some non-English-speaking illegal alien, which is what she probably has now. People who got babies, then didn't stay home to take care of them themselves, should all be shot.

Now that was a good idea. Nanny. For a while anyway. Taking care of a little kid was something she had experience doing. She'd go over there to Jan's house and casually befriend the kid, and then hit Jan up for the job. Jan would be so glad to have someone of her caliber around her little boy, she'd jump at the idea.

According to the faxed list, Jan lived in Hollywood. She found the street right away on the Thomas Guide. She would go and see Jan first when she got there on Friday afternoon, and then maybe that white-haired witch Marly Bennet.

SEVEN

MARLY BENNET believed that any ailment in the world could be cured by a chiropractic adjustment. That if her estranged husband had only had his spine cracked back into alignment, their marriage would have been saved. She was a passionate devotee of New Age practices who was waiting for the rest of the world to catch up with what she'd known for years about nutrition and meditation and breathing through the spine and high colonics.

She could convulse the others with stories about all the practitioners with whom she did business, like the woman in Malibu whose counsel she sought who channeled Marilyn Monroe and dispensed Marilyn's insights about show business and men. Or the herbalist who sold her a poultice to hang around her neck that would retard aging. But their most recent favorite was the story about the therapist who was helping her cure an inconvenient physical malady.

"I've finally stopped having urinary tract problems. Doctor Brotman got me to use my active imagination, to personify my bladder and talk to it," she announced last month.

Ellen moaned and rolled her eyes. "Here we fucking go," she said. "You know you're in L.A. when you start having confrontations with your internal organs. Can you imagine telling someone in Kansas, 'I took a meeting with my bladder?' They'd have you tarred and feathered."

"So what happened?" Jan asked.

"Well, she had me put two chairs across from one another and sit in one of them. First she told me to ask my bladder the questions as me, and then to move to the other chair and play the part of my bladder. It was remarkably telling. I said, 'Bladder, what seems to be the trouble? There is no apparent physical reason for my problem with you, and yet you persist in being irritable. Can you tell me why?' "

"You kept a straight face for that?" Ellen asked. She could never understand how the otherwise sensible Marly could put herself into the hands of yet another nutty quasi shrink with yet another wacko technique.

"Shh, you cretin, it's Gestalt therapy. Read Fritz Perls," Rose said, elbowing Ellen. "Go ahead, Mars. Then you moved to the other chair, and the bladder said . . ."

"The bladder said, 'Marly, I'm weeping for the loss of your youth.' " Marly looked around at all of them. "Isn't that fascinating?" she asked, narrowing her green almond-shaped eyes thoughtfully, as if she'd discovered something profound.

"You paid money for a session where you played Edgar Bergen to your urinary tract?" Ellen said irritably. "I was right, we are definitely in southern California. I think we all have to move. You three especially, because you have young kids. To make sure they don't grow up thinking this is the real world. Rose, see if you can get Andy to move his practice the hell out of here."

"Are you kidding?" Rose said. "I'm not moving. I'm putting in a call to my ovaries to see if they'll do lunch."

Marly's New Age material always had them laughing for hours. But as funny as it was, they all agreed that her A material was in the stories she told about Billy Mann, her soon to be ex-husband. A man she'd married when he was an out-of-work stand-up comic and she was the star of a long-running television series. Now she was out of work and he was a giant star. "The King of Late Night Television."

She told the others that the reason she started calling him that was because one day, a few years ago, they were having a conversation, or rather, she was talking and he was off in the ether and answering her questions by rote, so she said, "Billy? What is it?" And in a faraway voice, probably brought on by the stunning recent news that his 11:30 P.M. show was in first place, he said in amazement, "My God. I'm the king of late night television."

"Billy's such a narcissist," Marly joked, "that in the heat of passion, he yells out his own name!" Everyone agreed that her jokes were a hell of a lot funnier than the dumb ones Billy did in the opening monologue of his show every night. Unfortunately, to Jennifer and Sarah, their twin daughters, none of it was even a little bit funny.

They were the ones who since the separation were always waiting for their father to pick them up to spend the weekend at his house, and waiting and waiting until Marly looked at the clock and realized he'd flaked out on them again. Then her heart broke when she watched them unpack their little ballerina bags and cry themselves to sleep. It was an awful situation.

And all the while Marly kept telling the twins, "He loves you, he just doesn't know how to show it." Many nights she sat in the bedroom with the two canopied beds, soothing them, singing to them, until finally their breathing told her they were asleep. Then she went into her own room and cried herself to sleep, too.

GET IN BED WITH BILLY is what the billboards everywhere said. Billy's new show was about to premiere, and the advertising blitz to promote it forced Billy into America's bloodstream. Marly said she'd like to climb up onto one of those billboards with a can of red paint and write her addendum, YOU MIGHT AS WELL! EVERYONE ELSE HAS.

How Billy could ever want anybody but Marly was a mystery to anyone who knew her. She was a startling beauty, tall, with white skin and hair that had turned Harlow white prematurely when she was in her twenties. She had poodle-ish curls cascading all around a chiseled face and a smile of perfectly white teeth. In fact, everything about her was blindingly white. She drove a white car and dressed in white and had a white dog.

One night, in the middle of a screaming fight just before he moved out, Billy harangued her about just that. "I'm going blind from all the white! It makes me want to run around outside through the mud and then come in and dance on the carpets and the sofa, on the fucking duvet cover, and mess it up. I'm sick of white."

"Don't fret, sweetheart," she told him with the implacable ironic deadpan she used so well in her comedy performing. "As soon as you leave, the man I move in here will be black."

Billy had laughed at that. She could always make him laugh. But he searched her eyes to see if there was any truth in that.

"You're not seeing Arsenio, are you? I mean, that would be a mistake! He's not even on the air any more."

He knew she might not be kidding because she was a flaming liberal, which was another thing that drove him crazy. The way she fought the bleeding-heart fight for every injustice anyone could name. She was always on a tear about some liberal cause or other. Fighting for gun control or against oil rigs, against animal testing or for bicycle helmets. She was on top of every controversial issue. Always at some shopping mall or other, passing out pertinent leaflets.

And when her dazzling persona strolled through the Galleria, where she was speaking out on one issue or another that week, dressed in white jeans and a white cashmere sweater and white cowboy boots, pretty Marly Bennet still turned heads. The fans all remembered her from "Keeping Up with the Joneses," a television situation comedy on which she played Ali Jones for seven years. The character was the outspoken mother of seven children, and Marly's comedy timing, together with an intellect behind the eyes, had reviewers comparing her to greats like Eve Arden.

The show had been off the air for two years, and the acting jobs for women her age were rare, with only a TV movie now and then and a commercial once a year or so. But that wasn't enough, and she was worried. She went on interviews but did so reluctantly, hating the humiliation inherent in the process. Now and then she considered going into politics but decided there would be even worse humiliation in Washington.

This morning, after she dropped the twins at school, she came home and spent an hour on the Nordic Trac in the home gym she and Billy had built, then she took a bath. She was sitting at her dressing table putting moisturizer on her long white legs, trying to decide what to wear on a commercial interview that afternoon, when she heard the unmistakable *voom-bah* of a Ferrari pulling into her driveway. Billy.

From the bedroom window she saw him hop out of the car, watched the top of his head, balding a little in the middle of the blond curly hair. As he moved toward the front door, she felt her panic rise. What in the world did he want at her house in the middle of the day? She threw open her closet and tried to decide if she should change out of her robe and into something decent.

Ellen would tell her, "It doesn't matter how you look. He doesn't see you anyway, he only sees himself." Rose would tell her she should ignore the bell and pretend to be out. Of course her car was in the driveway, so she couldn't do that. And Jan, the only one of them who always believed there was still hope for Marly and Billy to get back together, would say, "Gussy up, honey. Make him eat his heart out."

Oh hell. She ran down the stairs through the large marble foyer and pulled the door open. Billy, still six inches shorter than she was, stood leaning on the door jamb, and she hated the way seeing him there made her melt. That wild blond hair and little-boy look of his made every woman in America want to pull him to her bosom and still did her in.

"Hey," he said, smiling his most adorable Billy smile. It was one of a repertoire of smiles Marly knew so well that one night, when they were still wildly in love, she'd described them and named them for him, and he'd laughed in her arms about how well she knew him. This was the one she called, "Howdy, Ma'am." It had a degree of reticence, a politesse, and a humility Billy didn't possess anywhere in his actual emotional makeup, only as an arrow in his performer's quiver.

"I have all the encyclopedias I need," Marly said, and he grinned.

"I was in the neighborhood and I thought I'd stop by and remind you that tonight's the first taping of my new show, so I'll be sending a car and driver to get the twins at around five-thirty, and if I could have them for two nights, I'd like to take them to Disneyland—"

"But your secretary and your publicist and your manager were all too busy to call and ask me those questions, the way they usually do?" she asked. He laughed at that, but it was an embarrassed laugh.

"Look, Mar, I've been a jerk. I know that. I made a mess out of our lives together and don't think I don't know it was all my fault. But I've been thinking all week about coming over to ask you if you thought that there was ever a way that we could all get back together and be a family again."

Marly stared at him, sure this had to be a dream. That any minute the phone would ring or the alarm would go off and wake her. This was not Billy Mann, TV star, her soon to be ex-husband, doing the impossible. Think carefully, her shrink told her, before you say anything to him. Don't let him get to you. So she took a long pause, and finally spoke.

"Billy." She felt herself trying not to tremble. "In my lifetime, I've seen a lot of things. Men walking on the moon, and the Berlin Wall coming down, and the end of the Cold War. I even saw the nutrition pyramid change so that carbohydrates are now better for me than protein, something I always wished would happen. So I know there are miracles in this world, and good ones, too. But I still don't believe that one of those could possibly be that you'd want to have a family experience. So what do you really want?"

In spite of her words she was drowning in hope. Being pulled down by the inexplicable possibility that the impossible had happened. But at the same time knowing it was absurd, childish, to believe it. No, a better word would be lunacy.

"Yes, but Mar, you're the one who always says you're invested in the idea that the human spirit has the capacity for change. And I know if you weren't, you wouldn't be working so hard with that shrink of yours, or signing up for all the self-help workshops you go to, or reading all the books about Eastern philosophies."

"True, but I'm the one who's doing all of that, not you, which

means you're not the one who's changing. So no, I don't think
we have a chance. At least not now. You'd need to do a lot of
work on yourself before I could ever go back." When the words
were out of her mouth, she said a little prayer that he'd give her
an argument.

"What if I start doing the work? Did a crash course, like the
Stanley Kaplan's, for becoming a good guy?"

"What if you did?"

"Would you give us a shot?"

She was choking on the words, yes, I love you, but what she
said was, "I have to think about it."

"Can I come in while you do?"

She sighed and stepped back into the foyer, and he followed
her, taking in the hall and then the high-ceilinged living room
that she'd redone three times since he'd left, just to keep busy.
"The house looks great," he said appreciatively. He'd never once
said that when he lived there.

"Thanks."

"*You* look great," he said, looking at her body in the white
Fernando Sanchez robe.

"Billy, what do you want? What is it? This is such a stunning
overnight change, you'll forgive me if I suspect it."

He was wandering ahead of her to the kitchen and she followed him on the cold marble floor, in her bare feet, having a
sudden rush of worry that she hadn't had a pedicure in a month
and that maybe her toenails looked bad.

"I don't know. Mid-life crisis, maybe. Looking at my life, sitting at that desk every night interviewing all those women, like
tonight my guests are that pig Madonna and that moron Kim
Basinger, and I know I'll be thinking 'Yeah? So what?' They wear
too much makeup, they push too hard, they need writers to
make them funny, and you don't."

In a sudden move, he hoisted himself up to sit on the center
chopping-block island, which was where he always used to sit
when he lived there, just where he used to like to sit on those
delicious nights when after sex they'd come down to the kitchen
to have a pot of tea. It felt so nostalgic to Marly that she hurried

to the stove, turned on the kettle, and looked in the brisker to see if there were any cookies.

"I don't know," he said. "Maybe I still can't do it."

Please, she prayed, whirling around, don't let him change his mind. "But I think I've grown up," he went on, staring out the window. "I think I finally get it. So what can I say? When I look back on my life, the only times I remember ever really being happy were the times I was in this house with you and the twins. I know we weren't always in sync."

Marly couldn't control a snicker.

"Yeah, yeah, yeah," he said, "you can laugh. You should laugh. We both know I was a dog. But I need to change. I want to be good for my family. And I think I can."

Marly stood completely still in the spot, afraid that her moving might make him reconsider again. "And did I mention that I really love you?" he asked. Oh, God. He hadn't said those words to her in years. She took two cups and saucers out of a cupboard and hoped he didn't hear them clinking together because she was trembling as she put them on the counter.

"Actually you didn't mention that," she said.

He sighed and looked long at her with very big, sad eyes. "Well, I really really do," he said and he put out a hand for her to come and take, which she did. And as he studied her hand that still had a white circle around the third finger from her recently removed wedding band, he said, "We both know I don't deserve it, but if you take me back, I swear you won't be sorry." Then he kissed each of her fingers.

"Don't do that, Billy," she said with zero conviction in her voice. She'd been celibate since he left. He took each of her arms in his hands and put them around his waist, then looked into her eyes. Sitting on the counter made his head higher than hers, which was probably the reason he did it.

"I love you, Mar," he said now, putting his hands in her white curly hair that had been piled on top of her head in the bathtub and was coming down, as a bobby pin found its way down her neck and into the back of the robe. She closed her eyes, knowing he would kiss her, praying he would kiss her.

Please don't let me ever wake up, she thought as his lips touched hers softly, then harder, and then he slid down from the counter and put his feet on the floor, while her silky white robe seemed to fall open without any help at all. And on the kitchen banquette, at ten-thirty in the morning, Marly Bennet was making hot, wet love with her almost ex-husband, and both of them were crying while the tea kettle whistle shrieked.

"I love you, I'll always love you, I'm so afraid." Marly wasn't sure later which of them said which of those words, or if both of them said them all. Afterward, they had tea and cookies, and when Billy stood at the door, he reminded her about the car and driver coming to pick up the twins at five-thirty to take them to his taping, and he said he'd call her tomorrow to find out what she thought of the show.

"A pain reliever," she said on the way back upstairs. That was the product in the commercial she was auditioning for today. Some pain reliever, though her agent, Harry, told her when he called that he wasn't sure which pain reliever. Usually she had more information to go on — what the character in the commercial was like, what income stratum, what lifestyle, so she'd know how to dress.

"Well, no pain relievers for this girl today," she said out loud, laughing a happy laugh.

EIGHT

BEFORE SHE REALIZED that a successful career could turn a relationship into a ménage à trois, with the career as the third being, Marly was happy. Her career had been moving along nicely before she met Billy, but she tried hard not to let the success get to her equanimity. She would not let her ego get inflated like the balloons in the Macy's parade the way she'd seen it happen to so many actors. So far she'd avoided having the obligatory entourage of managers, publicists, personal trainers, and masseuses.

When she and Billy met at the Improv, she'd been on "The Corner Bar," her first TV situation comedy, for two years, and her style as a gifted comedienne was already well respected. She had a healthy salary, loved the work, and was very hopeful about her future. And she knew she was doing something right when she was introduced at the tapings and ran out to take her bow and the studio audience went wild cheering for her.

She remembered reading an article about one of her favorite actors, James Cagney, who was quoted as describing his career as "just a job," something he did well but into which he didn't invest his soul. Marly was determiend to treat hers that way, too.

"Way bigger bucks," Billy said to her one night in the car as he drove her home from the taping. He came to nearly every Friday night shoot, because Friday nights at the Comedy Store and the Improv were the night when the polished, well-known stand-up comics got up to work. Low-on-the-totem-pole guys like Billy Mann were relegated to working during the week. At Marly's tapings he sat in a seat the network pages always roped off for him in the front row, and he cheered the loudest for Marly when she came out for her bow.

"Your character is breaking out. They should spin her off," he said to her in that inside lingo that bothered Marly when he used it.

"Thank you, honey," she said, sitting back with her eyes closed against the passenger seat of Billy's old Datsun with the ripped upholstery. She was pleased with the way the taping had gone that night.

"I think you hire a PR guy tomorrow and start a campaign to get them to give you your own show."

She laughed.

"I mean it."

She should have known then, and maybe she really did in her solar plexus, that Billy's ambition would be what brought them down.

"It's okay, Bill," she said. "I'll get there in time."

"Not if you don't step on people's necks you won't."

She remembered how he pulled his hand away from hers that night when she patted his hand to calm him down. "You have to ride the wave," he warned. "You only get so many of them. This is yours. Don't just let it move you around. Get on top of it."

She didn't feel his brand of desperation, his hunger. She had grown up in a world of abundance, with a handsome doctor father, an elegant picture-book mother, in a home and a town in New England out of Currier and Ives. Billy was a poor kid from a big Catholic family in which he had to be funny to get attention. And now, even though he was a history-making late-night star, no amount of attention ever seemed to be enough for him.

So when he started making it on television, he went hog wild. Not just for himself and his career, but for Marly and the twins Marly had carried after "The Corner Bar" went off the air. Billy was a hit stand-up comic guesting on other people's shows and making Johnny Carson laugh so hard the star had to put his face down on the desk. And after a while he was making very big money as a headliner in Las Vegas.

He spent every dime, on a new house, new cars, overly lavish birthday parties, trips in private planes, and on a staff of so many people that one day Marly found herself coming home from taking the girls to the park and asking some strange woman in a uniform in her kitchen, "Who in the hell are you?"

The woman was the special nutritionist bringing body-building meals for Mr. Mann. Too much, it had all been too much. Especially after Billy got his own show, when things started moving out of the realm of the real world. It wasn't the same as being an actor on a sit-com whom people stopped on the street and squinted at and asked, "Aren't you, uh . . . on that show . . . what's it called again?" This was different. This was about walking into every restaurant and watching people sit up and crane their necks, and about hearing the constant hum of his name, Billy Mann, Billy Mann, look, Billy Mann.

And people coming to the table when he was buttering his roll, or worse yet, making a toast to his wonderful wife, strangers thrusting their napkin and a pen at him for an autograph. And asking him personal questions and telling him which of his shows they hated and loved. Of course there was no way they couldn't love Billy.

It drove the twins crazy. Once they had to leave Disneyland because Billy couldn't go two feet without being mobbed. The twins were nine or ten then, and Marly remembered their, "Oh noooos," as each time Billy signed the autographs and amused the group who approached him. And just as he felt able to extricate himself and move his family away, another group of fans would move in on him.

"I'll call Eisner," Marly remembered him saying as they got back into the limo that brought them to the park, the big, long stretch limo that drove back on the freeway toward home before they even had a chance to go on one ride. The twins were both sobbing in disappointment. "I made a mistake thinking I could do this without advancing it," Billy said. "I should have called Eisner a month ago and just asked him to close the park for us," he said, looking guiltily out the window of the limo.

"I hate you, Daddy," Sarah said. "I want a real person for a father. Not you!"

Marly shook her head, remembering that sad ride home as she found a parking place down the street from the casting office. She took a deep breath and steeled herself for today's interview. A painkiller, she thought, pulling her rearview mirror down to take a last satisfied look at herself. "I'm ready for my close-up, Mr. DeMille," she said to her reflection and got out of the car.

In the reception area of the casting office there were a lot of women, chatting in that guarded, friendly way they did in these situations. Women who under other circumstances might have let their hair down with one another, in this room where they knew a big job was at stake, were tense and phonily sweet. Marly looked at them all and had a mad urge to stand up and say, "I just had the best sex in the world with the sexiest man alive. My husband, and he still loves me." But instead she floated along with her lovely inner grin.

She looked around at the different types, trying to figure out what the casting people were looking for. In this group there were the folksy-looking plaid-flannel-shirt types and a few perfect-hair types, and there was one very glamorous woman with black curly hair who was dressed in Chanel. And they were all up for the same part. She sighed and took a seat, waiting to go in. One actress emerged, looked flustered, and announced to everyone in the room after the door closed behind her, "It's an ice-cold reading, and they give you about a minute to look at the words," then flounced tearfully out of the waiting room.

Cold readings. Marly was good at those. Instead of giving you a long time to look at the script, they handed it to you, gave you a few minutes to look it over, and then you took your best shot, reading with one of the casting people. When it was Marly's turn to go in, she felt confident. She had always aced cold readings. And this would be for a one-minute commercial. In the past she'd read cold for miniseries, for heaven's sake. This would be nothing.

When the casting director saw it was Marly coming in, she stood and walked over to welcome her. "Marly Bennet, how are you?" she asked, and there was a reverence to the greeting that made Marly feel okay about being seen this way, as one of a group. After all, she told herself as part of the litany she always went through to make her feel more confident, her television career over the years had been substantial.

The only reason she was doing this was that at her age good parts for actresses were hard to come by. At least commercials were something to do, a way to feel you were working, still in the business, in front of the camera.

And this was the unfortunate way they cast the damn things. Unless, of course, you were a big name. Like Lindsay Wagner doing commercials for Ford. Not what they called a semi-name, in the middle class of the business, which was where Marly's career fell.

"This is Marly Bennet," the casting director said, introducing her to the assembled group, a few men in suits, a good-looking young man in shirt sleeves. Marly smiled her best smile. This would be a breeze, she would look at the dialogue, give her usual A plus reading, and get the job. She was head and shoulders above the caliber of actress she'd seen in the waiting room.

"She was Mrs. Jones in 'Keeping Up with the Joneses,' the casting director told the men, whose eyes were blank. "And before that she was Josie on 'The Corner Bar.' " Nothing. "And she's Billy Mann's wife," the casting director said, and then, as if someone had just plugged in the Christmas lights, suddenly all of their faces shone brightly in her direction. Marly felt her rage rise and her confidence fall, and she had to make a strong effort not to turn around and leave.

She was the one who had studied classical theater, she was the one who was working long before Billy ever stood on the stage at the Comedy Store. Why did everyone persist in introducing her as Billy's wife? But the casting director was handing her the script and she wanted a job, and what point was there in being childish about the way she'd been introduced?

"Look it over," the young woman said, and Marly had a flash of remembering when this young woman who was running the casting office was the intern to the now retired founder of the casting company. She was the kid who used to bring in boxes of take-out coffee and doughnuts. "I'll be reading with you, and when you're ready to go, tell me," she said to Marly. Dumb, that's all it was. To introduce her as Billy's wife.

Marly sat on a bentwood chair near a glass-topped table covered with résumés and photos of the actresses who were her competition and looked at the dialogue for the commercial. She didn't want to put on her reading glasses, so she held the script at arms length.

Later she'd rationalize away the whole incident by saying that her brain was only partially with it when she was looking at the script. She was thinking about her morning with Billy and the possibility that he might be coming home. The parts in the script were Suzy, Jane, and Grandmother. Marly felt as if she had a general idea about the dialogue and was ready to read. She looked up at the casting director.

"All set," she told her.

"Great. Let's go for it," the casting director said.

Marly waited for the casting director to give her a cue, but nothing happened. After a minute she looked over at the young woman, who looked at her questioningly and said, "Are you sure you're ready?"

"I'm sure," Marly said, then looked back down at the script. But the grandmother had the first line of dialogue. Good God, Marly realized, and then she almost burst into laughter as she saw what she hadn't before in her quick look at the material. The part of Suzy was for a toddler, Jane was the daughter in her twenties, who wanted her mother to take care of her baby, and they'd brought Marly in to read for Jane's mother. The grandmother.

If it hadn't been so funny, she would have wept. "Ahh, yes. Sorry," she said. "Let's start again." And then she read the grandmother's lines. Granted it was a very young grandmother who couldn't run after the little child to play because of arthritis, but a grandmother nevertheless. A good-looking Hollywood version of a grandmother, she would tell the girls tonight, and they'd die laughing.

Her audition was completely stilted and forced because while she read the lines, she was holding in a giggle. But later she thought that maybe it wasn't a giggle at all that had strangled her. "Thank you," someone said in that dismissive voice that means, "You've just wasted our time and yours." And Marly left, hurrying blindly through the room of waiting actresses, to pick the twins up at school.

Marly watched the twins approach her car. They were slim, with wild blond hair like Billy's. They love him, she thought as she watched them say a pleasant good-bye to some of their friends and then start an argument with one another as they walked. They'd be ecstatic when she told them he wanted to come home.

Maybe she'd stop at Gelson's to get the rest of the groceries she needed to make dinner for tomorrow night. Girls' Night, which for the first many years had rotated from one of their homes to another, had been headquartered at Marly's since Billy officially moved out, which was now nearly two years. It was the house that she and Billy bought after he started getting successful. Rose said it looked a little like Tara before the war, with a pretty white colonial exterior and a rolling lawn so green it made Marly very apologetic and defensive during the drought.

But the lawn wasn't healthy because of excessive watering. Its apparent health was due to the kind of care Marly, a perfectionist, gave everything in her life, and the irrigation set-up she had put in called a "drip system." Ellen said she was familiar with that system because it had provided all the dates she'd ever had.

There was a flower garden, a pool and cabana, and a very private hot tub where the four friends felt good about being naked, if that was possible at their age. The other reason the party was always at her house was that she was the best cook among them, so each time they came she made a glorious meal. Spent hours chopping away, and told them that when she did, she was healing her "inner Julia Child."

Tomorrow she would make a beautiful primavera sauce. As the twins' argument got louder, she ran over her grocery list in her head. And when she got to Gelson's Market on Sunset, the two of them came in with her, still bickering.

While they were waiting in line at the checkout, she saw Sarah's face turn pale and her eyes get wide, and she said, "Mom, look!" She was pointing to the end of the counter where they hang the magazines and the tabloids. And on the front page, the cover, in one of those full-page color shots they publish, was Billy. He was walking with his arm affectionately around some very young girl, who had to be no more than fourteen, and the headline said PARENTS ACCUSE BILLY MANN OF MOLESTING THEIR CHILD.

Marly walked over, and with a giant yank she wrenched the rack out of its holder and threw it on the ground. Then she went to the next counter and the next, pulling out the entire rack and throwing it over her shoulder so it hit the floor with a loud clang. And when the metal prongs wouldn't yield to her angry tugging, she ripped all of the copies of the tabloid out of the basket and threw them all around the market in a frantic gesture.

Soon the manager was trying to stop her, but she was hellbent on making her point, and she even knocked down a rack of Danielle Steel's latest paperback because it was in her line of fire.

"I bring children into this store," she shouted. "How can you allow this filth in here?" Later she told her friends that while she was going berserk in Gelson's, in the back of her head she could hear the voice of her ultra-proper grandmother, who once told her, "Men only want one thing, and that is to put their peters inside you." Marly had been horrified to hear that as a young girl. But now, all these years later, she was thinking how right on the money the old girl really was.

"Mrs. Mann," the store manager was saying. He knew her name because despite its vast size, Gelson's prided itself on being a friendly neighborhood market. "I'm so sorry. Maybe we can revamp the system and put the tabloids somewhere where children won't be privy to them. Mrs. Mann, please."

Marly was shredding copies of the *Enquirer*, then handing the shreds to the open-mouthed manager.

"Mom, please. Let's go home." The twins were mortified. They hadn't been old enough to understand when their mother stood on soap boxes to beg for support for the ERA, nor had they been in the courtroom when she fought the neighborhood in the valley that didn't want the shelter for battered women on one of their streets.

When the entire front of Gelson's in Pacific Palisades was trashed, Marly put her groceries in the ecologically responsible string bag she always carried to do her marketing, took each of the twins by a hand, and left to go home.

When she got there, she went upstairs to her bathroom and locked the door, sat down on the floor, and cried. That bastard Billy probably knew this news was breaking today, and he needed her and the girls back in his life so he'd look to the world like a family man who had been wrongly accused. Some lawyer probably told him, "Quick, go make a pass at your estranged wife and see if you can get her back." And she fell for it. Unfortunately she hadn't been to one practitioner who had an aphorism to cover this one.

NINE

HER KIDS *were sick of it. When they came over to visit her and they all watched TV together, one of them would be channel surfing with the TV remote, and a show or a commercial would flash by with Marly in it, and she'd say, "Marly Bennet! I graduated from college with her."*

She could tell by the way they exchanged looks that they were thinking, big fucking deal. Or one of them would say, "Oh, God, please don't let her start telling us again how she was the best one in the class, and now they're all famous and she's a Kmart shopper."

Polly was the only one who humored her about it all. Like that time when she was home sick from school. She came downstairs while her mother was watching "My Brightest Day," watching Jan do some big scene in a hospital room. She must have had some idiotic smile on her face, maybe she'd even been mouthing the words of the scene along with Jan, like some mental case.

"Was she nice, Mom?" Polly asked her when the closing-theme music was playing.

"Oh, yeah. And we were pretty good friends, too. She was the prettiest one in our class and I was . . ."

"The best actress, right?"

"Definitely. They all thought I was cool because I was from California. And Jack Solomon, a man who's now the president of a television network, was just some jerk who used to climb into the window of the dorm room at night and come to Jan's room when I was there, and we'd all sit on the floor, and we'd laugh and talk about how we were all going to be big in the theater some day. Probably in some rep company or regional theater, or on Broadway. Of course, after a while, I started dat-

ing your dad, and even though my parents were paying for me to live in the dorm, I mostly stayed at your dad's little place till we got married.''

She'd probably told that to Polly five hundred times, and now when she saw how hot Polly was with her boyfriend, she knew telling her that stuff had been a mistake. You weren't supposed to tell your kids you were fucking around so young, because then they figured it was okay for them to do it, too.

But it was worse to tell it to Polly, because it didn't take much to do the math that meant that the fucking around her mother had done was the reason she had been born. Why she came into the world, and her mother quit acting to take care of her, and then her brother, Jason, and then Kiki.

Once, just for a laugh, Polly had the idea of using Lou's video camera and directing a tape of her mother doing a few monologues. That great one she still remembered from The Glass Menagerie, in which Amanda Wingfield chastises her daughter for being afraid to go out in the world and take command of her life.

"Mom, you're awesome,'' Polly said afterward when they put the tape in the VCR and watched it together, holding hands. Tears were rolling down her daughter's cheeks, and that day Polly had looked at her with more respect than she ever had before.

And the kid was right. She was pretty goddamned good on that tape. Good enough to send it to Ellen Bass, which she never admitted to anyone that she did, with a letter saying give me a part in something, anything. But there was no response. Not a call. No fulfillment of her fantasy that one day the phone would ring and on the other end Ellen would be there, saying, "I'm sending the studio jet to come and get you. You were the best actress in the class. I have a part that only you can play.''

For a while, after all the kids were in school, she tried to do some work in regional theaters, in plays where she could rehearse at night and get Lou to put them to bed. One year she played the young wife in Barefoot in the Park at a local theater, and another year she played Patty in The Moon Is Blue. After Barefoot, when Lou brought the kids backstage they were really stoked. "Wow! Mom! You're better than a movie star,'' Jason said.

She'd seen the look of warning in Lou's eyes anytime she got caught up in thinking maybe there was still some way she could work as an actress, the look that meant "You do and I'll walk," so instead of acting she stayed home and played Little Mommy, the pet name that he called her for years. Right up until he left her for Polly's third-grade teacher.

And then the bastard, the fucking son of a bitch, when she was at her lowest, with no money, a lousy job, living in another lousy rented house, he found a fancy lawyer who helped him get the kids away from her. Last year in an angry argument over clothes, or some other stupid thing, Polly had shrieked at her, "I'm glad we're living with Daddy and Sharon. She's cool. She has a career. You're lame, mother."

Lame and old and unemployable. Maybe Polly's making that comment was what made her feel justified about taking the savings she'd been putting away for the girl's wedding and spending it on the trip to Los Angeles and this hotel room at the Sheraton Hemisphere that was fancier than any she'd ever seen in her life. On the fifteenth floor, with a view way below of the movie studio lot.

Right now down there, they were making television shows and movies. She could have been in those movies if she'd had the guts to leave Lou and go after what should've been her career. Before her gorgeous orange hair faded to this gray, before she started being menopausal crazy, with those hot flashes and waves of depression.

She had been embarrassed today in the lobby, checking in with her little duffel bag and her striped plastic purse, when the guy at the desk looked at her as if no one had ever made a deposit in cash before, but he took it. And now she stood against the window, looking down at the bright Los Angeles day, and watched as the trams that transported the tourists wended their way around the studio lot and past what had to be the commissary and the screening rooms.

And those buildings over there must be where the important studio executives had their offices. One of the executives was Ellen Bass. Ellen Bass, who was too busy to watch her tape. And maybe even Rose Schiffman had offices over there, too. That made sense. With a few secretaries typing up all of her movie ideas. She was even nominated for an Oscar a few years back, so everyone must be kissing her little ass.

After she went to see Jan, she would definitely mosey on over to the movie lot and look for Ellen and Rose. That way she might be able to kill two birds with one stone.

TEN

ROSE LIKED WAKING UP at five in the morning to write. To sit in her flannel pajamas with an afghan over her feet, while the house was still quiet and there was no chance the phone would ring or that anybody would drop by. Still in a dreamlike haze, she could close herself inside her cluttered home office and get lost in the words she scrawled on the turquoise lines on the yellow legal pad.

Later, when the day began in earnest, she'd turn on the computer and transfer the newly composed pages to the blipping, bleeping, intimidating high-tech machine she still didn't quite understand after months of instruction, yet somehow managed to operate by rote. But for her the brain-dancing, thought-weaving productive times were always during those still, dark hours, when she sat alone in her cluttered little space, sipping from a cup of very black coffee, using up the points on the soft-leaded Blackwing 602 pencils.

Sometimes while she worked, she imagined that she was a romantic figure, like the sensitive and perceptive Colette, reclining on a chaise in a flat in Paris, instead of the myopic and neurotic Mrs. Andrew Schiffman, lying on a convertible sofa in a house in Sherman Oaks. But soon Andy's alarm clock would blast, and her reverie would be shattered.

"Honeee?" "Mahhh??" The jarring sounds of morning called her back from the far reaches of her mind. Her husband and daughter, both cranky in the morning, rushed around getting ready to go off to work and school, and she had to help them through their morning rituals and out the door.

While she rehashed the dilemma between two of her characters in her mind, she made fresh coffee for Andy, who stood in the kitchen with the cordless phone under his bearded chin, simultaneously slathering peanut butter on his toast, and checking in on the condition of his patients — AIDS patients, cancer patients, some of whom looked last night as if they might not make it through to the morning.

While she decided how to open the love scene, she packed a lunch for Molly, who leaned on one arm, muttering sleepily about how Dad always made her late for school, pushing the cereal around in the bowl and reading "Cathy" out loud to Rose from the morning funnies.

This morning she absently made the lean turkey sandwich and cut up the fresh fruit, knowing attempts at good nutrition were futile, since in a few hours Molly would make a furtive trade with some enviable kid whose mom gave her corn nuts and bologna. From the table where her face was buried in the funnies, Molly said suddenly with a laugh, "Cathy reminds me of you, Mom. She's kind of ditzy, her office is always a mess, and she's a worrywart."

Daughters loved to blow the whistle on their mothers, Rose mused as she padded across the kitchen in her faded pajamas and her beat-up fuzzy slippers. She knew that from watching the behavior of Marly's twins, who were teenagers now and very critical of their mother. But at age ten, Molly seemed to be starting a little early. Probably because she was growing up in crazy, mind-blowing L.A.

"We're late," Andy said, hanging up the phone, filling his non-slip coffee mug, kissing Rose on the cheek, and ushering Molly toward the door to the garage. Rose followed, carrying the lunch box, which accidentally slipped out of her hand and crashed to the garage floor, making her have to stoop and open it to make sure the thermos was still intact.

"Mom's so nervous about her big meeting today, she can't see straight," Rose heard Molly tell Andy as they got into the car. And she was right. Poor old mom had a pitch meeting at a studio today, and she hated pitch meetings. As soon as she heard the garage door close, she topped off her mug with hot coffee and made her way to her bathroom to take a shower, practicing the key words of the pitch out loud as she did.

"Contemporary woman, high-tech arena, imagine Glenn Close or Meryl Streep." She felt nauseous, knowing what was ahead of her today. If only she could phone it in, mail it in, anything but get dressed in presentable clothes and sit in the overdone office of some interchangeable studio executive trying to sell an idea.

Selling her heart out, just like the vacuum cleaner salesman who once came to her family's little home in Cleveland, when Rose was seven, right after her mother died. It was a desperately sad time for them, Rose trying not to fall apart when her distracted father forgot to pick her up at school. And he was trying so hard to run his hardware store and the household at the same time.

"Maybe we need this newfangled gizmo," he said, shrugging to Rose while he let the salesman in the door. Rose sat in the same chair, smashed in next to her father, watching the mustached salesman present his product. Giving his overrehearsed spiel, his presentation, his pitch.

"Getta load of this," Rose remembered the man saying as he threw a bag of dirt on the floor, then showed Rose's father how his product so scrupulously sucked it up, and "Hold on to your hat for this . . . ," he said.

Little Rose, the glasses she'd worn since age five sitting on the tip of her nose, noticed the little beads of moisture forming on the salesman's bald head. Later she learned there was a name for the way the vacuum cleaner salesman had perspired that day. It was the reason she'd stopped wearing silk blouses to pitch meetings so no one could see her exude it herself. "Flop sweat." The reaction the body had when it knew there was no taker at the end of the sales pitch. The same reaction she had when she knew before she finished telling her story idea that the studio executive was going to say what her father told the disappointed vacuum cleaner salesman. "Thanks anyway."

At best the pitch meetings were uncomfortable and frustrating, but a necessary evil, so Rose forged ahead with them with the same get-it-over-with attitude she had about the dentist. It wasn't that she didn't know her material and believe in its worth, it was just that she was painfully shy. Most of the time she hid behind large tinted glasses and too-long black bangs and straight, shoulder-length hair in a style about which she said, "I'm trying for Dorothy Parker. Unfortunately, it's coming out Prince Valiant."

The lack of a mother in her life had made Rose Morris's shyness even worse. There was no one to reassure her that she was pretty or funny or smart, or to speak to about bras and tampons and boys. No one to tell her about the niceties of life that hardworking fathers didn't know about.

Once, a distant aunt who didn't care enough to take her under her wing, at least took the time to make a suggestion to Rose's father that he ought to sign the child up for ballet and tap classes to help rid her of her timidity.

But the idea of being looked at by even a small audience made Rose throw up in terror before every recital. So after two years she was allowed to give away the shoes and the tutu and come home after school and sit in her room and dream and make up stories.

The epiphany happened in high school when a play she'd written as a lark was a huge success, and it dawned on her that there was a way to be in show business, which she loved, and not have to perform, which she hated. Writing. A profession that provided simultaneous celebrity and anonymity for greats like J. D. Salinger could do the same for her. She declared it her major in college.

"It's the perfect career for my little mousekin," her father said excitedly when she told him one evening after school while they dined at the deli near his hardware store. Harry Morris had a childhood friend who'd become a well-known writer, so why not his daughter, too?

Carnegie Tech was heaven for her. In college she could sit in the back of a dark theater, listening to her friends alternately mutilating and glorifying the lines she'd written. Hearing words she could never say herself come from women she perceived as dynamic and outgoing and brave. Women she idolized not just for their beauty, which was radiant, but for their ability to stand in front of a group and emote.

"A great actor," one of their professors announced, "would shit on the stage if you asked him to."

That one made them laugh like loons back at the dorm.

"Be sure to include my bathroom scene," Jan hollered into Rose's room one day while Rose was typing away on her little Smith-Corona portable. "I need to prove how great I am!"

Right after college she moved to southern California, where her college boyfriend followed her and they were married. Now she was one of the small percentage of Hollywood women screenwriters who were constantly employed.

How ironic for her to find that the way most screenwriting assignments were won was by writers "pitching" their ideas to the producers or the studio executives. Selling, performing, turning on the potential buyer with a dazzling presentation of the story they wanted to sell. Just like the vacuum cleaner salesman who had thrown the dirt on the floor, then proved to her father that the handy-dandy machine could suck up the scattered debris, Rose had to throw her ideas out and demonstrate the way she would weave them together into an intriguing story.

Bookish Rose, who had long ago rejected being on stage because it frightened her so much, was now in a profession where it was mandatory to put on a show for some stone-faced studio person who held in his or her hands the fate of her next writing project. Working too hard, like the mustached vacuum cleaner salesman, to get the buyer hooked into the product.

Even after all the times she'd done it, she would still find herself taking a flustered beat to blink at her notes, trying to decipher them, knowing in a frenzy how easy it was to lose the interest of the people who had the right to say yes or no to whether her idea was worth the investment of their development funds.

Years ago an uncharacteristically kind studio executive said to her, after she'd presented the first sentence of her idea, then looked in a moment of panic down at her notes, "Let me stop you. I can tell you already, I love this idea, and I love your work. I want this, so don't be nervous, and don't think you have to make eye contact with me. This isn't speech class, you can look at your notes all you want. I'm buying your act."

She'd burst into tears of relief, continued the pitch in a choked voice without looking up, and when she was finished, he said, "I'll take it," and she walked out of his office knowing she had a a deal. That project had become her big hit film. The one people still rented repeatedly from the video store. The credit that was her ticket to subsequent meetings because she'd been nominated for both an Oscar and a Writers' Guild award for it.

The producers all remembered her film *Faces* and the way it made everyone laugh and cry. Since *Faces*, four years ago, Rose had five or six projects in various stages of happening all over town. "Development hell" it was called by the writers who made a living from it. Scripts she wrote, scripts she rewrote, scripts an agent tried to "package" by sending it to a star or a director who might be interested, but there had been no real action in a long time.

The idea she was pitching today had to be a winner. She loved it. The minute it crossed her mind, she knew it was exactly what the studios called "high concept." That was a term that meant the minute you told the idea to someone in one sentence, they could see its wonderful possibilities.

This one was about a love affair that started when two people met and fell in love via letters they exchanged on an electronic bulletin board. A kind of Cyrano for the nineties. It would have a great role in it for a grown-up woman. Someone who had been initiated into life, with older children and career success. There were dozens of actresses in the business who were longing for a part like this one. Every studio executive in town would know that, Rose told herself, so she was certain she could sell it.

"Oh, hi, Mrs. Schiffman," a pretty young receptionist said and immediately picked up a phone and buzzed a warning to someone somewhere in the heavily decorated suite of offices. Another pretty young woman hurried out of an adjacent office with a hand extended and said to Rose, "Mrs. Schiffman? Hi, I'm Stacy Craig, the director of John Pine's development? John really apologizes but he's been totally decked by the flu, and he asked if I could meet with you?" She spoke in that California-girl cadence in which every sentence goes up at the end, making it sound as if it's a question.

Rose wanted to leave. She looked at Stacy Craig and her first thought was, "I have dresses in my closet older than she is." Why didn't someone call her to postpone the meeting if John Pine was sick?

"Is that okay?" Stacy asked.

Rose was uncomfortable. She knew that going in and telling the idea to this person was a mistake. In fact, she probably shouldn't be bringing this particular idea to John Pine at all. It was a project she should try to sell to someone who would get it. A woman, who would understand the woman in the story. Like Dawn Steel or Sherry Lansing.

"I am such a fan," pretty Stacy said, shaking Rose's hand. "I've seen *Faces* ten times. It was so sad, and so fun?"

"Thank you," Rose said. So fun. The words made her cringe inside. It was an expression she'd cautioned her daughter not to use. An expression, she told Molly, that made the user sound stupid. "So much fun," she wanted to say. Maybe she should leave. Not take the chance that this child would understand her story, part of which was about the way a woman in her forties can't relate to any of the high-tech phenomena and ironically finds that a computer is running her life.

"So can we go into John's office and talk?" Stacy asked. Rose looked at the receptionist, who was also in her early twenties, and had an awful rush of realizing she and her project had been passed down to the D-girl, the nickname for the young women executives who work in development at the studios. John Pine had handed her off to Stacy, who would screen her idea so that he didn't waste his precious time until he heard from Stacy whether the idea had any viability.

Rose was sure that this young woman, whose frame of reference was so unlike her own, had almost no chance of understanding the point of the story. Yet Stacy was going to be the one who'd be the decision maker about whether the project lived or died at this company.

"Maybe I'll come back when John's feeling better," Rose offered, and Stacy's jaw tightened. The young woman had obviously been told to handle this, and she was not going to let it get out of her control.

"Um . . . well, it could be a really long time," she said. "So since you're already here and all . . . I mean, I could get the ball rolling?"

Rose felt shaky, but she wanted to turn this situation around. Hell, she thought, chances were John Pine wouldn't get this idea anyway, so she'd pitch it to the kid, think of it as a rehearsal, and try to get a meeting to pitch it to someone else next week.

In John Pine's enormous art deco office, she sat on a black hardback chair, and after Stacy efficiently opened a little notebook, Rose went through her idea, while Stacy took notes. After a while she felt the way she sometimes did when she improvised a bedtime story for her daughter and then watched the ten-year-old tap her feet with boredom.

Stacy didn't tap her feet. She nodded affably as she jotted things in the notebook, and now and then she laughed and smiled and said "Great, great," about some of the beats of the story, but Rose could tell she wasn't really getting through to her.

When she finished the pitch, she wasn't surprised when Stacy looked over her notes, then let out a long ominous sigh and said, "Well . . . great pitch. I like the arena, I like the journey the character takes, her arc is really well executed? And I'll run it past John when he's feeling better? And maybe he'll see it, but . . . honestly? And I have to be honest with you because I'm such a fan of yours? But without elements, hot elements, I don't see how this idea can work? And there's no way to get the kind of elements we need. Because here are the stats? The average age of women protagonists in 1992 roles was thirty-three? I mean this woman in your piece? She's way too old."

There it was. What was it Marly said last month? "I used to think the O word was orgasm. Now I found out it's 'old.' " The kiss of death.

Rose sighed and leaned back in the chair she'd chosen specifically because sofas were too cushy and cozy and made her too comfortable to stay focused on her pitch.

"You'd think that after *Thelma and Louise* something would have changed," Rose said, but she knew she was wasting her words. She put away her notes and rummaged around looking for her car keys in an outside pocket of the big leather bag she always carried with her.

"*Thelma and Louise* was a one-in-a-million shot," Stacy said, obviously parroting something she'd heard someone else say. She was trying too hard to sound like a seasoned pro. In fact, she sounded a lot like Ellen. "A freak thing?" She went on, "And, believe it or not, in spite of all the publicity it got, it didn't make any real money? So a script with a female over forty as the lead just ain't gonna happen," she said, shrugging. She probably thought using the word "ain't" made her sound folksy. "At least not at this studio. But we love you. And we want to be in the Rose Morris business? So come back, okay?"

Rose stood and managed a smile.

"Sorreee," Stacy said in the same little-girl way Molly answered when Rose scolded her about leaving her "My Little Ponies" out where someone could trip on them. She had an odd look on her face of regret combined with triumph, as if she wished the project from Rose could have been something she was eager to take to her boss. But it was combined with the satisfaction that she'd saved John Pine from wasting any part of his valuable day on some story that no one would want to see as a film.

"Thanks for your time," Rose said. She nodded to the receptionist on her way out and hurried down the steps and out of the building. In the parking lot, just as she was about to get into her car, she saw a group of executives on their way toward the building she'd just left, and one of them, surprise surprise, was the dramatically recovered from being "totally decked by the flu" John Pine.

At home, she warmed up some soup left over from last night's dinner, and while she ate, she looked again at the notes she'd used for today's meeting, wondering for a fleeting instant if the computer story could be adapted to accommodate a younger actress. Then she hated herself for even considering it. The whole point of the story, the part of the idea that had interested her in the first place, was the difficulty that people of a certain age had adjusting to the new technologies. A certain age. What if she was that age and couldn't get work ever again because of it?

She was putting on some comfortable clothes to get back to work on the spec screenplay she was writing, when the phone rang. "Well, kiddo, cream rises to the top." It was her agent, Marty.

"It also clogs your arteries and kills you," Rose said, "but please go on."

"Howard Bergman loves *Good-bye, My Baby.*"

"Really?" A giddy sweep of hope danced through Rose's chest. Howard Bergman was a very senior studio executive who could get a movie made. Ah, you fickle business, she thought. Only seconds ago she was sure she should forget the whole thing and spend her days answering the phones at Andy's medical office, and now she was back in the running.

"He just called me himself," Marty said, as dazzled as if it had been Moses who called him.

Good-bye, My Baby was a speculative script Rose had written and rewritten more times than she remembered. It was a story she'd worked on without an assignment, because it was something she needed to get out of her system. Putting it on the page had been a painstaking process, with the emphasis on the pain, because it was so personal, a tragedy from her own life relived each day she worked on it, cutting into her soul and letting her blood fall all over the script.

"He wants you to come in late this afternoon, if you can, and talk about a few changes, and he has some great ideas for casting."

Casting! Not just fix it, not just change it, not just punch it up. But Howard Bergman wanted her to come to a meeting where they had real actors in mind. Then maybe he'd give her a green light, make a movie, not just talk about it.

Good-bye, My Baby took her years to finish. But finally, with Andy's encouragement, she decided if she could get it down, even a little bit at a time, it would help her heal. Maybe it would give her some kind of closure about the death of her first husband, a man she had loved so powerfully, still missed so much, that her dreams were full of a reunion with him in some other world.

Closure, a pop psych word that meant you finally came to terms with something difficult in your life, and the coming to terms would set you free. But before she even got to the death-bed scenes, she wrote about their powerful bond, their recognition from the first day that they were meant to love one another from past lives.

The way he'd nurtured her, adored her, brought her out of hiding and helped her to feel womanly and wise. She would sob as she wrote about their love. And then, telling the truth about the nightmare of Allan's last days, it was too much. She knew there would never be any such thing for her as closure on that subject. Andy knew it, too, and he accepted it.

Some mornings while she'd worked on the script, she'd find herself curled up on the sofa with an afghan around her, sobbing quietly, remembering Allan's frail hand holding hers. His last good-byes and words of love. The way that two days before he died, he looked at her with as much of a smile as he could produce and said, "I wish we'd had a child together, so you could look at him and remember me."

"I'll always remember you," she protested, holding on to him. "I'll never stop loving you, dreaming of you, waiting to be with you." She remembered those last days, saying those words again and again, and the torment of losing her great love.

Scene by scene, she finally got the story down on paper. The part about the scholarly young resident who came into the room every day to check on Allan's well-being. A compassionate young doctor who would stop by after all the specialists and their complicated jargon were gone, a friend who could help Rose and Allan translate all the medical reports.

Patiently he would go over the information about the treatment and the side effects of the medication. Always sidestepping gently the news that Allan would never leave the hospital to go home with Rose, though she promised him and herself every hour that he would. And the most important thrust of the story, the character arc as the studios liked to call it, was the way the young wife had been forced to grow up, to step out into the world and become independent.

"So how about that for great news?" Marty asked her now. "Can you get to Howard Bergman's office at four?"

"Sure. I can get there. But what kind of changes is he talking about, Marty? I'm not going to let them make this if they want to do a *Love Story* kind of death. The last producer who was interested in this asked if I couldn't change the disease to something more attractive than cancer. I'm not going to sanitize it. The integrity of the piece has got to lie in the way the wife takes care of her dying husband under untoward circumstances. Real tubes, real hospital smells, and how she changes in the process. But inherent in that has to be the realities of a fatal illness."

"Look how you're already defensive," Marty said. "Don't do a jack story. There are so few people who can say yes in this *far-kaktah* business that when one of them likes your work, put on a little lipstick and go say hello to the guy. And if you want my advice, I wouldn't let a sale go down the toilet because of what they want to call the disease. If Howard Bergman wants to make the husband die of carpal tunnel syndrome, I would smile and say 'You know, Howie, that's a great idea.' "

"Well, that's where we differ, Marty. I wouldn't say that."

"Rose, listen carefully. Every year there are five hundred films produced. Also every year six hundred and fifty people are killed by lightning. That means you have a better chance of being killed by a lightning bolt than of having a film produced. In fact, in your case the odds are worse, because you already did it once. That's why you have to listen to me and go in and be nice to a guy who can make it happen for you again."

As soon as Marty hung up, Rose dialed Ellen's direct line.

ELEVEN

ELLEN Bass's office."

"Greenie? It's Rose. Is she there?"

"Hi, Rose. She is, but she's on the phone with Ron Meyer. Wait . . . she's just winding down. Can you hold?"

"Yes."

Ellen knew every studio executive in town and every producer. Either she'd worked for them or they'd worked for her at some point during her relentless scramble up the shaky showbiz ladder. She'd been a gofer, a production secretary, an agent, a producer, a network executive, a studio executive.

Once at a Girls' Night, Marly had asked Ellen about a director who was going to be testing her for a part in a film. Ellen squinted as if to search her memory, then nodded absently. "I may have fucked him," she said.

"Aggh." Jan had practically spit her wine across the table at that one. "May have?"

"Hey," Ellen said. "That was the seventies. This is the nineties. Do you remember everyone you fucked? I'll bet one month's salary you don't."

One month of Ellen's salary was a colossal amount of money. Rose always thought the story of Ellen's rise to power was a film in itself. Once she'd been listed in a magazine with top-earning female executives, and Rose's father had seen it, called Rose, and asked in amazement. "Could that be our little Ellen?"

Rose had been talking for years about writing a screenplay about the friendship among the four women. The years they'd shared, the way they'd weathered dozens of losses, five weddings, a terrible death, joyous births, an unusual adoption. Career vicissitudes that were like roller coasters. But every time she mentioned it, Marly's white hair stood on end and Ellen threatened to have her killed. Jan, naturally, loved the idea. "If you've forgotten any of the juicier stories about my past, call me and I'll remind you, Rosie," she said.

"Think of me as the Boswell to your Johnson," Rose tried with Marly. "The chronicler of your brilliant lives. You know it'll be a story filled with love and affection. A close look at aging in Hollywood. The three of you could all play the parts of yourselves. With a sock over the lens, of course."

"I'll put a sock somewhere other than over the lens, if you don't forget the idea and burn that damned file you have where you keep scrawling notes about us. God, I'd like to do a Watergate on your office and burn every reference to me," Marly told her.

The file in question was one Rose had kept for years, with notes in it about the ups and downs of the four of them, and by now there were tons of hilarious material in it. Which was what Marly was afraid of. "If you mention my relationship with Billy, I'll never speak to you again, and if you write one word about the twins, it's over between us. Think about it, Rose. Thirty years of a friendship. Are you ready to give that up?"

"Depends on who offers me more. You or Paramount," Rose joked.

"You already used my college romance in that movie about the coed and the professor, and I forgave you. You use my parents as characters every time you have to write WASPs. You wrote that story about the stand-up comic right after I started seeing Billy. I'm starting to feel the way Neil Simon's brother must feel. My life is used up."

"Not at all. I have a lot more stories to tell about you," Rose teased. "Thirty years' worth."

What Rose hadn't told Marly or the others, though Ellen knew it from experience, was that they had nothing to fear, since every studio exec who heard the idea told her the same thing, "Who cares?"

"It would be brilliant with Candy Bergen as Marly, Susan Sarandon as Janny, Goldie Hawn as Ellen, and Bette Midler as me," Rose said.

"Pass," was one producer's reply, accompanied by a yawn.

"Mia Farrow as Marly, Cher as Janny, Anjelica Huston as Ellen, and Diana Ross as me," she tried, just to see if anyone in another meeting was paying attention. No one was.

"Yeah, great, we'll call you."

"How about a miniseries? Farah Fawcett as Jan, JoBeth Williams as Ellen . . ."

No imagination. These people were dunderheads. Didn't they know anything? Who do you have to fax to get out of here, she thought, and laughed at the idea of using that question as a title. Maybe for an article about all the screenwriters she knew who were leaving crime-ridden, polluted L.A. and FEDEXing the pages of their scripts to the producers who had commissioned them. Writers who got the picture that the high-tech world of downloading computer files and sending instant facsimiles enabled them to work in Hollywood and live anywhere they liked.

Rose wouldn't be able to fax anyone to get out of there, even though she'd had more than enough of the business and the meetings and the egos and the insanity. She would, unfortunately, have to stay in L.A. forever because Andy, her husband of eleven years, had a career in a medical field that was the most forward-looking of all in this terrible brown-aired city. He was a lung specialist.

"One more second, Rose," Greenie said. "I hear her saying good-bye."

Ellen didn't say hello, she said, "Don't tell me you're not coming to Girls' Night. I'm going to probably get my ass fired because I'm leaving the second meeting this week before midnight, so you'd better make it worth it for me."

"Of course I'm coming," Rose said. "Andy already knows he has to come home early to be with Molly. I'm calling because I have a meeting with Howard Bergman this afternoon, and I need the scoop on his personality."

"He's cold," Ellen said. "I know a woman who was fucking him and who told me a story in order to illustrate to me what a thoughtful guy he is. Bergman was having his annual Christmas party, and about an hour before the guests were due, his butler of twenty years keeled over and died. Bergman didn't want to spoil the party, so he grabbed the butler under the armpits, dragged him into a closet, and left him there until the guests went home. And the woman actually said to me, 'Wasn't that sweet of him?' "

"Stop," Rose said, giggling.

"That's who he is. Frankly, knowing Bergman, I'm shocked he didn't prop the butler up, put a tray in his hands, and make him serve a few last hors d'oeuvres." They both chuckled. "That said, Rosie dear, keep in mind that he is a player and he only meets with a writer when he's really serious, otherwise he hands you off to a string of interchangeable D-girls, all of whom were born post–1970. What project does he have of yours?"

"*Good-bye, My Baby.*"

"Your best work," Ellen said. "I remember trying to get the putzes I work with to make that one over here. They wanted the woman to be widowed as she watched her husband die by flying out the window of the exploding World Trade Center. Listen, it's not going to hurt you to go meet with Howard Bergman. But be prepared. It'll be so cold in there, you could store your furs for the winter. And Rose . . ."

"Yes?"

"Just to put you in the mood, here's a joke that a writer told me today. Why is writing a screenplay like making love to a porcupine?"

Rose liked this joke already. "I don't know. Why?"

"Because it's you against a thousand pricks! Good luck with Bergman."

"Yeah, thanks a million, Maximilian."

Rose's stomach ached as she drove onto her second studio lot of the day, told the guard her name and that she was meeting with Howard Bergman, then found a parking spot. Bergman's enormous third-floor office was carpeted in white, with white plush sofas arranged with chairs in two seating areas around coffee tables.

At least, Rose thought with relief, in this meeting she didn't have to pitch, because they'd be talking about something she'd already finished. A script that Ellen said was her best work. Marty told her Howard Bergman loved it.

"Loved it," Howard Bergman reiterated as his cold, manicured hand took Rose's small, damp one. When his tall, slim frame stood near her, she had to look up to see his lined, handsome face. His smile was fawning. This was the kind of moment every seller lived on. The buyer was mad about the product.

"Did anyone get you anything to drink?" he asked her, so solicitously it occurred to her that seduction was seduction no matter what the hoped-for outcome. Howard Bergman was selling himself as a producer to her, but could have been selling himself as a lover the way he kept holding her hand and the way he moved her to a chair by putting an arm around her. Ellen was dead wrong. He wasn't so cold, she thought.

"Ummm . . . no. I mean, no thanks, I don't want anything." She always declined drinks at these meetings after she realized that if she drank them she couldn't make it through a whole meeting without having to excuse herself.

"Well, why don't we talk?" he said, and as if on cue, three young women with names Rose later remembered as Kim, Chelsea, and Heather, came in and pulled up chairs. And since she didn't have to pitch at this meeting and could relax, Rose settled into an upholstered white armchair. Howard Bergman sat on one of the white sofas, his long arms stretched out across the back of it as he spoke.

"I see this as a piece about the struggle between the life force and the triumph death ultimately has over all of us. A study in the futility of our fight, against that over which we ultimately have no control. And I see those sides represented by the characters in the material as you've written it now."

What the hell was this pretentious speech leading to? Rose wondered. Maybe, she mused, she should have rewritten it for

Ellen's studio and let them blow the husband up at the World Trade Center.

"But what I want to do, want you to do now," he said, "is to mine their souls, to play up the passion, really lean into the hot love story, because these people represent those forces at work."

"You mean," Rose asked, "you want more of the flashbacks to the love story about the couple when they first met and fell for one another and got married? Before the husband became ill?" she asked.

"No. I mean that in your story, you create a friendship between the wife and the young doctor. But what I know without question is that they should be fucking their brains out in the empty hospital bed with the curtain pulled around them and with the husband three feet away in a morphine stupor. The way I see it, she's so sure the husband is dying, she figures it's okay, and then the husband starts to make a remarkable comeback. And the young doctor decides he'll have to kill him. Wants her so much he has to murder his patient."

Rose had a cramp in her lower abdomen. The room was silent. She knew the three young underlings were watching her face carefully. Three young women watching to see how she would handle this. If she and Allan had had children together, she could have had daughters their age.

A morphine stupor. This would be one of those stories that, when she told it to her friends on Girls' Night, would make them laugh and shake their heads in disbelief. But now she had to come up with something to say to Howard Bergman, who obviously had no idea what her script was about.

"Well . . . ummm . . . I don't think so, Howard," she said, trying to stop her eyes from blinking furiously, hating her voice for sounding so timid, and trying to get a big breath so she could support it a little more to say the next as forcefully as possible. "You see, my woman character is in so much pain about losing her husband that she doesn't even notice what that doctor looks like for months, maybe even a year, after her husband's death."

Howard Bergman snickered. "That would never be the case," he said.

Rose flared indignantly. "That *was* the case."

"Irrelevant," he said evenly. "It wouldn't happen that way even if it did. You writers have a problem when you get bogged down in the truth. I realize you know about your life. But your life isn't a film, and I know about films. Nobody's going to believe, if I cast Tom Cruise as the doctor and Demi Moore as the widow-to-be, that she wasn't dying to fuck him, or fucking him already, and he wasn't thinking of turning the croaking husband's drugs up, high enough to take him out. That's a story for a hot picture. Not some vague idea that maybe the doctor and the wife learned something from the experience and maybe some day down the line, blah, blah, blah. I mean, who gives a shit about that?"

All of that was said with a smile frozen on his face. Tom Cruise and Demi Moore. Hah. Allan would have loved that casting, laughed himself silly over it. Andy would love it, too, the idea that goyish, handsome Tom Cruise was going to be cast as rabbinical-looking him. But what Howard Bergman was describing wasn't the film that Rose wrote, not the story she wanted to tell. She wanted to deal with the way the adversity of young widowhood made her into a woman, not turn it into some smarmy exploitive vehicle so two people could take their clothes off on-screen.

Her agent Marty and her friend Ellen the studio V.P. would both tell her to take the money and run. Her supportive husband Andy and her idealistic friend Marly would tell her to do what was in her heart. And Jan would simply tell her to be sure that there was a great part in it for her.

Allan, she thought, wherever you are, this is our story, so tell me what to do. Look down from on high and let me know what to say to this man. Do I tell myself that screenwriting is just my business and whoever gives me the most money gets to tell me how to do it? Do I sell it to him and let him throw me off the project to bring in someone who will do what he asks? Or do I tell him to shove it, and hope some other studio will want to make it the way I do?

She almost laughed when in her head she heard Allan's voice get back to her immediately with one word. "Run."

She stood and extended her hand. "Howard," she said, "thanks so much for taking the time to talk to me about this, but I don't think we want to make the same picture."

The minute she was on the road, she dialed Ellen's office. Greenie put her right through.

"So?" Ellen asked, picking up. "How cold was it?"

"It was so cold," Rose said, using a punch line from a very old joke, "that flashers in Central Park were describing themselves."

Ellen laughed. "You mean it was so cold his secretary had to put him in the micro and nuke him for three minutes before he could start the meeting?"

"I mean so cold that while we were chatting the Iditarod went crashing right through his office," Rose tried.

"Rosie, hon," Ellen assured her, "you and I both believe that good projects never die. With everything I know about this business, I promise you that *Good-bye, My Baby* will happen. In spite of all the schlock there is in circulation, there is still a respect around here, in certain circles, for quality work, and I swear to you it will get done.

"Sometimes I think about the book people in *Fahrenheit 451,* that scene that always makes me cry, where the people have had to memorize the books to keep the stories alive. A secret coterie of folks who care about the written word. So hang in and you'll prevail. Something will happen to set it moving and get it into the hands of just the right filmmaker. I just don't know what that something is, but I believe it'll happen soon."

TWELVE

SHE DIDN'T MEAN to shoot the gun. She didn't even think she knew how to shoot the gun. She just put it in her purse before she left home as an afterthought. Like everybody else, she'd watched all that stuff about the L.A. riots on TV, and even all this time later, she was afraid about going someplace where there was so much violence. So it just made sense to put the gun in her purse to protect herself.

Oh, Jesus. She'd been so nervous driving up that little winding road to Jan's, and then when she found that funny cracker box of a house sticking out over the valley, she thought for a minute she had the wrong place. She'd been expecting something like that house on "Dynasty" where the Carringtons lived. She couldn't get over that this was where a person who starred on some TV show could live. But that was the address all right.

When she saw the black Lexus with the tinted windows in the driveway, she knew it meant that Jan was probably home. Big deal, she kept telling herself, big fucking deal, she's your old college buddy. But she was nervous anyway. It didn't matter what she told herself, the truth was that her old college friend was a star.

When she finally got up her nerve, she got out of the car, walked to the door, and rang the bell, and after a little while Jan looked out one of those windows that were on both sides of the door, and she said, "Who is it?"

When she said her name, there was a long beat while Jan looked closely at her, and then her eyes went wide with surprise and she said, "No!" with real amazement in her voice, and then she opened the door and saw her there and said, "Hi, honeeee!" And gave her a big hug!

Not one word about how old she looked, or how tired, or that maybe *it was bad form to drop by like this without calling first or any formal shit like that. Just nonstop talk about the days at Tech and the stuff they did at Tech, and laughing about it. For a long time they just stood there in the front hall of her house, a hallway with toys all over it, laughing about the old days. She didn't tell Jan how she got her home address, and that was smart, because then Jan would have thought she was some kind of crazo who was stalking her.*

She couldn't believe she'd finally done it and that there was Jan O'Malley, not looking anywhere near as good as she looked on the show, when she had makeup on and all that, but still a big soap star. And she was trying to just act like some old buddy who happened to be stopping by. It was amazingly chatty and chummy, and they just stood there together in Jan's little house, a little house, not what she expected at all.

Jan's kid was playing upstairs, probably with the maid, and they could both hear him singing and laughing, so she said, "Aren't you lucky to have a son. I had kids." Then she realized she'd said it like that, as if they weren't hers any more. I had kids. "I'll show you," she said, and she was going to go into her purse and pull out pictures of her kids, but while she was reaching in to get them, the strap on her purse broke. Fucking piece-of-crap purse, and the purse turned over and everything went rolling out, magazines, papers, makeup, hairbrush, wallet. Shit!

As if she wasn't nervous enough, that really shook her up. Jesus, there she was picking stuff up off the floor, so embarrassed, but Jan was really nice about it and got down on the floor to help her, and then she saw the gun.

"Oh, that," she said, seeing the look on Jan's face. "My kids moved in with my husband, and I'm living completely alone, and that's why I have a gun. I even brought it with me here. Just let somebody try anything with me, I'd shoot them dead." And she laughed and picked up the gun and put it back into her purse.

That was when Jan got really freaked out. Her face went all tense and she said, "Look, I'm glad you stopped by, but I'm on my way out, so I have to get ready," and then her whole voice changed and it wasn't very nice. "You'd better go."

Go? There was no way she was going. She couldn't go. That wasn't her plan. She had what she was going to do all worked out, and she had to make it happen. Jan wanted to get rid of her, but she couldn't go yet.

So she tried to make small talk, to keep the light stuff going, but Jan was moving her to the door.

She wouldn't go. She wanted Jan to see pictures of her kids, and tell her how good she was with kids. If Jan's little boy came down and they started to interact, Jan would see how well kids related to her and think she was someone who ought to be around little Joey and give her a job, so she had to say the line she'd rehearsed, which was, "Can't I meet your son?"

She thought Jan would see that as something friendly to say. Meaning after all these years, you have a son, and I want to just take a little peek at him, I love kids. She thought she said that, too, I love kids. But by then Jan was hell-bent on hustling her out of there, probably because of the gun, and it really pissed her off. She was feeling sweaty and afraid and she said, "You know, I don't have a job, and you could hire me to take care of your son."

Well, that made Jan a little nuts. She was real shaky and she said, "Please get out of here. I didn't invite you, and I want you to leave right now," and her tone was so condescending. It was so I'm-on-top-and-you're-nothing that she decided not to move until she got her point across.

"I wrote you some letters," she said, feeling panicky now and knowing she had to get this in. "I didn't have this address when I sent them, so I mailed them to the studio, and you know what I got back? An autographed picture that you didn't even really sign, because I remember your handwriting. How could you let them send an old friend of yours an autographed picture with a fake autograph on it?"

"I'm really sorry. I didn't see your letters," she said, and it sounded as if she meant, you nobody, why would I see a letter from someone like you? "I get bags of fan mail, and if it came to the studio, it would get thrown into one of those bags, but I have a service that answers all of those," she said.

That really burned her ass, and she couldn't play the role of nice, chummy college buddy anymore. "Hey, I'm not your fucking fan, Jan. I'm your equal. You weren't the one who got the A's in acting, I was. I won the best actress award our senior year. Not you. And if you want to know the truth, which I'm sure you don't, the work you do on 'My Brightest Day' is real amateur shit."

"*Please just get out of here,*" she said. "*I'm asking you nicely to please leave.*" It didn't sound as if she was asking so nicely.

Then the kid's voice yelled out, "*Mommmmy,*" and she was so flustered that she answered for Jan, maybe for herself. Probably it was a reflex, after all the years of her kids hollering for her, but she said, "*Yes, honey?*" And Jan looked at her with a look that meant, *You are a lock-up case.* But by then she didn't care what Jan thought. She just wanted to see that little boy so much that she started for the steps, and Jan grabbed her. Grabbed so hard she pulled her sweater off her shoulders and said, "*I told you to go, goddamn it.*"

Well, that must have been what put her over the top. Sometimes Lou used to grab her like that in front of the kids. Like that time he grabbed her and, just for fun, cut off all of her long, beautiful hair in front of the kids. Well, nobody was going to do that to her ever again. Or talk to her in that tone of voice. For an instant she stepped away from the moment, and it was just like they were on the main stage at Tech again. Jan was the beautiful Adela in The House of Bernarda Alba, and she was the bitter, jealous Marterio.

"*Don't raise that voice of yours to me. It irritates me. I have a heart full of a force so evil that, without my wanting to be, I'm drowned by it.*" Jan looked full of fear now, and she was so bummed out by Jan's attitude, she was glad to see her be afraid. She reached into her purse and took the gun out.

She wasn't going to shoot Jan. She just wanted to scare her, get her to lay off and let her see the little boy. She wanted that little boy. To see him, that was all, but Jan ran past her now and started up the stairs as if she was going to go and try to hide the kid or something, and she went after her, not to shoot her, but to stop her, and then she hit her with the gun, hard, on the head, and after that the gun went off. Oh God. Oh my God.

Jan turned just before she fell onto the steps, with an awful, shocked expression on her face, and then she said — and this is the part that was so terrible to remember — she said, "*Oh no, what about my poor baby?*" And then she was lying on the floor, Jan O'Malley, her college friend. Jan was the prettiest one, and she was the best actress. Oh, God, and that was when she got out of there.

She fell into her car, and at first it didn't start, wouldn't start, made *that grinding sound it did when the battery was dead. Dead. No, please don't be dead. Then it started, and she floored it, and after winding around till she thought she was going to drive off the edge of one of those weird little hilly streets, she found her way to the Hollywood Freeway.*

Cars. There were too many of them in this city. She drove, weaving in and out of them, and finally she found her exit and the street where the hotel was, and she floored it up the long driveway to the parking lot and somehow made it through the lobby and back to this fancy room she couldn't afford.

She was sick from all the shit food she'd been eating out of the mini-bar. She opened the window and tried to take some deep breaths to keep from vomiting. This wasn't the way it was supposed to go for her in Hollywood. All she wanted was a job from one of them, and now she was, oh my God, a murderer.

THIRTEEN

JAN O'MALLEY, the actress who plays Maggie Flynn in the daytime drama 'My Brightest Day' was assaulted late this afternoon by an unidentified visitor at her Laurel Canyon home. Police said the forty-nine-year-old O'Malley was shot in the back, probably with a handgun, when she opened the door to her house, admitting the assailant, who argued with her, then shot her and ran.

"Detectives said earlier, 'We can assume Jan O'Malley knew the attacker, since her housekeeper, who was upstairs with O'Malley's young son, heard the actress arguing with someone who rang the bell and was admitted by O'Malley.'

Rose was reworking a scene from one of her screenplays in her head as she drove, so she was only half listening to the car radio when the bulletin came on the news. But she was sure she must have misheard what the man said. She was on her way to Marly's, and Janny was on her way there, too. She'd be there in five minutes, and surely Jan would come out to greet her and say, "It was a PR stunt, Rosie. Let's eat."

"Police say they know of no motive, and no arrests have been made thus far. Again, this just in. Jan O'Malley, Maggie Flynn on 'My Brightest Day,' has been rushed to Cedars-Sinai Medical Center, where she's been pronounced in critical condition, after a shooting at her Hollywood Hills home."

Rose turned down the radio, and her eyes went dim the way the lights in her house did when there was a power surge. It was at least ninety-five degrees outside, but she was cold and afraid and feeling too shaky to negotiate her car around the tight curves on Sunset Boulevard. As soon as she could make a turn onto a side street, she did and pulled her car into a parking place, leaving the engine running.

Cars whizzed by on Sunset as she pushed the telephone buttons entering Marly's number. After two rings, Marly's machine picked up. It was the voice of one of the twins. "Please leave a message." Marly was probably in the shower. If she hadn't heard the news, Rose couldn't leave a message on an answering machine saying that she was sitting in her car on some side street in Brentwood, shaking because she'd just heard Jan was shot. It wasn't a message you left on an answering machine, so she hung up. Maybe Marly knew about Jan already and was on her way to the hospital.

Rose held tightly to the steering wheel, then put her face against it and tried to decide what to do. Andy was on the staff at Cedars. She'd call him at home, and if he could find someone to stay with Molly, she'd get him to hurry there and find out if Jan was getting the best care possible. With the rush-hour traffic it could take Rose an hour to get to there herself, and it might be too late. Who in God's name would want to shoot Janny? It must have been a robbery.

But didn't the newscaster say it seemed to be someone Jan knew? Rose always joked about herself that she had a "Movie-of-the-Week" mind, meaning that the minute something eventful happened, she turned it into a story for a script, and she was doing that now. Maybe Jan was shot by the jerko producer of "My Brightest Day." Jan mentioned to Rose that he was always fretting about the sagging ratings of the show. Maybe he thought a scandal would be good for the numbers. What if it was the wife of that handsome actor who played Jan's lover on the show? A jealous woman who thought her husband's love scenes with Jan were starting to look too real.

Now she dialed her home phone on the car phone.

"Andy?"

"Hi, honey."

"Something awful . . ."

"I know, I've been trying to call you, too," he said. "I saw it on TV and then called the hospital to get the inside word. One of the neighborhood kids is coming to be with Molly, and as soon as she gets here, I'll meet you at Cedars. I would think the place is crawling with police, so I'll clear you and the others with security. I'm sure they have to be afraid the guy who shot her will show up at the hospital."

It was all so awful, so right out of some TV crime show, she wished someone would yell "Cut," and make it go away. Waves of anxiety moved through her. A minute before, this was the evening she'd been looking forward to all week. The evening she'd been smiling about all day, after the two stupid meetings she'd had this week. Now the worries that felt so big were absurd.

She put her foot on the gas and headed to the corner, then tried to nose her car into the flow of traffic moving east on Sunset, but none of the aggressive drivers would let her in.

"As far as I know, she's still alive," Andy's voice said over the speaker. "I reached one of the doctors at Cedars on the trauma team who told me that the bullet entered the upper part of her back toward her neck." Rose hated the way her doctor husband was giving her information on the speakerphone in that same clinical voice she'd heard him use with patients. She wanted to scream at him, "Don't tell me the bloody details. I can't stand it." But instead she listened numbly and watched the West Side commuters' high-priced cars move past her in a shiny blur.

"Luckily . . ." Andy's disembodied voice filled the car, and Rose wondered what in the hell he could possibly find in this situation that started with the word "luckily." ". . . it missed her aorta, but it collapsed a lung. It just nicked her spine and fractured off some pieces of bone from her upper thoracic and lower cervical spine, so she has an inflammation of the spinal cord."

"Andy . . ."

"She also had a blow to her head that made her unconscious, so they rushed her into surgery."

"Please get over to Cedars and make sure they're on top of this case," Rose said. A white stretch limo stopped and let her pull her car into the traffic, but the line of cars was slowing down, and after she'd gone only a few car lengths, the traffic was completely stopped.

"I'm on my way," Andy said. "In fact, there's the doorbell. It's probably Tracy Gellman to stay with Molly. I'm going to walk right out when she comes in, so I'll see you when you get there. Surgical ICU."

"Tell Tracy to lock the door and turn on the alarm, and — " Andy had clicked off. The traffic was still at a dead halt, and in her rearview mirror, Rose could see the woman driving a Jaguar sedan behind her looking at herself in her own rearview mirror, applying lipstick with a brush. "Janny," Rose said out loud. "Don't die. I'm on my way to help you come back. Hang in."

Her Filofax was lying on the passenger seat, so she riffled through the pages until she found Ellen's car phone number, but when she called, the line was busy. Ellen's car had call waiting, so the busy signal meant she had someone on both lines. Three less than were usually holding for her, Rose thought, as she pushed CLEAR and END.

Ellen always took the long way to the city over Cahuenga Pass and then west on Sunset, because her car phone didn't work in the canyons, and she liked to return some of her business calls, to get them out of the way while she drove. Tonight on her way to Marly's, she was in the middle of a conversation with Garry Marshall about the grosses on his newest picture when a click told her it was her call waiting, and she asked Garry to hold.

"Yo," she said, knowing the call beeping in had to be Greenie.

"Where are you, Ellen?" he asked her.

"In my leased German car, Greenberg of the Jacksonville, Florida, Greenbergs. Who wants to know?" Her last meeting tonight had actually ended at seven, but only because the "boys" were going to see a screening of a competitor's picture. They were all hurrying out the door tonight when Schatzman said to her, "I'll come in your car. Since the screening's at Universal, you can drop me back here."

"I'm not coming to the screening," Ellen said.

"Friday night services?" Bibberman asked her, overhearing. "Say Kaddish for your career." The prayer for the dead.

"El, I want you to get off the other line and pull your car over to the side of the road." Greenie's voice was too serious.

"Oh, shit," she said, trying to guess why the doom and gloom. "Did Bibberman freak out because I didn't go to the screening?"

"Ellen, do what I'm telling you!"

"Greenie, I'm on the other line with a director who can make a deal. I'll call you back."

"Hang up on whoever it is, and do what I tell you."

"Greens, I'm at Yucca Street in downtown Hollywood. A single white woman in a sixty-five-thousand-dollar car pulling over here would be committing a serious faux pas if she intended to stay alive. Didn't you read *Bonfire of the Vanities*? I know you didn't see the movie, because nobody did. Happily, it wasn't my picture."

"Get off the other line."

"You're pushy," she said and clicked to the other line to say good-bye to Garry Marshall.

"Garry? I've got a fire I have to put out on line two. I'll check in with you tomorrow." She sighed before she pushed the button again. "I just talked to my mother in Miami Beach five minutes ago, and Roger this morning, and they were both okay, so what requires stopping the car on my way to Girls' Night?"

"It's Jan," Greenie told her. "It's all over the news."

Rose knew a back way in to the underground parking at Cedars. It was an entrance she'd discovered in the months when Allan was sick and she was practically living in the hospital. Tonight after she drove up to the ticket machine and pulled out the ticket, she automatically steered her car into a parking space right near the elevator, and then remembered that this had been her regular parking spot. The one she pulled into on those mornings when she brought Allan a shopping bag full of goodies she hoped would cheer him.

Tonight when she turned off the engine, she sighed and sat

wishing she was anywhere in the world but at that hospital. She could hear the whine of an ambulance in the distance, and she tried to get herself ready to face whatever was happening with Jan.

Maybe she'd get up to the seventh floor to find that Jan didn't make it through the surgery alive. Maybe she'd be alive but close to death in the coma Andy described, and the friends would sit by her bed for weeks or months waiting, the way Rose had with Allan. Watching a myriad of doctors moving in and out of the room, shrugging their shoulders and saying what they had said to her so many times, "There's not a whole lot more we can do."

Rose was afraid she couldn't handle another hospital death-watch. Marly, Jan, and Ellen were all stronger than she was when it came to emergencies. They had practically carried her through those last weeks when she was saying her good-byes to Allan. Sometimes Marly would come and sit in the waiting room on the seventh floor, where Allan's room was, not wanting to intrude on Rose and Allan's last precious hours. When Rose eventually came out to take a breath that wasn't fetid with death, Marly would be there.

Together the two friends would walk up and down the echoing hospital halls, down to the twenty-four-hour cafeteria with its own heavy, greasy odor, to the gift shop in the lobby with its too-cheerful volunteer salesladies hovering.

And on the days Marly could get Rose to leave the building for a while, they'd stroll down La Cienega Boulevard to the Beverly Center, where the flashy stores would be a bright, distracting show as they walked. Sometimes they'd move side by side silently, sometimes Marly would jabber away in small talk invented to amuse Rose.

Ellen's visits to Allan were always early in the morning, on her way to what was then her low-level studio job, to bring him pirated videos of films that hadn't been released yet. Allan was a big movie buff, and during the long nights when he thrashed in pain and needed diversion, he loved to watch the previews of films on a VCR Rose brought in.

Jan worked all day on the soap, but she came to the hospital at night to check in on Allan and Rose, joking that she was really coming so that maybe she'd get lucky and "meet somebody." On the nights when all three friends showed up, after Allan fell asleep and Rose came out of the room, not wanting to go home in case he awakened and needed her, Marly, Jan, and Ellen would sit the deathwatch with her in the waiting room, able to make her laugh with their stories.

The levity the friends' visits brought to Rose, who was so bloated with grief she was sure she'd never laugh or love or work again, felt like a magic drug that momentarily blurred her pain. Even though the giggles soon segued into tears and then became sobs that seized and shook her. And each of her friends took turns holding on to her, hugging her silently, helping her let Allan go. How would she have ever made it through this life without them?

Thanks a million, Maximilian. Maybe that was the first time Jan told it, when Allan was dying. Rose remembered the way the other people in the waiting room had looked over at them disapprovingly when the four friends laughed at Jan's best story. Now she took a deep breath as she got on the elevator and pushed the button for seven. The elevator hissed up one floor from the underground parking, and at the lobby the doors opened for someone to get on. But no one did.

Rose spotted a group of paparazzi milling around outside the front entrance to the hospital. Probably hospital security wouldn't let them in. They must be waiting for some of the stars from "My Brightest Day" to show up, so they could snap some shots of the actors' concerned faces as they came to check on Jan. SOAP OPERA ACTRESS SHOT BY UNKNOWN ASSAILANT would make a great story for all the sleaze gazettes.

She saw one of the photographers glance through the glass door at the elevator and look at her appraisingly, not recognize her, then turn back to keep watch for somebody with a recognizable face to shoot, so he could sell the pictures to the tabloids. The elevator doors closed and Rose realized when it stopped again on the second floor that in this hospital, for the benefit of the orthodox Jews who were not allowed to press a button on Shabbat, the elevator stopped on every floor.

The continuous stops created an odd visual for her. In a script it would have said DOORS OPEN, ROSE'S POINT OF VIEW: orderlies on their break, chatting, CLOSE. DOORS OPEN, ROSE'S POINT OF VIEW: two doctors in suits, consulting, CLOSE. DOORS OPEN, nobody: just a piece of strange modern art on the wall, CLOSE.

Andy was waiting for her on the seventh floor in the surgical ICU waiting room. Rose was sure those were the same orange, peach, and pink silk flowers that had been sitting on that same Formica table when she sat here after Allan's last surgery. She remembered thinking then how tacky silk flowers were. Now Allan was long dead and the silk flowers were still there and poor Jan might be dead soon, too, and the silk flowers would outlive her.

Andy pulled her close against him, and she could feel his sweet furry face against her forehead. "I know how you feel about this place, and I guess I didn't think about it when we were on the phone, but on my way over here . . ."

"How is she?" Rose asked. She had to be able to tough it out, try to put the past out of her mind, to be there for Jan, didn't she? Maybe not. Maybe there were only so many hospital days one had to serve in this life, and she had done her time. She imagined someone stopping her on her way in to see Jan, saying "You don't have to do this, Mrs. Schiffman. You have a Ph.D. in hospital crisis."

"She's in recovery, she's still unconscious. She either fell or had a blow to the head. She has a subdural hematoma, so they not only had to remove the bullet but the blow caused the blood vessels under her skull to rupture, so they also have to deal with a collection of blood under her skull. The edema in her head is what's causing the coma."

Rose leaned into her husband and put her face against him, and after a minute or two she felt Marly's arms and recognized the scent of Joy, and then Ellen's scent of Norell, and now they all stood in a circle with Andy, too, holding on to one another as Andy told the others what he'd just told Rose.

"Poor Maria and little Joey. I went to pick them up and take them to my house," Marly said. "The police were there. Maria told me that she was about to bathe Joey and she heard a man's voice downstairs talking to Jan and Jan and the man seemed to be fighting. She said the bath was running when they heard a loud noise, but she thought it was just the front door slamming. When Joey had his pajamas on, she sent him down to be with Jan, and he was the one who found her."

"Oh, no," Rose said. "That poor baby."

"Do they have any idea who did it?" Ellen asked.

"The police I talked to when I went up to the house said that they're pretty sure it was some fan who broke onto the set the other day. Jan was shot with a thirty-eight-caliber gun, and that fan has one registered to him. They figure he probably followed her home and staked her out for a few days, and then today he got up his nerve and rang the bell," Marly said.

"Do they have him in custody?" Andy asked.

"Not yet, but they think he'll be easy to find," Marly answered.

"On the radio they said they thought Jan let the man in," Rose said.

"Oh, you know Jan. She probably thought she could reason with him and get him to leave her alone," Marly said.

"Never. She wouldn't let someone like that in. She was much too protective of Joey." Ellen shook her head in certainty.

"How could anyone hurt her?" Marly wondered out loud.

"If life was fair," Ellen said, "the guy would have gone over to my studio and mowed down the schmucks I work for."

Everyone laughed a little laugh and Marly said, "Or to Billy's," and then everyone laughed another pained laugh.

"Did you see the people out front?" Ellen asked Rose.

"What people? I came in the back way."

"The fans," Marly said, moving Rose toward one of the giant windows that overlooked the courtyard between the north and south towers of the hospital. "My God, there are already twice as many as there were when I drove in," Marly said, and Rose could see more than a hundred people milling in the now dark night, holding flickering candles.

"They have signs that say, 'WE LOVE YOU, MAGGIE FLYNN,'" Marly told her.

"It's so eerie," Rose said, shivering.

"What can we do, Andy?" Marly asked.

"Nothing but wait," he said. "I'll try to make sure we're updated on anything that happens. I know she doesn't have any parents left, but eventually one of us should call her sister and tell her how serious this is, in case she wants to come in from Pennsylvania." They all stood quietly, Andy with his hands in his pockets, rocking back and forth on his heels. They all knew that calling Jan's sister would mean Jan was about to die.

"They'll bring her to surgical ICU after recovery. It's right down the hall, but if they let you in to see her, it'll only be for a very few minutes, so I'm not even sure you three should stay here."

"Are you crazy? We're not moving an inch," Marly said, and Rose was sure those were the same words she'd heard her say in that same voice that time long ago when they stood together outside an abortion clinic, and the police warned them that the militant right-to-lifers were on their way. Andy knew Marly well enough not to argue.

"I'll be back in a little while," he said to all of them, then gave Rose a little hug before he moved with a brisk doctorly walk down the hall. The waiting area was grouped into sections. In one there was an older man reading the newspaper and a woman doing needlepoint. In another section a boy of about eighteen sat engrossed in whatever was being pumped into his ears from a Walkman, his big high-topped basketball-shod feet on the little coffee table.

The three women sat on the hard blue armchairs with uncomfortable curved wooden arms. The same chairs they sat in years before when Allan was dying. Ellen took off her cashmere Escada blazer and put it over her to serve as a blanket. Rose sighed and shuffled through some of the magazines on the table, and Marly somehow managed to get her legs up into a lotus position, which she sat in serenely with her eyes closed.

"Not exactly what we had in mind for Girls' Night," Ellen said.

"Not exactly," Marly said, opening her eyes. "Let's all hold hands right now and send Jan healing energy. Let's send white light to her injuries and put the idea out there in the universe that she's going to heal and be well." It was the kind of Marly statement that usually made Ellen roll her eyes at Rose, as if to say "Cut me a break. She's at it again." But tonight they were all united in their need to bring Jan back. So she took Marly's hand and Rose's, and they put their heads down for a long time. After a while they looked helplessly at one another.

"Janny was worried about her new contract," Marly told them. "And what she'd do if they didn't pick her up. I remember she said to me one night, 'Look what happens when we get to be this age. We're as disposable as yesterday's newspaper,' and I said 'Worse. At least yesterday's newspaper can be recycled.' "

"Gee, you knew how to cheer her right up," Ellen said.

"Believe me, I regretted it the minute I said it, and I thought about it all the way over here. I guess I was stressing about aging myself because it's been hitting me hard at every interview, too, so it's on my mind." She wasn't ready to tell them the story about her reading for the part of the grandmother. For a while they were all silent, Marly's cold hand still holding Rose's sweaty one.

"Remember Tennessee Williams's play *Sweet Bird of Youth*?" Marly asked. "How, when we were at Tech, we did scenes from it and I played Heavenly Finley, the ingenue? Tennessee Williams sure knew how to write great neurotic women. I keep thinking about the words of that character Alexandre Del Lago. The actress who ran away from Hollywood because she couldn't handle aging.

"She talks about getting old in the business, and she says, 'The screen's a very clear mirror. There's a thing called a close-up. The camera advances, and you stand still, and your head, your face, is caught in the frame of the picture, with a light blazing on it, and all your terrible history screams while you smile.' 'Your terrible history,' isn't that brilliant?" Marly said.

"I remember when you played Heavenly," Rose said. "And Alexandre was played by Betty Norell. Remember?"

"I do," Marly said. "Even then she was an incredible actress. She did that part so perfectly, and then she was one of the sisters in the García Lorca play, and she just mopped the stage with the rest of us."

"What's she doing these days?" Ellen asked.

"She's in England. It says in the alumni magazine that she spends the winters at that rep company Olivier started. I heard or read there was some kind of swap with American Actors' Equity so she could work over there," Rose said.

"I remember how at Tech we'd all get up there and fake our voices and try to make them fill the theater, but her big, booming voice just naturally did. And we'd work hard to create a character, using some tacked-on dialect or inappropriate walk. And Betty Norell would somehow become the character without all of that. When I watched her, all I could think was, how did they ever let me into the same drama department where someone like Betty Norell is my classmate? I'm the dope who played Carrie in the high school production of *Carousel,* and she's a star. She was so much better than all the rest of us," Marly said.

"How is it no one ever discovered her?" Rose asked. "I mean like Emma Thompson or . . ."

Ellen tsked and patted Rose's arm. "Little Rosie, I always want to ask you when you fell off the back of the turnip truck. You know being talented doesn't mean a damn thing in this business. It's so much about luck and timing and tenacity and trends. I see people every day who are brilliant and can't get arrested, and others who are knocking them dead all over the place, who are as dull as dog shit."

Marly shook her head as if she were trying to shake off what Ellen just said. "Janny always was afraid that she was one of those dull ones. She never felt secure about her work. She always joked that it was her body that got her into Tech, and after what just happened to her with Jack Solomon a few weeks ago, she was convinced she was right."

"Jack 'Mr. Television' Solomon?" Ellen said. "What happened with him?"

"Didn't she tell you?" Marly asked. "Maybe she was too embarrassed."

Ellen tried to remember if Jan had mentioned anything about Jack Solomon during one of those times when she let Jan ramble on on the phone to her. Sometimes she cleaned her desk or made notes and half listened. But she probably would have paid attention if it was something about that asshole Jack Solomon. Just because he was the man they all loved to hate.

"She didn't tell me, either," Rose said, pulling her legs under her to get warm in the overly air-conditioned hospital waiting room. Ellen kicked off her black suede Ferragamo loafers and put her black-stockinged feet on the coffee table in front of her.

"Oh, God, she was heartbroken by it," Marly began, and as she did, each of them thought how odd it was that in this unlikely venue, under these desperate, dreadful circumstances, an odd version of Girls' Night had officially begun. After all, the location was never really what mattered. What was important was that they were together, telling one another their stories.

FOURTEEN
The Man Who Would Be King

JAN'S A PISCES and her number is a three, so I knew right away when I met her that because she was a water sign she was going to be sensitive, with no confidence in herself. And I was right. For example, she always thought the letter they sent her accepting her to the drama department was a clerical error. That some day she'd be walking along the campus and someone would walk up, tap her on the shoulder, and say, "I'm terribly sorry, but you'll have to go."

She was so instinctual as an actress that she hated all the academic tearing apart of the characters they were teaching us. Once she came to my room in the dorm in tears, threw herself on my bed, and wailed, "Why do they keep asking us what the play is about? We're actors. We don't have to know what the play's about!"

I remember laughing at that. But in a way she was right. Some of the best acting I've seen is from actors whose work is the emotional seat-of-the-pants kind that comes from their gut. Jan has a great gut. She used to cut those acting classes where we had to be an animal or an inanimate object. I'd see her leaving the dorms with some guy, and she'd tell me, "I'm not going to be a banana today, Mars. I'm going out for a beer."

Most of all she hated the times we had to sit in the costume room until four-thirty A.M., doing some tedious job like sewing pearls on Desdemona's sleeves for the seniors' production of *Othello*. Or those nights when we'd sit in that freezing-cold cinderblock studio-theater, rehearsing some absurdist play until our minds were so blown out by exhaustion, it actually started making sense to us.

But it was Jack Solomon who always got us through those times. Remember how funny he was and how he could do imitations that would make us all die with laughter? We'd already be in that hysterical, heady state that my mother used to call "overtired." But Jack would make us fall apart because he was sincerely hilarious. He'd do his rewritten version of the absurdist play we were doing, out of the teacher's earshot, in gibberish or a Yiddish dialect, and we all broke up until we couldn't say the real lines anymore.

Jack's a Gemini. Talented, and sweet, but his greatest asset was that he wasn't threatening, even though at one point or another he'd made a grab for every one of us, but especially Jan. There was something so soft and vulnerable about Jan, and remember how angelic-looking she was? He used to love to corner her and ask her his favorite question, "When are you going to show me your tits?"

Of course that was in the days before anybody talked about sexual harassment. And Jan did what we all did then with those kinds of things, she cringed inside, gave him a hug, and shrugged it off, because he was a buddy. The one she used to let climb in the window of her dorm room, because it was okay for him to see us in our pajamas. She never really took him seriously.

I mean, she loved him. We all did. But never the way he wanted us to. Jan told me how insulted he got that one night when he managed to hang out in her room after the rest of us went to bed. She told me the next day how he'd pleaded with her for just a little kiss, which he probably hoped would inflame her.

She said when she opened the window and told him to go back out the way he came in, he told her she'd given him blue balls. Jan said unless he wanted them to be black *and* blue, he'd better get them and his ass out of her room.

But by the next day he didn't seem to be holding a grudge, and they were still really close friends. She even fixed him up a few times with some girls in the dorms she thought he'd like, but nothing ever came of it. Anyway, he made a really serious pass at her one more time at a party in our senior year. She said he was a little stoned that night, which was why he was so courageous. She just arrived at the party, and Jack cornered her in the room where she went to drop her coat. Remember that great black Dynel coat she had? It was so good-looking she hated to take it off.

Well, after she was sure everyone at the party had seen it, she walked in to put it on the bed in that apartment, and Jack followed her into the bedroom and closed the door. He put his arms around her and started doing his Marlon Brando playing Stanley Kowalski imitation, which always broke her up. She was laughing and hugging him back like a pal, and then he said that line that Stanley says in the play when he picks Blanche up and takes her off to bed. You know. "Tiger, tiger, put the bottle down. We've had this date for a long, long time."

Jan confessed to me back at the dorm that night, that there was a moment there when Jack Solomon could have had her. She wasn't drinking, and none of us had started smoking grass yet, so she couldn't blame it on some altered state of consciousness, but on that particular night, she looked at Jack Solomon and he looked sexy to her, really sexy, and she let him kiss her.

I remember the surprise on her face when she said, "That little Jew can really kiss. Not too slushy, kind of teasing, but very hot and knowing," and she said for that instant she felt a burning desire for him. We laughed so much that night, because after she thought a little about the burning desire she'd felt, she said to me, "You know, Mar, maybe it was just heartburn."

He was just starting to get his hand under her blouse, mumbling all the time how we wanted to see her tits, and she was going to let him see more than that, when something happened, I can't remember what it was she told me. Maybe somebody opened the door to the room, or somebody hollered dinner was served, and you know how Jan loves a good meal, so her mind came back into focus and she thought, Am I crazy? I was about to do God-knows-what with Jack Solomon. And she managed to stop the forward motion and rehook her bra and insist they go out to join the others.

So now you've got the picture. Well, as they say in the movies, fade out, fade in thirty years later. Thirty long, bloody years of all of us pushing, driving, going through hell to work in this business. Both Jack Solomon and Jan have worked hard. But she's an aging soap diva with thirteen-week contracts in which the producers have all the options. And Jack is a giant in the television business. You saw the *New York Times* article. There isn't anyone in the TV industry who has the kind of stardom he's achieved. He's better known than some of the actors on his shows.

So surely you'd have to believe that the rejection in the coatroom has to be a thing of the past. Right? And yet a few times, over the years, Jan has seen him and dropped hints about how she'd love to work on any of his shows, but he's never picked up on them.

He was the stage manager when she played Serafina in *The Rose Tattoo* at Tech, and she got a standing ovation every night. When we did *The House of Bernarda Alba*, and we all had to draw lines on our faces so we could look the age we are now, she played the ingenue and he was waiting backstage with flowers for her. Now if Jack wanted to, he could move her career up by light years just by getting some producer on one of his hit shows to give her a continuing role. And it wouldn't be charity. Jan's a terrific actress, and she's really been right for many of the parts.

I bump into Jack socially all the time and Jan did many times too, and afterward she'd call and tell me that he was so friendly. He'd kiss her and say, "You have to come over and see our new place." He asks about little Joey and how he's doing. Remembers her son's name and everything. She says he looks at her so lovingly it's as if they were right back in those days. Before he was big.

And she says all she can think of when she sees him is how that kind of bigness is bad for people. How people who have become that big start believing that they're really worth those ridiculously inflated fees they're collecting. And that their newly acquired celebrity friends really care about them. I see it all the time. With Billy, of course, all of us have seen what success has done to him. But with other people, too. There's even a paranoia associated with it that everyone's out to take advantage of you, which is only partly paranoia, because everyone is.

But it's easy to see why people are willing to pay the price of the paranoia, because of the power. Billy can have any woman he wants, and he has a staff of people who tell him he's great no matter what he does. Jack Solomon's shows are talked about everywhere you go. The articles about him in newspapers and magazines rattle on and on about the controversy around his outrageously brilliant shows. The way he's fearless about putting raw and real subjects on the air.

I always look at those photos of him in the paper, with that perfectly clipped mustache and those suspenders he wears now and looks so cool in, and I think, can this elegant-looking man possibly be that boy who climbed in the window of Jan's room in the dormitory almost every night for four years? And thirty years later he's snubbing her phone calls? I mean, it's hard to believe at his level he could still be holding a grudge about blue balls.

Well, for a long time it really didn't matter to Jan because things were going so well on the soap for her, and she was making a nice living, but then she watched them replace the actor who played her husband with a younger actor on the soap, and it made her nervous.

So she decided to drop Jack a note. Just a funny little note with references in it to the old days, not the blue balls incident, but the times he sat in her room, and the dorm mother would check up on her, and Jack would hide in her closet and after the dorm mother left, just to make Jan laugh, Jack would come out wearing Jan's robe and one of her hats.

She mentioned things she thought he'd get a laugh over. And she also mentioned that she didn't know how much longer she'd be on the soap, so that if there were any walk-ons on any of his shows, he should call her. Of course she was kidding about a walk-on. She'd heard that on one of the hospital shows that was on his network they were writing in some new characters, and she thought maybe there would be a woman doctor or something she could play. But she never heard a word.

Then a few weeks ago, just when she had some time off from the soap and was despairing, she got a call from one of her agents. The guy who covers all of the shows on Jack Solomon's network. Don't you love that we always call it that? Jack Solomon's network. As if the call letters were JSN. Anyway, the agent was a real sleazoid, if that's not redundant, and he said to Janny, "Guess what, babe! I think I got you a part on 'Doctors On Call.' Do you know the show?"

He tried to make it sound as if *he* was the one who had convinced them to hire her. You know how actors' agents always do that? They try to be heroes when the truth is, they don't do a thing. Jan didn't tell him that the president of the network was practically her brother in college. That he had obviously helped her get the part because of the letter she wrote, and that he was doing it through her agent to make it all legit. She just said, "Great. What's the part?"

And the agent said, "It isn't a big part, but it's a really juicy one. You play a nurse who's seducing some old rich guy. They know your work, you don't have to read for it. I'll send over a script."

Well, you know Jan. She was too nice to say, "No shit, honey, they know my work. The network honcho who's so big you can't even get in to see him used to wear my bathrobe, for God's sake." She just said, "Oh thank you so much."

So the script came to her house late that day. The character was described as "On the senior nursing staff, fortyish, sexy." The older man she was seducing in the scene was supposed to be a philanthropist with millions who's in the hospital, and she's hoping he'll fall for her.

It was a very hot scene and when she told me about it, I was delighted they were still writing parts like that, showing a woman our age with sex appeal. She ate like a saint all week so she'd look great on camera, she had her highlights done, her skin looked great, and the night before the shoot, the show sent over some new pages.

In the scene as written, the nurse was alone in the room with the man, and while they were talking, she unbuttoned the top two buttons on her uniform. Now everyone knows that this particular show, "Doctors On Call," is famous for its shock value. The kind of show that Jack Solomon champions and that makes his network number one. But Jan never thought the scene was going to go any further than that. So then she looked at the new pages, and it said, RENEE RIPS THE TOP OF HER UNIFORM AND AS BUTTONS POP OFF, SHE FLASHES HER NAKED BREASTS AT MR. MARKHAM. In the story the rich guy was old and sick, and he had a heart attack when he got a look at her naked breasts.

But it didn't say, AS RENEE RIPS HER TOP OPEN WE CUT TO MR. MARKHAM'S FACE. It said, she flashes her naked breasts. Well, she called me that night in a panic. She said, "This is television, so there's no way they can show bare breasts, right?" And I remember thinking, well, if they can, it'll be on Jack Solomon's network. And then Jan said what I was thinking, which was, "Why would America want to see the naked tits of a forty-nine-year-old woman anyway?"

It was too late for her to reach anyone that night, so I told her to go in in the morning and talk about it with the director. Her call was at six-thirty in makeup, but she was up at five, as nervous as if this was her first part. She needed it to be good so badly.

She went into her kitchen and took Lipton tea bags and put them in ice water and then laid them on her eyes for a while, so by the time she went into the studio any puffiness would be gone. She knew she was supposed to go into makeup with a clean face, but she put on a little foundation and some blusher, because she figured maybe Jack would come down to the set to visit before she was made up, and she wanted him to think she still looked good.

Well, she got to the studio with such high hopes. At last Jack was going to do all the things for her career that he was able. Though he hadn't called her, and this had all been handled by third parties, she was sure he was about to surprise her with the long-overdue display of friendship.

But when she arrived, there wasn't even a dressing room for her, just some little nothing of a trailer, with a piece of masking tape on the door with her name written on it in grease pencil. For a minute that hurt her, but she'd just seen her shrink the day before, and they spent a lot of time talking about expectations and how they can really do you in. So she tried to release all those scenarios she'd had in her head, that Jack would send her flowers with a card saying "Old friend, welcome to my network."

While she was in makeup, one of the ADs came in, and she told him that she really needed to talk to the director, and the guy said, "Yeah, okay," but nobody came by to talk to her. In fact, after her makeup was on and her hair was done, she sat backstage thinking, Jesus Christ, here I am, an actress who's been on a soap opera for fifteen years, earning a six-figure salary, and these people are walking by me as if I'm some extra.

She went back and sat in that little doghouse of a trailer for a long time. There was a phone in there, and she called me. I was meditating, and I heard the phone and something told me to answer it, and she told me what had happened so far that morning.

She said, "I'm feeling as if I'm Blanche Dubois. That everything good about my life is in the past. That I'm relying on the kindness of not exactly strangers, but some old school chum to give me a part. And I'm not even sure about how I'm going to play the damn thing. I mean for sure I'm not going to take my top off. And the director isn't breaking his neck to come in and work on it with me, or to tell me if there's a body double or what."

While we were talking, the AD came to her trailer and knocked and said that the director was ready for her, so she said good-bye to me, and out she marched. The director was in his fifties, and she felt comfortable enough with him to make light of her concerns about the scene. You know, doing jokes about flashing.

She said he was very gentle and very soft-spoken and, as it turned out, a real method kind of guy. Usually television doesn't like that kind of director, because he spends too much time talking to actors and wastes money. She was afraid. She'd been out of the loop for fifteen years. When you work on a soap for that long, you're out of touch with the realities of the business. You never go on auditions, never have to know what projects are happening.

Besides, there was always that great naïveté Jan always had about the world. For example, she went crazy when she saw Demi Moore naked on a magazine cover. And she called me after I told her to go and see *The Crying Game*, shrieking, "I don't believe it. I don't believe they let some guy play a woman, and then all of a sudden he takes off his clothes and you see his actual penis hanging there. How could you tell me to go and see that?"

Well, the director on "Doctors On Call" turned out to be really good. He talked to her about being in the moment, all that great Stanislavski talk. About the given circumstances of her character, about what Renee's objective was in the scene, and how she would go after getting it. He had his arm around her and they walked over to the bed, and the actor who was playing Markham ran some lines with her, but it was all really low-key, and she was feeling good.

And the next thing she knew, it was quiet on the set, and the lights were on, and the director, who she was starting to think she'd like to take home with her because he was very sensual, suddenly said "Action." They were shooting MARKHAM'S POV, which was camera on Jan all the way, and the actor was feeding her the lines from behind the camera. And she was really into it.

She felt great. As young and slinky and hot as a *Cosmo* cover girl, and when she got to the part where Renee rips open the uniform, she said she never even gave it a thought, just ripped it open. She told me, "I stuck my naked chest right out there, and I heard that actor gasp a death gasp and the director yelled 'Cut, and print!'" People on the set were applauding, and everyone was coming over and congratulating her while they changed the camera angle, and the hair lady came over to comb her, and she said it was really powerful and that she got hot just watching.

They shot all the angles and it went very quickly, and when they finished, she asked a few people if Jack had been on the set, because she figured even if he was there, he'd probably lay back so she wouldn't be nervous if she saw him. But everyone told her he pretty much stayed away on shooting days because after all he had a whole network to run, but they assured her he always came over and watched the dailies and would be there to see her scenes when the producer saw them.

So she went home feeling very strong and up and positive. She never sounded better. She told me she was on one of those today-is-the-first-day-of-the-rest-of-your-life kind of highs. She was even trying to think of ways to break her deal with the soap and go out and do freelance acting, figuring after people saw her in that scene, they'd be calling her left and right.

In the morning, when a huge bouquet of flowers arrived, she was still so turned on, she ripped open the card. It said, I SAW THE DAILIES AND YOU WERE UNBELIEVABLE, LOVE, JACK. And it was on his own business card, written in his own handwriting, not by the florist. Naturally her mind was racing. Maybe Renee would become a running character, maybe she'd finally made the leap to prime time TV.

She put the card down and was trying to decide if she should put the flowers on the coffee table where Joey might be able to get at them or if they'd be better on the dining room table, when she realized she'd put the card face down, and there was something more written on the back of it. So she picked it up and looked at the other side.

You know how, like the rest of us, she has to hold anything at arm's length to read it these days? I always tell the twins, "Don't even show me that book, I am much too old to try to find Waldo." Anyway, Jan held the card at arm's length and looked at the back of it, where Jack had written, P.S. THANKS FOR FINALLY SHOWING ME YOUR TITS. And her whole body went cold.

She couldn't believe she'd gone to him, her hat in her hand, her heart on her sleeve, you know all those expressions that have to do with being humble. To her, that note was like one kid saying to another, na, na, na, na, na, na! I can make anybody do anything I want. Shoving his power down her throat.

She felt as if she'd been completely set up by this power-happy man, who knew she was groveling when she sent him that note, who knew she was at a low point, and who had to use his show to humiliate her.

"Maybe that's not what it was," Rose said. "Maybe he just thought it was a hot part that would get her some attention."

"No," Marly said. "It was the last show of the season, and somebody Jan knew went to the wrap party, where they sometimes do a gag reel, you know, of out-takes, of goofs people make, and things that go wrong. And the person told her that the last shot on the gag reel was a close-up of her bare breasts, and then over it they supered the words SPECIAL THANKS TO JACK SOLOMON. Apparently it got a big laugh. She called to tell me that, and after she did, she cried so hard she had to hang up."

FIFTEEN

ELLEN shook her head in angry disbelief. "So thirty years later, Jack Solomon gets to see the tits he missed out on in college. The lowlife. This is a man who could get on the phone and call any casting director and within ten minutes have a hundred young, beautiful women parade naked through his office. But he did that? The lousy bastard." She picked up her loafer with her toe and dangled it there, watching it and shaking her head in disgust.

"Well, not that I'd ever want to defend him," Rose said, "but Jan could have refused to go in once she saw those pages in the script."

"Yes, if she'd been thinking clearly," Marly said. "But her clash with Jack Solomon was an interaction of their neuroses. The healthy behavior for Jan would have been for her to call him on the phone, or better yet, to go in to his office and say, 'I need this, Jack. Please do it for me if you can.' And the healthy behavior for Jack would have been to call her when he got her note, not to have his people call her people.

"But they were both inextricably linked in the myth of who they were in college, still carrying the baggage of thirty years ago, so neither one of them could confront the other. She was the girl he couldn't get, and he was the boy she feels guilty and stupid about rejecting every time she sees his name in the paper, because now he has more power than anybody in the television business. And they each brought those feelings to the transaction. By being afraid of him, she was in league with him on this."

"You're exactly right," Ellen said.

"I know. Isn't it remarkable how sane and lucid I can be about other people's lives, and a blithering idiot about my own?" Marly asked through a laugh.

"Pretty shitty," Ellen said, and she stood and stretched.

"But you can understand why she was afraid. We have that groove in our brains now, because it gets proven to us again and again that the people in those positions are rude and greedy and unfeeling," Marly said pointedly.

"Watch it," Ellen said.

"If the Ferragamo fits, honey . . ." Marly said.

"I'm not going to get into that same fight with you again," Ellen said, collapsing back on the chair. "I'm sorry to be the one who has to always remind you that when Ethel Merman sang the song, the lyrics were 'There's no business like show business,' not show creativity, or show warm and friendly."

"I know, I get it, it's all about money," Marly said. "But remember the days when we all used to believe that 'talent will out'? And we slaved away, studying and working because we thought our technique would get us the jobs, not the fact that we knew the guy who produced the show?"

"Yeah, and we also thought Rock Hudson was macho, and Werner Erhard had the secret to life, and what about sexual harassment?" Ellen said. "We should have only known it was called that."

"True," Rose said. "I was so naive I thought Long Dong Silver was the name of the flatware pattern I registered for when I got engaged."

That made the others laugh a loud peal of laughter that made the man and woman across the large waiting area look over uncomfortably. The boy with the Walkman was sound asleep with his head back.

"Now, that's naive," Marly laughed just as she noticed the two men who turned the corner on their way to the elevators. Marly recognized one of them as Ed Powell, the producer of Jan's show. Every time she'd seen him before, at a party or when she went to visit Jan on the set, he was nattily dressed in some expensive-looking suit. Tonight he was dressed in a rumpled sweatshirt and sweatpants, and his hair was askew as if he'd jumped out of bed and hurried over to the hospital. He was with another man in his fifties who wore a tweed blazer and dark glasses.

"Hello, Ed," Marly said, standing. Ed Powell looked over at her, his eyes narrowing, probably as he tried to remember her name, and then gave her a nod of semirecognition. "Oh, yeah, hi there. I'm real sorry about Janny. I know she's your close friend, and I'm real sorry," he said uncomfortably. "I just talked to one of the docs, and he told me she's out of surgery and they're going to be moving her into recovery any time now. But she's in a coma."

Then his eyes looked faraway; and he thought out loud. "I think that's what we'll tell the papers. In a coma, don't you think?" he asked turning to the other man. "I've got the press downstairs crawling up my ass for some buzz about her," he said to Marly, then turned back to the man. "I think for now, just your basic coma ought to do it. Get them to print that it looks really bad and that she's probably dying. Then if . . ."

"I'm Hank Brand," the man with the sunglasses said as he extended his hand to Marly in a tone that implied, 'We both know Ed Powell's a boor not to have introduced us.'

"Oh, Christ, I'm sorry," Ed Powell said. "Hank Brand is the publicist for my show and this is . . . uh, Billy Mann's wife."

"I'm Marly Bennet," Marly said coolly, and she shook the publicist's hand.

Ed Powell's body English said he didn't want Marly in the conversation any more. He turned his back to her, edging the publicist away to talk privately, but Marly wanted to hear what they were saying, so she followed closely behind them.

"Then if we make it sound as bad as possible," Ed Powell said, furrowing his brow, "and she pulls through, it's a full-out miracle, and we really go through the roof the day she comes back. We bring her on during sweeps week, in a wheelchair, and we do a whole big . . ."

Marly couldn't stop herself. She put her hand on Ed Powell's arm. "Excuse me, Ed. Are you saying you're going to exploit this disaster to promote your television show?" Both men looked at her with the same kind of light annoyance they would have if she'd been a waitress at the Beverly Hills Hotel who just spilled water on their table. "That's a mistake. It's irresponsible for you to put harmful ions out there which could have an adverse effect on Jan's recovery."

Ed Powell looked long at Marly, then smiled at his colleague. "Harmful ions? That's a classic. I'll have to remember that for one of the characters on my show." Then he looked back at Marly with a patronizing smile and added, "One of the crazy ones." Then he gestured with his head down the hall toward the elevator, said, "Let's hit it, Hank," and moved off.

Marly's first instinct was to run after him and pummel him. To tell him he was killing Jan, to tell him if Jan died it would be on his conscience forever, but she knew he didn't have a conscience, so she took a chance that maybe she could get to the press agent instead.

"Hank, wait. I know we've just met, but I need you to hear me. This is very important to Jan. Life-or-death important. Because we all know ideas are what kill people. Surely you've read Deepak Chopra or Louise Hay? You understand that the way we perceive the world is the way we make it, don't you? That's why you have to tell the press that Jan is doing well. Those messages are transformed into molecules that reach her cells."

She heard the begging in her voice, but worse than that, she knew how ridiculous she must seem, trying to explain those ideas to this particular man. Knew that in a year she and the girls would laugh about this, but at this moment she was certain it was the most urgent cause in the world.

Ellen and Rose walked over to where she and the press agent were standing. Hank Brand didn't acknowledge them. He had an expression on his face that looked as if he were trying hard to hold in a laugh. Probably he couldn't wait to regale the other vultures he worked with by telling them his story about this dippy woman.

"Mrs. Mann," he said, "the company I work for represents 'My Brightest Day,' and that means Ed Powell is my employer. If he says Jan O'Malley's dying . . . what can I say? As far as I'm concerned . . . she's dying." Then he smiled a tight little smile and he moved off down the hall.

"I'd like to kill him," Marly said.

"I'd like to hire him," Ellen said. "Anyone who's that blindly loyal . . ."

Marly leaned against the wall. "When I think of all the times I defended the press, and the First Amendment, and the right to print stories that drove other people mad," she said. "And now I'd like to take the assault weapon I've fought so hard to have banned, and mow them all down."

"Mar," Rose said, "remember what Lenny Bruce said. The word isn't the thing. Let people say what they want. When the time comes, we'll go in and be with Jan and tell her she's okay. And she will be."

"Who knows better than we do that they print lies every day?" Ellen said. "I've seen articles about myself in the trade papers saying I was getting jobs I never even heard about, buying projects that never crossed my desk, dating men I've never even met. But I laugh it off because I know the lies don't affect reality." Marly wasn't looking at her. "I know you know that, too," Ellen said.

Marly slowly turned to look at Ellen with pained eyes. "Are you trying to tell me you've seen this week's *Enquirer*?"

"I am," Ellen said, "this morning at the newsstand at the commissary."

"I saw it too," Rose said.

"And?"

"And I think Billy was probably talking to some young fan, and an overzealous photographer thought he'd make something out of it. Period. Billy's a loon, but he's not a child molester," Ellen said.

"We don't believe it for one second. And nobody else will, either. Ignore it," Rose said. "Those papers are garbage. One of my friends was in the market with her six-year-old daughter a few weeks ago waiting at the check-out line, and the child tugged at her and asked, 'Mommy, what does Oprah mean?' "

Marly laughed. "You're right," she said. "But it's awful. For me, and for the twins. And Billy. He's already under a lot of pressure. There's been such a buildup about the new show and how great it's supposed to be, and he's competing with all of those other late-night shows and he's panicked about that. I looked out the upstairs window at the top of his head and noticed a little bald spot, and I'm sure he's worried about that, too."

That made them laugh. "Do you think he worries about aging?" Rose asked. "With men in show business it's probably called 'The Dick Clark syndrome.'"

"Only without the 'Clark,'" Ellen said, and the three friends laughed.

"All men in this business are crazy. Do you think maybe there's something in the ink in *Variety* that goes directly to their brains?" Marly asked as they moved back to the chairs.

"No. I think it's men in general. In Molly's class, the girls have a poem they've been saying since kindergarten: 'Girls go to Mars to get more candy bars/Boys go to Jupiter to get more stupider,'" Rose said and they laughed.

"How do those little girls already know the battle lines are drawn?" Ellen asked.

"Andy seems so sane. I want a man like that," Marly said. "But I guess our relationships mirror us, and that's why I've spent so much time clinging to the idea of Billy. Because something in me required the drama that's a part of his package. And that was why the two of us got stuck at some impenetrable contact boundary that I couldn't transcend."

"What in the hell does that mean?" Ellen asked.

"To put it in that psychological jargon of which she's so fond," Rose said, "it means Billy's a schmuck."

Marly laughed, but her body remembered the thrill of Billy inside her that morning. She wanted everything he'd said to her to be true, for there to be some explanation about the tabloid picture.

"Jan used to tell me if she could give up smoking, I could give up Billy. She used to tell me I just had to detox my system of him and I'd be fine."

Rose didn't mention that she knew Jan went back to smoking after quitting for three months, or that Jan was still seeing a man she'd been hooked on for more than ten years. Or that Marly just talked about her in the past tense, as if she were already dead.

"I even went to one of those Coda meetings. It's a twelve-step group where you work on letting go of co-dependent relationships."

"What was that like?" Rose asked. "Is there a movie in it?"

"Only if you're co-dependent on Julia Roberts," Ellen said, and Marly snickered.

"I sat there listening to everyone's story and thought, I don't *want* to learn how not to be co-dependent. I like being co-dependent. I just need to find the right man to do it with. Someone who wants to be co-dependent with me as we co-depend into the sunset together."

"God, if what you said is true and our relationships mirror us, then I'm a vampire," Ellen said. "I haven't had one in so long I don't even know how to talk to anyone who doesn't reply 'Meow.' Of course I did have a few beauties in my life, which may have scared me off forever. And I'm sure you both recall them."

"We do," Marly said.

"You even had one in the lockup ward," Rose said.

"Thanks for remembering," Ellen said, "not to mention a few who should have been."

"She did? You did? I don't remember that," Marly said.

"Yes you do," Rose reminded her. "That weird Norman Braverman. The tall one with all the wavy black hair she was with for a while."

"Oh yes," Marly said . . . but the lockup ward? I didn't know he was put away. Tell me."

Ellen, remembering with a smile, told them the story of Norman Braverman.

SIXTEEN
The Snake Pit

Six WEEKS after Norman Braverman dumped me because he couldn't make a commitment, he was committed to a nuthouse in New England. I liked to tell myself that the little putz's incarceration was a direct result of realizing he'd walked out on the greatest woman he'd ever known. That one morning he woke up screaming my name, knew he'd lost me forever, and in torment and despair turned in all his sharp instruments, checked out of Hollywood and into a bin.

But the truth was, nutsy Normie's trip to the farm of funniness had nothing to do with me. This was a man who was certifiable long before we met. Unfortunately, in my own needy state of mind I neglected to notice the clues. And there were a lot of them. Number one, he was the only man I ever knew who faked orgasms. He'd put himself inside me, and within seconds I'd feel him get soft.

I tried not to take it personally while I watched him writhe around on top of me making moaning noises so I would think he'd lost his tumescence due to an explosion of passion. But anyone who's been around, even a little bit, knows for certain that after passionate explosions there has to be evidence of same. After a Norman Braverman explosion, despite the sound effects, there wasn't so much as a drop.

Number two, crazy fucking Norman couldn't decide if he had a life wish or a death wish. For example, he ate bran by the box and exercised seven days a week for at least two hours a day no matter what the weather or his condition. But he also smoked more than a pack of cigarettes a day, then drank himself to sleep every night.

Number three. The guy was neat, no, not neat, a better word would be compulsive. As in when he left the bathroom, he folded the end of the toilet paper into an origami triangle, the way maids do in hotels to let you know they've been there to clean up. In fact, Norman's mother, who frequently came out to dinner with us, liked to tell a story about just how neat Norman was when he was growing up.

"He ate all of his food symmetrically," she bragged to me one night. "Normsie wouldn't take a bite out of one side of a potato chip unless he could take a bite of equal size out of the other side." Now I happen to have a son myself, and I knew the behavior she was describing was so nuts that if my kid had it, I'd take him by ambulance to the nearest shrink. But this was a woman who thought everything her forty-year-old bachelor son did was genius. And she called him on the phone several times a day to tell him so.

Which leads us headlong into symptom number four. A few of those calls happened to come in on a Saturday night when I had a baby-sitter at my house taking care of Roger, and Norman and I were at his house, in bed. Trying to make love. But when he heard his mother's voice on the answering machine saying, "Hi, darling . . . ," he pulled himself away from me, shushed me as if he was about to take an urgent business call, and left me lying there while he chatted and dished with her.

You're probably asking yourself why I stayed with him. Maybe because I was a single mother desperately trying to find a father for my son. Maybe because I'm shallow and he was very good-looking. Tall and lean with thick black wavy hair and turquoise eyes. Or more probably, I was hooked into him, because there's something about people who walk the thin line between sanity and bananas that's charismatic.

But even more to the point, there was something in my own bottomless need that understood Norman's. Both of us were in a trough period in our careers that year. Norman had lost three big clients, and a fourth was threatening to walk out on him. I had just been fired from Fox and didn't have a prospect in sight. One month I'd been mentioned in *Los Angeles Magazine* in a column about female studio execs who were called "Movers and Shakers in The Biz," and the next month I was counting the cans in my pantry to see if there was enough Chunky vegetable soup to last until I got another job.

Actually, the embarrassingly true reason I allowed Norman Braverman's nutsy behavior to roll off me with about as much interest as he did, and continued to have this so-called romance with him, was that I was on the rebound from another relationship when I met him and desperately needed someone, anyone, to cling to. So I went on pretending he was the man for me, closing my eyes to the fact that he wasn't the man for anyone, particularly himself.

But the writing was on the wall, in this case a padded wall back east, in a lock-up building where Norman had been held for a long time before I even heard about it. It was at a brunch at the home of Joel and Sally, the couple who introduced me to Norman, that I got the news. I'd already decided that I wasn't going to go to the brunch, and I left the invitation sitting on my desk for weeks before I called to R.S.V.P. because I was afraid Norman was invited, too, and I'd have to see him there and face the discomfort.

He had handled our breakup in such a cavalier way that even though I'd wished for months to somehow get the nerve to do it myself, when Norman did it first, I was devastated. We were at his house one morning, it was summer, and Rogie was at sleepaway camp, so I got to be at what Norman jokingly called "grown-up sleep-away camp."

We'd had a so-so night before, and Norman was blowing his hair dry while I put on makeup at the bathroom counter next to him. And out of nowhere, with the dryer's screaming noise filling the air around us, Norman said, without ever taking his eyes from his own reflection, "Ellen, I've been thinking a lot about the two of us, and I've decided I'm going to have to pass."

"Pardon?" I said, dropping my Fabulash mascara wand, and

noticing in horror when I grabbed it up from the ecru sisal bathroom rug that it had left a little line of dark brown fibers next to my foot.

"I mean, we can still go to dinner tonight, but as far as the future goes, I'm giving it the Marty Robbins," he said.

"Who?" I asked, putting my foot on the mascara spot so Norman wouldn't see it, probably forcing the makeup so deep into the pile that it would never come out.

"Marty Robbins," he said. "Get it? El Paso."

I didn't get it until I was driving home. Giving it the Marty Robbins? Marty Robbins sang "El Paso." Pass. He was passing on having a relationship with me. The cleverness made me want to throw up. Made me sick that I'd ever spoken to a putz like Norman Braverman, let alone been intimate with a man who ends a relationship by telling you he's giving you the Marty Robbins.

Sally swore to me when I finally called to R.S.V.P. that there was no chance that Norman Braverman would show up at the brunch, so while Roger went to a movie with a few of his friends, I went to the brunch. Who knew that the reason Norman wouldn't be there was that he was in occupational therapy, making a trivet out of popsicle sticks? That news came later.

It was a pretty, sunny Sunday morning at Sally and Joel's, and I was chatting with some of the other guests over the poached salmon, which I hadn't touched because I was certain it had to be going bad in the sun. When the ice in my glass of Evian melted, I went inside to get some more. Just as I was heading back outside, I saw Joel hurry down from upstairs. When he spotted me, he walked purposefully over and pulled me into a corner of the living room.

"I guess you've heard about Norman?" he asked.

Heard about Norman. Oh no, I thought. By the look on Joel's face I could tell that he was about to break some real bad news. He's going to tell me Norman's getting married to someone else, was my first neurotic thought. That some other woman has accomplished what I couldn't.

"He's in a hospital," Joel told me confidentially. In a hospital,

I thought. Well, that's good news! Great news for me because it means he's definitely not coming to this party. I guess he's giving it the old Marty Robbins. Ha, ha! The schmuck.

"And it's very serious," Joel said. His face was pale. Oh, God, I thought, my elation busted. Very serious is ominous, and now terror tightened my throat. Very serious had to mean Norman had a communicable disease, which because of our close association, I was about to learn that I had, too.

"Mental ward," Joel said, putting a smile on his face, in spite of the chilling words he was offering, so that the couple walking by us, an agent from CAA and his actress client, wouldn't guess that Joel was telling me something horrifying about someone those two probably both knew. Of course, at that moment, to me, Joel's last two words felt like the best ones I'd ever heard, because they meant that whatever Norman had wasn't contagious.

"The poor son of a bitch," Joel said, and I had to laugh to myself that "poor son of a bitch" was a long way from the description of a man who, only a brief few months before, in the days when Joel and Sally wanted to fix me up with him, was described as "a real upstanding fabulous guy. A great catch!"

"He calls me every few days from the pay phone in that place," Joel said with sadness in his eyes, and for a fleeting instant, I was sure a joke was going to come next. That I was the dummy who had fallen for the old mental-ward set-up, and that any minute I'd have to laugh at myself over it. But then Joel pointed to a telephone in the living room, where the hold light was blinking. He called me a few minutes ago, and while we were talking I mentioned that we were having a party today, and that you were here and, Ellen . . . he wants to talk to you very much."

"He does?" I said. And I was really flattered. "Really?" Now the important question here should be, why did it thrill me to hear that a lunatic wanted to talk to me from the pay phone at the fruitcake factory? Why was my heart pounding as if I'd just been informed I'd won the Oscar for my last picture? Why was I panicked about what I was going to say to the little bozo who had dumped me in such a shitty way?

"You can take it upstairs," Joel said, walking me to the bottom of the steps.

I walked slowly up the stairs, and when I arrived at the top I scouted around for a place where I could sit and talk to Norman privately. I picked Joel and Sally's cool white bedroom, an idyllic-looking spot with one of those damask duvet covers on a big marshmallowy-looking comforter, and what seemed like a dozen huge white square pillows across the head of the bed.

I was having performance anxiety worse than I ever have when I go in to meet with the biggest stars, or talk story with the biggest writers. So I sat down and tried to collect myself while I stared at the flickering light on the hold button calling to me from the phone on the glass bedside table.

What does it look like at the other end of this call? I wondered. Is Norman in a straitjacket, while a big impatient male orderly who looks like Lurch on "The Addams Family" holds the receiver of a pay phone to his ear? I glanced around the room at the photos of Joel and Sally and their three daughters. Family pictures of the kind of family I actually thought for one desperate moment I might have when my son gave me away to Norman Braverman. Which might have worked if I could have kept Norman hard and/or off the phone with his mother. The phone.

I put my hand nervously on this one, then picked up the receiver, harboring the hope that maybe crazy Norman had only been allowed three minutes per call, and because I'd walked upstairs too slowly, he was now being dragged back to his room by the orderly, who would not be dissuaded by the offer Norman was probably making to represent him and get him a part in a major motion picture. "A second lead," I imagined Norman shrieking, "with your name above the title."

"Hello?" I said.

"Hello, gorgeous," Norman said back. And you want to know who's really crazy? When he said that, I had an inexplicable rush of feeling. A sorrow that made me instantly lose all memory of the passionless sex, the smoking, the drinking, and did I already mention his mother? Somehow at that moment, which must have been a very lonely and low one for me, I could only remember every good thing about him. The sweet way he kissed, the gentle way he dealt with his temperamental clients, the funny stories he used to like to sit and tell me at the end of his long work days. The way he promised he'd be a great father for Roger.

"I hope I'm not spoiling the party for you," he said. "It's just that when Joel told me you were there, I realized how much I wanted to hear your voice and tell you, probably too late, how sorry I am if I hurt you."

"Well, thank you for that, Norman," I said, wondering if he knew that I knew where he was calling from, or if Joel was supposed to have kept that part a secret. I was trying to decide if I should tell him that I knew he was in the cracker mill or not, when he said, "I guess you know where I am," putting an end to that dilemma.

"I do."

"Did Joel tell you that I'm in James Taylor's old room?" he asked, in what had to be the ultimate in Hollywood kitsch. Name-dropping the guy who inhabited the room in the booby hatch before you did. I think I countered with, "How nice. And how long will you be staying?" in the same way the desk clerk at Brown's Hotel asked me last summer when I checked in.

"Hard to say, gorgeous, hard to say," Norman answered in a sweet, sorrowful voice. "I could be in here for a long, long time. I'm in real bad shape. If I wasn't, do you think I could have ever walked out on a gem of a girl like you?"

Well, if you didn't notice before what a fool I am, this ought to clinch it, because the minute Norman said that, I forgave him not only for giving me the Marty Robbins, but for every injustice during our romance. I actually felt better about everything that had happened between us, even though I suspected that only minutes earlier, this same person probably told his therapy group that he was Louis the fucking Fourteenth. The flattery made me feel so okay about everything that when he asked me the next question, I immediately said, "Of course."

"Would it be all right if I called you from here now and then? When you're at home? So we can really talk? Maybe I can explain away some of the awful things I did to you, and if you'll let me, I'd like to talk to Roger. I loved Roger, and I know I must have hurt him, too, when I broke up with you."

"Oh, Norman. He understood. But he misses you too," I heard myself lying. My son didn't even look up from his Legos when I told him Norman Braverman and I were through. "And of course you can call me at home. Any time!" What was I thinking?

At the risk of having you call the *casa de pistachios* to tell them to warm up the James Taylor suite for me, because this is as nutso as I ever got or ever hope to get, I will admit that what I was thinking was that I could save Norman Braverman. That I would be the one to pull him out of this terrible state of mind, of which impotence must have surely been a temporary symptom, and turn him into a new man.

I would have my mother fly out from Florida to stay with my son, and I would rush to the cuckoos' nest, bring Norman treats, read to him through the bars or the barbed wire or whatever they put him behind. And soon they would take my darling Normie out of the jacket with the very long sleeves and send him home under my aegis, the picture of mental health.

By the time I left the brunch, I was a woman with a mission. My plan was clear. After Norman and I got back to Los Angeles, I would have a restraining order slapped on his mother and change the phone number, and soon we'd be making plans to get married, making fiery love, and maybe even making a little sister or brother for my Roger.

But when two or three weeks went by, and Norman hadn't called even once from the pay phone at the wacko ward, my Florence Nightingale complex cooled, and I began welcoming fix-ups from yet another couple with yet another alleged great guy.

At the same time I was trying to get any job I could, but the work situation was dismal. My bank account was getting so low, I was afraid my son and I were going to have to move to Miami Beach and live in the old folks apartment building with my mother. It was another dateless Saturday night, and I was in my

sweats, watching television and feeling sorry for myself, when
the phone rang.

"Hi, gorgeous," Norman said. This time my heart didn't skip
a beat, it just thudded a little.

"Norman, how nice to hear from you," I said, leaving off the
word *finally*. "You sound good." And he did. Probably a hell of a
lot better than I did that night.

"Yeah, I feel great, even though I'm still here," he said, sounding as chipper as if "here" meant a luxury hotel in the Caribbean.
"People have been writing to me and sending me things, and I
really feel as if a lot of folks out there care about me."

"That's great," I said, thinking I should have sent him some
baked goods. Maybe something appropriate. Like a box of nut
bars. I also felt very much like I wanted to get off the phone. Norman wasn't my boyfriend. He wasn't even my friend. He was a
guy who gave me the Marty Robbins and who was probably
only calling me now because everyone else he tried first was out
on a Saturday night.

"In fact, you want to hear the cutest?" he went on. "Yesterday
I got chicken soup delivered in dry ice from Barbara."

Barbara? Did he mean Walters? If only I knew how he was
spelling it. Maybe it was Barbra Streisand.

"Very cute," I said, wishing I hadn't let Roger spend the night
at a friend's, because when he was at home at least I had a
Scrabble opponent.

"I've also had two or three really long conversations with Bob
over these last weeks. In fact," Norman told me, "just between
us, there's a very good chance that when I get out of here, I'm
going to close a deal with him."

"Bob?" I asked absently.

"Redford," he said, "and maybe Paul Newman, too. He actually stopped by here on Tuesday. He lives in Connecticut, you
know, and it's so close he figured we'd take a meeting instead of
talk on the phone, but they told him I wasn't allowed to have any
visitors. The nurses were so thrilled to meet him, they're still
talking about it."

"Oh my God," I thought, sitting up straight and startling the cat off my lap as I really took in what Norman just said. This was worse than I imagined. This man was having agent's madness. It made sense. When an agent cracked, lost his marbles, went around the old proverbial bend, wouldn't he have delusions that big stars were seeking him out and trying to sign with him?

This poor man. I was aching with sympathy for him now, realizing how far gone he really was. Poor baby, I thought, poor thing. This was someone I had once really cared for. Maybe my reasons for being with him had all been wrong, but we had shared intimacy, and time, and hopes for the future. And now this unfortunate creature was losing his grip, a casualty of the pressures of show business.

"And how are *you* doing, Ellen?" he asked, but I knew it was just to be polite. Well, I thought, at least his madness has left him with a sense of civility.

"Me?" What could I say? I wasn't going to complain to a man who was probably phoning me between shock treatments that I was worried about being unemployed. Somehow, I came up with enough small talk to fill a few minutes. News about Roger's soccer team, movies I'd seen, the weather. I was relieved when he finally said, "Call you again," as his sign-off, but judging from what I now knew was his condition, I didn't think he'd be calling again.

"I look forward to it, Norman," I said, and I put the phone down, feeling devastated for him.

The next morning, when I had just said good-bye to the real estate broker who was coming to take a look at my house, which I'd decided I'd better sell, Bill Haber from CAA called and said there was a great job opening for me at Worldwide Pictures. "Go take a meeting there with the senior V.P., Peter Goldman. He'll love you."

Worldwide Pictures had a great reputation as a forward-looking company, and they hired a lot of women. I knew a few of the women executives, and I thought I'd fit in well there. I was feeling hopeful. Maybe I'd saved the house. I hustled my ass into that meeting, and I knew right away Peter Goldman and I were on the same wavelength. We loved all the same films, we had similar ideas for future projects, he had a great sense of humor, and when I left I felt confident.

I called Bill Haber when I got home. "Goldman loved you," he said, "but he still has a few more people to see, and then he'll send his top two picks to meet with Harvey Springer. Springer will be the one who decides."

Weeks went by. I still didn't hear. Just as I sat writing checks that I thought were going to deplete everything I had left, I got a call from the real estate lady asking if she could show the house, and I realized I'd been praying that nobody would want it. In full-out depression, I was about to set a time with her when my call waiting beeped, and I told her I'd call her back.

"Hi, gorgeous," Norman said. "So what's happening?" I remember marveling that he sounded a hell of a lot better than I was feeling. I remember also resenting the fact that garden-variety neurotics like me were painfully in touch with reality, and lucky psychotics like him got to live in the ether, where it must be nice.

"Not much is happening here," I said, not mentioning that my heart was aching because it looked like I'd have to sell my sweet little house. "I'm still hanging in, and I've had a few meetings around town trying to get a job. Right now my best prospect is over at Worldwide. I had a preliminary meeting with Peter Goldman, and now I'm waiting to see Harvey Springer."

"Well, I'm sorry to say this, Ellen," Norman said, "but that's not going to happen." And then he was quiet. What did he mean? What wasn't going to happen? Did he mean I wasn't going to get the job at Worldwide Pictures? Had his voices told him?

"What isn't going to happen, Norman?" I asked, trying to sound patient and not patronizing. Why, I wondered, did I ever tell Norman Braverman it was all right to call me? Why was I having this bizarre telephone relationship with someone who was now going to insult me, when I was feeling rotten enough already?

"The job at Worldwide isn't going to happen," Norman said.

"I mean it's nothing personal, Ellen. You'd be good in that job, it's just that there are too many women in that department already. And Peter Goldman can't make a decision because he won't even be there next month, and neither will Harvey Springer."

"How on earth would *you* know that?" I asked him, and I almost laughed as I did, because I knew this conversation was in the same category as the one about chicken soup from Barbara or Barbra, and Bob Redford calling, and Paul Newman coming to visit him. It was part of the psychosis, the colossal ego that accompanies that kind of illness, that makes everything anyone else says or does somehow revolve around the patient. Now Norman believed that my potential job was something *he* was controlling.

"Because when I come in, I'm making a clean sweep," he said. "Cutting back the chaff and really running a tight ship." I decided that the mixed metaphors were probably a symptom of his disease, too.

"What are you talking about, Norman?"

"Didn't I tell you that I'm going to be running that studio by the first of next month?" he asked me. "I sent back the contracts this morning." His voice was more animated than I'd ever heard it. All I could think was whatever those drugs were, I wanted some, too.

"Norman, that's great," I said. "I'm so happy for you." Meanwhile I was thinking, boy oh boy, this must really be hard for his mother, even though as I already mentioned, hard and his mother, in my experience with him, seemed to be mutually exclusive.

When we got off the phone, I sat at my desk, staring, for a long time. Joel was right, this man was a poor son of a bitch. But I couldn't worry about it anymore. I was a single woman supporting a child, my mother, and some felines who turned up their noses at ordinary cat food and got too snarled to be groomed at home. Maybe I'd better figure out if I could be an independent producer, start looking for projects, come up with ideas, and of course, pray hard that I'd hear from somebody at Worldwide about my meeting with Harvey Springer.

My mother called from Miami Beach a few times to see if I was okay, and I knew she was worried. I remember how the three of you took me out to dinner and kept calling me, too. Marly even brought over a few bags of groceries one day. Then one morning Sheppy Cherbak called to see if I wanted to meet for lunch. Sheppy's a wonderful writer, and someone I've been close to for years.

Now and then we meet and complain about the business or romances or just life in general. But I was so depressed by then, I didn't want to get out of my sweat clothes and make myself look human to go out.

"I don't think so, Shep," I said.

"In the Valley," Sheppy tried, meaning it could be casual. "For a hot dog." I've known Sheppy since I first arrived in Hollywood. He's funny and we always laugh together, and over the years he's seen me looking worse than I looked that day. I really needed to be cheered up, and I knew it would be fun to laugh with him, so I said okay, and we agreed to meet at one o'clock at the hot dog place next to the newsstand at the corner of Ventura and Van Nuys.

I got there a little bit early, on purpose, so I'd have time to browse through the colorful rows of assorted magazines, which has always been a favorite pastime of mine. I love the flashy covers and the eye-catching headlines. I stood there for a while picking and choosing which of the tempting ones I would buy, excited by the number of choices.

When I was holding a few favorites and was walking over to the guy who wears the change belt so I could pay for them, my eye caught the headline of *Variety* and for a minute, all the traffic on Van Nuys Boulevard stopped, and so did the people walking by on Ventura Boulevard, and so did my heart. I had a giddy, dizzy feeling that I was losing my grip on reality when I read: BRAVERMAN MOVING TO TOP WORLDWIDE POST, MAKING CLEAN SWEEP. "Norman Braverman, former actor's rep, announced today that he would bring deals with Robert Redford and Paul

Newman with him when he helms studio pic exec post next week."

When Sheppy got to the corner, he came over and stood next to me and wanted to know why I was sitting on the curb looking pale. I told him it must just be because I was hungry.

SEVENTEEN

GOOD GOD." Marly was laughing at Ellen's story. "It's true. The inmates really are running the asylum. That's unbelievable."

"But absolutely true," Ellen said. "Which is why now when I deal with the jerkoffs at my studio, I remember that at any given time, they may have had a visit to the booby hatch, and then everything they do makes sense to me."

Rose nodded knowingly. "Can't you see the board of directors, looking over the résumés of all the people who applied for the job of studio boss, and finally one of them says, 'Eureka! This guy's perfect. He'll understand the way we think! He's been locked up for being a paranoid schizophrenic.' "

"Jan's coming out of recovery," they heard Andy call to them. They turned to see him standing at the end of the hall gesturing for them to come with him. Ellen put her shoes on, and they all hurried to follow Andy along the long hospital corridor.

Just as they stopped at the double door to the recovery room, it opened, and two hospital orderlies wheeled out a gurney, which moved forward with a clanging bump over the metal sill and into the corridor. As it came closer, they could see that Jan was on it.

She was unconscious, with a tube down her throat, and a nurse with a bellows was squeezing breath into her. Her head was bandaged, and her face was purple with bruises. She was hooked up to IV fluid that hung from rolling poles on wheels, which the two men wearing green surgical scrub suits moved forward next to the bed. The friends stood at fearful attention watching her go by.

Rose felt a weakness in her thighs, and she was sure her knees were about to give out under her; Marly's arm went around her waist, as if Marly knew she would need steadying. Then Ellen moved closer to her, too. They held tightly to one another, watching the odd float bearing their comatose friend as the men moved it through the door to the surgical ICU.

When the door closed behind Jan's gurney, Andy took one of Marly's hands in his, and Ellen's hand in the other, while Rose stood with her back leaning against him in their small circle, and he spoke quietly.

"The bullet damaged her lung, but that seems to be functioning normally with the tube in place. That nurse with the bellows will hook her up to the ventilator and she'll breathe on that for a while. There was also a collection of blood underneath her skull that they were able to suction out. And her head is bandaged because they had to go in and cut through her skull to get the blood out.

"She's still unconscious, and it'll be a matter of time before they know whether or not there was damage to her brain underneath the pool of blood. There might be some inflammation to the spinal cord where the bullet hit her. She hasn't been moving her legs, and there's no way to know now if she'll regain normal function. But they seem to be hopeful that she'll be conscious within the next few days."

"When can we go in?" Marly asked.

"The nurses need to become familiar with her and stabilize her," Andy said, "so I'd say it'll be at least an hour until they'll let anybody in."

"Is she going to survive this?" Rose asked. "What are they saying about her chances?"

Andy shook his head slightly. "In cases like this, it's impossible to say."

Marly couldn't listen to any more. She had to walk away, hugging herself as she looked down the hospital corridor, her trembling face struggling to hold in the tears of anger and sadness. She remembered when Jan's sister, Julie, had tried talking Jan out of adopting a baby at age forty-five because she was too old. She'd laughed about the way Jan had dismissed the warnings.

"Julie," Jan said sweetly, "even if this little baby grows up and gets married as old as thirty, I'll still be only seventy-five. Young enough to dance at his wedding." Now Janny might not dance at Joey's wedding, or even walk down the aisle.

Maybe she wouldn't even live until the morning, and then what would happen to the sweet little boy? Surely Jan had made some kind of will, assigning Joey's guardianship if anything happened to her. Marly tried to put the thought out of her mind that there was even a small chance the custody of that angelic boy could go to her. She had wanted another baby so much when the twins were still small, but the rise of Billy's mammoth career and the dissolution of her marriage had made that unrealistic.

Besides, Jan would have specified that everything she left behind, including Joey, go to her sister in Pennsylvania, Marly thought. The sister who told her not to adopt the baby in the first place. She shivered when she realized she was already writing Jan's death sentence with those thoughts.

"Shouldn't somebody be calling Julie?" she asked, turning back to the others.

"I have Julie's number," Rose said, paging through her Filofax, muttering to herself as pieces of paper flew out of it onto the floor. "I know I had it here someplace, because last summer when Jan went back to see her, I talked to her a few times, when she called to get medical advice from Andy, so I have the number . . . somewhere. Damn, I'm a such a goddamned flake. I have to find the number so I can call Julie and tell her. Oh, here it is. I'm going to call her."

Andy put his hand on her arm. "Honey, I think you should probably wait a few hours. We'll definitely know a lot more about Janny's condition by then. Why don't you three go down and get something to eat?"

"He's right," Ellen said, "let's try to get something downstairs."

Rose felt too queasy to eat, but she hoped maybe food would calm the gnawing acid hole in her middle she was attributing to terror. "I guess," she said, and led the others to the elevators, which seemed to be taking forever to arrive, so she pushed open the door to the stairwell, and Marly and Ellen followed. They walked single file, seven flights down the metal steps.

"I should have brought along the dinner I made for Girls' Night," Marly said when they opened the door to the basement floor and the greasy smell of the hospital cafeteria enveloped them. In the low-ceilinged basement cafeteria there were only two other diners, some women at the far end who were chattering loudly to one another, who were as dressed up and bedecked with jewelry as if they were going to a party.

Rose was the first to take a plastic tray from a pile and slide it along the metal shelf that ran the length of the sparsely stocked buffet. She chose a sticky-looking pasta salad under Saran Wrap, and a Diet Coke, hoping the caffeine would zap away the sleepy feeling that often tugged at her when she felt afraid. She fought a yawn as she put the can on her tray.

Ellen put a tuna salad sandwich on her tray. Marly took a banana and some yogurt, then reached into the glass case where the desserts were lined up and put her hand on a bowl of red Jell-O. "I think we all should have some of this," she said, putting a bowl of the shivering red cubes on each of their trays. "My treat. Maybe the taste of it will take me back to my childhood." But when they got to the table, she looked at the bowl on her tray and changed her mind. "I just remembered," she said. "I had a lousy childhood."

They sat at the end of a long table, unwrapping and then picking at the barely edible food. The two women at the end of the room seemed to be looking over at them now and gesturing and whispering, and Rose, who noticed their behavior, decided it had to be because they recognized Marly. They were carrying their trays of dirty dishes to the conveyor belt now, and they couldn't resist stopping to stare. Then they approached the table with a tentative yet adoring look.

"I'm sorry to bother you," one of them said to Marly. "But I really wanted to tell you just how much we loved you in every episode of 'Keeping Up with the Joneses.' "

Marly smiled. "Thank you so much," she said.

"You are such a gifted comedienne. There hasn't been anyone like you except for maybe Lucille Ball."

Marly warmed to the lavish praise. "Oh, how nice of you to say that."

"And we know it must not be so easy to be so funny, under the circumstances of your life." Marly stiffened. "We know you're getting divorced, but we want you to know we think it's for the best. You got rid of him before he turned into a real pervert."

"Poor you," the other one said. "And your poor daughters. I saw the *Enquirer* today, and I am sure he's guilty as sin, and I'm glad you're not a part of his sick life any more."

Marly's face was now frozen, and Rose could see she was trying to decide how to react.

"I wish I had something with me for you to sign," the first woman said. "My daughter would be so thrilled to have your autograph. You don't by any chance have anything with you that you could give her with your name on it?"

"I don't have anything," Marly managed to say through clenched teeth.

The woman exchanged a glance that said they didn't believe her. "Yeah, well it would have been nice," one of them said. "Too bad." And then both of the women turned to walk away, and as they did, one said in a confidential voice all of them could hear, "She could have given you a deposit slip, a napkin, anything. But they think they're too good to take the time with you. Meanwhile, she hasn't had a good part since that Jones show went off the air."

Marly stood, and in the voice Rose remembered her using when she played Portia at Tech, she said to the exiting backs of the two women, "I'm in this hospital because one of my best friends is near death. I'm hurting and frightened and trying very hard to be polite, so it's my fondest hope that you'll do the same and turn around and apologize for your rudeness," she said. Ellen and Rose exchanged looks. Not knowing whether to stop her, to tell her to ignore the women's obnoxious behavior, or to laugh.

Both of the women turned, with scowls on their faces, and one said, "Apologize? Who do you think you are? You're as bad as that jerk you married."

Rose remembered later that Marly had a smile on her face as she picked up a bowl of Jell-O from Rose's tray, took a cube and threw it at one of the women, and then another and another until she had to move on to the second bowl. It took the women a few seconds to understand what was happening, then they looked down at their rhinestoned outfits with the red blobs melting and sliding down the front, and when they did, one of them got the Jell-O right in her hair. In horror she put her hand up to her head and shrieked at Marly, "I hope you and your sex-maniac husband go to jail!"

"You Hollywood slut," the other one shrieked as they both turned and ran out of the cafeteria, and Marly kept throwing with that same good arm she used when she coached the twins' softball games, until the last cube of Jell-O was gone.

"Way to go, Mrs. Jones," one of the black food attendants hollered out to Marly, and in return she saluted him with a victorious fist in the air. Ellen and Rose were still laughing when Marly wiped her hands off on a paper napkin. Rose took her own napkin and cleaned up some of the Jell-O from the floor.

"Jan always says I'm too combative," Marly said, helping her.

"How observant of Jan," Ellen said.

"But what can I do? People like that think my life is their business, and it drives me wild. The plumber who comes to fix my shower asks me about Billy's girlfriends, and the dry cleaner wants to know how much I'm getting in the divorce settlement. Women have stopped me on the street and said, 'How could you let that adorable Billy go? He's such a doll, I'll take him any day.'

"One day I actually shrieked at one of them who said that, 'Oh, really? Well, when he wakes up in the middle of the night and has to watch his own videotapes to make sure he's alive, and other women mail him their recently worn underwear, which he so sweetly shows you, and he sometimes sends his bodyguards when he's too busy to pick up the kids . . . enjoy, baby!'

"They don't know that he's what Jung calls a *puer aeternus*, an eternal boy. Wearing his penis on his sleeve. No, I'll bet even boys have a greater sense of responsibility, don't they? Didn't Roger when he was a kid?" she asked Ellen. But before Ellen could answer, she laughed out loud at herself. "I am over the top," she said. "I haven't thrown food at anyone since summer camp," and she laughed a laugh that was a breath away from tears.

"It's good for you to let it all out," Rose said.

"Her? Are you kidding?" Ellen said. "She lets it all out more than anyone I know. You and I are supposed to be the emotional Jews, and she's the one who's always venting her rage."

"You're right," Marly said. "I think I've been letting too much out. Always too big, too much, a complete reversal to the pent-up good girl my parents tried to get me to be. Billy used to call me the unWASP. He said my temper was one of the things that hurt our marriage. And I'm worried. Not only because of Billy, but two things happened within the last few months to make me think I may have hurt what's left of my career, too."

EIGHTEEN
To Have and Have Not

I ALWAYS thought as I got older that fiery anger that sometimes grabs me unexpectedly would level off. That eventually I'd become a nice mellow old lady. But even though the old lady part is coming true, I feel as if I'm more full of rage than ever. And this isn't just a little umbrage over some political issue, this is outrage at everything that crosses my path. Maybe it's hormones, maybe it's living in L.A.

For a while I thought it had to do with my abandonment issues around Billy moving out of the house. But I decided that was too facile an explanation. On closer examination, I think it has to do with my inability to face aging and all the implications that come with it. Like the idea that I'm no longer eligible to create babies, and that maybe I should have had many more after the twins were toddling around.

I also can't bear the idea that unless someone has a part for me in some show or film or even a commercial, I can't create artistically, either. That I'm at the mercy of a business that wants me to be obsolete. It all makes me feel so out of control, and that's the way I find myself behaving. Also, the twins are at the age where they're very independent, they mostly need me to drive them from point A to point B, and pretty soon they won't need me for that, either. So I feel obsolete as a caretaker, too.

Lately I've been painfully aware of the fact that I had to find something that was just for me. The way my mother keeps telling my retired father, "Get a hobby or you'll die, Thomas." And that's why I campaigned to get elected to the board of the twins' school, and became co-chair of the school's country fair, and a few months ago I accepted the presidency of my neighborhood committee.

Recently the big issue we dealt with in the neighborhood committee meeting was how to stop the damned production companies from filming on our streets all the time. The location scouts love our area because it's always so picture-perfect, but they block our driveways with their big trucks and the mobile dressing rooms. The noise pollution is awful, and the kids can't play outside their own homes. Everyone, including me, was really eager to see them stopped. So I initiated a petition for everyone in a radius of a few blocks to sign, and we worked out a whole system of how to prevent the film crews from coming here so often.

What I'm saying is, I am occupied with things other than just the occasional interview. And when I do get one, I try very hard to put it in perspective, but I always walk in with a colossal chip on my shoulder, thinking, "Why are they making me audition for this? I have miles and miles of film they can look at. They can screen every episode of every show I've ever done and spare me the humiliation of humbling myself by sitting in front of a group of yawning people and reading lines I could say even in my sleep. But they never do.

A few months ago, I went in to read for an advertising agency casting a series of national spots for a new car. I was hoping it would turn into the kind of thing Lindsay Wagner does for the southern California Ford dealers. A spokeswoman, with an ongoing relationship to the product, in a very classy kind of showing.

Well, in spite of my bad attitude, I got to the casting office, and everyone there couldn't have been nicer and more respectful. The director was someone I'd worked for years ago, and he came over and gave me a big hug, and the man from the agency was there, and he said, "This meeting today is just a formality, you're the one we wanted for this, and all we really wanted to do today was say hi."

I walked out of there feeling absolutely great. They sent me straight to wardrobe and the clothes were wonderful and I was all psyched up to shoot on Friday. When I got home, there was a message on my machine from Harry, my agent, saying they were paying me top dollar, and the shooting schedule would arrive that night. It was going to be an A plus experience all around.

When the messenger arrived with my shooting schedule, I told the twins I got a job, and they were thrilled for me. They gave me high fives and said they wanted to come on the set and watch me the way they always did with their dad. Once I overheard Sarah talking to a little friend of hers who came over to our house to play. The other girl said to her, "I know your dad is Billy Mann, who has that TV show. But what does your mom do?" And Sarah answered, "She goes on interviews."

At last one had paid off.

I didn't even open the envelope with the shooting schedule in it until after dinner, and when I did, I laughed out loud. The commercial was shooting on Friday morning at eight A.M. and the location was Albermarle Street. The street that runs perpendicular to mine. I could walk to work. I live two houses from Albermarle Street.

Then I remembered. My God! The neighborhood committee! After all we worked on about putting a stop to the filming around here. There would be hell to pay if this production company got a permit to shoot on Albermarle Street. There was no doubt they'd have to have the shoot moved somewhere else or get into a big brouhaha with the committee. My committee! But what if the production company won the battle, and the angry neighbors looked out of their windows to see that the star of the commercial they were fighting was me? Their own president?

It was insane that of all the streets in this city they picked Albermarle. It had to be some kind of cosmic lesson to me. A moment in time meant to teach me something. Maybe how to deal gingerly with things instead of always pulling on my army boots and marching in with guns blazing.

I decided I was going to be very diplomatic. I'd call the producers and tell them that because of my ironic position as both president of the neighbors committee and star of the commercial, I was in a position to warn him that the neighbors would be hostile to them, and they ought to try and find a different location, or end up in an unnecessary battle. The solution seemed pretty simple. They could just change the location of the shoot, and the neighbors would never be the wiser.

In the morning I called the production office. And the same receptionist who I'd met on the interview treated me as if she were an immigrant arriving at Ellis Island, and I was the Statue of Liberty. "Oh yes, Miss Bennet, so nice to talk to you." She told me her boss was out, but I gave her the lowdown to give him on the neighborhood committee and why he should change the shoot to somewhere besides Albermarle Street. And at about eleven, while I was in the garden, I heard my phone ring, so I ran in.

It was the producer of the car commercial. He was ever so sweet, and frankly I felt a little guilty being in cahoots with him and warning him about the neighbors, but my mother always taught me that the best choice is the one that blesses the most people, and I knew I was doing what was good for everyone concerned. He seemed very grateful for the tip, and he said he'd get back to me with the new location. That was Wednesday. I never heard a word all that day. All day Thursday went by, too.

Finally, at about five on Thursday, I called the producer's office, and the machine picked up because they were gone for the day, so I called my agent Harry's office to see if maybe my new shooting schedule and revised script had gone to his office by mistake, instead of coming to me. Harry's secretary sounded kind of tense when she heard it was me, and after a minute she put Harry on the line.

"Marly," he said in a very solemn voice, "I hate to be the bearer of bad tidings, but you've been released."

"I've been what?"

"Released. From the car commercial. They're not using you."

I felt sick. I'd been one thousand percent sure this time. There was no doubt that I was the only one they wanted for the commercial. "Why not?" I asked him. "What happened?"

"They said they decided not to go ahead with you, because you were being difficult."

Difficult? The word stuck in my chest. Difficult? I couldn't believe it. Now you all know that I have had reasons in my life for being called difficult. Sit-ins where I've been removed by police officers, marches where I've carried the banner right up the lawn of the White House. Which one of you was it that peeled me off President Reagan at that luncheon when I wanted to kill him for his silence about AIDS? That was when I was difficult. This was not.

I had worked at handling this conflict with a ladylike suggestion to make the producers' lives easier on the shooting day. Well, now I was so enraged I threw the phone across the room and did what I always do when I'm frustrated and crazed. I cleaned out closets. In one downstairs cupboard in the family room, I found a bunch of old photo albums of Billy and me with the twins when they were toddlers, and I think I probably sat there for two hours crying over every picture.

On Friday morning when I got into the car to drive the twins to school, we couldn't make a left turn onto Albermarle Street because the trucks from the commercial shoot were blocking our way. I was about to make the right turn, but naturally I couldn't help it, and I looked left to see what was happening. I won't even discuss the fact that my impotent little committee, including me, hadn't done a thing to put a stop to it. What really hurt like hell was to see that standing next to a shiny red car was an actress having her face powdered by a makeup man, and from the back she looked exactly like me.

I guess I must have been sitting there staring for a long time, because all of a sudden I was looking into the face of one of those rent-a-cops who work on those sets. And he leaned into my car window and said, "Sorry, lady. You can't make a left turn here. We're shooting a commercial for a car, so you can't drive down this street."

"Mom," Jenny asked me, "weren't *you* supposed to be in a commercial for a car today?" I knew I would have to tell the twins what happened, but I couldn't figure out how I could possibly explain it. How could I teach two adolescents that honesty doesn't pay? I wasn't moving yet, and the officer was getting miffed.

"I told you, no left turn, lady," he said to me nastily.

Difficult, difficult, difficult. No, I would prove to myself that I had control. Not me. I would release the angst into the white light the way my yoga teacher tells me to when we're doing our deep relaxation work. I would breathe into my spine and breathe out with love.

"Thank you, Officer," I said, and miraculously I didn't run him over. I simply made a right turn and headed for school. "There was a misunderstanding between me and the producers of the commercial," I heard myself saying to the twins, "so I didn't get the job after all." But they'd already lost interest in my plight and were chatting about someone in their class.

After I dropped them off, I called my manicurist from the car phone and she'd just had a cancellation, so I went in and got my nails done. And then I did several errands, hardware store, nursery for some new plants, and then I stopped and did a little grocery shopping. When I got home and put everything away, I noticed there was a message on my machine, so I played it back and it was Harry saying, "Get over to Goldstar Casting right away and see Delia Katz. It's for a big national spot and they asked for you, and look gorgeous because they want an elegant mature woman, and that's you."

I tried not to react to the word mature, and called Harry's office to get more information, but a machine answered and I realized they were probably all at lunch. Delia Katz has used me several times before. You remember her? She's a tough little New York type with that street accent, who doesn't mince words. I once heard her tell some darling character actress, "Yer lookin' like a fat cow. Take off the weight or yer dead."

Look gorgeous, I thought. Dear God. I was in my white sweats, and at that moment I didn't know if I had any gorgeous left to look. I tried calling Goldstar Casting and asked for Delia Katz, but she was at lunch. I asked for her secretary, but she was out, too. The receptionist said they'd be back at two.

It was one o'clock, so I decided to hurry up and shower, wash my hair, put on my makeup, and just be at the casting office at two when they got back from lunch. While I was putting on eye liner, I realized my hand was shaking. I was nervous. I've been acting for thirty years and I still get nervous before I go up for one of those things.

I'd only driven three blocks when it started raining. I couldn't believe it. It hadn't rained in months. All anyone talked about was how Los Angeles was in a drought, but on this day when I had to look gorgeous, it was pouring. So by the time I got out of the parking lot and into Delia Katz's office on Melrose, all the pouf was out of my hair. I didn't have a mirror, but I could feel that my makeup was already that kind of muddy it gets when the weather's very damp.

It was one of those tiny reception areas, some shabby little chairs around the room and some old trade papers on an end table. There was a receptionist's desk, but nobody was sitting there. In fact there wasn't a sign of anyone. I was glad. That meant this wasn't a cattle call. It always feels so eerie when I open the door to one of those places and look into the faces of ten other actresses who look just like me.

Well, as I said, on this day no other actresses were there, and I was glancing around to see if there was a mirror so I could check the condition of my hair, when the door from one of the offices opened, and Delia Katz herself emerged.

I was wearing very high heels and she was wearing completely flat shoes. And you remember what she looks like? With that frizzy yellow hair? And too much makeup, as if she was wishing she was one of the actresses. Very chunky and so short she was looking right into my belt buckle. I said "Hi, Delia," expecting she'd give me a big hello, but she looked up at my face and there was no recognition in her eyes at all.

It was very strange. For a minute I felt like Jimmy Stewart in *It's a Wonderful Life*. Remember that scene when he finds out what the world would be like if he'd never been in it, and he sees his friends and nobody recognizes him, and even his own mother slams the door in his face?

"It's Marly Bennet," I reminded her, figuring she'd had a memory lapse about my name, which happens to the best of us, particularly at this age. And she *is* about our age, I mean she's been around for years. I remember when she first started out, forever ago, at Screen Gems. Besides, she had to recognize me, since according to Harry's messages, she was requesting me for the commercial. But still her expression showed nothing. "Harry Berman said you were looking for me," I tried.

Her response was to look at her watch, then back at me. "Yeah, I was, Marly Bennet," she said, kind of sing-songing my name. And her face, which isn't too pleasant to begin with, had the nastiest little expression on it I'd ever seen. "Do you know what time it is?" She asked me, out of pursed lips that made her look like the Wicked Witch of the West.

Well, all of a sudden it was as if I'd never lived the forty-nine years I've lived. As if I wasn't a well-respected actress for years, a pillar of the community. I felt as if I was a bad child being scolded for something, and I didn't know what. And I was so shocked that a little funny voice came out of my face, and I said to this Mammy Yokum of a woman, "Oh. Uh. Time it is? Well, let's see. Is it . . . two uh? I mean, I . . ."

"It's two o' fuckin' clock," she bellowed up at me. "I called your agent at nine o' clock this morning. Where were you this morning? At ten o' clock? At eleven o' fuckin' clock?"

"Me? Oh, I was . . . well, at eight I was dropping my girls off at school and . . ."

"Yeah, well if you want to have a life and work in this business," her nasty, mean, contorted mouth informed me, "you better go out and get yourself a beepah."

"A what?" I asked, leaning forward because I thought I'd misheard her. But it was the New York accent. A beepah.

"A beepah," she sneered. "Holy Christ! Even my teenage daughter has a beepah."

A beeper. She was telling me that if I wanted to have a life of my own and still be in commercials, I had to go out and get set up with the thing that Andy wears to tell him that his patients are in a life-and-death situation, so he can rush to their aid. A device which, when it goes off in Rose's house, means that a human life is in danger. Not that there's a part available in some goddamned meaningless television commercial.

"I cast that part at twelve-fifteen, and I closed the deal before I went to lunch," she said, twisting the knife. And then without a "good-bye," or a "sorry," she walked past me into one of the other offices in the suite, while I stood there in my now flat hair and my sticky, overpainted face and my best white silk suit, which was spotted from the rain. And after a minute or two of digesting what had happened, I turned and walked out the door into the rainy day.

I just walked slowly and miserably to my car, even though the raindrops were pelting down on me. I guess I was hoping it would look as if the raindrops were causing what were now big mascara tracks down my cheeks. I was furious at myself. What in God's name was wrong with me? I couldn't let another incident like that go by. I couldn't let that woman get away with that behavior. My entire body was throbbing when I turned and walked back into the casting office and called her name.

"Delia," I called out in my biggest Carnegie Tech voice.

"Yeah?"

"I want to talk to you, right now."

"Well, you'll have to wait, I'm on the Ameche," she hollered back out, meaning she was on the telephone, because Don Ameche once played the part of Alexander Graham Bell and that's a cute thing some people like to call the phone. Well, the cuteness made me even surer I was doing the right thing by coming back and confronting her.

"Then get off it," I said. My heart was banging, and I walked into that little office right to where she was sitting, ripped the phone out of her hand, slammed it into the cradle, and said, "And listen to what I'm going to say."

Her face was fuchsia when she looked up at me. "Hey, who the fuck do you think you are?" she said, but I was sure there was a little flash of fear in her eyes.

"No, Delia," I said. "The better question would be who the fuck do you think *you* are? Because all of the evidence up to now has it that you've been behaving like a nasty, odious little drunk-with-power troll. Not just to me but to every actor in this business. And I need to know why you think it's okay to turn your condescending sneer on actors who need the work, want the work, count on you to understand them, and have to prostrate themselves in front of you while you strut around here acting as if you have some talent superior to ours."

"Get a grip, Marla," she said, getting my name wrong on purpose. "I can ruin you."

"No you goddamn well can't. You can't ruin me because I have mental health and a wonderful life and children who love me and friends who are there for me and confidence in my talent. My wellness is what has enabled me all these years to be able to tolerate walking into a room of people like you who want to demean and criticise people like me. A bunch of idiotic flea brains like yourself who think they have to say something in a meeting to prove they're worth their high-paying, no-talent-required jobs, so they say something negative. People like you destroy all the good in this business."

"Hey, you were late. It's not my problem," she tried, but I was on a roll.

"Terrified sycophants who are feeding off the talented people. Little leeches who are so panicked that someone will realize one day that they have zero to contribute and fire them, so their fears come out in lousy behavior to everyone around them. And you know what I'll bet, Delia? I'll bet all of that pent-up hate you have has collected at the top of your head and it's what's keeping you so short and twirpy."

And hearing myself say that brought me back. Made me burst into laughter, giggling at the insanity of what I was doing and what I just said, and looking into her bugged-out eyes and realizing that the reason I was now looking into her eyes instead of over her head was that I'd actually lifted her from her chair by the collar and was nearly choking her to death, to the point where she was wheezing out what she wanted to say next. And it was such a cliché that when she did say it, I just kept laughing into her frightened little face.

"You'll never work in this town again . . ."

"Oh come on, Delia. That's such shitty dialogue from such a bad, dumb movie that it's funny," I said, and that was when I dropped her, and while she was adjusting her clothes, I said, "You don't control who works here and who doesn't. You're just another little casting grunt. You don't have that power, and you can't frighten me the way you do every other poor soul in this mean and vicious business in this awful city that's so morally bereft that God is trying to warn us by shaking us the way a parent shakes an errant teenager. I'll work whenever I damn well please," I said, brushing my hands together in a gesture of extreme distaste, as if to get any trace of her off them. And then I stormed out of her office.

"You'll pay for this, you over-the-hill piece of shit . . ." I could hear her screaming after me. But I kept walking, and when I got outside the rain had stopped, and the sun was shining down on me, and I was glad I'd gone back in there and said what I did.

"And was there any aftermath?" Rose asked, as the fluorescent lights in the hospital cafeteria buzzed, making it sound as if there were a fly trapped inside one of the long white bulbs.

"Oh, not to speak of . . ." Marly said wistfully. "Except that I haven't had a job since then."

NINETEEN

"IT'S BAD news," Rose said as she saw Andy come into the hospital cafeteria. His stethoscope was hanging around his neck and bumping against his body as he moved. "I can see it in his eyes."

"They're having trouble stabilizing Jan's blood pressure," he told them when he got to the table. "Her condition is looking pretty serious. I think one of you should call her sister and get her to come out here." He looked almost apologetic, as if he knew they'd been counting on him to use some medical magic to fix Jan. Telling them it was time to call Julie was a portent of doom, and Marly closed her eyes as if to shut it out. "I mean, I'll call her if you like," Andy said. "But I think it'll probably be better coming from one of you."

"And tell her what?" Ellen asked.

"I think she ought to have a chance to get here," he said. "Sometimes family members like to say good-bye even if the patient is comatose."

"I'll make the call," Rose said, and was immediately sorry she volunteered. What could she say to Jan's poor younger sister, who would certainly fall apart when she heard? She'd probably get hysterical, and Rose would have to calm her. Jan and Julie were more like mother and daughter than siblings. Jan always talked about her sister the way a doting mother talked about her favorite child.

"Julie's the jock, not me," she'd say after a tennis game. "Nobody can hit the ball the way she does." Or she'd leaf through a magazine and spot some great-looking dress, and instead of wanting it for herself, she'd say, "I'm going to call and see if they have it in Julie's size." Rose was sure Julie would want to get on the next plane to L.A.

"There's not a whole lot more I can do here right now," Andy said, "and Molly's baby-sitter needs to leave, so I think I'll go home and pay her and send her off. Call me if there are any questions, or if there's anything I can take care of," he said, giving his wife a kiss on the cheek. "I told the nurses in ICU to let you in when they think it's okay. They usually only allow family in, and only one at a time, but I think they'll probably let you all in tonight."

"Because you insisted?" Marly asked.

"Must be because he told them it was Girls' Night," Ellen joked.

But Rose knew exactly why the nurses were willing to break the rules. "Because it's probably her last night?" Rose asked her husband, and Andy nodded sadly.

"No, it isn't," Marly insisted, but without her usual conviction.

Andy waved a helpless little wave to them all and left.

"Let's go up, and I'll call Julie," Rose said, moving her glasses to her nose so she could peer over them and look at her watch. It was nine o'clock. Midnight in Pennsylvania. Maybe if she got through, Julie could call the airlines tonight and book an early morning flight west. As the three friends moved together through the oily smell of the cafeteria and back to the elevator, their arms looped around one another's waists, Rose wished she could go home with Andy.

Get into her own cozy kitchen and make a piece of toast and jelly and a cup of tea, then crawl into bed under her comforter and sleep. Not spend the night on a hard chair in a hospital. Not go upstairs to call a woman she barely knew and give her the worst news of her life. She promised herself as the elevator rose to the seventh floor that after she accomplished the hard task of calling Jan's sister, she'd go back down to the cafeteria and reward herself with the brownie she'd been eyeing earlier.

"Remember to tell her Joey's surrounded by people who love him, because I know he'll be her first concern," Marly said.

"Tell her I can have a studio driver pick her up tomorrow if she needs a ride," Ellen called after her as Rose moved down the hall toward the phones, glancing down as she passed the big windows at the dark street below, to see that the legion of Maggie Flynn fans, their ranks somewhat thinned, were still out there.

She remembered Jan's anxiety when the company her sister worked for went under, and Julie found herself unemployed. "Don't worry, honey-lamb," Rose heard Jan say affectionately into the phone one night. She had arrived at Jan's to take her out for a birthday dinner, and Jan had gestured for her to wait while she finished talking on the phone with Julie. After a few minutes she gave Rose a look of distress. "I'll send you a check every month until you get back on your feet," Rose heard her say reassuringly. When she hung up that night, Jan shrugged helplessly at Rose and said, "I'm all she's got."

At the bank of pay phones, Rose stood for a while, cleaning her glasses with the hem of her black blazer, trying to formulate what words she'd use to break the bad news. When Julie said she didn't have any money to pay for an airline ticket, Rose would tell her that wasn't a problem. Then she'd call Western Union and wire her enough to cover her travel expenses, or charge the ticket to her own credit card, to be sure Julie could get here to say what might be her last good-bye to her sister.

Finally she steeled herself, then dialed zero and the area code, and then the number she had for Julie in her Filofax. There was a bong after she punched in her credit card number, and a computerized voice saying "Thank you for using AT and T." The phone in Beaver Falls rang twice before a man answered it, with that odd Pennsylvania dialect Rose remembered the four friends used to try to imitate when they were in school in Pittsburgh.

"Hallow?"

"May I speak with Julie O'Malley, please."

"Whozis?"

"My name is Rose Schiffman, I'm a friend of her sister Jan's."

"Oh yeah. Holdon. N'kay?"

"Yes." While she waited nervously, Rose wondered how many times bad news had been transmitted through this phone she was holding. How many people had stood just where she was standing, at the phones nearest surgical ICU, having to say, "I'm sorry to have to tell you this, but . . ."

She was the one who had called Allan's family in New York on his last day. To tell them it was only a matter of hours until he'd be gone. She was the one who managed to say the words, "You'd better come as soon as you can." She was the one who had heard Allan's mother wail, "My baby," on the other end of the line, and his father taking the phone to say, "Oh, no, oh dear God. We'll be there tonight."

"Hallow?" Rose heard the fear in Julie O'Malley's voice.

"Julie, this is Rose Schiffman, do you remember me?"

"Yeah, hi, Rose. Sure, I remember you. And I already know about Jan. It was on the local news here," she said. "I called over to the hospital, but they put me through to some nurses' station and nobody there would tell me anything. Is she . . . ?"

The local news. Of course, Jan was a big enough star to have this be all over the news. Rose felt stupid for not having called Julie immediately. "She's still alive, but she's not doing well," Rose said. While she was filling Julie in on as many details as she could, trying to be gentle, she imagined Julie dissolved in shocked tears at the other end.

This was the kind of news you should give to a bereaved family member in person, at a time when you could put your arms around them, be there to comfort them when they lost control. After she'd told Julie everything, she was silent, and there was no sound but the hush of the long-distance line, until finally Julie spoke.

"Rose, you're real nice to call me," she said, "and all I can say is, I hope she lives through this. She's a good person. But if she doesn't make it, I can tell you one thing for damn sure. I'm not takin' that adopted kid of hers. And even though we never discussed it, I'll bet anything she left him to me."

A tremor ran through Rose, and she took in a deep breath and tried not to cry. She held the phone with her left hand and put her right hand over her mouth, as if to stop any angry words from rushing out.

"I mean, not too long ago," Julie went on, "Jan told me, and she was kidding around with me at the time, but she said, 'You better hope I die young, girl, because in my will, I left everything including the bobby pins to you.' Which, believe me, I'll take. But I'm the one who tried to talk her out of taking in some kid whose real parents are God knows who. You know what I mean, Rose?"

Rose felt as if she'd been kicked. "No, I don't know what you mean," she said, leaning against the wall next to the phone.

"Well, here's the deal. Last month I let my boyfriend move in here, and we have a great thing going, and he's already raised a few kids of his own. So, believe me, the last thing he wants at this stage of his life is somebody else's kids."

Rose wanted to hang up, but instead she calmed her anger with long, deep breaths and listened to Jan's sister rattle on about her boyfriend and their great life together, and finally, when she couldn't stand to hear another word, she said, "Julie, . . . will you come out to California to be here, in case Jan doesn't come out of this? I'll take care of the cost of the airline ticket. I'll pick you up at the airport, and you can stay at my house."

There was silence, then Julie said, "No. I'm not coming out. Thanks for the offer, Rose. But I don't see what good it would do."

"Julie, Janny loves you as if you were her child. Maybe hearing you in the room could bring her back," Rose said. "Maybe if she thought you needed her, she'd find her way up and out of this coma. I mean, my husband's the doctor, not me, but what if the way these things work is that the unconscious person fights her way back to consciousness when she knows how needed and how loved she is? I'll call the airline now if you . . ."

"It's a nice thought, Rose," Julie interrupted, "but I don't believe that's the way it works. Anyway, call me back if you find out that Janny wants to be buried back here near my parents."

"I'll do that," Rose said, and hung up the receiver. She felt weak and sad and tired. Poor Joey. Jan's little baby. Julie was probably right. Jan would have left his guardianship to her. She leaned against the wall and tried to collect herself. Finally she needed to sit down so badly, she just slid into a heap onto the floor, next to the bank of pay phones. She was staring straight ahead when Marly came around the corner.

"Oh, hon, what is it?" Marly asked, hurrying over to sit next to her.

"All Jan's sister had to say was that she'll take any money Jan leaves her, but she sure as hell doesn't want *him*, meaning Joey, and she won't even come out to say what might be good-bye to Jan."

"Maybe it won't be an issue, maybe Jan'll be okay," Marly said, and she took Rose's hand, but when Rose looked into her big green eyes, the fear that Jan probably wouldn't survive was there. "I came looking for you because I think maybe we should walk down there and try to get into the ICU." They both stood and walked back toward the waiting room.

Ellen was pacing when they arrived. "Doesn't it strike you as odd that there are no police around here?" she asked when she saw them. "I would have thought the hospital would be surrounded by them. I mean, there's some man walking around out there who shot our friend, and he could come back and try to finish her off. I'd think there'd be a cop at every door of this hospital. Certainly on this floor. I'm going to go down to the lobby and find out what they're doing about securing this place."

"I'll come with you," Rose said, thinking again about the brownie in the cafeteria. Maybe while Ellen threw her weight around with security, she'd go and get the brownie.

They were standing by the row of elevators when the up arrow above one of the doors was illuminated, then there was a whoosh and the doors opened. A round-faced woman in her late thirties looked at the three of them. She had curly brown hair and was dressed in an inexpensive navy pants suit, with a white shirt underneath and a scarf tied clumsily around her neck.

"Is this seven?" she asked them. "Surgical ICU?" She held the bucking elevator doors open with the same hand in which she held a battered brown briefcase.

"Yes, it's right around the corner," Marly answered.

"Are you ladies going up?" she asked them as if to offer them the elevator car she was vacating now that she'd determined she was in the right place.

"No, down," Ellen said.

"Oh, okay," the woman said and let the elevator door close with a hiss behind her. She smiled politely, then moved off down the hall as Ellen impatiently pressed the down button again, and they saw her turn around and look at Marly.

"Aren't you Marly Bennet?" the woman asked.

"Get out the Jell-O," Rose said under her breath as Marly nodded and the woman walked back to where they were standing. The woman pulled a badge out of the pocket of her jacket.

"I'm Detective Rita Connelly from the West Hollywood police department. I'm investigating the Jan O'Malley shooting. I was just over at the house snooping around, and so I thought I'd come by here and see how she was doing. I recognized Marly Bennet because I used to love watching 'Keeping Up with the Joneses.' And I put you together with Jan O'Malley because of this," she said.

"This is Rose Schiffman and Ellen Bass," Marly said. "We're all close friends of Jan's."

"Ahh," the policewoman said. "College friends, right?"

"How did you know?" Rose asked. Rita Connelly shuffled through her briefcase and pulled out a plastic bag through which they could see a sheet of glossy fax paper.

As Marly leaned in to look at it, she could smell the musky odor of cigarettes on the policewoman's clothes. The fax paper had a list of names of some of the West Coast drama alumni from Carnegie.

"You can all look at it," she said. "Just leave the Baggie on it. It was in the foyer of Jan's house," Rita Connelly said. "It looked as if it had fallen behind an umbrella stand."

"All of our names are on there," Rose said.

"Why don't we go sit down?" the policewoman asked, and they all walked back into the waiting room. All of the other people who had been there were gone. Rita Connelly shuffled around in her briefcase. "Anybody care if I smoke?" she asked, pulling out a box of Marlboros.

"The hospital might," Ellen said, and Rose smiled inside, knowing that under ordinary circumstances anybody lighting a cigarette in Marly's presence was subject to a lecture about what their murderous secondhand smoke was doing to others. While Rita Connelly lit a cigarette, the three friends leaned in to look at the typed sheet in the Baggie. Each alum's name was followed by a career update. But unlike the lists that were in the alumni magazine, this one had each graduate's home address next to it. Jan's name and address were circled. And so were all three of theirs. Next to each of their names someone had written a word or two that the handwriting made hard to decipher.

"Anyone know why she'd have this?" Rita Connelly turned her head away from them to blow out the cigarette smoke.

Rose looked carefully at the policewoman, taking her in. You know you're aging when doctors and police all look like such babies to you, you worry about putting your life in their hands, she thought.

"Maybe Jan was going to do some fund-raising for the school," Marly said.

"Jan? There's no way she'd ever be able to hit anyone for money," Ellen said. "She didn't have the time, or the personality it takes to call and do that. Jan's the person other people ask for money. She's a soft touch, but she could never be a hustler."

"And besides, if this is a list of people she was going to call, why would she circle her own name?" Rose asked.

"That's not Jan's handwriting on there, either," Marly said. "Those words. What are they?"

"Looks like 'nanny,' maybe 'receptionist,' and that might be 'proofreader,' " the policewoman said. "The list was faxed to someplace in the 619 area code. That's San Diego." Then she took another drag of the cigarette, and as the smoke came out, she asked, "How's she doing?"

"Not great," Ellen said.

"Tell me about what was happening in her life. Anybody hate her? Envy her? Resent her? Want her out of the way for any reason?" There were no ashtrays anywhere because the hospital had a no-smoking policy, so with an ease that meant she'd done it before, Rita Connelly removed the cellophane from the Marlboro box, held it open in her hand and flicked the ashes into it.

"Everyone envied Jan," Marly said. "She was beautiful and warm, and even though on the show she was a 'bad girl,' the fans loved her. *TV Guide* recently called her a 'soap diva,' but not because she was temperamental, God knows. She was anything but that, but because her character had grown into such a powerful figure on daytime TV."

"There were lots of weirdos around that show," Ellen said. "Even one of the women writers, who didn't like her, and a wacko who sat outside the studio every day and told the guard he was going to marry Jan someday."

"Yeah, I know about him," Rita said. "We're looking for a guy right now who broke into the studio and onto the set this week. He might be harmless. On the other hand, we have to check it out. Any of you ever argue with her?"

"We all argued with one another," Ellen said, "but not in any dangerous or threatening way."

"And I'm sure you can each account for where you were at four o'clock this afternoon."

"I was in a meeting at a movie studio in Culver City with the producer and three of his staff," Rose said.

"I was in an executive meeting at a studio in Burbank with my colleagues," Ellen said.

"I was in Gelson's Market in Pacific Palisades tearing up copies of the *National Enquirer* that had photos of my children's father on the cover," Marly said, thinking after she did how that event seemed to have taken place weeks ago, and that Billy making love to her . . . dear God, could it have only been this morning?

The police officer thought about what each of them had just told her and looked at them with what seemed to be admiration, or maybe she was mocking them. "You three are some high-powered ladies," she said.

"Believe me, Rita," Marly said, sighing, "like everything else in this town, it's all an illusion."

"You telling me?" Rita said. "I've worked this precinct for twelve years, and I've seen it all. Brought people into this hospital in conditions you wouldn't believe, with God knows what stuck into every orifice of their poor beat-up bodies. And most of the time there's some press agent outside the emergency room, trying to tell not only the photographers, but us, the police department, who saw it all, that it never happened. You have to love it," she said, stubbing out what remained of the cigarette on the bottom of her shoe, blowing on the butt and putting it into the little cellophane holder she'd made.

"I was in a lawyer's office in Beverly Hills once a few years back," Rose said, "going over one of my contracts, and while I was waiting for him to finish on a phone call, I walked around his office and found myself looking out the window and had a great view of the Beverly Hills streets and shops. And all of a sudden I saw ten police cars pull up outside of Van Cleef and Arpels. And within seconds I saw a roadblock go up, and uniformed cops with guns out were surrounding the place. All of this while the lawyer was talking away. I remember watching it all very calmly, waiting to see the director rise up on a crane to get a long shot, and to hear the word 'Cut!'

"I was sure I was seeing some studio filming a movie on the streets of Beverly Hills, because we're so used to seeing that around there every day. And then the lawyer got off the phone and we got down to business, so I stopped thinking about it. Well, the next morning I opened the L.A. *Times,* and there was an article on the front page about Van Cleef being robbed, while I watched. And I thought, there's so much pretend around here, I just figured the robbery was pretend, too."

The policewoman laughed. "Yep, I was there that day. The guy had twelve hostages in the jewelry store. But we finally got him out." She shook her head and laughed, as if remembering a fun time.

"I have to ask you this question," Ellen said, "because I've got a project in development about a young woman who wants to be a cop, and I'm curious to round out her character. What is it that makes a woman pick a career in law enforcement?"

Rita Connelly frowned, thought about her answer, and then smiled. "I guess I thought it was going to be sexy. That it offered excitement, drama, meeting bigger-than-life people, having thrilling experiences."

"And now?" Ellen asked.

"Now I know it's full of men who are so worried about the size of their genitals, they take it out on everyone who crosses their path. Not to mention corruption, graft, dishonesty, back-stabbing, and fear. But by now it's too late because it's all I was trained to do, and I'm supporting a few people and some pets, too."

"Jesus," Ellen said. "Did you just say those words or did I? That sounds just like my experience with show business."

"It's about as bad, except *you* get the big car and the fancy salary." All four of the women laughed. "So did Jan O'Malley have any serious boyfriend? I mean could this have been about a romance that went bad?"

"No," Marly said.

"Absolutely not," Ellen said. "She hadn't been seeing anyone in a long time."

"She was completely focused on her son," Marly said.

Rose felt nervous. This was a question only she could answer, and if she did she'd be revealing a secret Jan had been keeping from the others. But what if the secret had something to do with the shooting?

"The answer to that is yes," she said quietly. "Jan was seeing someone."

Marly and Ellen looked at her in surprise.

"She was?" Marly asked.

"Tell me about it," the police woman said to Rose as she pulled a small spiral notebook out of her purse.

TWENTY
An Affair to Remember

ANDY always tells me that one of the reasons I'm a writer, a person who lives in the world of her own fantasies, is that even at my age I'm still a romantic schmuck. To give you an example that he likes to use to prove that, he reminds me that in nineteen-whatever-it-was when Jan was so crazy for Terry Penn, and she told me he was going to leave his wife to marry her, I believed it. Okay, so I was already chopping liver and deviling eggs for the wedding. I really wanted Jan to be happy.

I was at her house one night when Terry called her, and my temperature went up just overhearing Jan's side of the phone call. "Oh, honey, me too. Oh, God, I want that, too," I heard her say a million times. And I've got to tell you, when she walked into the den where I was sitting fanning myself with a book, she was as glassy-eyed and lovesick as if they'd just been having at it in the next room.

"Oh, Rose, we can't live without one another any more," she said to me, and I immediately asked about Susan, because everyone knew that Susan and Terry Penn had what was perceived as the perfect family. Terry was a handsome actor turned producer and then studio executive. Susan wasn't a beautiful woman, but because of all that money and all those homes, she had her picture in the paper all the time. And she had that status that wives of men with that kind of power are granted. Like Candy Spelling and Patsy Tisch before the divorce.

"Does he ever talk about his marriage?" I asked her. I never had a married man, except the ones who were married to me, so what did I know about how they behaved?

"Oh believe me, Rose, it's no marriage," Jan said, hugging a throw pillow to her chest as if she were a teenager at a pajama party talking about her steady. "I mean, it is what it is. He likes the way they look together in *Town and Country* magazine."

That was her way of telling me that Terry and Susan Penn's marriage only existed for practical reasons, like homes and money and appearances, but not for the important thing, which was wild passion, intimacy, and romantic love, and that's what he had with Jan and couldn't live without in his day-to-day life for one more day. According to Jan. She told me that's what he told her all the time.

Jan was the first "other woman" I'd ever known in person. Andy says I have yet to learn that every one of them, without exception, believes exactly what Jan just said. I told him I don't want to know how he knows that. Okay, Janny may have been kidding herself, I mean all of us are guilty of that in some way or other. But I love her so much and always have for a million reasons. And one is because she always has such a funny take on everything.

For example, we both hate to exercise, but we'd go together to those sweaty, music-pounding aerobic classes and work out, and I'd look in the mirror at Jan in the row behind me and she'd make these tortured faces at me, and then one day in the locker room at the health club she said to me, "Rose, I've definitely decided, I'm not doing the aerobics anymore. I'll do the Nautilus machines and build up my muscles, but I'm not going to get myself all sweaty."

"That's a mistake," I told her. "Andy's a doctor and he always says no matter what, you have to do the aerobics. They're crucial for your heart."

Janny looked over my shoulder at herself in the mirror, sucked in her stomach, and said, "Who cares? Nobody can *see* your heart." We laughed over that for weeks.

"Terry Penn will never marry her," Andy told me again. I remember it was when Molly was very little and we were sitting at the beach in Santa Monica, watching her play in the sand. I had just told him about the beach house Terry rented for Jan in the

Malibu Colony for the upcoming summer months, but he shook his head, and I hated his certainty.

"He will. He loves her."

"He won't."

"He might," I said, backpedaling.

"I'll tell you what," he said. "Let's set an outside time. You can even pick the date. And if Terry Penn doesn't leave his wife by X date, you'll treat me to the vacation of my choice. And if he does, I'll take you anywhere you like."

I couldn't understand how my husband, who loves my friends, could bet against Jan's happiness and not believe that Terry Penn would do what he'd been promising Jan for more than a year. To tell his *Town and Country* wife he was leaving her for my passionate friend, explain gently to his kids, who would understand and would want to come with him to live in the big house where he was moving Jan, and where soon the two of them would have a family together.

Isn't it awful that I was so ready to see Terry and Susan fall apart? But you know how I get when it comes to my friends? I didn't know Susan Penn, and I was very worried about Jan's survival. I could just picture her on the grounds of some grand estate. Finally taking a breath from the years of taking care of herself and her sister. I guess I believed the fairy tale that some handsome rich prince was going to save her, just the way she still believed it in those days.

"Six months?" Andy asked me. I counted off the months on my fingers. Six months would make it October, a great time to go to Hawaii. That's where I would make him take me when I won the bet about Jan and Terry, who at that moment I was picturing making love in the beachfront bedroom of the Malibu house. I imagined Terry swearing to her that soon they'd be out in the open, swearing on something sacred, which I found myself hoping wasn't his children's lives, in case Andy was right.

In the second week of October, Andy and I went to the Heritage House in Mendocino, and I paid for it all. The rooms, the meals, and the good red wine. Terry was still stalling and Jan was still letting him, and that was how Andy and I had those two glorious days in Mendocino on my VISA card, and by the way, it's beautiful up there at that time of year.

Andy wasn't exactly gloating, but the lesson he was trying to teach me was that men know men, which was how he knew that a man like Terry Penn was not about to give up what he had with Susan Penn just because he liked to get laid.

In November I had a big rewrite to do on a screenplay, and Andy suggested I take a few days at The Oaks at Ojai and he'd get his mother to come and stay with Molly, so I could get my work out of the way. I love The Oaks, it's one of my favorite places to hide away, so I did, checking in by phone once a day at home. One day when I called home my mother-in-law told me that Jan had called twice, so I called her back.

She really just wanted to chat about her romance with Terry, but when she heard I was in Ojai, she decided that getting Terry away from Los Angeles for an afternoon and up to Ojai would be a great idea.

"We'll drive up and take you to lunch," she offered.

I was on the spa plan, seven hundred and fifty calories a day, and starving to death. A lunch date sounded like heaven to me, so I agreed. I was nervous about it. I'd never met Terry Penn, but I'd read the articles about him in *Time* and *Vanity Fair*.

I was waiting for them at a restaurant in Ojai, feeling like an escapee from the spa, when they walked in. The minute I saw Terry Penn, I understood viscerally why Jan couldn't let him go. It wasn't just Terry's breathtaking good looks. There was something about his presence that was magnetic.

I've met many movie stars, and always they seemed so much less than I'd imagined they would be. Terry Penn was more. Dramatically handsome. And boy did he flash a heartbreaking smile at Jan's friend, whom he'd come here to impress with the fact that he was taking a day off from running an entire studio to meet me. Didn't that mean he'd eventually leave his wife?

And he obviously loved Jan. I could see it by the way he held on to her, looked at her. I cursed myself for not making the time on the bet with Andy twelve months instead of six, because now that I was meeting Terry Penn in person, his devotion to my friend was obvious. By Christmas, maybe just after Christmas to avoid a painful holiday season for his kids, I knew he would leave Susan and marry Janny.

When Jan left the table to go to the ladies' room, Terry Penn put his tanned, manicured hand on my pale, ink-stained one and looked deeply into my eyes. It was like locking eyes with the snake in *The Jungle Book*, Molly's favorite video. He captured me with those eyes. I fell into them so easily that if things had been a little less otherwise, meaning if I hadn't been so happily married, and Jan wasn't my beloved friend, I probably would have just left with him myself before she came back. He said, "I love her. I'm going to marry her."

Those eyes were his secret. I imagined him in meetings with big stars and famous directors, catching their eyes in the same way and saying, "I'm going to make this picture. I'll commit forty million dollars to it right now." And they were stupid enough to believe him, too.

Well, now we're up to about four years ago in this story. Terry finally separated from Susan Penn, a moment that made Jan and me at lunch one day, if you can imagine, in the middle of the day at Bistro Garden, order a bottle of champagne, and toast, of all things, true love. He was now taking Jan out in public, to screenings, to cocktail parties. You remember, because we were all worrying that he might actually really marry her and then what would she do?

Jan was feeling so good that she couldn't wait until that night to see him so she could tell him the news about the adoption lawyer who had called her to say that he had a baby who would be available to her right away. But that night when she told him, Terry laughed in her face. He told her she had to be, and I quote, out of her "stupid fucking mind."

"Oh, you have a problem with that?" she said, trying not to back down since it had taken her so long to get up the nerve to call the lawyer in the first place. "Well then, why don't you make me pregnant?" she asked him, clenching her back teeth and waiting to see if he'd take the challenge. And when he laughed and told her that they were both a little long in the tooth for that, she lost it, maybe because she knew he was right, at least about her, and she felt hurt and stung and old and as if she'd wasted her life. They had a giant fight, and he walked out. Remember that Girls' Night right before she went to pick up the baby? She was a basket case, but she was determined not to stop her life, so she adopted Joey and you know the rest.

When I told Andy what happened, he asked me if I knew how the weather was in Hawaii that time of year and if I cared to put any money on anything. I hated him and Terry Penn and all men. But a few weeks went by, and Janny called to tell me that Terry had called and come over apologetically with a big teddy bear for the baby and was now visiting regularly and kitchy-cooing little Joey.

They were back to dating, and she even joked that she told him, "No sex until after the baby's six weeks old." She also said in Terry's behalf, knowing there wasn't a whole lot to say for him, that on the nights they went out and her housekeeper, Maria, couldn't sit with Joey, Terry paid the baby-sitter.

Anyway, one night they went to a big awards event at the Beverly Hilton. It was a dinner dance. Jan was at his side while all the sycophants came over to kiss Terry Penn's behind. Now we all know how someone like Terry Penn can change the life of anyone in the creative community. So everyone scrapes and bows and tries to get in his good graces, hoping the way they hope for the winning lottery number that he'll say, "You get the part," "You do that picture."

Jan told me how he sucked in the attention, took sustenance from it, kissed the women and hugged the men and laughed with them, and as they walked away, he'd still be wearing the big smile on his face and making derogatory remarks to her about every one of them.

She told me afterward that as she stood in that ballroom next to him that particular night, she felt in her stomach that something was really wrong. As if someone had opened a window and let in a frozen blast of wind, because she was suddenly blown away by what a dishonest person he was, or to use her term, "a lying sack of shit."

She said she knew he had lied to Susan about where he went on those nights and days when he was sneaking off to meet her, but that was different. This was lying to everyone, about everything. "You look so great. Your picture was the best. Your script knocked me on my ass." And it alarmed her to see those people walk away with their feet off the ground thinking Terry Penn loved their writing or their film or them. Just the way she thought he loved her.

"Let's dance, honey," she kept saying to him, feeling weak and nauseous and suddenly dowdy among this glittering crowd where Marvin Davis's wife was wearing a ring the diamond of which covered her entire finger. She told me she thought maybe if they danced, and Terry felt her body close to his, he would remember who they were together.

"In a minute," he promised Jan, just as Jane Fonda threw her perfect arms around his neck.

Jan went to the ladies' room and splashed cold water on her face. He had to marry her. She called me that night from the pay phone in the ladies' room at the Beverly Hilton. Andy must have been at the hospital. I was half asleep, but I grabbed the receiver, and I knew as soon as I heard her teary voice it was going to be about Terry Penn.

"Rose, what am I going to do?" she asked, trying to talk softly so the glitzy women moving in and out of the ladies' room would think maybe she was just checking in with her answering machine or calling her baby-sitter.

"You have to set boundaries," I told her. "He'll push you to the wall. He *has* pushed you to the wall. As Ellen would say, 'Tell him to shit or get off the pot,' " and as I said that, my instructions were punctuated by the sound of two toilets flushing in the ladies' room. Poor Jan, that poor girl was crying softly into the phone.

"You're right," she said. "I know you're right. And I'm going to do it. On the way home tonight. I'll tell him this is it. We're engaged or it's over."

"Janny," I said, "that's not enough."

"Right. As soon as his divorce is final, we're married."

"You got it," I told her. There was another flush. "Call me in the morning and tell me it worked." I couldn't get back to sleep. I pictured Jan and Terry in his limo as it sped over Laurel Canyon. I knew she'd be strong. I was positive Terry would agree to marry her. Dr. Andy Schiffman, my beloved, would be shocked.

Love conquers all. I still believed it, and so did Jan, until she got back to the table and Terry wasn't there, and when she looked around the room she felt close to death when she saw him on the dance floor with the gorgeous star of one of his up-coming movies. A woman whose looks are so perfect you think they can't be real when you see them in photos. But every feature, hair, skin, body, is just what you always wished yours was from the day you opened your first magazine. Jan sat at the table where the other two remaining people were male studio accountant types in a heated discussion about grosses.

She wanted to go home, but she was afraid to leave. She didn't want to look at Terry and the young actress, but couldn't stop her eyes from going to them, seeing their bodies pressed tightly together, the flirtatious looks passing between them as they laughed and talked, and then didn't his lips brush away that thick lock of hair from her forehead?

When the song was over, Jan steeled herself for Terry's return to the table. He'd tell her that dancing with that actress was just business. She would insist that it was time to leave. Make him come home with her. In the car she would tell him, "No more." Set boundaries. But she knew by the expression on his face when he was on his way back to the table, greeting his fans as he moved, that it was too late for that.

"I think we should go," she tried softly.

"What?" Terry was on, he was hot and high on his own racing blood, and Jan was full of that fear you have when you know they're slipping away and there's nothing you can do about it.

"Go, leave, have to pay the baby sitter . . ." was what came out, though she knew as she was saying those words she should be taking another tack. That fancy uptown man didn't give a damn about baby-sitters or her son. He was out to snare a new woman into his bed, and Jan was what her mother used to call "corned beef hash." Which means what you do with yesterday's meat.

Terry pulled some cash out of his pocket, because he was the one who at his insistence always paid her baby-sitters. "Here. You go ahead. I've got business to take care of. Take the car, honey. And I'll call you in the morning." As in beat it, you bimbo.

Of course he didn't call Jan in the morning. A week later when she bumped into him in the studio commissary, he said, "Angel face, we almost made it work, didn't we?" And walked away. Three months later, as soon as his divorce was final, he became engaged to the actress he danced with at the party. It was all over the papers. On the Sunday of their wedding, Molly and I picked Jan and Joey up at her house in Laurel Canyon, and the four of us went to the Santa Monica pier so the kids could go on the rides. While Molly took Joey on the bumper boats, Jan and I sat on a bench and she wept.

"It's not going to be a marriage, Rose. I mean it is what it is. He likes the way they look together in the couples section of *People* magazine. I mean, she's too dumb for him," she said. I ached for Jan. I remembered that day in Ojai how, like the bumpkin Andy always says I am, I truly believed it when that man told me he would marry her.

For a while after that she dated Larry Hodgens. Remember him? He was a darling guy. A civilian, meaning he wasn't in show business. A few people mentioned the odd fact that Larry looked a lot like Terry Penn. "He's like Terry Penn with character," someone said at a party. But I guess that didn't work, because very soon after that she got bored with him and stopped seeing him.

I watched the articles in the magazines about Terry Penn and his new wife, and watched them have one kid and then two, and the wife's career kind of fizzled out after a few bad movies. Once I saw them at a screening, and that formerly gorgeous young woman now had a frazzled, beaten look, and she was wearing a dress you shouldn't wear if you're chunky, which she had become.

Anyway, about a month ago, I was in my car coming from a meeting, and I realized I had Joey's birthday gift in the trunk of my car and I was right near Jan's, so I stopped over, and we had coffee and I got to see Joey and watch him do all the latest cute things he had learned.

When the phone rang and Jan had to take the call, I went into the powder room to make a stop before my long ride home, and after I washed my hands and was about to go back out into the kitchen, I couldn't believe it when I heard Jan saying into the phone, "Oh, honey. Oh, God. Me too. I want that, too." It was suddenly as if I'd been thrown back all those years, and I knew with a sick feeling that she had been, too.

I looked at my face in the powder room mirror and tried to compose it into the expression of someone who hadn't over-heard those words, and I waited until I heard Janny hang up the phone before I came out of the bathroom.

"Well," I said, feigning innocence, "I guess I'd better hurry on home." But when I looked at Jan's flushed cheeks and she looked at my lying face, we both knew what was happening.

"Terry and I have been back together for a year," she confessed to me.

"But isn't Terry still married to that actress?" I blurted out.

"Oh, Rose," she said, before I finished my question. "It is what it is. It's not a marriage. And he's going to leave her. I'd say within the next few months he and Joey and I will start looking for a house."

I drove home, feeling that sad about-to-cry feeling in my face, but no tears came. And then I remembered what Jan said to me that day so long ago at the gym about the aerobics, and I realized she was wrong. Anyone who looked could definitely see her heart.

TWENTY-ONE

SHE WAS seeing Terry Penn again," Marly said sadly, as if she'd just heard that someone she loved had gone back to drugs after rehab. "A few times I asked her if she ever ran into him. We called him the Prince of Power. But she always changed the subject. Now I know why."

"Because she knew you'd tell her she was choosing to be a victim and creating futility to avoid commitment," Rose said.

"And as usual, I would have been right," Marly said. "Besides, it takes one to know one."

"Why hasn't Terry come to the hospital?" Rose asked. "By now the shooting has to be all over the news."

"Because he'd have to explain it to the second wife he's been fucking over," Ellen said.

"You can't possibly think that Terry and Jan had a fight and he was the one who shot her?" Marly asked Rose, but the policewoman answered the question.

"Doesn't sound like the kind of guy who would soil his hands. Naturally we'll check him out, though," she said.

"What if it was Terry Penn's wife who shot Jan?" Ellen asked. "Like in *Presumed Innocent*."

"I think you've been producing too many movies," Rose said, and the others laughed. The moment was interrupted by a shrill beeping sound. The detective unbuttoned her blazer to reveal not only her beeper, but a gun in a shoulder holster. She stood.

"I have to call in. Where do they keep the phones around here?"

"I just realized I have one with me," Ellen said, opening the zipper on her black Prada purse and pulling out her cellular flip phone.

"Cool," Rita Connelly said as Ellen handed it to her.

"Not as intimidating as the paraphernalia you're packing," Marly said.

Rita punched some numbers into the small, flat telephone. "Connelly," she said, followed by a few "Uh-huhs." Then she pushed END and handed the phone back to Ellen.

"They brought in that guy who broke onto the set of 'My Brightest Day,'" she told them. "He has a gun registered to him that's the same kind that was used to shoot your friend. He says he can't remember where it is. Sounds like he could have found his way over to her house. I'm out of here, ladies. Here's my card if you need any more advice on the movie about that woman cop."

Then she stopped and looked at the three of them and said, "I have three kids, and I know how tough it's going to be on that little boy if he loses her." She put her thumb up. "I'll hold a good thought," she said, and then she hurried down the hall and out of sight.

There were just hospital sounds for a long time. Elevator doors whooshing, a floor waxer in the distance, an ambulance outside with the sound of the siren getting closer.

"Isn't it interesting," Ellen said, "that despite appearances, which nobody knows better than we do how they can always be deceiving . . . that that woman is one of us."

"I think there's a film in it," Rose said, smiling, "a small unpretentious film about how what we are inside doesn't always reflect—"

"Hey, Rose. Let me tell you what to do with your small unpretentious film," Ellen said and gave her a playful punch on the arm.

"Why in God's name if that fan showed up at Jan's house, would she ever let him in?" Rose asked them, her glasses catching the strange fluorescent lights. "That's the odd part."

"Let's go down there and be with her," Marly said and they

all stood and moved back down the hall to surgical ICU. Ellen pushed the buzzer on the white plastic box next to the door.

"Yes?" A woman's voice replied to the buzz.

"I'm Ellen Bass," Ellen said to the box. "Jan O'Malley's friend. If she's stabilized, we want to come in and be with her."

"I'll be right out."

After a minute, the nurse opened the door. She was a blonde in her sixties, with very black mascara caked on her lashes. One at a time she looked at Ellen, then at Rose, and when she got to Marly, she smiled. "I know you," she said excitedly. "I loved every episode of 'Keeping Up with the Joneses,' and that other show you were on about the bar. I'm genuinely sorry about your friend."

"Thank you," Marly said.

"I always watch 'My Brightest Day' too. She's so beautiful and talented." Under all the hard eye makeup the nurse had a warmth in her eyes. "She's stable, but she's still in what they're calling a light coma. Doctor Schiffman mentioned that you'd want to come in together, and I think it would be a good idea for her friends to be with her and to keep talking to her."

"So do we," Ellen said, moving past the nurse into the ICU, where ten equipment-filled rooms opened onto a monitoring desk, above which hung ten computer screens, one for each patient. Two other nurses sat at the desk chatting. Five of the rooms had patients in them, hooked up to inexplicable machines and tubes.

"I know you don't particularly like a group in these rooms," Marly said to the nurse, "but we really are her extended family, and I think if what you're saying is true, our being with her is going to mean a lot to her recovery."

The nurse patted Marly on the arm in a motherly way, then said, "If I were you, I'd talk as if she was being included in your conversation. Because hearing is the last sense to go, and I've known people to come out of comas and describe conversations they heard in the room around them from family members who figured they were too out of it to hear. But before you go in, could I just trouble you for an autograph for my daughter, Miss Bennet? Her name is Jessica." Marly smiled an assent, and the nurse produced a pad and a pen. She wrote a message and her signature for the nurse's daughter.

"I'm Nancy," the woman said. "And this is Shiela, and Kari," she said, gesturing to the two nurses at the desk.

"This is Rose Schiffman and Ellen Bass," Marly said, and the nurses smiled a polite hello.

"Ellen Bass? Ellen Bass is out there?" They heard a man's voice call out weakly. "Nurse, do me a favor. Get her in here."

The nurse looked behind her toward the cubicle from which the voice had come, then back at Ellen. "That's Mr. Zavitz, Fred Zavitz, do you know him?"

"Does she know me?" the man's voice said. "We're family!"

"He just had a lung removed and he's in very delicate condition, but I guess it's okay if you go in and see him." The nurse smiled and shrugged.

Fred Zavitz was an old-time producer. When Ellen was a gofer at Screen Gems, he had a deal at Columbia Pictures, where he produced half a dozen movies. And he was always nice to the kids who worked on the lot. In the days when Ellen worked on "The Monkees," next door at Screen Gems, she liked to creep onto the sets at Columbia and watch them shooting the feature films. Katharine Hepburn and Sidney Poitier filming *Guess Who's Coming to Dinner*, or Gregory Peck filming *McKenna's Gold*. And Fred Zavitz would tell his secretary Libby to make sure to get Ellen a pass or to give her a bogus delivery to make to the set so she could get in the door and watch them shooting.

The thing in the bed was skeletonlike, but somewhere in and among his features, Ellen recognized Fred Zavitz.

"Hiya, Freddy," Ellen said in as jovial a voice as she could muster.

"Ellen, darling, why are you here?" he asked, as if he was hoping the answer was that she'd come to see him.

"One of my good friends is in here, Fred."

"I'm sorry to hear it, dear, but listen, while I've got you here, take a minute. I have a great story to tell you."

Ellen leaned against the wall of Fred Zavitz's cubicle and tried to look interested. It was the least she could do for a man who'd just had a lung removed.

"My son and I haven't spoken in twelve years," Zavitz said, stopping to lick his dry lips, then going on. "So now I'm dying, I mean let's not mince words here, I'm basically on borrowed time. So who do you think is the specialist in the field of medicine that I need the most? You got it! So unbeknownst to me, my doctor calls him in to consult on my case, and we're reunited. Now that's a movie. I could put a writer on that thing and have it ready in a month's time after I get out of here. Provided, of course, that I get out of here. It's got irony, it's got pathos, it's got big, juicy parts. I see Paul Newman as me and Sam Shepard as my son. Hey, listen, if she wanted to, Joanne Woodward could play my wife."

The nurse, who was back in the room now taking Fred Zavitz's pulse, looked at Ellen as if to urge her to indulge him, but Ellen didn't need her cue.

"Newman and Woodward would be great, Freddy," Ellen said. "They haven't had a good vehicle together in a while."

"Am I right?" the pale, bony man in the bed asked, then winced.

"Shall I get you something for the pain?" the nurse asked.

"Not now," Fred Zavitz told her. "I'm in a meeting."

"I like it, Fred. You call me when you get on your feet, and if I can't use it, I'll make sure you get it to somebody who can."

"You're a doll," Fred Zavitz said. "A regular doll. Say, listen, I hope your friend is feeling better. What did she have?"

"We're not sure. But it might have been a fan who loved her too much," Ellen said, and went to join Marly and Rose, who were standing next to Jan's bed. Rose was trying not to recoil as she looked at Jan's bandaged head and her corpselike face. Marly was holding Jan's hand and talking to her inert body.

"Janny, everything is okay. Joey's at my house and he's just fine. The twins will hug him and kiss him and play with him as if he were a doll, and tomorrow morning when he wakes up, I'm going to promise him that you'll be back soon, because you will.

We're sending you wellness vibrations and the white light of our love."

"Janny, you realize you fucked up Girls' Night," Ellen said, "so I wish like hell you'd wake up and tell us about Maximilian Schell. I can use the laugh."

"Me too," Marly said.

"This is like a scene from 'My Brightest Day,' " Rose said. "If I'm not mistaken, they even have a permanent ICU set on their stage because so many people on the show find themselves in comas. Janny, Maggie Flynn would not tolerate this. She'd throw off the bandages, be wearing a shocking pink nightgown and marabou mules, and tell them all she was on her way to Paris."

"Janny," Ellen said, "a police officer told us they think they may have the man in custody who did this to you. They took him in for questioning. They think that guy who broke onto the lot was the one." There was a sudden spasm from Jan, and they all held their breath, hoping it was signaling her awakening, but then she settled into the same placid state she'd been in before.

"Janny, come out of this and get old with us. It won't be so bad because we have each other. We can be crotchety, wrinkled ladies at the Motion Picture Convalescent Home. Race our walkers down Ventura Boulevard and put Krazy Glue in Jack Solomon's Polident," Rose said.

"Janny," Marly said, "I know how you felt about what happened to you with Jack Solomon. You felt seduced. But it was no big deal. We've all been seduced. Billy seduced me this morning. He came over and wanted to make love, and I agreed because I've missed him so much, and now it's all over the papers that he's being accused on some child-molesting charge. So now I feel like he was just hoping to get me to be on his side when it all came down."

It was the first Ellen and Rose had heard about Marly's visit from Billy, and Rose saw the hurt on her face and understood now why everything the ladies in the cafeteria said had made her so crazy.

"I'm sure we've all done things we wish we hadn't," Ellen said. "Hell, I gave one of the Monkees a blow job."

Marly shrieked, "You don't mean it! Which one?"

"Does it matter? It was when I worked for them. One day in a dressing room at Screen Gems."

Rose and Ellen laughed loudly, and through the glass they saw the ICU nurses glancing over at them. "Which one?" Ellen wondered aloud, her brow furrowed. "I don't have a clue. Maybe it was Mickey Dolenz. Or Peter. Hah! Peter something." That made Marly and Rose laugh even more.

"Peter Gazinya! Remember that joke from when you were a kid?" Rose laughed and took off her glasses and wiped her eyes.

"You never told us that before," Marly said.

"I guess at the time I was too embarrassed," Ellen said through her laughter. "I don't even remember why. I hated all four of them," she said. "I couldn't wait to leave that show."

"I have a memory like that," Rose said. "About six months after Allan died, the lawyer who was handling his estate fixed me up with a man who was visiting from England. The lawyer said, 'Nothing serious, Rose. It'll just be someone nice to take you to dinner.' Well, the man was very attractive and after I'd had three glasses of wine, and you know what that can do to me, the guy told me that the reason he was in town was to close a deal on a picture with Marlon Brando."

"Uh-oh," Ellen said, "we all know how Rosie loves Marlon Brando."

Rose flushed. "So then he said that he was staying at Marlon Brando's house, and that Marlon was in town on a rare visit from Tahiti, and he asked if I wanted to meet him. And I nearly melted down. 'Marlon will love you,' he told me. 'He's crazy about petite, dark-haired women.'

"Aside from the fact that I love Marlon Brando, I also had been thinking for years about a great movie idea for him, and all the way over to his house, in my half-smashed state, I tried to remember the details of the plot so I could tell them to Marlon, and I was high enough to believe that he was going to love the idea and sign on the dotted line to star in my movie. I kept thinking, I'll tell my agent, 'This is an idea for Marlon Brando,' and he'll say, 'How do you think you're going to get Marlon Brando, Rose?' And I'd say, 'I already have him, Marty!' "

"Let me guess," Ellen said. "You got to the house, there was no Marlon Brando, and the Brit jumped you."

"Have I told this story before?" Rose wondered out loud, and Marly and Ellen laughed. "In the morning, I remember telling myself, 'I'm a widow, Allan and I didn't have sex for a very long time because of the illness, I forgive myself.' And on my way home, I realized that the house I was leaving was off Coldwater Canyon, and even people who buy those maps to the stars' homes know that Marlon Brando's house is on Mulholland Drive."

Marly tsked, and smiled a how-foolish-we-all-are smile. "Why we let ourselves be conned," she said. "And boy have I let myself be conned a few million times in this life. By salespeople, by charlatans, by my kids, and always by Billy. There was one story I haven't told any of you before now because I felt so awful about it. I think I'm just getting to where I can tell it now. Janny will enjoy it especially."

"Was it more awful than blowing one of the Monkees and not remembering which one it was?" Ellen asked, laughing.

"Much more," Marly said. Standing over Jan's bed, her sentences punctuated by the breathing machine attached to Jan, she told them.

TWENTY-TWO
The Power and the Glory

IT'S TAKEN ME nearly fifty years of existing on this planet to become reasonably conscious. You all lived through it with me, and you know my philosophy has always been "Any road up the mountain," and you've watched me try them all. I've been ested and Rolfed and T.M.'d, not to mention the fact that I know Marianne Williamson personally and once sat at Werner Erhard's dinner table. I'm constantly seeking the word, the teacher, the teachings, the way to heal the planet and myself in the bargain. And through it all I have finally evolved a theory about human behavior, and here it is.

If you listen carefully to what somebody says about themselves during the first fifteen minutes after you make their acquaintance, they'll tell you everything you need to know about them forever. In fact, the seeds of why your relationship with that person will succeed or fail can always be found if you look back at those minutes.

Example. A few years before I met Billy, there was that man Ronny Bates, who I met at a wrap party of some show over at MTM. He was very good-looking and very bright and while we were standing at a buffet table that the caterer had decorated with baskets of vegetables, Ronny picked up a whole red cabbage and joked, "I'll do anything to get a head in this business." Instead of realizing his truth was coming out in jest, I thought that was funny, and when he asked me out, I said yes.

Ronny was struggling to get anything produced, and his company was foundering. I knew he liked the idea that I had a big part on a hit television series at the time. Meaning I guess he liked the cachet of having me as his date at events he had to go to in the business.

I was wanting to be in love so much that I kept trying to be in love with Ronny, but the chemistry just wasn't there, and I always had nagging doubts about his character, so I pounded it into a friendship, and for a long time if either Ronny or I had an event to attend and no date, we'd each call the other. He's very attractive, a good dancer, very gregarious, so it worked out well. But I'll get back to him.

Then I met the illustrious Billy Mann, and speaking of telling you everything you need to know in the first fifteen minutes, on the fateful night I met Billy at the Improv, where he was a struggling young comic doing stand-up for no pay, he told me proudly, "Television is my life!" Have I made my point about the first fifteen minutes telling all? I mean, didn't *that* turn out to be the awful truth?

After we married, and Billy's career took off, people came out of the woodwork. After that first night that Billy guest hosted "The Tonight Show" and scored so big, there was no doubt that he was going to have his own show and own the town, and everyone was after him.

But some people were too intimidated to call him, so instead they called me. Can you get him to appear at our charity event? they'd ask me. Can you get him to do a guest spot on our show? Can you get him to endorse this product? People I hadn't seen since high school were calling as if it were yesterday. First they'd reminisce about old days I barely remembered, and eventually, and I always knew it was coming, they'd hit me for one thing or another about Billy.

Coincidentally, although I believe it was Werner Erhard who always said "There are no coincidences," I bumped into Ronny Bates again on the lot at Fox one day, just after Billy and I separated. I was feeling very blue and I was out of work and I had just come out of an interview where I knew I gave a lousy reading. And on my way to my car, I bumped into some woman who was at Tech when we were there, I forget her name, but now she's writing self-help books.

She said, "Wow! Marly Bennet! I read in *TV Guide* that you're married to Billy Mann." I was feeling very sorry for myself, and I said, "Well, we're living apart now," hoping for a shred of sympathy, hoping that maybe a woman who wrote those books might offer me some great insight into how to recover from a broken heart.

"Is it amicable?" she asked.

"Well, kind of," I told her. "I mean, we have children together, so we're trying to be as civil as possible." And then she said, "Well, is it civil enough for you to call him and ask him to put me on his show? I have to promote my book, and it's very important for me to get publicity."

You know me, I was so enraged I was just about to rip her face off when Ronny Bates walked up. "I mean, we are old school chums," she was saying, "so maybe you could just use your influence to get me a five-minute spot?"

"Billy doesn't decide who's on the show," Ronny said to the woman very firmly, and I wanted to kiss him, he was like the cavalry rushing in to save me. "The producers and the talent coordinators make those decisions, so Marly can't help you."

The woman introduced herself to Ronny, but when she found out he was just an out-of-work producer, she quickly decided she had better places to be and left. When she walked away, he said to me, "Can't people be insensitive assholes? Let's go get a cup of coffee and bad-mouth everyone in town."

It was the perfect thing to say to me that day, and we went to the commissary and dished and had a great time. I was so lonely and he seemed so interested in me that all of a sudden I was having these pictures in my mind of how some day, down the road, we'd laugh and ask ourselves why I'd wasted all those years of being married to Billy, when Ronny and I should have been together all along. About what a nice step-father he'd be to the twins. And so what if he wasn't a big hit in the business? Billy was a big hit, and look what a miserable human being he was.

Anyway, finally Ronny got around to admitting that he had an agenda, too, but that it had nothing to do with Billy. What I mean is, while we were sitting in the commissary and I was already as far down the road in my fantasy as whether or not the twins would accept him, he got around to the fact that he needed something, and that his bumping into me that day wasn't an accident. But what he needed wasn't from Billy. It was from me.

Ronny wanted to produce a "Movie of the Week" about battered women, and he knew I was very involved in the setting up and funding of a shelter for them, and he asked if I could help him get into the shelter to see what it was like, so he could talk to some of the women and really get a feel for it. I told him that would probably be impossible, because the most crucial element of the shelters was their privacy.

I told him there were secret locations for the shelters, and special codes for entering, because the whole point of the shelters is the safety and security of the women and children who stay in them. He said he knew that, and that he felt a profound responsibility, and those were the words he used, profound responsibility, to make his movie honest, and that the only way it would be technically correct and accountable to the seriousness of the problem was if he really got to know the situation from the inside.

How many years will I have to live here, work here, and have the rug pulled out from under me to know how people lie? I think I was so flattered in the hailstorm of Billy's popularity to feel that someone wanted something just from me that I forgot to think about the awful material Ronny Bates had been connected with in the past. I also submit this as one of the worst things I've ever done, because I wanted Ronny back in my life, needed someone so much, that though my intuition told me not to be his entree into a world that was so fragile, I did it to keep him interested in me.

I said I'd help him, and that night when I got home I called around to some of the friends I'd made, caseworkers, and volunteers who helped staff the houses. I gave them Ronny's rap about how they could help him represent the shelters in a responsible way by meeting with him.

It still amazes me that no matter how sophisticated people are, and no matter how protective they are of their privacy, there's this little bug that gets under their skin, that makes them think, "Wow, show business. Maybe my aunt in Cincinnati will see this, and know I had something to do with it." So they agree to do things that they don't necessarily think through.

I know I didn't think it through, and pretty soon there was Ronny Bates, thanks to me, suddenly in everyone's face at the shelter, very intrusively asking them questions they didn't even want to answer to themselves, let alone to this show-business jackass. A real Hollywood kind of guy wearing what I noticed for the first time in the tiny living room of the shelter, because it stood out so much in that environment, was too much gold jewelry.

I knew I had made a grave mistake, right after he sat next to one of the women and said, "Okay if I tape this, hon?" Battering of yet another sort, and I was the accessory. So after he left that day, I asked all of the women if they felt in any way violated by him, and they all said, "Oh, no. It's important to get the word out to women everywhere that these shelters are havens, places where they can come without feeling the kind of intimidation they live with in their lives, and Ron told us that by talking with him, we were helping those other women. So we're cool about it. We want to know when it's going to be on TV."

I didn't have the heart to explain the development process to them, and how Ronny Bates didn't even have a deal on the material anywhere, and what the network system was like. In fact I'm sure a lot of the people I deal with at these places don't even know I'm an actress, let alone Billy's estranged wife.

Well, pretty soon Ronny Bates was at the shelter more than I was. One night he popped in and dropped off the leftovers from a big luncheon he'd just had at his house. I mean I know it was a nice gesture, but he dropped off caviar at a shelter for women who can't afford to buy themselves tuna fish, because if it stayed in his refrigerator, he was afraid he'd eat it, and it's very high in cholesterol.

These are women who jump at any sound, who fear that any minute there'll be a knock at the door, and it'll be their estranged husband showing up to blow their faces off with a gun, and this little hustler was stressing over his HDL to LDL ratio in front of them, while he unpacked the Beluga. Isn't it remarkable how I fall for every crumb bum on the earth?

When he finally had a story and a writer for the project, he asked if I would please read the script for authenticity, and he told me he'd like to give me a producing credit on it for doing that. Well, you know how few and far between the acting jobs can be? So I figured for a second that maybe this was the beginning of something new for me, and I told him to send the first draft over as soon as it was ready.

A few days later it arrived, and I was feeling very pleased with myself in my new role as producer. I remember sitting down at my desk that morning with a mug of coffee, feeling every inch an executive, thinking what I'd buy myself to wear to the set the first day the movie was shooting. Maybe a black wool crepe suit.

And then I read the script, and as I turned each page, I felt more and more nauseous. The part of the woman who was the overseer of the shelter was a dominatrix. She hated the women and treated them like whores and slaves. She conspired with the husbands, lied to the wives, fed them swill, and took advantage of them sexually. I actually had a physical reaction. I felt chilled and sick and sure he must have sent me the wrong script. So I dialed Ronny's house. But his machine answered.

I remember leaving a flustered message. Something like "Ronny, this can't be the script we talked about, the responsible message about battered women. They'll think they're going from the frying pan into the fire if we show them this point of view of shelters. That's no good. I mean, to begin with, none of it's true. And it really is irresponsible to depict it this way. So as your colleague and the technical adviser on this project I have to tell you, you can't sell it this way. Because you can't let people see it in this terrible light."

As the twins like to say to me when I say something to them that doesn't hold any water at all, "Yeah. Right." That's what Ronny's failure to call me back meant. Yeah. Right. Your job is through, bitch. You got me where I wanted to go, now back off.

But you know me. No opinions lightly held. I believe it was Werner who said that the essence of communication is intention, and I am always on a straight course when it comes to intention. When my manicurist told me her right-to-life group approved of shooting doctors to "save babies," I threw the table over on her in the middle of a fill. She had acrylic in her hair, and "Fiesta Red" on her blouse right next to her pro-life pin.

The point is, I wasn't going to let Ronny Bates get away with this. I called him again and again, and one night, off guard, he answered the phone, and I didn't even say hello, I just said, "You can't do it. I'll fight you. You have to make it right." Naturally he greeted me with a big phony warm greeting, as if he'd just been about to dial my number to tell me what he told me then.

"You're right, Marly, you're a thousand per cent right. I screamed at the writer, gave him notes." Him . . . did you notice that? Why not a woman writer? "And I promise, you'll be really proud of it. The network loves it, everyone is hot for it. You have to know I learned so much because of you, and I will not let you down."

I sighed, thanked him, and hung up. Fool with me, will he? I actually thought that. I actually told myself that I had showed him he was not going to pull a fast one on these women. That he was not going to get away with any of that sensationalistic exploitation garbage as long as he had me on board. I would class this project up so high, if ABC didn't do it, we'd go straight to PBS.

I even mentioned it to Billy one night when he came to pick up the girls. The question "So what're you up to?" had become a sore spot between us, as you can imagine, since he was now the biggest star on late night, and I was not getting callbacks on interviews. But that night he happened to ask me that question, and I said, "I'm probably going to be producing a film." It was so grand to see the shock on his face. As big a star as he is on TV, what he really wants is to be a movie star. So I didn't mention it was a movie for television.

"No shit?" he said, and I'm so sick, the fact that it impressed him made me want to get my producing credit very badly. So when the revised script came, with the new blue page inserts, I poured the coffee and went back to my desk and started reading. I was incensed to see that virtually nothing was changed. I mean, things were definitely different in the script, but if anything they'd gotten worse.

Now the dominatrix was molesting the battered women's children. I lost it. I called Ronny and got his machine and like a crazy person, I screamed into the phone. I said I realized that he only had his own interests at heart all along, that I knew now that he'd led me to believe he was one kind of person and turned out to be just another Hollywood phony instead. I remember screaming "You can't do this to people," into the phone, and then realizing not only that I was crying but that the person I was really talking to when I said all those things was Billy.

It took Ronny days to call me back, and when he did I was out, so he left a message on my machine. It was right after one from Billy saying he was in meetings so late that he couldn't pick the girls up, during which a woman's voice was laughing in the background the entire time he was speaking.

Then came Ronny's message, in which he spoke slowly and in a patronizing voice that made it sound as if he were speaking to a child of two. "Marly, we start shooting this MOW on Monday. The network is so happy with it, they want to make a big overall deal with my production company. I heard what you said, I have made many of the changes you suggested, and I am messengering you over a copy of the shooting script so you can sign off on it, and let me know if you do or do not want your producing credit. All the best to you and the twins."

The script didn't arrive until Sunday night. If there were any changes, they were for the worse. Husbands were making harassing phone calls, women were sneaking drugs into the place, one of the women was a Satanist and trying to convert the others. I have never been so appalled by anything in my life. I didn't sleep for one minute that night, and after I dropped the girls off at school, I drove like a crazy person over to the studio.

I had no idea how I was going to get on the lot. I didn't have a pass, I didn't have a clue what stage they were on, I only knew which studio, but I was possessed. I drove up to the gate, and heard myself say to the guard, "Hi, I'm in the cast of *Shelter.*" That was the name of Ronny Bates's movie.

The guard picked up a clipboard, on which he obviously had a list of names of the cast, and I didn't know who any of them were, so I couldn't give a fake name. "Your name?" he asked. Clearly he had never seen "Keeping Up with the Joneses."

"I'm Marly Bennet Mann," I said. He looked for a long time, probably under B and then under M, and then he looked at me and said, "I don't have you on here."

I was afraid the next move was the guard calling the set, and Ronny hearing my name and trying to keep me off the set, and I didn't know what to do. Now, you know how neat I am? So my car is never a mess, but for some reason on that day I had the kids' stuff all over the backseat, and some clothes I was planning to take to the cleaners on the floor in front of the passenger seat, and a whole pile of mail I needed to go through, and a copy of *People* magazine my mother had sent me from back east because there was a picture in it of me and Billy leaving Spago after Swifty Lazar's Oscar party.

So for some reason I decided that was the way to go, to get me onto the lot. To use what I hated the most, which was exploiting Billy's name the way every other dog in this town wants to. But I grabbed the magazine, opened it to the page called Glitterati, at this awful picture of me with Billy waving a fist at the camera, and thrust it out the window at the guard. "Here," I said. "This is me. Mrs. Billy Mann." While he was looking at it, I flashed on Judy Garland in *A Star Is Born,* saying, "Hello everyone, this is Mrs. Norman Main."

The guard was smiling now. We know how everyone loves Billy, don't we? And then he looked back at me and said, "You're his wife? Boy, that must be fun. Go ahead." I let him keep the magazine, and hated myself, but this was for a worthy cause. I was going to march on that set and raise hell. I was going to terrorize Ronny Bates until he closed down production. I am so stupid, I actually thought there was something I could do.

I stopped a young woman who might have been a production

secretary, walking across the lot, and she knew where they were shooting, so I found a parking place and walked over to the stage, pulled the big, heavy door open, and crept through the cool darkness to the set.

It was very dingy. It was supposed to be the bathroom in the shelter, which in reality is very sunny and welcoming. I know because I worked on making the real shelter look that way, and Ronny Bates knew it, too, because he'd spent enough time there. There was a big crew and a lot of actresses milling around who I didn't know but who seemed as if they were chosen because they looked tawdry, when the truth was that most of the women I'd met in the shelter were very vulnerable looking.

I stood quietly for a while and then watched as a nearly naked actress walked into the bathroom, and the actress who was playing the woman who oversees the shelter was watching her get ready to take a shower. That was it. I walked over to where Ronny was standing chatting with someone, and I could see he was shocked to see me walk in there.

I summoned every ounce of assertiveness training I ever had, and I said, "Ronny, this is criminal. You're sending the wrong message to women who will be scared away from something they desperately need to change their lives."

Ronny smiled a self-conscious smile and said, "Marly . . . come over to the production office and we'll talk about it."

"We'll talk about it right here," I said, hoping I was embarrassing him. I saw him blanch, and then he said as loud and clear as he could, "Marly, get the fuck off my set, get the fuck off this lot. If you don't, I'll have some of my crew carry you off bodily. Stay out of this, or I'll make you sorry you didn't."

I looked around hoping someone would step forward and say I don't know what, maybe, "You can't talk that way to her, she's fighting for truth and honor and justice. This production is shut down for being a bad example to caring people everywhere!" Ha. Everyone on the set was completely self-absorbed. The actresses were yakking to one another and flirting with the crew, one of the cameramen was reading a paperback, no one was even listening.

I was motionless for a minute, and then I remembered him in that buffet line years ago at that party when he picked up the cabbage, and what he'd said. "I'd do anything to get ahead in this business," and I wished like hell I'd paid attention to my first-fifteen-minutes rule. And even though I don't believe in Werner anymore, he did say we are all God in our own universe, and I created that situation. So I went home and waited for the show to air.

It got a forty share, and right afterward Ronny Bates bought himself a house with a tennis court in the hills. Somewhere I believe, right near the house that's reputed to belong to Marlon Brando.

TWENTY-THREE

SHE FOUND the hospital with no sweat at all. She had good directions that she got by calling. It made her laugh when the person on the line told her, "You make a right on George Burns Drive, then you park at the Marvin Davis Building, then you walk through the Max Factor Tower, which is across from the Steven Spielberg Building." Maybe only people who were big in show business were allowed to be sick there. Maybe when they picked you up off the street after being hit by a car and they took you to the emergency room, somebody at the entrance had the job of asking, "Can we see your résumé? Have you made enough money in this industry for us to let you in?"

She did all the things they told her. Burns to Davis to Factor to Spielberg, and then she was in the lobby, looking at the uniformed guard, who wouldn't let her go upstairs. Jan was in a coma close to death, at least that was how all the news reports were making it sound. So if the others were there, and they had to be there, at least one of them had to, they'd never know anything. They'd welcome her, the way Jan had, hug her, and ask her about all the things she'd been doing. She'd tell them she just happened to be in town visiting friends and she heard about poor Jan on the news, and they'd all commiserate.

Perfect! She'd say how heartbroken she was, and perhaps they should organize the memorial service. Because surely at the memorial service all the old friends would be there, and one of them would have a job for her. But the goddamned guard shook his head at her. "I'm sorry," he said. "Doctor Schiffman gave me explicit orders that only people whose names were on this list could go up. And I can't violate that. So if you'd like to call Doctor Schiffman, or you can find some way to get your name on this list . . ."

She tried to read the list upside down, but when the guard saw what she was doing, he turned it over. Goddamn him. Goddamn the fact that she parked her car in a pay lot, figuring that after she visited the hospital, someone would give her a parking validation, and now they wouldn't even let her in.

"Thanks," she muttered, and sauntered away, trying to figure out if she could spot a stairway that went up, and after a while, when the guard wasn't looking, she could somehow find her way to Jan's floor. The chilly night air blew into the lobby as a handsome man with a Tom Selleck mustache pushed the door open, and his entrance caught the guard's attention. He was dressed in a tux.

"Hey, Frank," the man said warmly to the guard.

"Mr. S.," the guard said, standing, and flushed and put out a hand for the man to shake. "How's everything, sir? All of your shows going well this season? The staff here sure goes bananas when your camera crew is out there. One of the other guards told me he was going to join the professional extras union, after the last time one of your hospital shows was shooting exteriors here and he was in them." The guard let out one of those apologetic self-conscious laughs people sometimes use when they're in the presence of someone who intimidates them.

"That's nice, Frank. Listen, I was just across the street at Chasen's at an awards dinner, and I heard some very disturbing news."

"Sorry to hear that, sir, is there anything I can do?"

She was sitting now on a sofa with her back to them, but in the black night the window became a mirror, and in it she watched the guard and the man chatting away, and she was shaking because she realized the man had to be Jack Solomon. She could turn around right now and say, "Jack, it's me," and maybe he'd be thrilled to see her. And the bad news he was talking about had to be . . .

"Jan O'Malley, a lifelong friend of mine, is in here, and I want to go up and see her. So point me in the right direction, will you, Frank?"

"Oh, yes, Mr. Solomon. She's on seven in surgical ICU. Not doing too well, from what I hear. I'm sorry to break it to you, since she was your friend, but that's the word. There was a big press conference just a little while ago, and they were very pessimistic about the prognosis. But you go on up, sir. And maybe things will have changed."

"Thanks, Frank," Jack Solomon said, and breezed off toward the

elevators. Jack Solomon. They'd had pajama parties together in the dorms. She sat on his lap all the way to New York. Why hadn't she called out his name?

Seventh floor, ICU, she thought. How can I get there without going by that lying little weasel of a guard who said your name had to be on the list and then he let Solomon go up but not me. I should have killed them both. Should kill the guard now and go up. Why didn't I at least have the guts to show myself to Jack and beg him for a job? I'm too afraid. That's why I married Lou, that's why I put having kids in my way and didn't come to Hollywood before, because I was always too goddamned afraid.

TWENTY-FOUR

THE REGULAR SOUND of the breathing machine was hypnotic, and the cold temperature and soft light in the room made the whole atmosphere sleep-inducing. Ellen yawned, and Rose stood to adjust the blankets around Jan.

"I'm worried that she's not warm enough," she said, like a mother hovering over a sleeping baby in a nursery.

"I'm glad they let us be with her," Marly said. "I have a real sense that she knows we're here. That she's hearing us and our stories and that somehow it's helping her."

"I probably should call home and see if there's a message on my machine saying I'm fired," Ellen said, opening her bag and pulling out her cellular phone. "Is this okay?" she asked Marly, "or will my bad movie studio molecules bring evil energy into her space?"

Marly forced a smile. "I forgive you for that," she said, and Ellen dialed. After a minute she pressed one of the phone's buttons to activate the rewind on her home answering machine.

"Look at this, Janny," Rose said, moving close to the bed, "isn't modern technology something? It enables a studio hotshot to run her business right out of the intensive care unit."

Ellen was listening to her messages, and after a few minutes while she did, she smiled and then laughed out loud. "I have to play this back for you," she said to Rose and Marly. "It's a message from Greenie, and it's hilarious. Here." She pushed a button and handed the phone to Rose, and Rose and Marly put their heads next to either side of the flat little receiver to listen to the playback from Ellen's machine.

"El, it's Greenie. I'm sorry to even call you with this bullshit, and I hope like hell that Jan's going to make it, and that all is well at Cedars, but I figured you'd call your machine and I needed you to know that after you left tonight, Bibberman pulled a full-out shit fit.

"He turned around from going to the screening and came screaming in here and said, 'Tell her that besides missing the screening tonight, she walked out so soon, we never even talked about our Monday morning meeting with Jodie Foster. I told her yesterday that if we can get Jodie to direct this project, I think we can get Julia Roberts and Geena Davis to star. Then our foreign distribution will pay the difference. You can also tell her if she leaves one more meeting early, she can go back to carrying coffee to the Monkees.'

"I was very calm," Greenie continued. "I said, 'Bibberman, darling, if you turn on the news, you'll learn that one of Ellen's best friends was shot and is in a coma at Cedars, where Ellen can be found sitting at her bedside. You wouldn't understand that kind of caring, so I suspect you'll be trying to reach her there. She loves this friend, Bibberman, in a way that you have never loved, and probably no one has loved you. More than a deal with Jodie Foster, more than, and this may shock you, even a deal with Julia Roberts and Geena Davis. She is probably planning to stay by this friend's bedside for a long time.'

"Well, don't you know the little asshole actually took a moment and looked down at his Cole-Haans as if he was feeling a slight twinge of remorse. For an instant I fooled myself into hoping that maybe there was a God looking over show business after all, that maybe somewhere behind that ugly facade of heartless, bloodless studio exec, the man had a soul. Until he looked up into my big blue eyes and said what he thought was a statement of having his priorities straight. 'Tell her to call me as soon as her friend dies!'

"I wouldn't have left this message if I didn't think it would make you and Rose and Marly laugh out loud. I love you, and I'm praying for Jan."

They were all laughing, the laughter tinged with disbelief at

Bibberman's megalomania. "A bigger asshole has never lived," Ellen said, putting away the phone, looking up when she heard the buzz of the ICU door. And through the open portal of Jan's cubicle, they could all see who was entering.

"I spoke too soon," Ellen said, realizing before the others who the dapper-looking man was who came breezing toward them as if he were one of the doctors on the hospital staff. "Here's someone who's an even bigger asshole. Did they forget to spray in here? How did he get in?" The nurses at the desk all nodded a nod of familiarity to Jack Solomon, whose appearance had been dramatically transformed for the better by his success. He had a slim physique, carved daily by a personal trainer out of what once had been a round little paunchy body, a great hairstyle trimmed and shaped regularly by a great barber, a perfectly shaped mustache that looked great on him, custom-tailored clothes that fit to perfection, and a swagger of confidence that was unquestionably sexy.

Tonight he was wearing the best-looking tuxedo ever made. And the only remnant of the former schlemiel who once climbed in the window of the girls' dorms, to be their platonic friend, because that's all that was available, was the occasional trace of a New York accent.

"They know me here," he said by way of explaining his easy access. Then he opened his arms wide as if he expected at least one of them to come over and hug him. "I shoot my shows all over this joint, so I can go anywhere I want . . . and by the way, it's nice to see you, too, Feinberg."

Ellen was deadpan.

He always called them by their last names when they were at Tech. "Bennet and Morris, can't you teach her how to watch her language?" he asked now, looked at his watch and said, "It's still the family hour." When he realized not one of them was going to come to him, he moved forward and put an affectionate arm around Rose. "I can't believe I was right across the street at Chasen's at an awards banquet, and out of nowhere Norman Lear leans over and asks me if I saw all the fans outside the hospital when I came by. I guess I was on the phone in my car when

we passed Cedars and didn't notice, so I said 'No, who's dying?'
And he said 'It's a terrible tragedy about that actress and what
happened to her today.' And then he told me who it was, and I
was so stunned I left right in the middle of my chili. How is
she?''

None of them spoke as he moved past them and looked into
the room where Jan still lay motionless, and then closed his eyes.
"Oh, Christ," he said. Marly made a shushing gesture and ush-
ered all of them away a few yards to the heavy door that separated the ICU from the hall. Rose and Ellen followed.

"We think she can hear us," Marly said softly.

"What can I do for her? I'll pay for specialists. I'll hire a private eye to find the guy that did it. I've got private eyes on the
payroll of two of my shows. I'll call one at home right now," he
said, pulling a phone out of the pocket of the tux jacket.

"Put that goddamned phone away," Ellen said. "You narcissistic putz. No one wants your help. I heard you fucked Jan over
so royally she couldn't even say your name without bursting
into tears. What's with you, you power-happy schmuck?"

Jack Solomon did a comedy take, looking back over each of
his shoulders as if he were looking behind him to see who Ellen
could possibly be accusing of doing something to hurt Jan.

"Pardon me? I did something bad to her? What in the hell did
I do to her? This I have to hear. I had the producer of my highest-
rated show bring her in to do a plum part that I hand-picked out
of one of the best scripts because I knew it was a part that had a
chance of going into a major story line. I knew she could chew
the scenery with it, and she did. We tested that episode, and that
scene went through the frigging roof. I sent her flowers afterward and told her so. You people are out of your fucking minds
calling me power-happy."

"But you got her the part with no ulterior motives, right?"
Ellen asked. "No old grudges. No power trips to get even for the
fact that you couldn't have her back when we were at Tech?"

Jack's face fell, and he shook his head and clucked his tongue.
"You've been hanging around with those lowlifes at Hemi-

sphere too long, Feinberg. They may do things like that. I sure as hell never would."

"Then what about the card?" Ellen asked him as if she were a prosecutor in a courtroom. "The card you sent with the flowers?"

Jack frowned and thought about it, as if he didn't know what card she meant. Rose couldn't stop looking closely at him, marveling at the fact that he was aging so well. His mustache had strips of gray in it, but the rest of him had never looked better. He'd become a great-looking middle-aged man.

"You mean because of the P.S. about finally seeing her tits?" he asked.

"Her breasts were used as a joke," Marly said.

"Not at all. As an integral part of the story line."

"Yeah, sure. That show and some of the rest of the shows on your network exploit women like crazy," Ellen said.

"And you used them on the gag reel," Rose said.

"I don't make the gag reel, the editors of the shows do that," he said, his brow furrowed with annoyance that she might think that he had something to do with a job so menial. "I just show up at the party. And the joke I made to Janny about seeing her tits was the exact same joke I made to her thirty years ago, when she always patted me on the head and laughed it off. But now I make that joke and I'm bum-rapped as sexually abusive? We're allowed to be sexy on television now, and why shouldn't we be? Sex is part of life. This isn't the fifties. No one wants to watch 'Beat the Clock' any more. So I just dropped the B and the L."

Marly emitted an outraged sound at his joke. "Get out of here, Jack. Go back to your party at Chasen's, and leave Jan with people who care about her." Jack ignored her and turned his anger on Ellen.

"Besides, Feinberg, my network's known for nice juicy hot passion. Your studio makes movies that have guys' brains blowing out their ears. Why are you better than me?" Ellen was silent. "Listen, ladies . . . I'm not going to get into a pissing contest with you three. I'm a good guy. I give money to the UJA, I support my parents. Remember Betty Norell? I even sat on the phone with her daughter, who called my office in such a panic they put her through to me because the girl can't locate her mother and she thought maybe Betty was in L.A. Like I would know, or give a shit, where Betty Norell, who I haven't seen in thirty years, would be. But did I say I can't take the call? No. I sat on the phone with the kid because I'm a good guy."

"Shh," Marly said, because at that instant she thought she caught sight of Jan seeming to have another one of those spasms, a restless tossing movement that might signal her awakening. They all hurried to the door and waited to see if there was any sign of her becoming conscious, but now only the blipping machines were active. Jan continued to lie still.

"Sometimes," Jack said then, in a voice that sounded as if it might crack any second, "in my office during the day, I turn on that soap of Jan's and lock the door, and sit there with a boner just like I used to get when I sat in the dorms staring at her. Because my whole life, Jan O'Malley was for me like that blonde in the white Thunderbird was for Richard Dreyfuss in *American Graffiti*. The wet dream who always haunts your life. I loved her, I still love her. I watched those dailies of her flashing her boobs in 'Doctors On Call,' and it was all I could do to keep from doing a Pee-wee Herman imitation in my own screening room."

"Mr. Class," Ellen said, but Jack ignored her. Now he had one arm draped around Marly's neck and another around Rose's.

"I used to love those nights in the girls' dorm on Morewood Avenue. It was Morewood Gardens, but remember how the boys used to call it 'The Cherry Orchard'? And you four were gorgeous. You should have worn signs on your chests freshman year that said 'We're Virgins, We're Pretty, and We Know It.' Hey, I'll bet you ten million bucks I can describe the pajamas every one of you wore, and it's thirty years ago, for Christ's sake."

"We can't handle that bet, Jack," Ellen said. "You're the one who makes the big bucks in this group." Jack was still looking into the room at Jan, deeply into his reverie of their youth.

"Janny had those slinky see-through pink baby dolls, and

then when I wanted to grab her after I looked through them and saw that killer body under there, she'd slap my hand. And Rose Morris, always a sex symbol, you had those green-and-black checked flannel pajamas, and old Marly the WASP. Hah! You had the long-sleeved, high-neck Lanz nightgown. And Feinberg, what in the hell did you have?" He thought for a minute, then lit up. "A Tech sweatshirt. Didn't you always sleep in an extra-large Tech sweatshirt?"

"I still do," Ellen said. "Which may be why I'm still single."

Marly was openmouthed. "My God. You were right about every one of our pajamas," she said. It was obvious he had melted her by recalling those details. Marly was a sucker for sentimentality. They all knew that, including Jack, who turned to her now to play his vulnerable scene to the hilt.

His eyes filled, and he nodded a nod that said, And you thought I was heartless, as he put his hand on Marly's face. "You see, Mar," he said, "you're the ones who pin the idea of a power trip on me. You give it that spin because you have some fantasy about my life that isn't true. Because we all know that if I wanted to, in my position, I can see all the tits, excuse me, ladies, breasts, in Hollywood all day and all night. So why would I ever humiliate someone I love? And you know what else? Something really important?"

"What?" Marly asked, falling for it hook, line, and sinker.

"I hate hospitals, and I think I'm gonna vomit."

Rose laughed out loud. "You do? Two of your shows take place mostly in hospitals."

"I know, and it's why I stay in the office instead of being on the sets of any of those shows. I get sick to my stomach. I think I'm gonna go accept my award, and have one of you call my office tomorrow and leave a message about how Jan is coming along."

"What's the award for, Jackie?" Ellen asked. "Sincerity?"

"Humanitarianism," Jack Solomon said, then turned to her. "You ought to try it some time."

"Thanks for stopping by, Jack," Rose said as he walked toward the outer door.

"Hey, Morris," he said, pointing at Rose. "You're a good little writer. I'll give you a job on any of my shows any time." He smiled his best and warmest smile before the door to the hall closed behind him, and the three friends stood near the nurses' station looking at one another.

"He's a piece of garbage," Ellen said.

"Shh," Marly said, "don't forget that hearing is the last sense to go. Besides, maybe he means it. I had no idea he loved Janny that much."

"Neither did he, it was all an act," Ellen said.

Rose sighed as they settled back into what were becoming the familiar plastic-and-metal chairs crammed into the cubicle around the bed where Jan lay.

"If he lies and treats people badly, it will come back to him," Marly said. "I really believe it. I think there's a balance out there, and you get what you give. Maybe not right away, but it happens."

"I think about that all the time," Rose said. I did something awful once that I'm sure is coming back to haunt me now. And I dream about it and worry about it, and I know I've never told any of you the story, because I was too ashamed."

"I hope Marlon Brando's in it," Ellen said. "And I hope this time you actually had him."

"Marlon Brando is not in this story . . . but close. This one is about Manny Birnbaum."

TWENTY-FIVE
The Invisible Man

RIGHT AFTER GRADUATION, I went back to Cleveland to pack up my things and move here, and before I left, everyone told me that the first thing I should do when I was settled was to call Manny Birnbaum. Manny was the best writer in television, with a list of credits that would make your mouth hang open. And in the forties, when I was a toddler, he was a close friend of my Dad's from their high school days. I remember hearing all the stories about how Manny moved to New York to "seek his fortune," and when he made it big, all the friends at home were as proud as if they'd done it themselves.

He wrote "The Garry Moore Show," and "The Jack Paar Show," and "The Dick Cavett Show." My father, who in those days had a little hardware store and appliance repair, and drudged away there making keys and taking apart toasters, felt touched by the glamour every time Manny's name went by on the television screen.

He would always call me in to watch the credits on a Manny-written show and say, "Here it comes! Manny Birnbaum. There it goes! Did you see it, Rose?" My father liked to brag that he could tell which shows Manny worked on without even seeing Manny's name at the end, because he could recognize Manny's slam-bang sense of humor anywhere just by hearing it.

Eventually Manny found his way from New York to Holly-wood, and of course, much later, I did, too. When we all first got out here in sixty-six, Manny was already a veteran writer, and his career was blazing. I was intimidated and afraid to call him, but my father kept sending me notes telling me I was crazy not to, so finally, after I'd been in town for a few weeks, I nervously dialed Manny's home phone number, hoping he wouldn't be there. But he was.

When he heard it was Harry Morris's daughter calling, "little Roselah," he invited me out to what was to be the first of our traditional monthly lunches, at Jerry's Deli in Studio City. In those days I think he was working on "The Andy Williams Show."

He was a cute little round man with a cloud of black hair around the edges of a bald head, and he had a great nice-uncle sweetness to him. I jabbered about my life, and what I wanted to do with it, and I remember before we parted that day, Manny said for the first time something he was to tell me at least a hundred more times, which was: "A writer is a person on whom nothing is lost."

Over the years he attributed that quote to Robert Frost, Edna Ferber, James Thurber, Roy Gerber, and maybe even Thomas Jefferson. "And you, maidelah," he always added, "are going to be a good one. Just from talking to you, I can tell that you see stories everywhere."

He encouraged me and helped me as patiently as a saint, reading my first feeble pages while we waited for our orders to come, and he and I both munched on the crunchy kosher "new" pickles Jerry's Deli always had sitting in plastic bowls on every table. Sometimes he'd still be reading over the soup and bagel chips, and I had trouble eating because my stomach was flipping around nervously while I watched his face for a reaction to my work.

Eventually he'd put the papers down on the table and gently tell me, first of all, the things that were good about what he read, and even more gently, not what was bad, but how I could make it better. Then he'd bring a little comedy relief to the moment, by dazzling me with the funny material he was working on for George Burns or Bob Hope.

And I felt so lucky that he was taking the time. I knew what a genius he was. In a writing class I was taking at UCLA Extension, my teacher was talking about some television show and spoke in awed tones about a certain quirky brand of comedy scene he referred to as "a perfect Birnbaum." Manny was a legend in television comedy.

In nineteen sixty-eight, when I married Allan, Manny and his wife were at the wedding. Remember? He was the one who stood up and made that hilarious toast that everyone was quoting for months afterwards. Manny is one of those people who can be funny about anything. He can pick up the telephone book and improvise a hunk of material for twenty minutes that will have you gasping for breath and wiping away tears of laughter from your eyes. He's what a producer I once worked for called "a comic entity."

As you know, I'm not a comic entity. I write drama, stories about human frailty, stories about pain. And there weren't a lot of jobs for twenty-two-year-old women in television in those days, not on the writing staffs. So I took a lot of writing classes, and while Allan was going to graduate school, I worked as a hostess at the International House of Pancakes while I wrote at night. Finally after a million false starts and a number of years, I sold an episode of a television show called "Cimarron Strip."

Which was pretty funny, considering my only experience with anything Western before that was when I was five, and some guy with a flea-bitten pony came around to my neighborhood and took pictures of the kids, wearing the photographer's sweaty cowboy hat, sitting on the pony. Then he sold the pictures to our parents for too much money. Which is to say, I was not exactly Louis L'Amour.

My dad still has the picture of me on that pony on the wall. Anyway, that episode got me more jobs in television, and then you remember I got an assignment to write a feature film for Universal, and my name was in the trades all the time. I had enough money of my own so that once I made the mistake of trying to pick up the check when I went to lunch with Manny, who gave me a little slap on the hand and said, "Don't insult me."

By now it was the early seventies, and Manny was skinny from working out at Gold's Gym, which he had started doing at the advice of his doctor, after he had what he called a "squeez-ing" in his chest that scared him into getting into shape. And the cloud of hair had not only turned white, but now it was down to his shoulders, and he wore it in a ponytail, which he pulled through a hole in the back of a cap with the words Writers' Guild on it. But these days, instead of regaling me with the funny sto-ries, Manny was complaining a lot.

I remember coming home one day and telling Allan how I figured Manny's curmudgeonly attitude probably was due to old age. He was, after all, in his sixties. But Manny said it was because he was feeling victimized by a prejudice he was starting to feel in the business, which he couldn't name.

He told me there had been a noticeable shift in the way people were treating him, a disrespect for what he'd brought to the tele-vision business, for his writing style. That he was somehow being perceived as too old-fashioned to be a part of what was happening in the business at that moment.

I didn't know what to say. The complaining made me uncom-fortable. By the end of the lunch, just because he was Manny, and being funny was what he did best, he was making jokes about it, and I was relieved. I didn't want to sit around with some kvetchy old guy over pickles if it was going to be depressing.

I had a lot of work to do and didn't want to interrupt a writing day to hear about how stupid the network executives were. That was a given. In fact it seems to me, I was so busy with my own assignments that I had to cancel what Manny called "our consti-tutional" once or twice. So the next time I saw him was a few months later. I was pulling my Mustang into the parking lot at Jerry's, and Manny was waiting for me, sitting on the hood of the old Cadillac he drove.

"Hey, kid," he said every time I pulled into the parking lot of Jerry's Deli. That day there was something distracted about the look in his eye. In fact, I remember as he stepped forward to meet me, he was almost hit by a woman in a Mercedes who was back-ing out of the space next to the one I was pulling into.

I knew from a few phone conversations we'd had that re-cently Manny had been doing something very tough for him, which was calling up comics he'd worked for in the past, and if he got them on the phone, saying, "Listen to this joke." Then he'd try the joke out on them, in the hope that they'd like it and buy it from him.

Most of the time they did like it, and bought it, because Manny's jokes are topical and very funny. And when someone tells you how witty some of those big stars are, it's usually because Manny told them, or should I say sold them, what to say. But you can't really make a living or a life out of selling jokes door to door, and that's why Manny was more depressed than the last time.

"So what's new?" I always asked, hoping that today he'd light up and say, "I sold a pilot idea to NBC, and I'm starting to write it." But instead, that day he fogged up and said he was going to tell me something, but I couldn't tell a soul. I promised, but he still didn't tell me what the secret was, until we were at our usual table, which is outside on the sidewalk, where, at no extra charge, as you eat your soup, you can inhale the fumes from the buses that go by on Ventura Boulevard.

"I'm working the night shift at Kinko's," he told me. I was sure it was a joke, since comedy writers love using words with the letter K in them, because for some reason the sound of the letter K is supposed to be funny, ergo his choice of Kinko's, which is the name of a chain of copy and printing stores. "I have to do it if I want to eat," he said. "So far, I've added a little humor to a couple of guys' business reports. But that's as good as it gets."

When I realized he wasn't kidding, the enormity of what he was saying hit me. Not that there's anything wrong with working at Kinko's. All of the people who have helped me there, to get a manuscript Xeroxed, are sweet and nice and courteous. But for Manny Birnbaum to be working there, to support himself, was like Walter Cronkite selling freeway flowers.

"Why Kinko's?" I asked.

"Because after all the pages I've Xeroxed for myself, I know how to do it real well for other people," he said. Then he added, as if to reassure me, "I'm on the midnight-to-six shift at the one in Reseda, because I don't know anyone in Reseda, and there's very little chance that at that hour, in that location, Brandon Tartikoff is gonna walk in there and spot me.'' There was no disguising the shame Manny was feeling, and instead of being the selfish little brat I'd been the last time, it occurred to me that I had to hear him out and help him because I owed him in spades.

''What can I do to help you?'' I asked him, thinking it felt like such a short time ago when I stood in my family living room, looking at the black-and-white screen, when the television was still an exciting new toy for our family, thrilling to the sight of Manny Birnbaum's name. But it really had been a long time, and instead of being venerated and consulted and revered by an industry he'd helped to make successful, Manny was out on his ass.

''Nothing, maidelah,'' he said. ''But thanks for asking.''

The next day I got on the phone and called John DiMaggio. John was a writer I knew from when we were both on the Writers' Guild show committee. He was a sweet, funny man who had a hit comedy series that had been on television for five years.

We chatted for a while, and I knew he knew I wasn't just calling him to shoot the breeze. Pretty soon I could tell if I didn't get to the reason I called, he was going to hang up, so I said, ''Listen, I'm calling to tell you that if you need someone really strong on your writing staff, you'll never guess who's available. Manny Birnbaum!''

John was quiet for a little while, and then he said, ''No kidding? Boy, was I a fan of his. Remember that routine he wrote for Tim Conway and Carol Burnett about the fat couple? A classic.''

''I'm telling you,'' I said hopefully. ''He's the greatest.''

''Yeah,'' he said and then sighed. ''Thanks for the tip, Rose. You're nice to call,'' and I thought maybe I'd pulled it off. Made John DiMaggio think I was offering him a hot property, and that maybe he had a job for Manny. I was about to give him Manny's phone number, when he said, ''Because I remember you telling me that he's an old friend of your dad's. Gotta hop,'' and he hung up.

Meanwhile, you know how fickle the business is. Well, things were starting to slow down for me, too. I was falling into some tough times myself, and though I'd been going around to a lot of meetings, I wasn't getting any assignments. I had a meeting one day with some producer who was looking for a writer to adapt a novel, and before the meeting, I took the novel apart and made a zillion notes on how I'd do it, and after my big enthusiastic pitch, the producer shot down every idea I had.

Now I remember that day as if it was yesterday, feeling down about that meeting as if it was the most important thing in the world. Driving home over Mulholland thinking I had to get a job soon or my eligibility for Writers' Guild health insurance would be threatened. And when I got home, I saw Allan's car in the driveway, and I wondered with this very odd foreboding why he wasn't in the office. Somehow I knew with a sinking feeling that the reason he was at home was going to be something terrible.

My father, I figured it had to be about my father. That my father was dead, and someone had reached Allan at his office, and he had come home and was waiting to tell me the news. It was something awful like that. I knew it. I hurried into the house and I looked at Allan's beautiful face, and there was, without a doubt, doom in his eyes.

He said, "Baby, sit down. I have to talk to you about something important," and I could feel my heart in my throat because I knew it was going to be very bad. But I couldn't imagine how bad, until he told me the doctor thought he had cancer, and he was going in for surgery the next morning.

Everything else fell away after that. For the longest time nothing mattered but the results of Allan's surgery, the bad news about how aggressive the disease was, bringing him home for a few weeks, then taking him for more tests, more treatments, more surgeries. And somehow making it through those days with the horrifying realization that our love story was ending.

One day when I had a quiet moment, I looked at our financial picture and it was pretty bleak. So while Allan slept, I tried to write, tried to come up with ideas to pitch, and had some half-hearted meetings in which I knew before I opened my mouth to pitch them that my ideas were dull.

It was a few months after the first surgery, and I was getting into my car after a bad meeting at Warner's one day, needing to hurry home and make lunch for Allan, though he was hardly eating anything by then, when across the parking lot I saw Manny Birnbaum.

I waved, and he came over and hugged me a big fatherly bear hug, and I cried in his arms. From exhaustion, from pain, from frustration. He said it was ironic that he was bumping into me that day, because he'd been entertaining an idea that he wanted to try out on me. He said there was a new comedy show coming on, on ABC, that was "staffing up." They were looking for writing teams, and maybe he and I should go in and try to get the job together.

"We're perfect for the show because it's about a young married woman who lives with her father, so we bring both characters' points of view to the party." When I didn't answer, he sold a little harder. "Listen, with your characters and my jokes, maidelah, we could be a hit."

He was so sweet and so hopeful to a dishrag of a person whose husband was dying and who thought she'd never have another creative notion for the rest of her life. Write a show with Manny. A comedy. Obviously he needed me to average out the age problem he was having at the network. And I needed him, because I was sure the right side of my brain was gone forever.

"Yeah?" I joked, and where I found humor at that moment I'll never know. "But what if it ends up having *your* characters and *my* jokes?"

"Then we're dead in the water," he said, grinning.

"Manny," I said, wiping my eyes, thinking what an angel he was, and how he didn't need the additional burden of someone as crazy as I was then. "You don't want me as a partner. I'm in the worst emotional shape I've ever been in. I cry at the drop of a hat, I can barely think straight most days."

But Manny dismissed my excuses with a wave of his hand,

and soon we were meeting at my house during the hours when Allan napped. And mostly the meetings were about Manny getting me up to speed so that if we could get a meeting for that ABC show, I'd appear to be "a comic entity," or in the worst case, they wouldn't think I was a complete moron.

We read the pilot, and a breakdown of the characters, and talked them and worked them for days. We knew we were ready for the meeting when we had what we thought were ten strong story ideas. And I'd be lying if I didn't admit that the lion's share of the work was Manny's. His genius came shining through. He had heart and warmth and trickery, and on top of that he could find something funny about everything.

The truth is, though I contributed a little, I knew that essentially I was Manny's front. Like Woody Allen in the movie with Zero Mostel. Manny could write the script in his sleep, and he didn't really need anything from me but my presence in the meeting. It was a thought that ordinarily would have awakened me in the middle of the night, feeling awful, but in those days I was awake all night anyway. Putting the blanket back over Allan, crooning to him to get him back to sleep as he lay in a hospital bed in our bedroom.

You can imagine how comedic I felt on the day of the meeting when I tell you that I knew a few hours later I was taking Allan into the hospital for what I suspected was going to be his last visit there, or anywhere.

"We killed 'em," Manny said, giving me five when we got into the elevator after the meeting. And I guess he was right, because the three jerky producers of the show laughed at everything we said in our very rehearsed, highly controlled, created-by-Manny pitch. "Those little stiffs were pishing in their jeans," he said happily. "And you were a trooper," he said, realizing my attention was only halfway there, and pulling back a little on the high.

That night Allan was admitted to Cedars, and I stayed with him until midnight, then went home to get some sleep, and at nine in the morning when the phone rang, it woke me. I jumped to grab it with fear that Allan had taken a bad turn during the night. It was my agent. "They want you," he said, "but they don't want him."

"That's impossible," I said. "He's the one. He's the brains, the talent, the ideas. I'm completely incapable of doing that show without him. It's a comedy."

"They say they want rich characters, which they can get from you, and they can fill the jokes in later."

"That's not how it works. The jokes and characters have to be written by the same person, otherwise they're not organic," I said, knowing I was quoting Manny. "Why don't they want him?"

"Because he's old, his ideas are old, his jokes are old-school shticky. They don't understand him, Rose."

"They're incompetent dunderheads," I said, enraged.

"You want to hear what they're offering you?" my agent asked.

At the foot of the double bed where Allan and I had slept locked in one another's arms for so many years was the as yet unreturned hospital bed, with the IV pole next to it, a cold, awful reminder of the past months, and what I had yet to face. Not just the expense, but the head-ringing, hospital-sitting nightmare that might last for the next six months. At least if I had a project, something not only to do, but that could bring in some income . . .

"What are they offering?" I said, hating myself for asking.

The number was ludicrously high, as so many television salaries were in those days. "But more than that," my agent said, "I told them your situation, and they told me you don't even have to come in, you can work wherever you want and send it over to them."

The hospital. I could stay near Allan, be where he needed me to be, and still have a writing job, a high-paying writing job, and extend my health insurance benefits for a long time to come. A writer is someone on whom nothing is lost, so you can bet the irony of what was happening, if I let it, was not lost on me.

When Allan came out of surgery that afternoon and was "resting comfortably," I called Manny and asked him if he could meet me at Jerry's Deli at four o'clock. I saw by the look on his face when I drove in that he knew why I wanted to talk. I got out of my car, and he stepped forward and took my hand.

"You know what?" he said. "It's too late in the day for soup. I think maybe I'll just have a bagel and some iced tea."

I had a speech rehearsed, and I was going to make it as soon as the Ventura Boulevard bus went by, but I never got to say anything but, "Manny . . ."

"Maidelah," Manny interrupted, but he didn't look at me, he looked at the pickles. "The business is changing. It's not what it used to be, and younger people are taking over who have ideas I don't understand. So if you want to know what I think, I think you should grab that job, because you'll be wonderful for the show. And the show will be wonderful for you."

"What did you do?" Ellen asked her as Rose leaned back now in the hard hospital chair.

"I took the job. Somehow I rationalized that I could do it without him, though I knew I wouldn't be brilliant at it, or even good, but adequate. Which is what I was, and the show was canceled a few months later. Probably because they were too stupid to hire the writer who could have saved it."

"And Manny? What happened to him?"

"He died a few years ago. In fact, the funeral was in Cleveland because he wanted to be buried near the rest of his family. My Dad went to it, and afterward he and some of the old friends went back to pay their respects at the home of some of Manny's cousins. My father called me later, and he was stunned.

"He said Manny died broke, but worse than that he died brokenhearted. He hadn't written a word in years, he had a will, but all that was in it was his old Olivetti typewriter and some manuscripts he was donating to the UCLA archives. And some instructions for his funeral and burial. On his tombstone he wanted it to say three words, 'But seriously, folks . . .' "

"This business . . ." Ellen said sadly. "This fucking killer business."

TWENTY-SIX

SOME of the people in the crowd outside the hospital saw her coming out the door, and one of them, a woman in a quilted parka with the hood up, said, "Hey, don't feel bad. None of us could get in, either."

She was amazed when she looked around at the ranks of fans that they had camp stools and coolers and warm clothes, as if they were prepared for the Rose Bowl parade or something. It made her think they must have done this kind of thing before.

That fat guy even had a Watchman, one of those little portable TV's that work on batteries, and he was tuned in to some newsbreak and then announcing what he heard to the other people. All of them were standing the vigil for Maggie Flynn. Not Jan O'Malley. Not one of them even mentioned the name Jan O'Malley. They were all talking about Maggie Flynn.

"They think they got the guy who shot Maggie," the fat guy said, and several of the others moved in closer to him. "They just said he's been arrested for questioning. Some nut who broke onto the set the other day looking for her."

Hah, she thought. As if this guy wasn't a nut himself, standing in the damp night, outside a hospital holding a candle because he was worried about some fictional character.

"I can tell you one thing for sure," the fat guy said. "That man is lucky it was the cops that found him and not me, 'cause I'da killed him with my bare hands, no questions asked. Anyone who hurts Maggie deserves to be dead."

She could hear on his television that the network had now cut away from the newsbreak, and back to some sit-com where the audience was laughing that fake canned laughter every few seconds. The blue shadow of the TV cast a flickering light on the fat guy's big, round, double-chinned face.

Two women who looked as if they were probably a mother and daughter, both with big dark circles under their eyes, stood with their arms around one another's waists. They were both holding those big, thick, twenty-four-hour candles and looking forlornly up at the towering hospital building. "I think they owe it to us to come out and tell us if Maggie's okay," the younger one said in a choked-up voice.

"Are you nuts? They don't care about us," the fat guy said, with a sneer of disdain at the girl's naïveté. "Pretty soon they'll send a cop out here to bust us for trespassing or loitering or some shit like that. You watch. I'm at all these things. That's what they did to us when we went up on Sunset to that shrine for River Phoenix."

"Maggie deserves to die," a bony woman with glasses said. "She's been stepping out on Aubrey, and if this guy didn't shoot her, I'll bet Lydia would have killed her anyway. Everyone knows Maggie was having sexual relations right at Flynn Laboratories with Phillip Jenkins."

"Shut up, Lois," a man who was probably the woman's husband said, poking her in the side. "She's not dying. She's going to be okay."

These people were too strange. They actually thought the person who was in the hospital was Maggie Flynn. Didn't they know it was Jan, her friend from college? They were insane to talk about the people on the show as if they were real.

"What if she dies, Mom?" the girl with the raccoon eyes asked.

"Oh, it'll be okay. Remember what happened to Aubrey? If she dies, she'll probably show up in the Caribbean or someplace like that."

Why was she standing out here? She wasn't one of these little weirdo fans. She told Jan that, too. She was a better actress than Jan had ever been. And those letters she sent to Jan in care of the show got shoved into the same bag as the letters these kooks wrote to her. She was Jan's old friend, and they wouldn't even let her go up to see who else was visiting her. They let Jack Solomon go up. Probably right now he was chatting away with Ellen Bass, that cunt, who never wrote a note back to say she got the audition tape. She wished now that she'd shot that bitch, too.

"You know sometimes they die on those shows, and they come back, and sometimes they're gone forever. My guess is, they'll just find someone else to be Maggie."

For an instant the idea slammed through her that if Jan died, the show would be needing to recast the part of Maggie, and she could play it. But then she knew that was absurd. I'm not glamorous enough, she thought. And the old feelings of envy were like hot lava in her chest. Even in critical condition in a hospital, Jan O'Malley was bigger than she'd ever be. She was nobody, just like the rest of these people on the sidewalk.

"What did I tell you?" the fat guy said as a police car driving down the street pulled up beside the curb just where they were gathered, and two officers got out.

"Time to go home now, folks. This is hospital property and they don't want you out here disturbing the peace," the tall bulky one said, in a patronizing voice that sounded like he was talking to a bunch of dogs. The crowd was dispersing. People were blowing out their candles and moving off down the street.

Wouldn't they all be shocked, the fans and the cops, too, if she suddenly put her arms out and said, "Cuff me, copper. I'm the one who shot her. Take me in and throw me in jail!" That would get their attention. But she didn't say that. Instead she turned quietly and walked away into the night, down the street to the parking lot to find her beat-up old car.

TWENTY-SEVEN

J ANNY, I know your spirit is strong in there, and you're longing to talk to us. If you can hear me, and I know you can . . .
squeeze my hand!" Marly had tried those words on Jan repeatedly over the last hours, but Jan was unresponsive. Ellen
stopped herself from saying, "Give it up, goddamnit. If she
could talk to us, she would." She was glad when Marly finally
moved to the floor, where she sat in a lotus position, her back
against the glass wall of the ICU cubicle.

Each of them felt the lateness of the hour in her chilled, exhausted body. Rose and Ellen sat on either side of Jan's bed.
Ellen had pulled over Marly's unused chair to prop up her legs,
and her body was slumped down in her own seat to make a
makeshift bed. Rose tugged at the sweater that was sticking to
her body and gazed down at the steno pad on her lap, the one
she always carried in her purse so every now and then she could
jot down an idea for one of her projects.

They were talked out. For hours they'd gabbed nonstop, and
just the way the nurses had advised, they'd included Jan in the
conversation, remembering the stories, rehashing their mutual
past, retelling the old jokes. Now there was no sound but the
steady breathing in and out of the ventilator.

Ellen yawned and looked at her Rolex. "My God, it's nearly
eleven-fifteen. There's a TV in here. Maybe we should watch the
end of the news."

"Do you think it's okay?" Rose asked, looking anxiously over
at Jan, worried that the TV news might be too harsh for her. "I

mean the news is always unsettling under the best of circumstances. Maybe Janny shouldn't . . ."

"I think it's just part of carrying on as if all is well," Marly said. "Why don't you go out and see if it's okay with the nurses?"

Rose went out to the nurses' station to get a remote control to operate the television, and in a minute she was back with one. She pushed a button, the TV buzzed on, and she clicked around until she found the local news, then turned the volume to soft. They listened to stories about a robbery in Van Nuys and a fire in Malibu, and then there was a commercial for Yoplait yogurt and another commercial for Nike.

Then, almost startlingly, there was a full-screen shot of Jan looking back at them. It was a publicity photograph Jan particularly loved. It was well lit, she wore a pretty, open-mouthed smile, and her eyes were dancing. Marly emitted an audible moan of sadness. The voice, they heard over the shot was Kelly Lange's. She was the anchorwoman on NBC.

"Earlier this evening, police officers dispersed a large group of fans who stood outside of Cedars-Sinai Medical Center in West Hollywood. The group, which numbered in the hundreds, was waiting for some word on the welfare of actress Jan O'Malley, who plays the part of Maggie Flynn on the daytime drama 'My Brightest Day.' "

Now they rolled a videotape of the exterior of the hospital, and as the anchorwoman spoke, there was a background of Jan's fans with their signs and their candles. A microphone was in the face of a fat man who said, "We want to know that she's doing okay, we love her, and if she can get our message up there in the hospital, 'Maggie, we're praying for you.' "

Now they cut back to the newsroom, where the pretty, perfectly coiffed, blonde anchorwoman said, "West Hollywood police have made an arrest in connection with the Jan O'Malley shooting. The suspect being held for questioning is Filbert Borzak, a longtime fan of O'Malley's. Witnesses told police that earlier this week, Borzak broke onto the set of 'My Brightest Day,' on which O'Malley has appeared regularly for fifteen years. Jan O'Malley, still in critical condition at Cedars-Sinai tonight.

"That's all for this Friday evening. Stay tuned for the new Billy Mann show, premiering right after this. Billy's guests are Kim Basinger and Madonna."

"Oh God," Rose said.

"A perfect end to an otherwise perfect evening," Marly said.

"Another asshole heard from," Ellen said.

"I can turn this off," Rose said, holding up the remote and looking quizzically at Marly.

"No, leave it on," Marly said, and then, to make sure she wasn't sounding too eager, she added, "Janny loves Billy. She'll get a kick out of hearing his jokes."

There were commercials, followed by more commercials, and then a big-band sound, playing Billy's theme, and a spray of cuts of Billy from the old show. Pictures of Billy dressed in every imaginable costume, Billy with big-name guests, images flying by that gave you the message "This is one giant star, so don't even think about changing the channel, because you're in for a great time."

One of the nurses stood in the doorway with a concerned expression. Marly was sure she was about to tell them to turn off the TV because the noise was disturbing the other patients, but instead she tugged at a pocket glass door that would shut the sounds of their room off from the rest of the ICU, and slid it about three quarters closed and walked away. Rose turned down the lights, and they all pulled their chairs into the best position to watch the wall-mounted television.

The incongruity of sitting in that desperate little room, with Janny on a ventilator, and all of them watching Billy, gave Marly chills. This would be Billy taped a few hours after their tearful lovemaking, their promise-filled parting, Billy knowing his name was being destroyed by the press, and that his adolescent daughters were in the audience.

"Heyyy, how are ya?" he asked the audience. Lots of whistles and hoots and Billy smiled his ain't-I-adorable smile, and Marly felt her hands clutched into fists, wondering if he was going to take on the *Enquirer* and the smut they wrote about him.

"Did you hear about the new doll they're manufacturing this year? Divorce Barbie. She comes with Ken's things."

There was a big laugh from the studio audience.

"Of course, if you have kids, you know that can't be true, don't you? Because Ken doesn't have a thing." Another laugh. "Did you ever look? Tell the truth, when the kids were asleep one night? I mean it could be because Barbie took it in the divorce. But I don't think so. I think he never had one in the first place. And I'm worried. My daughters are getting too old for those dolls, so they gave them to me to take to the rummage sale at school, and I got to the school to help them take inventory, so I opened the box and there was Ken. I think it was Ken, it might have been Aladdin, they're relatives, and he was naked as a jaybird, and I thought if this is what these girls are raised on, they're in for a terrible shock!"

"Good ol' Bill is doing the quality material," Ellen said. "Open the season with penis jokes. His usual fine taste."

"Not that I'm implying that there should be Flasher Ken, raincoat sold separately, or to be politically correct now, he'd be called Sexual Harassment Ken, but . . ."

He was getting big laughs, and Marly saw the confident look he got in his eyes, which meant he knew he was on the money, happening, funny. Marly found herself grinning, and when she looked at Rose and Ellen, they were smiling, too. The next few jokes were about the Clintons. Billy loved to do material about them.

"Al Gore, Bill Clinton, and Hillary all go to heaven," he was saying now. "When they arrive, they go in to meet God, who is sitting on a heavenly throne, and God says to the vice president, 'And, in your brief time on earth, what have you done for mankind?' and the vice president says, 'Well, Lord, I was an advocate for the environment. I fought to save our world from . . .' "

There was something odd about the audio on the television. As if there was an echo, and Marly thought that it sounded as if maybe the nurses had turned another television on in the ICU, or maybe another patient in an adjacent room had turned one on, but Billy's voice seemed to be reverberating.

Now he was doing the part of the joke where God asked President Clinton what he thought he had done for mankind, and then he imitated the President's southern accent and the imitation was perfect. It got a huge laugh from the studio audience. And now God asked Hillary what she thought her contribution was . . . and Rose must have heard the echo, too, because she stood to close the pocket door all the way, and when she did, she gasped.

It wasn't another television they were hearing. It was Billy Mann himself, in person, standing in the doorway of Jan's room, reciting the monologue along with Billy on the tape. "Never mind what I did, pal. You're sitting in my chair . . ." was the punch line. Billy on TV said it, and so did the real Billy. Ellen glanced up at him, and then Marly saw him and stood, not knowing what to say, afraid she looked as disheveled as she felt.

He was wearing red sweat pants and a Lakers sweatshirt and a brown leather bomber jacket, and he looked pale. "Hi," he said, looking into Marly's eyes, but the sad smile on his face was one Marly couldn't identify, though she'd been sure she knew them all. This one was almost afraid, very contrite, filled with concern, and surprisingly it felt sincere. He looked over at Jan, then closed his eyes as if the sight of her was too hurtful. He shook his head and opened his eyes and asked Marly, "Is she going to make it?"

"We don't know," Marly said, wondering what she should say, about this morning, the picture in the paper, anything, everything. "We're waiting."

Both Rose and Ellen stood tentatively. They both knew that to Billy they were the enemy. After all, who did a man hate and fear more than his estranged wife's best friends? Three women who knew about every dumb thing he'd ever done and said to Marly and the twins. Three lifelong loyal friends who had held Marly's hand through the separation, railed at her to confront him when she'd been too accepting of his childish behavior. Insisted that

Marly swear she'd never "yes" him the way everyone in his entourage did. These were the very friends who had nagged her into promising them she'd go and fight for sole custody unless he stopped disappointing the twins the way he often did.

But even if he did hate them for all of those reasons, Billy moved forward to each of them now with a hug that said that what happened to Jan transcended all of that. Billy on the TV was telling the audience to stand by because he had a great lineup of guests, and when he said the names of the female stars, the studio audience whistled and stomped raucously. Rose picked up the remote from under her chair and clicked off the TV.

"I went back to your house with the twins after the taping because I heard the news," Billy said. "We canceled our plans and went back to your house to see if you were okay. Maria told us you were here, and all three of us played with Joey until we tired him out and he went to sleep. God, is that kid cute. What in the hell is going to happen to him?"

Marly raised a finger to her lips and tossed her head to the side to indicate Jan and said, "He's going to be fine, because Jan's going to be fine. We're all counting on it." She wanted to throw her arms around his neck and say, "Let's go home." He'd gone to her house to see if she was all right. It was a step toward human.

"That was sweet of you, Billy, to stay and play with Joey," Rose said.

"Billy's a Capricorn and a two," Marly said, her eyes never leaving his as she riffled around in her purse feeling for a hairbrush, which she finally located and pulled through her white curls. "And they have tender feelings for children."

"New show looks good, Bill," Ellen said.

"Yeah, thanks," Billy said. That was usually all the opening he needed to launch him into what Ellen would call "more self-examination than there is a self." A deep discussion about the way his timing had improved, how bonded he'd become with his writers, how his input into the production elevated his show

from the usual late-night claptrap into something more mean-
ingful.

But he didn't take it. "The twins wanted me to bring these
signs they made." He unrolled two papers he was carrying
under his arm, one that read GET WELL, AUNT JANNY, Love, Jennifer, and the other that read I LOVE YOU, AUNTIE JAN, Love,
Sarah.

"Oh thanks, Billy," Rose said. "I'll get some tape and put
them up."

The ventilator huffed in and out and nobody spoke for a
while.

"Mar," Billy said, "I hate to quote another talk-show host, but
'Can we talk?' I mean the twins told me you had the cleanup
crew at Gelson's working overtime today. So I thought maybe
you'd let me say a few words to you on my own behalf before I
go back to the house to make sure all the children are asleep and
safe."

"For example, what words?" Marly asked nervously.

"For example, surely you're not buying into that shit? That
little girl in that picture with me on that newspaper is Greg and
Sandy Weber's daughter. He's one of the guys over at the agency
who represent my production company. Their daughter was
walking with me out of the Bruin Theater and her parents were
two feet behind us. Greg Weber is suing that paper because the
kids at the high school are all tormenting the poor little girl. Mar,
these are the tabloidians who brought you 'Elvis is alive and a
Hassidic rabbi in Miami Beach.' "

"You mean he's not?" Ellen said.

Marly was leaning wearily against Jan's bed, holding nervously to Jan's hand as if she were afraid Billy's tirade might
damage Jan further. It really was too much, completely inappropriate for Billy to have come here tonight. He could have waited
until Jan was improving, or at least until Marly was at home to
talk about this. Instead of bringing their painful relationship to
the intensive care unit.

She knew her friends were waiting for her to act, to stand up for herself the way she did for every other issue on earth, to tell him to go away. To refuse to fall for his con anymore. So she summoned her courage and tried to organize her thoughts.

"Billy, without insulting you or hurting your fragile ego, I need you to hear that I have more urgent problems to deal with right now. Life-and-death problems. I'm not going to let myself get all caught up in some battle that will compromise the energy I require to focus on taking care of my friend and her child.

"I've wasted more than enough of my life mourning the unfulfilled expectations I had for our marriage, and now, when I'm confronted with how precious life is, it makes me absolutely certain I don't want to waste another minute on the shallow concerns you and I spent years making important."

"So, Mar, does that mean that everything you and I talked about this morning is out the window? Because some sleaze gazette buys a picture of me from one of those paparazzi leeches, you're going to forget all that we did and said this morning and send me out of here? Look, I know this is a terrible time to talk, and a terrible place and a horrifying situation. But I want you to know I lived on this morning all day. Why do you think I was cooking on that show tonight? Because all the way to the studio, and sitting in that makeup chair, I was saying, 'My baby loves me, and we're going to make it work.' "

"Gee," Ellen said. "Musta been some hot morning."

It made them all laugh out loud. "So what's it going to be?" Billy asked, as straightforwardly as he'd ever said anything in his life. "Are you going to take me back? Yes or no?"

Marly thought about it, then suddenly her eyes opened wide, and she gasped and then laughed.

"I think it's yes," she said. "I mean Janny thinks it's yes," and then, though her face was lit up like a Broadway marquee, she was crying. "She just squeezed my hand! Once. For yes."

"There must be a kink in her IV," Rose joked, and Billy gave her a look that said "Stay out of this," but Ellen and Marly laughed.

Billy went to Marly and put his arms around her and spoke, not caring that Rose and Ellen heard every word. Probably figuring they'd hear about it eventually, so why not just let them be there when he said it. "I've been fighting so many demons for so long, honey. Let me come home and help me make a life with you. I really want that."

Marly's face was as full of blush as it was the day she and Billy walked down the aisle. "I'm going to go, but if it's okay, I'll stay at your house tonight, to be with the twins and Joey while you're taking care of business here. Then, when you get home, I'll be—" Marly interrupted him.

"No, Bill," she said. "You can't stay there. I have to give this lots of thought. To make a decision from a stable place. Not here in this room, at this moment."

"Yeah, Bill," Ellen said. "Some people don't think they have to do everything in front of an audience."

"I'm going," Billy said to Marly. "I love you." Then he took Jan's hand out of Marly's and held it and said to her, "At least I know one of you is on my side," and without looking at any of them again, he was out of the room.

"Now that was the real Billy Mann show," Ellen said.

Rose just sighed.

Marly looked at them both. "I want to believe him, but I'm afraid in a few months he'll change his mind again, and I'll be kicking myself for being a pushover."

The ventilator sucked in and breathed out, in and out.

"Happens to the best of us," Ellen said.

"It'd probably be a hell of a few months, though," Rose mused.

"True," Marly said. "Full of apology, good behavior. I see it with the battered wives who take their men back. All the hopefulness, the unreality that comes with new beginnings, but it's a Band-Aid, and pretty soon it falls apart. And I can't do it to the girls. It's one thing for me to be sucked in by it, but I think kids have enough to go through without having to be dragged through their parent's problems, too. You were always so protective about Roger when you were getting your divorce, when you were dating. How did you do it?" she asked Ellen, who shook her head.

"Are you kidding? I fucked up all the time. Colossal fuck-ups. I made mistakes with that kid that we still laugh about. Life lessons were botched left and right. In fact there was one story that still gives me a guilty stomachache. I mean, now it's funny because we survived, at least it's funny to Roger. He brings it up and laughs. But talk about doing things you're ashamed of. This has got to be my entry."

Marly was back on the floor in her lotus position, and Rose put away the steno pad so Ellen could tell them what happened.

TWENTY EIGHT
Little Caesar

DURING MOST of the seventies, my life was a complete disaster. After I gave the podiatrist the toe, he managed to make it out of the marriage and California without giving me anything for our son. Not only that, but he took everything that was worth anything in our cute little house with him, so in one week I went from being *très* Pierre Deux to very Pier One. And all I wanted was to be the best mother and the best provider in the world to make up for the fact that I knew Herb Bass would never be there for Roger.

I was desperate to make a good life for Rogie and me, so I took any and every job I could get to support us. And some of the situations were pretty scungy. I started out on "The Glen Campbell Goodtime Hour," where Glen may have been having a good time, but I was not. I was the coffee girl, the receptionist, and the runner.

I got picked on by the writers and the producers, hit on by the guests, and Glen called me Arlene for the whole two years. "Paper Moon" was a better experience, in fact it was where I first got to know Jodie Foster, because she played the Tatum O'Neal role in the series. Another was the second go-round of "Sonny and Cher," which I should have known wasn't going to last when she was on TV with her ex-husband and pregnant with Greg Allman's baby. That great big demographic known as Middle America just didn't cotton to it.

So when the ex-Bonos went off the air, and I couldn't find another job, somebody told me there was an opening working for Ziggy Marsh. I laughed when they first said it, because if anybody represented the scourge of show business, that little reptile was it.

Remember Ziggy? He's still around. I see him at the studio now and then, and he hasn't changed one bit since those days. He's still a caricature of what an agent's supposed to be. Short enough to buy his clothes in the boys' department. Once, years ago, I bumped into him at the May Company when I was shopping for Roger, and Ziggy was trying on kid-size jeans. He also has the yapping temper of a dog who was bred down to teacup size and whose nerves got all out of whack in the process.

The part that always amazed me about him was that he somehow managed to get his own name in the paper more than the stars he represented. Usually it was for cocaine arrests or being rushed to a hospital because he was one breath short of OD'ing, or because he'd just beat the shit out of his wife. But somehow he managed to weasel his way into the careers of a lot of top stars, who I guess figured maybe it was good that he was a snake in the grass, since he was *their* snake in their grass, so that made it okay.

I mean, I understand the theory, because I always tell people who ask my advice about agents, "Don't ever be represented by one you want to sit with at a dinner table. You want someone who's an obnoxious killer." Well, Ziggy qualified in spades for that.

Anyway, I guess the little lizard liked my résumé, or more likely he'd probably gotten laid that morning, but he was in a rare good mood the day I came in for my interview, and he hired me on the spot as a kind of assistant and sub agent. Roger was nine years old, and I was in dire need of money, so I jumped in with both feet, figuring if I paid a lot of attention to how the agent business worked, maybe I'd grow up to be Sue Mengers, a lady agent who I always thought was cute in her aggressive way.

Well, the way things worked in the Ziggy Marsh office was that anything was okay, as long as it got you where you wanted to go. You know Ziggy's wife is Andrea Caldwell, right? Andrea Caldwell, who's about as gifted an actress as my ugly Aunt Sadie, only my ugly Aunt Sadie is prettier. So if somebody wanted one of Ziggy's big clients for a project, they knew that the price was that they had to put Andrea in a small part in the same film. That was a given.

And he was always on the take. People were shmearing him all the time with free trips and cars and drugs, trying to get him to push his clients to take their deals or show up at their charity events, and if they didn't give him a little something sweet on the side, he ignored them. He was the lowest.

When people asked me where I was working, I was so embarrassed, I'd say the Ziggy Marsh Agency so fast and so slurred, that I know a lot of people thought I was saying the William Morris Agency. Not that that would be something to brag about either, but at least it wasn't scumbag city.

I stayed because the pay helped me put my kid, who was very smart, in a private school, and barely make the tuition. Also, I was getting the residue of the shmears. I sold the motor bike someone gave Ziggy and he gave me, and I used the money to take my son to Florida to see my mother one winter. And I still have the treadmill someone gave Ziggy, who already had one.

Anyway, there was one client Ziggy always wanted but couldn't get near, and the client was John Travolta. It was right around the time of *Saturday Night Fever,* and Travolta was blazing hot. Guys at Pips were wearing white suits and pointing their finger to the sky when they danced, and everyone was whistling "Bein' Alive." Ziggy tried getting Travolta on the phone, going to Santa Barbara to see him, having Andrea invite him to a party, but Travolta wasn't interested.

Meanwhile I'm packing lunches, driving car pool, rushing in to the office, working all day, and paying a sitter to pick Roger up at school. And by the end of the day I'm always exhausted, so when I get home from work and I'm cooking dinner and Roger asks me, "Hey, Mah, want to buy some raffles so I can have lunch with the guy from *Saturday Night Fever*?" I don't even think about it. I say "Sure," and give him ten dollars, and he gives me two raffles, and I fill them out and then I do the dishes.

In the morning, on the way to school I have four nine-year-olds in the back of my wagon, Roger and his friends Bobby and Tommy and Richie, and I half listen to their conversation because I'm worried about whether or not I reminded Ziggy that he's having lunch that day with Tony Orlando and Dawn. But when I tune in, I realize that the kids are saying that Ed Milstein, Richie's father, is John Travolta's business manager or something like that, and John Travolta has agreed to have lunch with the kid at our school who sells the most raffles.

I couldn't get over how sweet it was of a big star to do something like that. When I got out of my station wagon to take Roger's Indian Village out of the back, because I wanted to help him carry it into the classroom, since it took us three weeks to make it and I would die if it fell apart, I saw Esther Milstein. Apparently she was the one who balls-out called up Travolta and asked him to do a favor for the school, and she was really strutting.

It was, without a doubt, a coup. I congratulated her, and she told me that we were printing three thousand raffles, a thousand more than last year, and that her daughter Debbie was already in the lead in sales, even though Debbie had already met Travolta a few times in her Dad's office.

The race to sell the raffle tickets was always hot and heavy, but this year it was the biggest. The phone in the tiny school office rang off the hook and Olga, the seventy-year-old receptionist, joked that she was now answering the phone by saying, "John Travolta Elementary."

A week or so later, I was at Ziggy's office in the middle of ten different things, and Roger called me from school to say he was sick, and the sitter wasn't due to pick him up for three hours, and I couldn't get ahold of her to get her to go pick him up early, so I had to run up to the school.

I remember what he had. It was one of those kid things, where it wasn't contagious, but he felt too lousy to stay in class, which meant I obviously couldn't leave him there. But I had to go finish my work, so I took him to the office with me, and I made sure he had crayons and paper, and that he was quiet while I got my stuff finished.

I was on the phone, and then in the Xerox room, and lost in

thought, when all of a sudden I was passing Ziggy's office and I heard Ziggy saying to somebody, "So, uh, let me get this straight. It's the guy with the white suit from *Saturday Night Fever* who's comin' to the school?" And then I heard my son's voice say, "Yep, he's coming."

"To have lunch with the kid who sells the most raffle tickets?"

"Yep."

"So, like what if that child wants to bring someone along to the lunch?" I heard Ziggy ask Roger, who must have somehow wandered into his office, while I was making copies of a contract. "Is that part of the deal?"

"You mean a friend?"

"I mean his uncle. Me. I mean if you win, can I come, too?"

"Oh, I'm not gonna win. There are some kids who already sold fifty tickets. I only sold two to my mother."

My stomach was sinking because I knew what was coming. I knew Ziggy Marsh could and would write a check for all three thousand five-dollar tickets if he felt like it, call it a business write-off, and it would still be less than he and Andrea paid for the hors d'oeuvres they served every year at their fancy Christmas party.

"Yeah, well, hows about I make you a deal?" I hear this asshole say to a nine-year-old boy.

"Okay," my baby answered.

"I'll buy a thousand tickets from you, this minute, and that'll probably guarantee that you'll be the winner."

"Aaarigght!" Roger said.

"If," Ziggy that little schmuck, says to him, "you take me to that lunch with the guy from the movie."

"Sure!" I hear Roger saying as I walk into the office.

"I'm doin' business here," Ziggy says to me with a cutesy smile on his face and his little size-seven feet on the desk.

"Yeah, Mom. Business," Roger says. "I'm gonna win the prize."

I felt sick. I don't know why. I mean, the truth was, the five thousand dollars was going to go to the school. It would finance scholarships to kids who were in need. Why did I care that it came from this vulture, who was using a kid's contest to try to feather his nest?

"I mean, this is okay with your mom. Isn't it, Mom?" Ziggy asked me, grinning, because he knew I knew exactly what he was doing, and that I, his toady, was in a vulnerable place.

"I guess," I said. "Why not?"

"Then it's a done deal. You get the tickets and give them to your mom, she can fill them out for me, and I'll write a check to your nice school for five grand."

"Five hundred dollars?" my innocent little Roger says, his eyes wide with shock.

"Five thousand dollars," Ziggy says, his face flushed with pride that he's just suckered in some nine-year-old.

In those days I couldn't afford to write a check to the building fund at my kid's school, so what I gave to them instead was my time, as limited as it was. I would go in on a Saturday and tag things for the garage sale, or help build scenery for the school play. And that particular month, all of the mothers were coming in on the weekends, and while the kids played on the field, we made skirts for the booths for the fair.

At one of those sessions, one of the women suggested that with the success of the John Travolta idea, we were doing so well with the tickets, that maybe we shouldn't limit ourselves to the three thousand tickets, that maybe we ought to print up more and sell five thousand tickets. Someone also suggested, as a joke, that maybe we should sell kisses from John Travolta right at the fair and that she'd personally ante up her life savings for that.

Esther Milstein thought it was a good idea to print more tickets, and so did everyone else, and I made a mental note to find out if it was possible that anyone was even close to Roger in ticket sales, though I couldn't imagine that any other child would sell a thousand tickets.

What I hadn't counted on was the aggressive marketing techniques of Joanne Lee, a sixth-grader who was in the school on a scholarship. Joanne's mother was a manicurist in a beauty shop in Beverly Hills, and the little girl went to the shop every day after school and sold tickets to all of her mother's customers, and everyone else who came to the shop.

About three days before the fair I heard from Esther, and maybe she said it to give me a goose so I'd get Roger to work even harder, that Joanne Lee had sold fifteen hundred tickets. She was ahead of Roger, or should I say ahead of Ziggy, who had gone on a rare vacation to Fiji with his abused wife, Andrea.

I clutched. I knew I'd better track Ziggy down and tell him his lunch with Travolta was in jeopardy. I also knew that Andrea Caldwell had taken him to this resort called Turtle Island, away from all phones, as a test of his love, because their marriage was on the rocks, and she insisted he go to a place that remote so he could prove to her that she was more important to him than show business.

Maybe I should leave it alone, I thought, let things take their course, let the deserving Joanne Lee win the lunch with Travolta, and show that little dog Ziggy Marsh that money wasn't everything. But then I got a grip and realized that doing that could put me back out on the street with no job, and I'd just found out that Roger's teeth were coming in crooked and he needed braces.

Maybe I should buy the additional raffle tickets myself, and hope that I was doing the right thing and that Ziggy would reimburse me when he got home and found I had covered for him, to make sure he'd have lunch with John Travolta. But then I added it up and realized that to buy five hundred tickets, which would only put Roger even with Joanne Lee, would cost twenty five hundred dollars. I had five hundred dollars in the bank.

I had to call Turtle Island. If Ziggy took my call, breaking the deal with Andrea Caldwell, she might leave him. If he didn't take my call, and the raffle deal fell apart, he would kill me. It was her marriage or my life, so naturally I picked me.

There was one phone at Turtle Island, and the line was always busy. By the time I got through, it was eleven at night in Fiji, and the person who answered was not happy to take my message for Mr. Marsh. Two days went by and I never heard back. I had called him from his office, so even if he didn't get my message, at least he'd be able to see on the phone bill that I did try to reach him.

On the morning of the fair I called Turtle Island one more time, and the line was busy again. I was worried, but I told myself I had done my best and that was all I could do, and I went off to the fair. The school grounds looked beautiful. The parents' committee had done a fabulous job with balloons and crepe paper.

I worked in the cold-drink booth, and Esther Milstein worked in the throw-the-Ping-Pong-ball-in-the-goldfish-bowl-and-win-a-fish booth right next to it. Esther was supposed to be the one who was going to pull the winning raffle ticket from the basket, and she'd been waiting for the headmaster to come and get her, but for some reason, the little brass band, led by the music teacher, was suddenly playing a fanfare, on the far side of the field.

The music was what made me look over and see that a lot of people had gathered around the bandstand, where the headmaster himself was standing with the basket of raffle tickets. I didn't hear what he was saying to the assembled families, but he was getting a few laughs from them, because he could, when he turned it on, be very charming. "Esther," I said, "come on," but Esther was busy transferring a goldfish from its bowl into a plastic bag full of water for one of the kids who'd just won it, and she didn't hear me.

By the time she was ready to walk over there with me, the headmaster had already announced the names of two of the raffle winners, and as we made our way over to that side of the field, he was announcing the third.

Esther looked at me as if to say, "What in the hell is he doing?" But by the time we got near the front of the group we knew, because that was when he said, "And finally . . . the winner of the lunch with John Travolta, star of *Saturday Night Fever* . . ." I looked around trying to spot Joanne Lee, hoping to see the joy on her face when she won. And the headmaster said, ". . . is the student who sold the most raffle tickets, Roger Bass."

Rogie shrieked with joy and jumped in the air and ran to the stage to have his hand shaken by the headmaster. I was dumbstruck. I knew it wasn't true, but people were now circling me, congratulating me and telling me they were envious, and asking me what I was going to wear to the lunch, and I looked around and this time I located little Joanne Lee, whose face was frozen. And next to her, with the same stoic mouth-set, was her mother. But their empty eyes, devoid of disappointment, told me they'd been prepared for that announcement.

I watched the headmaster with a stiff smile walk back to his office, and as soon as Joan Casey replaced me in the cold-drink booth, I walked into his office, too, without knocking. I knew by his expression, which was a combination of embarrassment and resolve, that he'd been waiting for me.

"Mister Jenson," I said, closing the door to the office behind me, "I know my son didn't sell the most raffle tickets, and I need you to tell me why he won. Because I think he knows he didn't sell the most tickets, too, so tonight when the excitement wears off, I'm going to have to explain this to him."

"Mrs. Bass," he said, gesturing for me to sit in a chair opposite his desk, "I admire your principles for coming in here and questioning this. To use a well-worn cliché, children learn what they live, and I'm sure you're a fine example to your son. Now let me tell you the principle I used in handling this situation. Joanne Lee has a scholarship to the school this year worth ten thousand dollars. She needs another one next year. Thanks to the generosity of Mr. Marsh, your employer, not only will she have it, but so will four other students who might not have had the opportunity to come to this school. Do I make myself clear?"

The laughter and shouting from the children at the fair came drifting through the open window of the headmaster's office. I knew that a tax-deductible fifty thousand dollars to Ziggy Marsh was small change for a chance to have lunch with John Travolta. Could I ruin it for him? Could I make him take his dirty money back? Take away his generous scholarships to the school?

My eyes met Jenson's. A school administrator in tinsel town. A man who was responsible for the quality of the education of our children, and his salary at best wasn't a whole lot more than fifty grand. He had to hate a guy like Ziggy Marsh, and the only fly in his personal ointment might be if I spilled the beans to the board of directors about the way Joanne Lee had been screwed out of the lunch. I knew he cared about the school and thought the Hollywood people were the necessary evil he had to put up with to run it. So I got up and walked out of there and went back to the cold-drink booth.

A week later, on the following Saturday, Roger, Ziggy, and I had lunch with John Travolta in Santa Barbara. Travolta was so adorable I could have cheerfully jumped on him right there. He was charming to Roger, talking about flying airplanes and all the things kids love. Ziggy was on his best behavior and kept bringing up the business, but Travolta, not sure how this man he'd been avoiding for so long was in on this, was polite but essentially ignored him.

That night when I was tucking Roger in, he asked me what had happened. He had heard the buzz around school all week that Joanne Lee was cheated out of being the winner, so he knew something odd had happened. I sat on the bed and silently prayed for the strength to be honest and true without giving him details that would break his heart.

"Roger," I said, "I did a bad thing. I let my boss buy all of those raffle tickets from you because he wanted to meet John Travolta, and it wasn't fair and square because he influenced the way the raffle went, and Joanne Lee worked so hard selling the raffles at her mom's shop and she probably would have won. I'm so sick about it, I think I'm going to have to quit this job, and find another one, because I can't stay there anymore, and I want to apologize to you, because I let him do that for all the wrong reasons. I'm sorry, honey, I'm really sorry," I said and looked into his eyes, wondering if he understood.

Roger was sweet-faced, and his big hazel eyes blinked at me so innocently and even now when I think about it, I want to cry because he's always been such a great kid, and he said, "Yeah, well, Mom, you know what they say, don't you?"

And I said, "No, honey, I don't know what they say." And Roger shrugged and told me, "That's show biz."

Marly's laugh was tired. Rose didn't comment. When they both looked over at her, her head was thrown back against the back of the chair and she was sound asleep.

TWENTY-NINE

SHE SAT on the bed in the Tropi-Cal Motel in the Valley and counted the money she had left, laying it all out on the orange bedspread. She was still shaking from the move out of the Sheraton. In the middle of the night last night it had hit her that every breath she took was costing her extra. Like that little minibar. She'd been so excited when she saw all the stuff in it, figuring it was part of the cost of the room, and she wouldn't even have to order room service or go out to eat.

She could live on the free cheeses and the candy bars and cookies. Wouldn't have to go out and get food, or order from the hotsy totsy room service menu. So she ate practically everything in there. Then last night she discovered the little form on the top of the bar. The one you fill out to tell them what you ate so they can put it on your bill, the sheet where it tells you that the peanuts alone are six bucks a jar.

That's when she knew she'd better get the hell out of there. So this morning, holding her pile of cash like a kid who broke open her piggy bank, she checked out with her heart pounding while they added up the amount she had to pay, wondering if she'd have enough. And then she had to pay a deposit at this new place. The Tropi-Cal Motel. A true dive. And she only had eighty-three dollars left.

Eighty-three dollars was probably what Jack Solomon used to blow his nose instead of Kleenex. That tux he was wearing at the hospital probably cost thousands. Once they were on the same path, heading in the same direction, but she had veered off, planning to catch up with them later. And now all of them were in the bucks, and she was counting and recounting her last few dollars, hoping maybe she'd made a mistake and it would be eighty-four dollars or eighty-five.

What a dumb idiot she'd been wasting all that money on the Sheraton for appearances. *Thinking when she got to Jan's, after their chummy chat, Jan would say, 'I'll come and pick you up later and we'll have dinner,' and if that was the case, she'd be able to tell her she was staying somewhere good. But Jan didn't say that. Jan didn't want to have dinner with her, she wanted her to get her lowlife ass out of her house.*

And then that thing happened, that dumb accident. But at least there was real big news about that. Late last night on TV they were saying the police caught the guy who did it. The guy who did it! Maybe her luck was changing. Now maybe it was safe for her to go see the others. Go to their houses. She'd tell them she just got into town and heard the news on TV, and she felt so awful. And then she'd ask if she could do anything for Jan's little boy. She'd cruise by their houses.

She looked in her purse for the list of addresses, but for some reason it wasn't in there. Maybe she'd left it in the car. Never mind. She'd copied all of them down in her address book, so it didn't matter, and she could find them with the Thomas Guide.

It was a sunny, hot, smoggy day, and her car was like an oven when she got in. She opened all the windows and sat for a while looking at the street map, and decided she'd try Rose's house first since it was the closest. At a light she stopped next to a black Porsche with a young girl driver about the age of her daughter Polly. The girl's hand on the wheel had a gold watch and a few bangle bracelets, and rings on three of her fingers. I want that for Polly, she thought. And I'm going to goddamn get it.

People in this city were so rude. Especially on the road, where they just cut in front of you or they leaned on their horns if you took longer than one second to move after the traffic light changed. And then when they tore past you, they gave you the finger. She remembered reading a few years back how some really pissed-off people on the freeway were shooting at one another. She ought to pull out her gun and just hold it out the window at anyone who honked at her. That would shut the fuckers up. Hah!

The gun. She patted the big striped plastic purse to make sure she still had the gun. She had to do something about the goddamn broken strap on the purse. She couldn't afford to get a new purse until one of them gave her a job. Once she got a job somewhere and was settled in to some nice apartment, she'd go shopping and get herself some new things.

At Rose's street she made a left, then looked at the numbers until she found the house. Not bad. Not great, but not bad. She sat in her car looking up the driveway, wondering if she could really pull off a straight face when she saw Rose and had to say to her, "I felt so awful about Jan." Hey, she reminded herself, you're an actress.

She was startled when the door to Rose's house opened and a little girl came out with a basketball. She was tiny, but determined to shoot baskets into a hoop above the garage, which she was trying to do and not having much success. She would go down there and help her, tell her she was a friend of her mother's. Find out if Rose was home, just act as casually as if she were on a leisurely trip.

She already knew what she'd say if one of them looked cross-eyed at her clunker car. "Oh, I had to bring my daughter's jalopy. My car's in the shop." She got out of the car and started up the driveway, holding the big striped purse close to her, feeling the gun bump against her side. "Hi," she said, and the little girl looked at her.

"Hi," she said. She was smiling. She was only a few feet away from the kid, but then there was a loud noise which turned out to be a garage door opening, and a big black Mercedes backed out of the garage, and the little girl climbed in.

She could see the driver, a guy with a beard who must be Rose's husband, and as he got to the end of the driveway, he spotted her and stopped, and rolled down the automatic window. She could feel the escaping air-conditioning blow cold at her from inside the car. She could see the pretty little girl's face as the man asked, "Are you lost?"

"No, thanks, I'm not," she said.

"May I help you in some way?" he asked. The little girl was the age Polly was when Lou moved out. But Polly had never had the confident look in her face this kid had. It was a look only rich kids had, like they didn't have a problem in the world. Not the beaten look that means my dad's an asshole, and every night my mom cries herself to sleep.

"Uh . . . no. Thanks," she said.

She could tell that Rose's husband was waiting for her to walk away from their property, so she strolled past and up the street as if she was just visiting one of their neighbors and taking a walk. When he was

gone, she walked back up the driveway and all around the house, look-
ing into the windows.

Nice kitchen, she thought, pretty bedrooms, a little too froufrou for
her taste, and in the cute little office with papers all over the floor, she
saw Rose's computer where she did her writing, and all around it a
bulletin board with photographs on it. Pictures of that little girl, a few
pictures of the bearded husband, and then a lot of pictures of Rose with
friends. What had to be recent ones, and some old ones with her daugh-
ter when the daughter was a baby, and then that old one that she
couldn't believe she recognized.

She had taken it. She was the outsider who walked by that day. In
front of the dorm, Morewood Gardens, that the boys used to call "The
Cherry Orchard." They were all standing outside together, giggling
about some shit or other, maybe it was parents' weekend or something
because they didn't look like dramats, not wearing the usual jeans and
black sweaters. They were all dolled up as if they were going out to
lunch with their folks, and she walked by, and Rose said, "Let's ask
Betty."

They were so tight, such a cozy little group, they had to have their
picture taken all together. Rose and Marly and Ellen and Jan, to com-
memorate their friendship. Even now, thirty years later, she hated them
for being so close and so happy then. There were French doors on Rose's
office, and she tried turning the knob on one of them but it was locked
tight. She wanted to go in there. Just for a minute, to see what else Rose
had in there from the past. She tried another door and it was locked, too.

She would have gone back to her car then, but a truck drove up, one
of those little minicamper deals and a little Jap got out and pulled a leaf
blower out of the back, and some other equipment, and not six feet away
from her, a door from the house opened and a little fat Mexican lady
came out and started talking to the guy about what to do and what not
to do.

She watched them yakking away as the maid pointed to some ground
cover, and while they talked she led the gardener around the side of the
house, leaving the door ajar, so she slipped right in. Oh it smelled good
in there. That maid must be cooking something, because it smelled like
garlic and butter and it made her hungry.

She could see through the window that the maid and the gardener, rough life there, Rose, were in the backyard deeply into some conversation in some language, so she got all the way to the office. Inside Rose Schiffman's office. Jesus, she thought. This is where the magic happens. An Oscar-nominated movie was written in this very room. She felt excited, like Shirley MacLaine in Sweet Charity when she sings that song "If They Could See Me Now." She ran her hand over the keyboard of Rose's computer and then looked up again at the cork board with those pictures.

There was the one she had taken of the four of them. Now she took it down and held it at arm's length, so she could really see it, and the memory of it still stabbed her. Look at them, she thought, I hate them so much, I always did, and I still do, because they never even said, "Let's take another one with Betty in it." I remember feeling so shitful because of them. She was squeezing the push pin so hard it stuck in her hand while she looked at their faces in the picture. But now she heard the voice of the maid getting louder, and she knew she had to get the hell out of there.

She started to put the picture back up on the wall, and then she looked at it one more time and felt so bummed at them, so pissed, that she ripped it in half and then again, and then she threw all the pieces into Rose's wastebasket and managed to get out the door before the maid and the gardener got back.

In her car she looked at the Thomas Guide for Ellen Bass's street. It was a little one in Beverly Hills, south of Wilshire Boulevard. She'd go there next and check it out. Maybe the hotshot herself would be home, and she could ask her why she never took one minute out of her schedule to even dictate a thanks for the tape.

Once she got a job working at the studio, she'd make a lot of contacts, the business was about contacts, and pretty soon someone would say, "With that voice you ought to be acting," and then she'd have to tell Ellen she was moving on. Ellen would get it. She'd moved up in the world herself. She knew certain jobs were just stepping-stones to others.

When she found the street and the house, she thought she'd made a wrong turn. Ellen Bass could no way live in that little house. It was a nothing of a house. At least Jan's little house had a view. This looked like a brick box in a section that might be called Beverly Hills, but it *sure didn't look like it. The house was dark, so maybe she'd just park the car across the street and ring the bell.*

It was early in the morning on a Saturday, so unless Ellen Bass was shacking up with some boyfriend, she'd probably be there. It was hard to believe this was Beverly Hills. This was a street where some of the places were houses and some looked like apartment buildings. She walked up to the little porch and picked up the newspaper that was lying there.

She knocked and then rang the bell. She could hear it ringing inside, but no one came to the door. After a few minutes she walked around to the side of the house through the alley, past some big green trash cans, and then to the back gate. She had to laugh when she saw the little swimming pool that took up practically the entire yard. There was a table and chairs and two lounge chairs next to it.

This must be where the big-time lady executive sits to read scripts over the weekend, she thought, and she opened the gate. It was a clear, sunny, hot day, and the big tall palm trees that lined the street were barely stirring. She couldn't remember the last time she'd had a chance to sit around a swimming pool and feel the sun on her and just relax.

The grass around the pool scrunched under her espadrilles as she walked over to the pretty outdoor furniture. Prettier than in any ad, very white and tropical-looking. She put her big purse down on the grass and then she sat down in one of Ellen Bass's lounge chairs and put her feet up, and after a minute her whole body relaxed, warmed by the day. The turquoise, glimmering pool was almost hypnotic.

She was still holding the L.A. Times, *so she opened it to the Calendar section to read about what was going on in the business, and she even kicked off her shoes. This was what life was supposed to feel like. This was how big people lived. She was reading an article about violence in the media, nearly falling asleep over it, when a loud clang startled her.*

She could hear blaring rock music, and then a young, skinny guy with a flat-top haircut turned the corner. He was carrying a pole with a net at the end of it, some big plastic bottles, and a boom box that was blasting some bad rock station.

"Mornin'," he said to her as he dropped the stuff, walked back to a

little shed that must be where the pool equipment was, then came back out and picked up the long pole and eased it into the water. The music from his radio was too loud.

"Mrs. Bass awake?" he asked her over the sound.

"I don't know," she said.

"She was having trouble with her filter, but I'm not going to be able to look at it today, so if you tell her I'll be back Monday morning to look at it, I'd appreciate it. I mean, I might be able to get a part on my lunch break, and if I can, then I'll be back around three today, but I doubt if it can happen today, so will you tell her?"

"Yeah," she said, not sure what he'd just said.

He stirred the water around and poured some liquid from the bottles into the water and stirred again, and when he left, he said, "Have a great day."

After she'd finished reading the paper, she went to the front door of the house again. She rang the bell a few times, but there was no answer. To hell with it, she thought, and decided to move on to Marly Bennet's house in Brentwood.

THIRTY

THEY DOZED and woke alternately. Sometimes Marly lay spread out on the floor using her jacket as a pillow, and Ellen and Rose slept sitting up in the chairs. Nurses who moved in and out of the cubicle to check on Jan tiptoed around them, moving so silently that the three friends continued to sleep.

They were startled awake at six A.M., when a young, starchily dressed morning-shift nurse, who seemed inconvenienced by their presence, woke them by sliding the door open noisily and announcing that she had orders from the neurosurgeon to send Jan down to have another CAT scan.

"We need to see if the swelling has improved or become worse," she said in an all-business tone that had them gathering up their purses, slipping into their shoes, and walking groggily out of the room.

In the corridor they waited and watched as the bed was trundled out of ICU, and Jan's inert body jiggled as the orderlies bumped the cumbersome bed over the sill and into the hall. "Give 'em hell down there, Janny," Marly said softly.

Rose tugged at her sleeve, and they headed down the hall to the ladies' room. It smelled of a recent mopping with disinfectant, and Rose wrinkled her nose at the acrid odor and walked to the bank of sinks where the other two stood rinsing their faces.

"We look like the opening scene in *Macbeth*," Ellen said.

"After we get the results of this test, we ought to take turns going home," Marly said. Her white hair was wild around her pretty face. "I need to get to my house and make sure Joey's being taken care of properly. I felt fine about leaving him with

Maria because she's been his prime caretaker for so long, but we have to consider the effect of the trauma. We need to find him a child therapist right away, so he doesn't walk around with rage inside him for the rest of his life."

"And grow up to be a studio executive," Ellen muttered sleepily.

"As soon as we talk to the doctor, you can both go home for a while, and I'll stay," Rose said. "Molly has a play date today, and Andy will come back here to make rounds. So I'll just call him and ask him if he'll bring me some clean clothes."

They rinsed their mouths, Ellen ran a brush through her thick auburn hair, Marly lifted the top of her pouffy cotton-candy curls with a pick comb, and Rose pushed her hair back behind her ears. "It'll take them a while to do the tests. Let's go for a walk," she said.

Their heels clicked on the terrazzo floors as they walked down the hall into the elevator and then across the lobby, where a white-haired guard at a desk was reading a Stephen King paperback. Marly pushed the hospital doors open, and they stepped outside into the new day.

Silently, they moved together down Beverly Boulevard, past the Beverly Center. It was just dawn, and they could make out shapes in doorways of the sleeping homeless. A siren screamed, and an ambulance rushed past them heading for the hospital.

"Oh, what I would give to have my worst worry be Alex Bibberman, the way it was yesterday," Ellen said.

"Isn't it awful the way we need disaster to remind us what matters and what's nonsense?" Marly asked.

"You're right," Rose said. "There are days when I get caught up in the insanity and spin out on what I'm not doing, what I should be doing, what other people are probably doing, and worry myself into a frazzle. Last month I canceled my subscription to the trade papers because I realized that while I was reading them my stomach ached."

They moved swiftly, sometimes walking three abreast, sometimes single file, sometimes holding on to one another as they crossed the streets. At Fairfax Avenue, catty-corner to the snowy white CBS studio, they stopped for a red light, and Rose looked up and then smiled.

"Look," she said, and the others followed her gaze. It was a billboard for Billy's show. A giant picture of Billy with an ingratiating grin on his cute face. Marly's face melted into a mixed look of pain and adoration.

She sighed, and without taking her eyes from the billboard, she said, "It's so ridiculous, but I love him with that same kind of aching, overwhelming love we used to feel about boys when we were adolescents. I still get a rush every time he walks in my door. And it never goes away, no matter what name I give it, no matter what cure I take, trying to do away with feelings I've branded with every psychological term ever coined. And you know what? Werner said that life gets easier if we ride the horse in the direction it's going, and that's what I've decided I'm going to do. I'm going to call him and tell him I want him to come home as soon as he can."

She looked at her two friends and paused, waiting for the protests, for one of them to say, "Mistake! The man can't cut it. He'll just hurt you again." But both of them just nodded.

"I think if anyone made me feel that way, I sure as shit would set all the mental health books on fire and grab it," Ellen said.

Rose put an arm around Marly. "You'll make it work," she said.

Marly knew that they doubted Billy's staying power as much as she did, but they wanted it to work for her and were willing to support her through it. As the three friends stood on the street corner, oblivious to the traffic noises that were picking up, the L.A. morning sun rose in the sky. The Beverly Boulevard bus rumbled to a stop next to them and two women got off chatting away in Spanish and walked off down the street. The bus pulled away, leaving a cloud of exhaust, but they didn't notice that, either.

"I love you both so much," Marly said. "I want to say it now, because I wish I had said it to Jan more often. All I thought about last night while we sat in Jan's room was that I probably hadn't let her know how much her wonderful gift of friendship meant

to me. How I always loved hearing her voice at the other end of
the phone. How sometimes when I felt so low I could barely
move, I'd think about the stories she told that made me laugh so
much, and I was grateful that I had her in my life. So please, let's
not wait to praise one another, remind each other all the time of
everything we have together, and what that's worth."

"I love both of you, too," Ellen said, tears gushing out of her
eyes. Cars and trucks were whizzing by the busy Hollywood
corner. "I know I'm tough on you, Mar, and I hear myself doing
it sometimes, and I hate myself for it. You two and Janny have
walked me through this life at times when I thought I couldn't
take another step. When Rogie was little and I was so alone, the
times you three had us over for meals, picked him up at school
when I couldn't, gave him advice when he thought my advice
was stupid and yours was cool."

"We've come such a long distance with one another," Rose
said. Marveling while she looked at them through her own
puddle-filled eyes, that she not only knew the reason for nearly
every line on their beautiful faces, but the season when it was
acquired.

"Yeah," Ellen joked. "All the way to CBS." She took a tissue
out of her bag, and as she wiped her nose, she looked up and saw
two old Hassidic Jewish men walk by dressed in their long black
coats and black hats. This was the neighborhood of delis and
Judaica shops and kosher butcher shops, and home to many el-
derly Jews.

Ellen smiled. "My friend Artie Butler once told me that he
was supposed to meet somebody at CBS one day," she said.
"And the person he was meeting didn't know how to get there,
so the directions Artie gave the guy were, 'You go down Fairfax
Avenue, and the first place that doesn't have a chicken in the
window is CBS.' "

Laughing, and with their arms around one another, they
headed back to the hospital.

At eight-fifteen Jan's bed came rumbling off the elevator and
was wheeled past them in the seventh-floor corridor and back
into ICU. A few minutes later the neurosurgeon arrived. He was

a thin, balding man with kind eyes, who nodded to them as he moved in to the cubicle to examine Jan. When he came out into the hall a few minutes later, his expression was grim.

"Do any of you know if she has a durable power of attorney for health care?" he asked, looking at each of them.

"Oh, God," Ellen said.

"Her sister told me last night that Jan talked about a will in which she was planning to nominate her as the guardian of her son, so maybe the durable power of attorney for health care is with it," Rose told him.

"I can go to her house and look for a will," Marly said.

"It's necessary," the doctor said. "The prognosis is very serious. I reviewed the CAT scan, and her clinical picture has deteriorated since the imaging study we did before the surgery. The blow to her head caused massive damage and the edema is worse. There's a lot of pressure in her skull, and it's pushing down onto her brain stem.

"We can wait a few days to see if that changes, but I believe if we extubate her, it will only be a very short time until she dies. Right now I think we should hold off taking out the tube until we determine if her wish is for us to take extraordinary measures to care for her or not."

"What are the chances the swelling will go down?" Ellen asked.

"We don't know."

"I guess I'd better find out if she put any of that in writing," Marly said.

"When you do, you can call my office or have me paged here at the hospital."

When he was gone, none of them spoke. Marly shuffled in her purse looking for the key to Jan's that she had taken yesterday from Maria. When she found it, she held it up and said to the others, "I'm going to her house."

"Wasn't it taped off by the police?" Rose asked.

"No, the police who were there when I went by to get Joey yesterday told me that they only do that if the victim . . ." She couldn't make herself say the word dies.

"I'll walk out with you," Ellen said to Marly, "and be back this afternoon," she promised Rose.

When Marly drove up the narrow street and saw Jan's Lexus in the driveway, her chest ached with sadness. She parked her car in the carport behind Jan's and sat for a while. The distant sound of a leaf blower clacking filled the air. The little hill house was so isolated from the neighboring homes, it was easy to understand how someone could come there, shoot Jan, and get away without anyone noticing.

She turned the key and walked into the silent foyer. The area rug that usually filled the front hall was gone. Last night when she came, she saw Jan's blood on it. The police must have taken it away. There were toys still scattered around, and everything looked the same.

She took a deep breath as she walked upstairs, and when she passed Joey's bathroom, she could see the towels still strewn on the hamper from the bath Maria gave the little boy last night before he went down to find his mommy.

Jan had a desk in her room where she always sat to pay bills, and there was a small wicker filing cabinet next to it. Marly opened it and looked under W for will, but there wasn't anything. Then she looked to see if there was a file marked "Legal Papers," but there wasn't. So she went through each letter of the alphabet, through contracts and a file on Jan's sister's expenses, and bills to pay, and Joey's vaccination records, until finally she found what she wanted under M, because the lawyer's last name was Middelman.

She turned the pages until she came to Nomination of Guardians and scanned it quickly, "If it becomes necessary to appoint a guardian of the person or the estate of my minor child or children, I nominate my sister, Julie O'Malley, to serve as the guardian of the person and the estate of my minor child or children." The sister who doesn't even want to take Joey, Marly thought. What chance could he have being parented by someone who didn't want him? Why hadn't Jan, so sensitive about everything, understood that was the case? There were more papers and documents but there was no durable power of attorney for health care. Julie would have to make that decision, too.

When Ellen opened the door to her house, the cats meowed around her ankles in a frantic circle of fur. She went right to the pantry for the cans of cat food and stood at the can opener feeling them rubbing against her and purring. The sound of the can opener made her head pound. As soon as "the beasts," which was what her mother called them, were facedown in their bowls of food, she threw off her clothes, pulled on a nightshirt, and crashed into a deep and headachy sleep.

When she woke a few hours later, her head was still throbbing, and she staggered into her kitchen, noticing what she hadn't when she'd come in earlier. That there were twenty-nine messages on her answering machine.

She listened to every one of the twenty-nine and jotted down the names and numbers of the ones she had to return. "Ellen, this is Lindsay in Mr. Bibberman's office." Bibberman's secretary was on the tape six times. It was Saturday. Bibberman's secretary worked the same seven-day-a-week schedule as her boss. She was aggressive, ambitious, and knew she was giving up having a personal life as long as she worked for him.

"Alex," Ellen said when he took her return call. "If you're wondering about the meeting on Monday with Jodie Foster, I'll be a thousand percent ready for it. I'll see you there at nine sharp."

"Fine," was all he said, and he put down the phone.

Try to warm up your act a little, you putz, she thought. Not one concerned question about Jan. Not one drop of sympathy. "What did you expect?" she said out loud as she took a can of coffee out of the freezer. "You're in the meanest town in the world, in the most competitive business, with the biggest bunch of insecure maniacs who ever lived. You thought maybe there would be an 'Ahhh, poor baby.' Grow up."

While the coffee perked, she looked down at the rest of the list of people she had to call back and systematically returned them one at a time. When she came to the call from her pool man, a

message she'd listened to so sleepily she couldn't remember now
what he'd said, she decided to play it back and listen to it again
on the machine.

"Hi, Mrs. Bass. I told that lady who was sitting at your pool
this morning that I might not be able to come back today, but I
got lucky on my lunch break and found that part for your filter.
So I'll try and get by at around two or three. See ya."

She looked at the clock and it was two forty-five, then out the
back window and there in fact was Eddie, her cute hunk of a
pool man, just arriving, with that fucking boom box playing so
loud that when she opened the window, the music made her
think her head would explode. What did he mean when he said
that he told something to a lady who was sitting at her pool?

It wasn't Constanza, the cleaning lady. She came in on Mon-
days and Fridays and she wouldn't dream of sitting out at the
pool. Ellen shouted to Eddie, a yell to be heard over the music so
she could get his attention. When he came to the window, she
asked him about the lady. But the only detail he remembered
about her was a giant striped purse he nearly tripped over a few
times.

Why would anybody be sitting at her pool? That was impossible. Maybe Eddie had seen a lady at somebody else's pool
and confused it with hers. A big striped purse?

Marly drove home from Jan's trying to remember the books
she'd read about children and divorce, because the same principles of dealing with loss had to apply to Joey. Keep the dialogue going, acknowledge your own feelings of helplessness and
fear. No question is too silly, no fear is wrong. If you have trouble with an answer, it's okay to tell them, "I'm not sure what to
say to that, but I'll think about it."

As she drove west on Sunset, Marly called Sabrina Kleier, a
child psychologist she'd visited several times after Billy first
moved out. She was surprised when Sabrina herself picked up
instead of a service. When Marly told her what had happened,
the young child psychologist told her, "Find any photographs
you have of Jan and go through them with Joey, talk about Jan's

life, their life together, and how much she loves him. If you have photos of the adoption, take those out and show those to him. Maybe that will open some dialogue about how afraid he was when he found her."

When she opened her front door, the house was quiet. She walked from the door to the kitchen, trying to relive how it felt only yesterday making that same walk with Billy. She looked wistfully at the banquette, remembering the heat of their love-making, and then his tender words last night. He seemed to mean it all. But then he was a man who was paid millions to persuade America that he was sweet and boyish every night of the week.

She could hear squeals of laughter from the swimming pool, and when she walked outside, she saw her housekeeper and Jan's housekeeper, poolside as lifeguards, while the twins and Joey played in the water. Jennifer hoisted herself out of the pool and ran to Marly. "Is Joey going to be ours if Aunt Janny dies?" Jennifer asked.

Marly gave her a look that meant, "Don't say that!" and Jennifer said, "Sorry, Mom."

Joey waved from the water, where Sarah was pulling him around in a Donald Duck inner tube, and Marly went over to the pool and lay on her stomach so her face hung over the edge. Sarah floated the inner tube close to the edge, and both she and Joey gave Marly a tiny wet kiss on the cheek. She was relieved to see that he seemed to be having a good time.

"I'm going up to grab a shower and a few hours' sleep," she said. When she stood in the shower with the phone on the floor next to it and the shower door open in case Rose called from the hospital, she was shaking. When she finally pulled the curtains closed in her bedroom, got into bed and dozed off, she was awakened by Joey's screams. "I want Mommmmeeeee. My Mommmeeee."

Jennifer burst into her room. "Mom, he's doing it again. He's been screaming like that all night and day. When we took him in the water, he stopped for a little while, but he's always scream-ing." Marly put a robe on over her nightie and went downstairs, where the helpless Maria held the red-faced, agonized little boy.

"Let's talk about Mommy," Marly said to him. "Let's go get out the photo albums and talk about Joey's Mommy."

"Mommeee," Joey wailed, and Marly's heart ached for him.

The minute Ellen got back to the hospital to sit by Jan's bed, Rose left for home. Molly was at her play date and Andy was making rounds, and the house was silent. She was past sleep, so she walked into her messy office and tried to tidy up the papers. To sort them out. After plowing through a few of the piles, she found herself sitting on the floor, unmoving, in that daze that comes with the kind of broken sleep they'd all had last night. Her eyes scanned the photos on the cork board around her desk. The one at Marly and Billy's wedding where they were all laughing with their heads thrown back in joy!

When the phone jangled, she could feel it in her trembling body.

"Rosie."

"Marty, it's Saturday," she said to her agent.

"I tried to get you last night, but your daughter said you were out, and I really have to talk some sense into you."

"Why is that?" Rose asked. She was too numb to do her usual jokey exchange with him. Now she was looking at a picture of Molly and Sarah and Jennifer and Roger, at a Mother's Day picnic Ellen had thrown in her backyard. They were all in Ellen's pool, the little girls hanging on a grinning Roger, who was about seventeen at the time and still willing to come to parties with his mother's friends and their daughters.

"Because Howard Bergman told me you walked out of the meeting with him. Could that possibly be true?"

"It could possibly be," Rose said.

"Rose," Marty said, and she was so exhausted and so sure this was going to be something she didn't want to hear that she lay down on the floor and looked up at the ceiling of her office while he talked.

"Listen to me Rose. *Faces* was a long time ago. You need a current credit. When I pitch you for assignments, people are starting to ask me, 'Is she still around?' Let me sell that script to Howard Bergman, and you close your eyes and they'll bring in someone else to do the rewrite. That way I can tell people you have a project that's happening. Then maybe you can sell that story about the computer. Or that other thing about the women friends."

"No," she said.

"You're nuts," he told her. "But maybe you can afford to be nuts. You have a rich husband."

"My husband has nothing to do with this decision," she said. "Why don't you get me some more meetings on the computer idea?" she asked him.

"I tried, Rose. Everyone says the same thing. It's not castable. Nobody's going to buy a story that stars a middle-aged actress. They don't give a shit. And frankly, they're not so hot for ideas from . . ."

"A middle-aged writer?" she said.

Marty didn't answer. Instead she heard him say to somebody, "Tell him I'll call him back," then he got back on the line. "So I have one more suggestion for you."

"Which is . . ." she asked him, thinking she'd like to take a little nap right where she was, drifting, so tired, she just wanted to get Marty off the phone. Instead, to keep herself awake, she sat up and moved from the floor to the desk chair, picked up a pencil, and doodled while he talked, drawing cartoon eyes, which was what she always doodled when she was on the phone. Marly would probably attribute some dark meaning to the doodles.

"I represent a young gal," Marty said. Rose always hated that word. She made the eyes almond-shaped, and gave them long lashes. "And she is very, very hip. She took some courses at AFI, she's kind of punk-looking, pierced nose, that kind of deal, but don't be put off, because she's very bright. In fact she graduated from Harvard a few years ago. So, I had lunch with her yesterday and she said, 'Marty, people all over town want to meet with me, but at the moment I don't have any ideas.' "

Rose knew she should have put the phone down then, because she knew where Marty was going with this, but she stayed on the line with the same bizarre fascination people have when they stand and watch the paramedics pull bodies out of cars after an accident. Only this time it was her own body that was being pulled out of the car. He was telling her that she should go into a meeting with this young woman as if the idea had come from the two of them, and work with her and share the credit with her. It sounded horrifyingly familiar.

"Marty," Rose said, "let me make this real clear, okay? I've been a member of the Writers' Guild since nineteen sixty-eight. That's twenty-five years. More years than this girl has been alive. I have used more Blackwing 602 pencils down to their stubs than the number of days she has been on this earth, and I'll be damned if I will make like she's my writing partner so I can get into a meeting at a studio with some executive who will probably be the gal's age and wonder why Granny is along for the ride.

"May I also add that a writer is someone who does have ideas, so tell your client with the facial jewelry if she doesn't have any ideas, she isn't one." As she hung up, she thought with an ache about Manny Birnbaum. Then she looked at some notes on her desk that she'd made a few weeks ago. The notes were for a movie idea that had once seemed terrific to her, only now the idea didn't seem so hot anymore. So she crumpled the paper up. Then she turned in her chair and aimed the crumpled paper at the wastebasket.

She remembered how Allan used to do that and say, "And the crowds cheered as he scored . . . ," get the paper in the basket, and then say "two points!" She missed, so she went over to the wastebasket to pick the paper up and put it in. "Slam dunk," she said dejectedly as she kneeled next to the basket and righted the missed shot.

That was when she saw the pieces of a photograph in there and couldn't imagine what photograph it could be. So she pulled a few of the pieces out, and when she saw which one it was, she wanted to cry. Why would anyone take that precious photo of the four friends and destroy it? Was Molly acting out because she'd spent the last many hours at Jan's bedside? That wasn't like her at all. Rose cried quietly as she sat on the floor trying to put the picture together piece by piece.

THIRTY-ONE

SHE WAS in the motel room, eating a Big Mac for breakfast and feeling fat and crummy and disappointed. Before she left home, she'd figured that by this time she'd be calling to tell Polly, "Guess what, honey. I'm in Hollywood with a great job! And you can tell your dad, and that bitch Sharon, too!" Polly. She ought to call her. At least she ought to call her own answering machine to see if anyone was trying to get ahold of her.

When she reached into her purse to pull out the remote she had to beep into the phone to retrieve her messages, she felt the gun, and suddenly she was filled with fear that maybe the police would figure out the way they always did on TV that they had the wrong person, and then they'd come looking for her.

Nah, she told herself as she dialed her number at home. Police were only that smart on TV. After one ring she heard her machine pick up and her own voice answer and say in a way that Lou used to call "phony bullshit," but which she knew was theatrical, "I'm sorry I'm not here to take your call right now, but I really want to talk to you, so please leave a message after the beep."

Yeah, great voice. Ellen would be thrilled to have that voice add class to her office. She pushed the remote button, then heard the garbled, squeaky sound of the tape rewinding, followed by her daughter's voice. "Mom, I've been trying to find you for the past two days, and you haven't called me back. I know your car is gone, and I'm in a complete panic. Now it's Saturday. I'm calling to find out if you saw the news on TV, about your friend Jan? It's so awful. Call me back." Click.

"Yeah, this is Harvey over at the Floor Store, and I'm callin' to make sure you're comin' in. I don't care if you get germs on the filing cabinet,

I've got a month's worth of bills I have to send out, and all kinds of other stuff, so you better be here." Click.

"Mom. It's me. It's Saturday night. Where are you? I stopped by the Floor Store looking for you, and Harvey was really bummed because you didn't show or call. I figure you must be really super depressed about Jan O'Malley. I know you two were close and all. But the good news is I heard on TV that they think they got the guy who did it. So that's something, right? Talk t'ya later." Click.

"Mom, I have a confession to make. I was so shook about not being able to find you, I had this crazy idea that maybe you went to L.A. And then I was reading some article in the paper about that guy you know, Jack Solomon, and it talked all about the stuff he was doing at the network, so I took a chance and called information for the number of the network and asked for his office, and I got through to his secretary. I guess I sounded really upset because she put me through to him.

"Mom, he is so nice! He said if I ever come to town I should call him, and if I find you I should have you call him. He took my call because I said I was your daughter and you had disappeared. So, Mom, he must really like you to have them put me through when he's so busy. Anyway, please call me. Okay?"

"Yeah, this is Harvey again. I'm calling to tell you, you're fired. I had to do all the billing myself, and you didn't even have the courtesy to call me. So don't even come by on Monday for what I owe you. I'm keeping it and you can sue me." Click.

She went into the bathroom and put cold water on her face. She felt feverish and afraid. Now she didn't even have a job at home. And she didn't have any money. But there was actually good news in all of this. A pony in there somewhere, like that old joke about shoveling through the horse shit. And that was that Jack Solomon remembered her. Hah! He should only know that she'd been standing ten feet away from him at the hospital the other night. Maybe she should go over to his office at the network and pop in on him. Where the hell were those network offices anyway? She picked up her street map because there were landmarks on it. Maybe she could find them there.

Shit! Today was Sunday. Nobody would be in their office today. They'd be having barbecues with their families or brunches at the beach. Jack Solomon lived at the beach. She could drive out to his house in

Malibu. Malibu, just the name brought pictures to her mind of pretty young girls in bathing suits, the way she was once, the way Jack Solomon remembered her. How could she go out there and let him see her like this?

After a while she picked up the phone at the same time she pulled her address book out of her purse. Then she dialed nine for an outside line and the telephone number in Malibu. The least she could do was call him, apologize for Molly's panicked call. And her voice was still sexy. While the phone rang, she folded the greasy McDonalds' wrapper in half and in half again. She'd tell him she was in town to test for some film.

"Hello."

"Jack?" she said into the phone. She felt afraid and queasy but proud of herself for getting up the nerve to do this.

"No, this is Jason. Who's this?"

"Oh, is this Jack Solomon's residence?"

"Yes it is. I'm his son. Who's this?"

"Well, I'm an old college friend of his, and I was hoping to maybe say hello for a minute. I was in his class at Tech and I . . ."

"Hold on a sec. I'll see if he can talk. Dad! Telephone . . ."

Her heart was pounding. Jack Solomon had a son who sounded like a man. Of course he was probably in his twenties. Maybe he'd like to meet Polly. Wouldn't that be something. "Our children really should get to know one another," she'd tell Jack once the conversation got rolling. There was a whooshing sound in her ear, something from the other end of the line. Probably she was actually hearing the surf outside the Solomons' big, beautiful beach house.

Jack Solomon was going to pick up the phone any minute, and he'd be so glad to hear from her. Here's what she would say. "Hi, darling. Hasn't it just been forever? I've been working in England. But I really have been planning a move back to the states. Helen Mirren and I were just talking about it. She's doing that great detective series on PBS, and I'm here testing for a . . ."

"Hello."

"Jack?" Her heart was banging as loud as it used to when she stood offstage waiting for her cue.

"Um . . . my dad told me to tell you that he has to call you back later

or maybe tomorrow. So can I get your name and number? He's outside on the deck with some of the people from the network and . . . he asked me to get your name and number and he'll call you some other time."

Some other time. She hadn't even given her name yet, so it wasn't personal. It was just that a man like that was always busy. But if she left a number for Jack to call her back, the switchboard operator would say Tropi-Cal Motel, and then . . .

"This'll just take a second," she tried. "Maybe he could just excuse himself for a second and . . ."

"No. He told me to take a number," Jason said to her.

"I'll try another time," she said and put down the phone.

THIRTY-TWO

THE HOURS they spent in the hospital on Saturday night and all day Sunday had a timelessness to them which was punctuated now and then by the need for one of them to leave for a few hours to attend to the practical business of her life. But nearly every issue in their own worlds was on hold or in the hands of others as they sat by the bed, continuing to talk to Jan or to one another.

Sometimes while they sat, now bundled in sweaters to warm them in the chilled hospital room, Marly read in a tired voice from *A Course in Miracles*. But the doctor's dour-faced visits and Andy's helpless eyes when he came in to join them told them without words that there would be no miracles. When Marly went home on Monday morning, she called Julie to tell her the news and to discuss the will.

"I mean, what are the chances she can make it?" It wasn't just the miles that caused the distance in Julie's voice. "I knew she had me in that will for taking her little boy. But I sure as hell don't want to be the one who says 'pull the plug' on my own sister. I'd have nightmares about that for the rest of my life." Marly's mind was filled with a jumble of images as she stood in her own room that morning and told Julie everything the doctor said about Janny's chances.

She wore only a towel as she looked out into the backyard. At the iron-and-glass table under the gazebo Maria sat having breakfast, while Joey, who had left his cereal behind, happily chased a butterfly around the lush green lawn. And among her white lacy bedclothes, stretching lazily, after a night of sleeping there "to be available for the children" was Billy. Waiting for her to finish her phone call and slide in next to him.

"I don't want the responsibility," Julie said, "and I already told Rose that I don't want the boy. But maybe we can come to some kind of terms about him." Marly wondered if terms meant money. Of course she was talking about money. Julie was willing to sell her right to Billy's guardianship. Marly was too tired to scream, too pained to fight. When Billy tugged gently at her towel, she decided she had better things to do than continue this conversation now.

"Maybe we *can* come to terms," she said.

"And as far as the rest of it goes," Julie told her, "you three friends do what the doctors think is best." That was said in a voice that meant she was winding up this conversation.

"Thanks, Julie," Marly said and she put the phone down and sat on the bed just as a happy squeal from Joey rose from the yard. Then Billy was behind her kissing her neck and her back and moving her body against his under the warm comforter, telling her he loved her and they would work on it all together. He would help her decide what to do, he would make it all be right.

After their lovemaking, she thought, as he took her nipple into his mouth and the sweet sensations filled her body, she'd tell him she wanted to adopt Joey.

When it was Rose's turn to go home, she made Molly breakfast and took a long bath. It was one of those vague school holidays, teachers' conference day or something, she was sure she should have known about but didn't, so at about nine she made a play date for Molly and then drove her to the friend's house.

"Mommy, are you sad?" Molly asked her.

"I'm more than sad, honey," Rose said, making a left turn off Valley Vista onto a street that was filled with jacaranda trees, their lavender blossoms falling gently onto the cars parked along the curb, and she remembered how much Jan loved jacarandas. "I'm devastated about Aunt Jan. I've loved her very much for a lot of years, and I know when I lose her, my life will never be as wonderful as it might have been with her in it."

Molly hugged her mother knowingly before she got out of the car. "Love you, Mom. And if you're alone and it gets too tough, come and get me and I'll come home and keep you company. Okay?"

"Okay, honey," Rose promised. When Molly was safely inside her friend's house, Rose turned on the car radio to the news station, and as she drove up Beverly Glen she was only half listening when the news man said Jan's name, and then she thought she heard the words "released for insufficient evidence." They were saying that the stalker had been released. Good God. He had to be the one who shot her, and they released him.

When she spotted the old gray car parked in her driveway, she felt a surge of fear under her ribs. Andy wasn't home, and her house was isolated just like Jan's. She felt some relief when she saw that the driver of the car was a woman. But instead of pulling into the garage, she pulled up alongside the car, and honked and startled the woman who looked at her.

It was Rita Connelly, the police officer. Both she and Rose got out of their cars and stood facing one another in the driveway. Rita Connelly looked pretty and fresh in a red wool blazer.

"I heard they released that fan," Rose said.

"He found his gun, and it was a thirty-eight but not the one that shot Jan O'Malley. How's she doing?"

"There's been no change in her. I don't . . . there probably isn't much hope," Rose said and her face crumbled into a teary mask and she patted her hip where her purse usually rested, hoping to find a Kleenex, but she'd left her purse in the car.

"I'm sorry," the police officer said and pulled a handkerchief out of her own pocket. It smelled of cigarettes, but Rose was glad to have it to wipe away her tears.

"Mrs. Schiffman," Rita said, looking searchingly into Rose's eyes, "I called the alumni office at Carnegie early this morning, and they told me that the person they faxed that list of names to, the person who called them last week and said they needed the list to do some heavy-duty fund-raising, was you."

Rose's stunned reaction was to let out a sharp little laugh.

"Me? That's crazy. I never got that fax. The first time I saw it was when you showed it to me. I never would have made that call. Somebody must have used my name."

"Got any idea who would do that? Do you know anyone in San Diego? It was faxed to San Diego. Have you been to San Diego lately?"

"When Molly was two, I took her to the zoo there. That was eight years ago. Someone's using my name. How do we find out who it is?"

"Let's call the alumni office together and see if they can tell us what else the person said," Rita Connelly suggested.

While Rose looked up the Pittsburgh telephone number on the Rolodex in her office and dialed it, Rita Connelly looked around at the pictures pushpinned to the cork board. She also squatted and looked down at the pieced-together photo on the floor of the four friends in front of the college dorm.

"What happened to this picture?"

"I don't know. I came home and found it like that."

"Carnegie Mellon University Alumni Office. This is Dee Dee, how may I help you?" The voice from the speakerphone filled the room.

"Dee Dee, this is Rose Schiffman, the real Rose Schiffman, I'm here with Officer Connelly of the L.A.P.D. She told me she spoke to you earlier. We're trying to find out who really called you last week and asked for the West Coast alumni addresses."

"Mrs. Schiffman, I'm so sorry about what happened to Jan O'Malley. Of all people. I'm the biggest fan of 'My Brightest Day.' I even bring a little TV to work so I can watch it. And if you're the real Mrs. Schiffman, your voice sure fits a lot better with what I imagined after I saw you on the Oscars the year *Faces* was nominated. I mean, I remember paying attention because I knew you graduated from here, and when they had that shot of you sitting next to your husband, wearing glasses and all, and looking so timid. I never would have thought you'd have such a big voice."

"The caller had a particularly big voice?" Rita Connelly asked.

"She did. I mean it was that deep, foggy kind of voice. Of course Suzanne Pleshette is tiny, too, isn't she? And she has a voice like that, but anyway, the woman who called here and said she was Mrs. Schiffman sounded a lot like her. You know the one who played Bob Newhart's wife on his show? And I think she was on 'The Rockford Files,' too.

"I'm really sorry, Mrs. Schiffman, I take all the blame for this. As I'm sure you know, we really try hard to maintain the privacy of our graduates, but it seemed like such a good idea for some-one with your connections to send out a letter to solicit funds for the new theater, which is what the woman I talked to said she was going to do, so I got overly enthusiastic and gave out that private information. I hope it was okay."

Rose sank into the chair that faced her messy desk. "It wasn't okay. It was anything but okay," she said, and pushed the button to disconnect the phone. When Rita Connelly left, Rose called Ellen in the office, and when she wasn't there, Greenie suggested she try the car.

"Guess who was the person who received the fax with the alum names on it," she said when Ellen answered.

"Who?" Ellen asked.

"Me."

"What?"

"Somebody with a deep voice called the school and said she was me."

"Maybe it was Harvey Fierstein. When he's in drag, he looks a little like you."

"Funny. The cop actually came to my house because they let the stalker go for no evidence, so they're probably desperate to pin this on someone."

"Do you think anyone would believe that I saw Alex Bibber-man leaving Jan's house on Friday?" Ellen asked.

"Maybe." Rose laughed.

"Shit, there's an accident up ahead," Ellen said. "I'm going to be late for the frigging meeting. Call you later."

She was in the far-left lane of the 405 freeway, unable to

budge because there was an accident up ahead. She dialed her direct line at the studio.

"Ellen Bass's office," Greenie answered.

"I'm going to be late for the meeting."

"I don't even know why you're coming to the meeting. You're going through a big trauma, El. The meeting can happen another day."

"I want to get it over with," she said.

"Do you need me to come and get you?"

"You'd have to have a helicopter to get me out of here. I'm in the far-left lane on the 405 and there's a serious fender bender about a half a mile up."

"Bibberman will say you didn't leave early enough."

"I left at seven-thirty. It usually takes me twenty minutes. I was planning to be in an hour early to go over some notes for the meeting. I'm trying very hard not to cry."

"I'm not. I'm going to cry my eyes out. Hold on. There's your other line."

Ellen looked at the rows of unmoving cars, wishing that instead of laughing about yoga every time Marly mentioned it to her, she'd taken a few classes. Classes that would have taught her how to breathe through her spine or some other bullshit that Marly said helped her to relax. She couldn't remember ever relaxing a day in her life. Marly was right, the job was toxic.

Click, Greenie was back on the line.

"It may not feel like it today, but you're a lucky woman," he said.

"Yeah? How so?"

"That was Bibberman's secretary. Jodie must be on the 405, too, she says she won't be here 'til ten."

"Oh, Greenie, thank God."

The freeway traffic didn't let up for nearly an hour, and by the time Ellen arrived at the lot it was two minutes before ten. There was no time to stop at her own office, so she headed straight for Schatzman's office. She was running, when she heard a woman's voice call her name.

"Ellen?" She turned.

"Jodie."

"How are you?"

"I'm . . . okay."

She wished she looked as cool and collected as Jodie Foster, who now moved down the hall to catch up with her. Ellen wore a black straight skirt, a black silk sweater, stockings, and an Escada blazer, and Jodie was wearing a brown denim skirt, an oversized white T-shirt, and sandals. You had to be young to have the confidence to wear that to a meeting. Jodie Foster would be brilliant in Rose's *Good-bye, My Baby*. Ellen thought.

As they walked down the hall together, Ellen remembered Jodie's subtle performance in *Silence of the Lambs*. She was a complex and thoughtful actress who loved intelligent women characters. None of the women she played were ever dippy or gratuitously sexual. Wouldn't it be perfect for her to star in and direct *Good-bye, My Baby*.

But Schatzman called it romantic drivel, and Bibberman called it a woman's sob story, so Ellen had given up ever having it done there.

"Isn't Jan O'Malley a friend of yours?" Jodie asked Ellen.

"She is. One of my closest."

"I thought I remembered that. I've been following it on the news. I'm so sorry."

Ellen sighed. "Thank you." They were nearly at Schatzman's office.

"Do they know who shot her? Was it a fan?"

"There was a fan stalking her, and they arrested him, but they released him this morning for lack of evidence. And there was always a doubt in my mind about him being the one anyway."

They were in Schatzman's reception area now, and the secretary waved a little wave to Ellen to indicate that they ought to go in. "Because Jan's housekeeper said she heard the doorbell ring and that then Jan let the person in."

Ellen and Jodie were still looking at one another, but Ellen could feel the four men trembling with excitement as they all stood wearing their we're-great-guys smiles on their faces. "That sounds odd to me," Jodie said, and then she and Ellen looked at the men. And Bibberman, so eager to be the first to say something, to be amusing, to tell a joke even if it was a bad one, blurted out, "Maybe she let the guy in for a quick shtup."

Both Ellen and Jodie froze. Ellen looked at the nervous eyes of Schatzman and Richardson, and she could tell they both thought it was an idiotic blunder for a million reasons. Ellen felt as stunned as if Bibberman had kicked her in the face. She was shaking with anger and the need to speak her mind. But she took an instant to consider what it could do to her career.

Roger's tuition. Her mother's rent. It didn't matter. She couldn't hold it back. "Bibberman, do you ever listen to yourself?" she asked. Her voice sounded vexed, but she wasn't shouting. She was glad she hadn't screamed at him the way she wanted to. The skin on her face burned hot. She could feel Jodie standing coolly next to her. "I've seen you do some dumb things, but this one truly wins the dumbshit-of-the-year award. This is even better than that quote I read in *Esquire* where Katzenberg said about Molly Ringwald that he wouldn't know her if she sat on his face. You're not just a misogynist, Bib, that would be bad enough. You're rude, thoughtless, perverse . . ."

"Ellen, this can wait . . ." Schatzman tried to interrupt her, but now she couldn't control the avalanche of rage.

"No. It can't. Because this poor schmuck has finally accomplished what he's been trying to do, and I want him to know it. I want him to get that his idiotic language, his attempts at exclusion, his bullying that defies the Crips and the Bloods, and the abject humiliation he does so well, have finally made me able to say those two words he's been waiting to hear. I quit. I quit because I can't spend another day at a company with a colleague who would do shtup-the-stalker material not just to me about one of my best friends who is dying, maybe due to that stalker, but irony of hilarious ironies, in a room with, of all people, Jodie Foster!

"It's almost too idiotic to be true! It's one of those aren't-people-in-the-business-idiots stories we can all tell for years to come. And now you'll probably want me to take her aside and tell her how sensitive you are."

What she just said made her laugh. She was so beaten up, so wrung out, so stressed in every way, she couldn't stop her own giggles. "Bibberman, it's so awful, it's brilliant. And the only thing I can do about it is to quit. You win, I quit. I am longing to get out of here, to run away and do anything in the world but have to see your nasty little face one more morning. And Jodie, if you're as smart as I think you are, you'll leave, too."

Then she turned and walked down the hall and out of the building to her bungalow to pack her things, alternately laughing and crying.

THIRTY-THREE

WHEN SHE WALKED UP to the drive-on gate at Hemisphere studios, the guard in the booth was talking to a guy in a yellow Rolls-Royce whom he waved by. Then he leaned out to talk to her.

"Hi," she said, "I'm a friend of Ellen Bass."

The guard smiled. "Lucky you," he said.

"I'm going to run by her office and say hi," she tried, thinking if she could get past the guard, once she was on the lot she could ask someone where Ellen's office was.

"And your name?" the guard asked, picking up a clipboard.

"My name?"

"Is she expecting you? If she is, her office left us your name."

"And if she doesn't know? I mean, I was just in the neighborhood and . . ."

"I'll call her office and clear you."

Her name would just draw a blank or, worse yet, bring a sneer from that snotty secretary of hers. "I want to surprise her," she said.

"Lady," the guard said to her, "over at Universal there was a guy who showed up not long ago and wanted to surprise everyone in the executive office building with an Uzi. Not that I think you look dangerous, but I like this job, and the rule is, I have to have you cleared or you go away, even if you're Arnold Schwarzenegger or Sylvester Stallone. That's the rule."

A tram full of tourists passed by just behind the guard, and she could hear the young woman in the red jacket who sat at the front of the tram speaking into a microphone, saying something about "the office buildings where all of the important decisions are made, just on your left, and behind it, the studio commissary. And further along you'll see *a group of bungalows where a select group of executives have their . . ."*

"I've known Ellen Bass for thirty years," she said quietly.

"Doesn't matter," the guard said.

"I guess not," she said, then turned and walked back toward the motel. She'd go in and have a cup of coffee and then pack her car and hit the road. She had nothing left. She had to go home. Back to that dumpy apartment and gray life in San Diego. Her money was almost gone, and she couldn't get to any of her old friends, couldn't get near them. People here spent their lives trying to get these big jobs and careers so they could be famous and in the public's face, and then once they made it, they had guards at gates.

Maybe she should try to get a regular job, a waitress job, just for now, until she could communicate with Ellen and convince her to hire her. Goddamn Ellen was right across the street, and she couldn't get to her. There had to be a way. In the motel coffee shop she sat at the counter, where there were no other customers, and ordered a toasted English muffin and some coffee, and when the waitress handed her somebody's used L.A. Times, she knew the woman recognized a kindred down-on-her-luck spirit.

The item on the police letting the guy go was on page three, and she tried to look nonchalant as she read it, but it made her sick. How could they let him go? What if they started a big investigation and somehow figured it was her. What if Jan got better the way they did on those soaps and told the police to go and find her. When she looked up and saw a police car pull up at the curb, she felt like vomiting.

"You on vacation here?" the waitress asked when she slid the plate with the toasted muffin in front of her. She was a soft, pudgy woman with a round, friendly face.

"Yeah," she said, trying to look like she was okay, and opening the little tin of strawberry jelly, but when she stuck a knife in it, the jelly oozed red like blood.

"We got coupons that can get you on that tour across the street for less than half price," the waitress said, as if she were talking to a child. "If you feel like it, you could check it out. I've never done it, but some of my customers have, and they say it's a ball and a half."

She swiped some jelly across the muffin, but she was just doing that to avoid the woman's expression, which was "You're a charity case, so I'll be nice to you."

"It's usually thirty bucks, but I think with these coupons, it's only about ten or twelve or something like that. Any interest?"

The knot in her chest cleared up when she saw the cop take a newspaper out of one of those coin machines at the curb, get back in the black-and-white, and drive away. "It's supposed to be Hollywood at its finest," the waitress said. She wanted to say to her, "Lady, I should be a star at that studio, not begging for coupons to go on some tram with a bunch of fat guys in Hawaiian shirts."

"The tram rides right through the sets of the shows they're shooting, and they point out the way they do all the stuff you see in movies. It even goes right past the office of the hoo-has who make the movies, and the big deal commissary. One of these days I'm gonna go over and do it myself."

When the waitress put the tab down in front of her, she slid a coupon along with it, and said to her with a wink, "You ought to think about going on over there, girl. It'll cheer you up."

THIRTY-FOUR

WITHIN HOURS all of the bookshelves in Ellen's big, airy, bungalow office at Hemisphere Studios were empty. The dozens of books and screenplays and photographs, which until that morning had jammed the white lacquer shelves, were now almost all packed into moving boxes, and the open boxes lined the walls of the room.

A warm breeze blew through the open window and rustled the to-do list Greenie had put on the desk, a list on which nearly everything was crossed off. The only items left in the room, besides the furniture, were the TV and the VCR, which both belonged to the studio. He sighed, thinking there was still the bathroom to finish, but Ellen would have to clear that room out herself so she could decide what she wanted to save and what she wanted to toss.

"I remember the day we moved into this office with such high hopes, and now look at this exit, like Jews running from Cossacks," he said.

Marly, dressed in faded jeans and a black cashmere sweater, her white hair pinned up by a black barrette, had arrived from her hospital shift to help. She insisted she had to help Ellen make a fast exit from Hemisphere Studios. She said it was something she was good at because of her work with battered women. "It was never in Ellen's life myth to work for those men," she said to Greenie as they loaded the last few boxes, "and this is what's supposed to happen."

"Honey, it's a myth to call them men," Greenie said. "They're mice. And this is one mean, fuckin' town." He was measuring a piece of tape to the proper length and then cutting it with a scissors. "One of my friends, a woman producer, made a great movie that bombed at the box office, and afterward she said to me 'Gee, I don't know why they say it's cold in this town. I got fifty calls from people telling me they felt awful that my movie was such a financial disaster! Wasn't that sweet of them?' Sweet my adorable tush. If the picture had been a hit, not one of those jealous jerkoffs would have dialed her number."

Marly walked from box to box, taping each one shut, while Greenie followed her and marked the box with some reference to its contents. "They were so pissed at Ellen for her style of saying good-bye, they cut our phone lines," Greenie said. Ellen was outside in the parking area, but through the open window of the stucco cottage she could hear him.

"Which I guess is nothing, since one studio exec we know disagreed with the biggie and came in to find his office furniture on the lawn. So get this," he said. "I went over to the commissary to get an apple for myself, and I tried to call Ellen from there to see if she wanted one, too, and when I dialed the number, the studio operator got on the line and said, 'Sorry, sir, that number is no longer in service.' I said 'The fuck it isn't! You'd better put me through, you puppet of the Armani Advantaged, or I'll come over there and strangle you with the switchboard wires.' "

Marly let out a hoot of her most outraged laugh. "What'd she do?" she asked.

"She hung up on me, natch. She couldn't defy them."

Ellen lifted a heavy box full of scripts that fell into the category of writing she loved and which she'd tried to get the "boys" to do, but on which they'd passed, "and pissed," she thought as she put the box into the trunk of her car. Now maybe she'd have a chance of seeing the projects through at another studio. She felt light with the relief of knowing that after today, she never had to set foot on this lot again. That she was freed from the churning, stomach acid–producing anxiety she'd felt every time she'd walked into a room with that heinous group of executives.

"They gave her less than a day to get out of here. The car lease guy is coming to her house tonight to pick up the BMW," Greenie said.

Ellen smiled. Greenie was as glad as she was to be getting out of this place. She'd already had a call from Jodie Foster about a job, or at least about some projects they could do together.

"Schatzman knows that Ellen made every deal that was worth anything last year. In fact, she saved his heavily used ass a few times, and still he let all that sexist shit go right past him, like he wasn't even hearing it. If you ask me, they're all a bunch of . . ."

Greenie's tirade was drowned out for Ellen by the voice of the tour guide on the approaching tram, ". . . brilliant studio executives who develop and nurture the fabulous films you stand in line to see," the guide was saying in a saccharine voice. "Some of those executives have offices in the one-story bungalows on the left." The sound of the tram full of tourists, trundling by her office at regular intervals, had become such a usual part of her day, such a part of the studio's revenue-producing business, that Ellen rarely thought much about it.

Sometimes when she was on a long phone call, she'd look out the window and study the faces of the passing tourists, wondering who they were and what their lives were like. But mostly she'd learned to block out the sound and the interruption the trams full of curious tourists caused when outdoor shooting had to pause as one of them clanked noisily past a set. She'd learned not to grit her teeth when she was in a hurry, in her car, to get somewhere on the back lot, and found herself behind one of the noisy metal vehicles, having to inch along and overhear the same cutesy spiel repeated by the tour guide to the eager tourists who had paid thirty bucks a head for the privilege.

Today it was Rose's little white Mustang convertible stuck behind the tram. As the tram finally rumbled along on its way, Rose tapped a little hello beep to Ellen, then pulled into one of the spots nearby.

"Rosie?" Ellen asked nervously. "Is it . . . ?"

"Jan's the same," she said. "Maria left Joey with Billy and the twins and drove over to the hospital. She asked me if she could sit with Jan for a while. They've been together for a long time, and I understood. So I came here, but . . ." Her eyes were blinking furiously behind her glasses, the way they did when she was angry. "I drove up to the guard and said I was coming to your office, and he said you no longer worked here. I said I knew you didn't but I was coming to help you move . . . and he just shook his head and shrugged his shoulders."

"Oh, God," Ellen said. "When Marly got here, the guard was still clearing people to come here, but now they must have been told that I'm off limits." She shook her head. "I can't believe the fuckers have gotten to the guards, too."

Rose was fuming. "I've known that guard for years, I've been here a thousand times in the last twenty-five years. I said, 'Frenchie, what do I have to do to get on the lot?' He said, 'You have to be cleared by someone who works here, Rose.' He was giving me a tip. Telling me if I could get clearance from somebody else, he'd let me go by. So I pulled over to the side and got on my car phone and called Will Staple's office, and his secretary cleared me. What is wrong with those people?"

"It doesn't matter," Ellen said. "It just reaffirms my resolve to get as far away from these nasty lowlifes as I can. Maybe we can even get *Good-bye, My Baby* made, Rosie, by somebody who will understand it. I sent it over to Jodie this morning, and she already called to say she loved it."

Rose hugged her.

"Sure, sure, now Rose shows up, when all the work is finished," Greenie teased through the window when he spotted her out there. "Get in here and tote those boxes."

Rose grinned. "I'm on my way," she said and started for the bungalow. Ellen closed the trunk of her car just as another tram rolled up the street. ". . . brilliant studio executives, who develop and nurture the fabulous films you go to see. Some of those executives have offices in the one-story bungalows on the left."

Ellen walked into the office and looked at the passing tram out the window. At least they had tinted those windows, so she could look out but the tourists couldn't see in. Good-bye Schatzman, so long Bibberman, she thought, good-bye tours. I won't miss you.

On the streets of the back lot, the trams moved like snails to give the tourists time to snap pictures of the famous sights they remembered from their favorite films. But around these executive offices, since there was so little of interest for them to see, sometimes the tram drivers had been known to put a little weight on the accelerator.

So the tram was clipping along at a pretty good pace at that moment, and Ellen wasn't a hundred per cent sure, but for an instant, she looked at the wistful face of a woman, a passenger on the tram who was leaning on the rail, who looked strangely familiar to her.

A woman who was older, no, maybe not so much older, but haggard and tired-looking, with graying-at-the-temples-hair. She was wearing a black cardigan sweater and carrying a big striped purse. She was so familiar that it gnawed at Ellen as she walked over the threshold into the office.

The bathroom, she thought, coming back to the reality of the move. She wondered if Greenie had packed up her things from the pretty tiled bathroom in her bungalow. When he saw her on her way in there, he called out, "I did most of it, but there are still a few little things I wasn't sure about, so they're on the counter." Absently, later she remembered it was absently, she went into the bathroom and tossed the remaining cosmetics into the half-full moving box on which Greenie had marked E.B. BATHROOM STUFF.

"Thank God for Jodie Foster," she heard him saying. "Otherwise I'd be looking in the *L.A. Times* for employment opportunities. And I have zero skills. All I know how to do in this world is to say, 'Sorry, she's very busy!' That qualifies me to do what? Answer phones for Heidi Fleiss!" Ellen and Rose laughed at that joke. "Well now, at least we're looking at possible jobs."

Tampons, hair spray, lozenges. *Jobs.* A vent brush, a blusher brush, a tube of lipstick in a color she no longer wore. *Receptionist. Proofreader. Nanny.* That's what those words meant that someone had written next to all of their names on the list. Jobs. An empty bottle from an old prescription of an antibiotic, prescribed by Dr. Andrew Schiffman. She tossed it into the wastebasket. A bottle of her cologne. Norell.

Betty Norell. The name hit her, and when it did, so did a lot of other thoughts that rushed at her like an oncoming train. *Chichester. If only it were open all year round, I'd never leave the place.* That's what Randy McVey said in the meeting. Chichester was the theater started by Olivier, and Rose said that's where Betty Norell worked in the winter.

She put the cologne bottle down on the counter and walked into the office, where the others were taping the last few boxes. "Who remembers what it said on that list? The one Rita Connelly had with all of our names on it."

"Names and home addresses," Marly said.

"And some other words that somebody wrote on it," Rose said, "like nanny, and . . .

Jobs. Proofreader. Receptionist. "The list was made by Betty Norell," Ellen said. "She thought she'd come here and one of us would give her a job. Next to Rose is where it said proofreader, next to me it said receptionist . . . and Jan . . . next to Jan it said nanny." She was pale and fearful. "What did Jack Solomon say the other night about her?" she asked.

"Oh, some long story about how her daughter was searching for her and he was such a good guy he took her call, even though he was in a meeting with God or somebody like that," Rose said.

Greenie looked up from the last box. "That name sounds familiar," he said. "Betty Norell." He was processing the name. "Is that someone you know?" he asked and shuffled through the box he'd been about to close. "She sent you a video ages ago," he said to Ellen. "No," he sighed. "It's not in here."

"What kind of video?" Ellen asked.

"You know, like all those kooks out there who send in their home tapes, all those people out there who read articles about you and think you can make them a star. I just figured she was one of those, so I put it in the cupboard with all the rest of them. I had no idea you knew her. I mean, I think in her note she said something like, 'Hi, Ellen. Take a look at this and let me know if you have a part for me.' But they all say that, try to sound so chummy. In fact, now that I think about it, I think she may have even called here, but wouldn't say what she wanted, so I didn't put her through. I mean, you get dozens of calls like that a week."

"Can you put your hands on the video?" Ellen asked.

"Maybe," Greenie said and tore the tape from one of the sealed boxes. "Who is she?"

"She was the best actress in our class at Tech," Marly said.

"Betty Norell shot Janny," Ellen said, sitting because she didn't think her legs could hold her any more. And then she put it all together for them, all the thoughts that were rushing around in her mind. She collected them and then blurted them all out. Starting with the fact that the list the police found in Jan's front hall had jobs next to each of their names. It was faxed to San Diego, where Betty Norell lived, to someone who said she was Rose but had a voice that sounded like Suzanne Pleshette. A voice that was so deep Maria could have mistaken it for a man's voice.

"But I thought Betty Norell spent winters in repertory in England," Rose said. "At the theater started by Olivier. What's it called? Chichester. That's what it says in the alumni magazine."

"That's what she writes in to the people who put together the alumni magazine," Ellen said. "They don't check. I could tell them I owned the world and they'd put it in there. But it's a lie. Chichester is only open in the summer."

"Why tell that lie?" Rose asked.

"Maybe because it's the dream we all had for ourselves at Tech. To never sell out. To only do important work. To be true to the theater," Marly guessed. "I know I'm jealous every time I read that."

"Yes!" Greenie said suddenly, pulling a video cassette out of one of the boxes and then out of its sleeve. "Shall we?" he asked and shoved it into the VCR. There was a black screen, then a hand-lettered sign that said, BETTY NORELL SWANSON, THE GLASS MENAGERIE. PRODUCED BY HER DAUGHTER POLLY SWANSON. After an instant there she was, with gray hair, a lined face, the way she'd looked in *The House of Bernarda Alba* when she played the ugly jealous sister.

"As you know, I was supposed to be inducted into my office

at the D.A.R. this afternoon," she said in the character of Amanda Wingfield in *The Glass Managerie*.

"I remember when she did a scene at Tech from this and she played Laura, the daughter," Rose said.

"We all used to play the daughter, dear," Marly said, and Greenie turned up the volume on Betty's voice. It was a great, deep, resonant sound.

"But I stopped off at Rubicam's business college to talk to your teachers about your having a cold and to ask them what progress they thought you were making down there," she said, and her performance was already powerful. She had just spoken a few lines, but her instincts about the character were so strong, her ability to lose herself within the role so sharp, that she was well into it. That expression on her face was the look of a mother whose dreams had all crashed to the ground.

Ellen put a cold hand on her own hot face. The woman she was seeing was the woman on the tram, the woman carrying a striped purse. The striped purse Eddie the pool man had seen when Betty Norell came to her house looking for her. Probably she was the next one to be attacked. The way she'd attacked Jan. But why? It didn't matter why.

"She's on the lot. Call security," Ellen said out loud. Her voice was filled with terror. "I saw her go by on the tour, a few minutes ago. She probably took the tour to get on the lot, and she must be planning to shoot me next." Betty Norell, the best actress in the class, had sent her a tape, and she'd never watched it. Betty Norell was the one who shot Jan, and now . . .

"The phones are dead," Greenie reminded her.

"Well, I may be, too, if you don't get through, now! Call from my car. Tell them they have to cover all the trams and find a middle-aged woman carrying a big striped purse."

Greenie grabbed Ellen's keys and ran out the door to her car.

"My God, I just remembered," Rose said. "A long time ago, right around the time Allan was so ill, I got a letter from her. It was sent to my agent's office because the Writers' Guild won't give out our home addresses, but they will tell people who want to reach us who our agents are, and she said something like, 'I know you're some big fancy hotshot now, and don't have time for someone like me, but you better help me.' I thought it was so mean-spirited, and I was hurting so much from my own loss, I never answered it."

"But why would she want to kill you? Not returning somebody's calls isn't a reason for murder," Marly said. "If it *was*, the whole William Morris office would be dead." Nobody laughed.

"Who knows. Jealous, enraged at what she perceives is our unqualified success," Ellen said.

Greenie entered, red-faced. "Security says they can't do anything for you. They told me if you have problems, you'll have to take care of them yourself," he said.

"Then let's go," Ellen said.

"Where?" Rose asked.

The video was still on and now Amanda Wingfield was saying ". . . little birdlike women without any nest, eating the crust of humility all their life!"

"Ellen, this tour is so huge, and if you think you saw her go by a few minutes ago, she could be anywhere now," Greenie said. "There are shows, and rides, and stores, and stands, and booths, and thirty thousand people a day doing them. You've been back there often enough to know how nuts it would be to try and find her. Besides, what if she has a gun and figures out that you're looking for her? Let's call the police and let them take care of this."

"Fine, call Rita Connelly at the West Hollywood Police station. Tell her to rush here. But by the time she does, this woman could be gone. I'm going to find her. She shot our friend." Ellen pulled her car keys out of Greenie's hand and rushed out the door of the bungalow.

Marly looked at Rose. "I think this falls into the category of Turkish prisons and backs of ambulances, kiddo, so we'd better go, too."

The dark-tinted windows of Ellen's BMW made the squintingly bright day look grayish to Rose as she slid in.

"Where are we going to look first?" she asked, leaning forward from the backseat and talking to Ellen, who was backing the car out of her parking place.

"I don't have a fucking clue," Ellen admitted.

"I've never been on the Hemisphere tour," Marly said.

"Well, don't say I never take you anywhere," Ellen said, and she floored the car up the hill toward the tour center.

THIRTY-FIVE

Rose ENVIED the camera-toting, summer-clothed groups of people, walking with their arms around one another from the parking lot to the ticket booth. A large group of Japanese tourists were having their photo taken together, laughing and jockeying for position in front of the HEMISPHERE HOLLYWOOD sign. A photo, she thought, taken of the four of them at Tech. What in the hell was it doing ripped up and in her wastebasket? That particular photo.

This morning when Antonia, her three-day-a-week cleaning lady, came in, Rose asked her if she knew anything about it, but her cleaning lady looked at the pieces Rose had assembled, and she shook her head.

"I never thought I'd see the day I'd actually pay to do this," Ellen said as she parked. The three of them got out of the car into the glaring sunny day, and walked over to the ticket kiosks to stand in line behind a large noisy family with seven children, all under the age of twelve. "While we're waiting, we'd better figure out if we're staying together or splitting up, if one of us takes the shops and another one takes the rides and another one takes the shows until we find her."

"And more important, what we do *if* we find her," Rose said. "I'm afraid. If you're right, she could still have the gun. I turned down a big offer to do a rewrite on *Kindergarten Cop* because I hate guns."

Ellen slid her company MasterCard under the glass to the woman in the ticket booth and held her breath, wondering if the studio schmucks had canceled that, too, but somehow the charge card she used for all of her expense account items must have slipped their minds, because it cleared, and the woman handed her three tickets and three brochures.

"Are we having fun yet?" she asked Marly and Rose, and nudged them through the turnstile. Inside the gate they stopped to psych out what they were going to do, and Rose and Ellen looked at Marly, who had her eyes closed.

"What the fuck are you doing?" Ellen said. "Asking your bladder where Betty's hiding?"

"I'm getting in touch with my natural knowingness, which is going to help me intuit how we should best do this," Marly said softly, her eyes still closed.

Rose saw Ellen's impatience rise, and she was feeling angry herself, and afraid, and not so sure that all of this wasn't some manifestation of Ellen's being forced to move off the lot in such an ugly, stress-provoking way. Betty Norell had been a nice, quiet girl at Tech. She tried to remember the times they'd interacted in those days. To picture her in her mind, in the dorms, in the cafeteria.

Betty had run downstairs with her the day she and Allan were pinned. Stood next to her. And Betty . . . one memory stopped her, and chilled her. Wasn't it Betty Norell who had snapped the now torn picture of the four of them? Wasn't she walking by them one day right after Marly got her new camera, and they were all laughing and carrying on and taking pictures of one another and were dying to have a picture of the four of them together. Didn't Betty Norell walk by, and didn't one of them ask her to take that picture? That had to be a coincidence. Even if she was here, in town, even if she was the one who shot Jan, there was no way she could have found her way into Rose's home office.

"We should stay together," Marly said. Rose was feeling cold in the blazing-hot day.

"Yes, stay together," she said, relieved. She wouldn't have known what to do if she was alone and suddenly looked into the eyes of Betty Norell.

Ellen didn't have an idea or a plan, so after a minute she agreed. "Okay, we'll stay together. First let's walk, and look over the crowd and see if we spot her. The trams all look alike, but after a while they empty out down below at the centers where there are shops or rides or shows. Let's try to figure out what she'd want to do here. I mean besides kill me? Not spend money, not go on rides, maybe see the make-up show? Or the stunt show?''

She was brainstorming. Rose recognized the style. Just the way she did sometimes with other writers. Nonstop talking on the subject, in the hope that somehow from the unconscious tumble of words a valuable idea would surface. ''What attraction on the Hemisphere lot would interest a frustrated actress?'' Ellen asked herself out loud. She stopped a passing red-jacketed tour guide. ''Can you tell me what displays here are interactive? Which ones actually use people from the audience as part of the show?''

''Uh . . . well, let's see . . . ,'' the young man said, thinking. ''There's makeup, they make you up as a monster, you ladies might enjoy that. Or, there's the shooting match. They dress some of the folks in Western gear and they have a fake shoot-out with some of our stunt guys. And . . . oh yeah. There's a real good one over at the looping and dubbing stage. Some of the people in that audience get to put on a headset and then put their voice to a star's face, and then those guys play it back on the screen and it's totally cool. You ladies might like that one. The only thing is, there's a long line, so you might have to wait about fifteen minutes or so. But it's worth it.''

''Thanks,'' Ellen said, and hurried ahead with the others following close behind her.

They wove in and out of baby strollers and laughing teenagers and large groups of tourists with guides translating what they saw into their native languages. Actors dressed in costumes of Dracula and Frankenstein and King Kong romped past them, entertaining the noisy, boisterous throng.

On the Western street there was a large group of spectators, and all of them were looking up at a cowboy standing on the roof of an old western saloon. Then, from around the back of the saloon came a nervous-looking man, obviously a tourist volunteer, dressed in studio cowboy attire, designed to get a laugh, with the too-big hat and the chaps and a big silver star that said SHERIFF pinned to his barrel chest.

"Git your hands up, sheriff," the cowboy on the roof called out, holding his gun on the little dressed-up man below. But the tourist, doing what he'd rehearsed, pulled the blank gun out of his holster and pulled the trigger. The man was so short and the stunt man so high up that when the shot rang out, the gun wasn't even aimed at the stunt man.

Nevertheless the stunt man contorted his face, clutched his chest, fell to the roof, and then as the audience moved back gasping with horror, they watched him tumble off the roof to the ground in a brilliant fall. The tourist blew at the end of his own gun in a gesture of triumph, and the crowd cheered as the stunt man jumped to his feet and took a bow.

Ellen scanned the crowd nervously, but there was no one there who looked like Betty Norell. "Let's go," she said, and Marly and Rose followed. At the entertainment center they wandered into shops filled with thousands of images of the characters in their films, on their television shows. Every possible merchandising gimmick was there.

"Don't move or I'll kill you," said a deep voice and Rose spun around to see a man holding a Hemisphere 50 soaker water gun at his wife, who frowned.

"Oh, Harold, put that down," she said, "and come and look at these sweatshirts."

The clothing, the videos, the viewers, the dolls, the jewelry and key chains and mugs and posters. All of them caught the bright sunlight of the warm day as the tourists pulled the items greedily from the shelves, then waited in long lines to pay their money for the overpriced junk.

"Special effects," Ellen said, tugging at Rose's sleeve. "Let's go there."

The guide had been right. There was a big line at the special effects studio. There was a show going on at that moment, and the number of people in the line probably meant they would have to wait through at least one more seating before it was their turn to go in.

"She could be in there already," Ellen said. "I guess I'll have to make like a suit," and she fished in her purse, pulling out her wallet, and from it a photo ID the studio policy insisted all employees carry. "Wish me luck," she said, and moved aggressively up to the front of the line, where a red-coated male employee who looked like a bodyguard stood at the door.

Rose and Marly watched her talking to him, showing him her ID, and then saw the way his eyes lit up. Most of the young people in these tour jobs were in their early twenties and had aspirations to stardom, so meeting an important studio executive was a big deal to them. Ellen seemed to be smoothly informing him why she and her friends had to go in to the stage right now on a business matter. There would have been no reason for Bibberman and company to tell the tour people that Ellen was persona non grata, so the young man, dazzled by her ID, nodded in approval. Ellen gestured for Rose and Marly to join her, and they moved ahead to enter the sound stage, where the demonstration was already in progress.

They edged along quietly until they were standing at the top of the bleachers full of people, just near the steps to the control booth. Ken Moss, a sound man Ellen recognized because he'd worked on a few of her pictures, explained to the audience what they were about to see. Ken was a good-looking mustached blond of about forty-five.

"In film," he said to the group of a few hundred, "audio and video are always recorded separately. The sound tracks are recorded by the audio person, who you can't see right now because he's back in that booth, and the video obviously by the camera people. When dailies, which means the film shot each day, and any of the rough cuts of the film are shown, they're projected double system, which means the audio and the video are playing separately but cued up, or in sync.

"Once the film is cut to everyone's satisfaction, it's prepared for completion. To do that, the picture is color-corrected and the various sound tracks are worked on. There are three separate sound tracks at this point. Dialogue, sound effects, and music."

A piercing scream made Ellen jump and the other two hold on to one another, until they saw it was a restless baby a mother couldn't quiet. The embarrassed woman stood and walked out with the now screaming baby as Ken went on. "Dialogue tracks are corrected and enhanced by looping. That means the sound plays on a continuous loop, sent to an actor through a headset, and he or she speaks the dialogue to match the picture projected on a screen in front of him or her."

Rose and Marly and Ellen scanned the group. It was dimly lit in the studio, but not one of the people there remotely resembled Betty Norell. Rose sighed with relief. Let the police find her, she thought. Let Rita Connelly with her gun do this. "She's not in here," she whispered to Ellen. "I don't see her."

Ellen nodded, and the three of them started for the door. "Sometimes," Ken said, "the actor will turn out to have the wrong voice for a part, and the film will have to be revoiced. A voice-over actor will be brought in and work with the director to put his or her voice to the part already acted by someone else. So let's say Joanne Woodward has played the part," he said, and the stage got dark as Joanne Woodward's face came up on the screen.

It was Joanne Woodward years ago, in some old film like *Rachel, Rachel,* and the print was in black and white. "But we're going to pretend that Joanne, brilliant actress that she is, simply wasn't able to get the emotion the director wanted, so the director had to call in another person. And that person was our volunteer from the audience, who is backstage, and will she please come out now, and her name is . . . What's your name, dear?"

"Betty," they heard a deep, rich voice reply.

And all three of them froze. They had been an instant away from walking out of that sound stage, and now they turned to see Betty Norell in a spotlight next to Ken, who was guiding her to a stool next to a microphone on a podium. "Betty, you have a lovely voice," Ken said.

Betty smiled and clutched her big striped purse close to her body. "Thank you," she said.

"Betty has so kindly volunteered to improvise a little scene so that we can loop, if you will, Joanne Woodward with Betty. Inserting Betty's voice into the film. To show you what the process is like we call revoicing. And if she's really good at being Joanne Woodward, we'll see if we can get Betty a date with Paul Newman." The audience laughed, but Betty looked very uncomfortable.

"When we've finished, we'll play it back, run the new sound against the film so you and Betty can see how it works." The friends were close together now, behind the audience, afraid and mesmerized at the same time. "So, Betty, you put this headset on, and face the screen, and when you hear the beeps, you start doing a speech. Anything. Your grocery list will be okay, or you can recite a poem you learned in elementary school, a little speech that's about two minutes long, because that's the length of Joanne's monologue. Are you okay about this?"

Betty nodded. "Good. Well, I'm going to run up into the booth now, and Betty's going to revoice Joanne," Ken said, and he hurried off the stage. The three friends watched him lope toward the booth, spotting Ellen as he did, and smiling in surprise, then blowing her a kiss before he disappeared.

Betty sat on the stool with the headset over her frowzy hair, with an odd faraway look in her eyes as if she were getting into a role and thinking about the character's given circumstances. Her posture changed, her carriage was suddenly commanding and interesting, fascinating to watch. And when Ken's voice came from the booth and said, "Okay, Betty, I'm about to roll the sound," she took a deep breath. The picture rolled, and after a moment Joanne Woodward's lips moved and Betty began.

"Sometimes having great wealth makes people lonely!" she said, as her deep, rich voice filled the studio. Rose put her hand on Ellen's arm and squeezed. This was the beginning of a speech she'd heard before, but she had to remember when. From some play, but she couldn't remember which one it was.

Betty was getting into it now. "A cultivated woman, a woman of intelligence, can enrich a man's life, immeasurably," she said, as Joanne Woodward's lips moved on the screen. "I have those things to offer," Betty said, with just a trace of the southern dialect that any actress would want to use for Blanche DuBois. And of course, that was it, Rose remembered, Blanche's speech to Stanley in *A Streetcar Named Desire*.

"... and this doesn't take them away."

People in the audience were stirring uncomfortably. They had expected this to be funny. They had figured this would be some person who would be doing what they would do if they had been chosen, which was to blunder through the scene. After all, they had just spent the morning in a fake tornado, having bogus Indians shoot at their tram, having the Loch Ness monster rise from the waterway as they crossed, and all the other hilarious things that had happened on the tour so far. They couldn't understand why this woman was so serious, and so dramatic, saying these things that sounded as if they really were lines from a movie.

"Physical beauty is passing. A transitory possession. But beauty of the mind and richness of the spirit and tenderness of the heart, and I have all those things, aren't taken away, but grow! Increase with the years!"

"Hey, she's good," Marly heard someone in the row in front of them whisper. "She must be a shill."

"I'm going to the booth," Ellen whispered and quietly hurried out of the back row, up the four steps into the control booth, and closed the door behind her.

"How strange that I should be called a destitute woman, when I have all those treasures locked in my heart," Betty Norell said with her head held high the way Blanche would, but the broken voice gave away the character's terror.

She was getting to the guts of the role perfectly, just the way she had so many years ago at Tech. In fact, now, in the spot where Rose thought she remembered Tennessee Williams's stage directions asked for a choked sob from Blanche, Betty Norell emitted a choked sob, then managed to pull herself together as the rapt audience looked on.

"I think of myself as a very, very rich woman!" Betty said. "But I have been foolish, casting my pearls before swine. You and your friend Mr. Mitchell. He came to see me tonight. He dared to come here in his work clothes! And to repeat slander to me he got from you! I gave him his walking papers. But then he came back! He returned with a box of roses to beg my forgiveness."

The film stopped, and Joanne Woodward's face was frozen in stillness on the screen. "Betty!" The voice over the PA was Ken's. "You're wonderful," he said, "but I have to stop you here and ask you to . . ."

"Don't interrupt me," Betty snapped, angrily reeling around and looking in the direction of the booth, and she put her hand up in a salute to shade her eyes from the light, as if that would help her to see into the booth. "I wasn't finished," she said, enraged by the rude interruption. "The important part is coming up. I don't want to stop yet."

"Well, ladies and gentlemen, we've discovered a star," Ken's voice said with what sounded like amusement, "with a star complex to match. I know, Betty, I know that you want to go on, very much, but now it's time for me to do my job and play the scene back so everyone can see what a good job you did." Betty was flushed with embarrassment and anger and with a melodramatic move, she pulled a gun from her big striped purse.

"I want to finish the scene," she said, and the audience exploded with laughter. They were right. She *was* a shill, and this was another funny stunt, like the one with the Indians. "I'm not kidding," Betty said, her eyes wild with anger at their laughter. "I'll kill anyone, everyone," she said, but the audience thought that was funny, too.

Rose and Marly held on to one another, and then they heard Ellen's voice over the PA.

"Betty, it's okay. Everything is okay. This is Ellen Bass."

Betty looked around nervously, then up at the booth.

"Who?" she asked, squinting in the direction of the voice.

"Ellen Feinberg. Remember me?"

Betty's eyes were wide. "Is it really?" she asked. She was trembling.

"I work here, Betty, at this studio. I think you went past my office a little while ago."

"I know you work here. I've been following your career from day one! My plan was to get off the tram and try to find your office in that big glass building, but when I stood up the guy said we couldn't get off the tram there. They wouldn't even put my calls through to you. Who do you think you are, Ellen, treating people so badly? I sent you a tape and you never even watched it."

"I did watch your tape. I've been very busy but I managed to watch your tape just recently, and you were sensational in it," Ellen said in a voice Rose knew was phony, and that Ellen probably used fifty times a day with actors and directors and writers she had to brush off nicely. Betty pouted grudgingly, holding the gun on the audience in general.

Rose heard someone in the audience whisper, "What in the hell's going on here?"

"I even called your house to make you an offer," Ellen said.

"What kind of an offer?"

"A part in a movie I'm going to make."

"Like shit," Betty said, her doubting eyes angry with a look that said they'd been disappointed too often to fall for this.

"I did. I talked to your daughter."

"You're lying. My daughter doesn't even live at my house."

"I know, but she was there, looking for you. She was worried because you'd been gone for a few days and nobody knew where to find you," Ellen said.

"Yeah? What's my daughter's name?"

"Her name is Polly," Ellen said. "Betty, I know she must be proud of your talent. So am I, Betty. I still want to offer you a role in a film I'm making."

"You're a fucking liar. Everyone in show business is a liar. Phony, lying assholes. No-talents who think their money makes them hot shit."

Rose squeezed Marly's arm, and then she whispered, "You've got to admit, she is right about that."

"It's a great part, Betty, and you won't even have to test for it, because I already have your tape. So put the gun down now, and come up to the booth."

Betty looked confused, and very afraid. "Ellen," she asked in a voice filled with worry, "do you think I look old?" Marly emitted an audible pained sound. It was the question the close friends often asked one another, and the loving answer was always, "You look sensational."

"Betty," came the reply from the booth, and Rose heard the emotion in Ellen's voice, "I think you look sensational."

Betty harumphed as if she didn't believe that lie, either. "Jan said I looked good, too," she said. "And I thought she looked wonderful. I didn't want to hurt her. I didn't want to."

"Betty," Ellen said, "wait till you see me. My belly's so round these days, I have to buy my control-top panty hose in industrial strength."

A big laugh swept through the audience. Rose was terrified that the laughter would make Betty shoot the gun, but instead Betty laughed, too. "So do I," she said, but she didn't drop the gun. "Tell me about the part in the movie," she said, very serious now, and turning suddenly to hold the gun on a woman who had dropped something noisily in the front row. The audience gasped. They were getting to the point where they weren't sure what to make of this whole scene.

"It's called . . . Good-bye, My Baby. And the woman is a mature, womanly adult who . . . has a dying husband," Ellen improvised.

"Yeah . . . and what happens?"

"We're trying to get Kevin Costner to play your husband," Ellen said.

Betty lit up. "Swear to God? I love Kevin Costner," she said, and that was when she dropped her arm for an instant, and the burly guard who was standing at the door tackled her and another one grabbed the gun. The audience on the sound stage loved it, and they all burst into wild applause.

"Oh, God. I didn't mean it," Betty said. "Don't hurt me. I didn't mean to kill her. I only wanted to get into the business . . ."

Rose put her face on Marly's shoulder. She couldn't bear to watch Betty's struggle as they carried her away, through the door of the sound stage.

"Thank you, ladies and gentlemen," they heard Ken's voice saying over the PA as the lights came up. "Next show in ten minutes."

"He never even played the film back," Rose heard someone say in the line as the people filed out of the sound stage, and she and Marly went up to the booth to find Ellen.

THIRTY-SIX

WHEN THEY ARRIVED at the hospital that night, they were asked to wait because the doctor was still in with Jan. While they stood at the nurses' desk, Ellen noticed that the cubicle where she'd visited with Fred Zavitz was empty. A young frizzy-haired nurse she hadn't seen before sat at a computer keyboard, typing.

"I guess Freddy Zavitz made it out of here," Ellen said to the nurse, who looked up distractedly, then focused on what Ellen had just said.

"Oh, they took Mr. Zavitz away a few hours ago. He died of cardiac arrest."

Ellen leaned sorrowfully against the nurses' counter and listened to the plunking of the computer keys. A nurse came out of Jan's cubicle, and a few seconds later she was followed by the neurosurgeon. He stopped when he saw Rose and Ellen.

"You can go in and talk to her now," was all he said.

Ellen walked slowly past him and into the room and over to the bed, seeing Jan's face without a tube in it for the first time since the shooting. Her cheeks were gaunt, but her skin was luminous, and her expression was peaceful.

"Janny," Ellen said, standing close to the bed. "Betty Norell is in police custody. She was arrested this afternoon. She won't hurt anyone else. I can't imagine how she could ever hurt you. She was at the studio looking for the rest of us when we caught her." Rose stood back as if waiting in line for her turn as Ellen went on.

"I wanted you to know that so you wouldn't worry. I also want to thank you for all the joy you've brought to my life from the day you borrowed my red crepe evening dress and left it in some fraternity boy's room, and could not only not remember which guy, but which fraternity . . ." She laughed a tiny shrill laugh at what she'd just said.

Rose watched her through wet eyes, seeing all the bravado and savvy of Hollywood honcho stripped away leaving Ellen Feinberg, the girl whose room had been next door to hers in the dorm. The girl who got the munchies before she smoked the dope. The funny, vulnerable way she was before the divorce and single-motherhood and before she dated or made a deal with what she liked to call "every asshole in Hollywood," and became so toughened up by it all.

"I want you to know I'll always keep the promise I made to you at Joey's adoption ceremony when I said I'd help to be responsible for his welfare forever," Ellen said. "And I had a little boy once, and he turned out damn good, so you know I know what to do," and then the runaway emotion made her have to turn from the bed and lean on Rose. Her thick auburn hair covered her face as she held Rose tightly and trembled but couldn't say a word.

After a little while she moved to a chair, and Rose walked to the bed and put her hand on Jan's arm, above the plastic hospital bracelet. The IV tubes had been removed too, and she was able to take Jan's slender hand in her own. "Janny, the other day Julie and Marly talked on the phone for a long, serious time, and they came to the conclusion that because of Julie's life being up in the air at the moment, and because Marly and Billy are going back together, that Joey would be better off living with Marly and Billy. Ellen and I think so, too. Marly jokes that she's semiretired anyway so she'll have a lot of time to devote to him, and she loves him and the twins do, too."

"We all thought that would be okay with you, and Julie said she'll come out and visit and be with him as often as she can," Ellen lied, moving back to the bed.

Both of them looked up when they heard the sound of the pocket door sliding open and waved a little wave to Marly. Each of them choked back the kick of emotion they felt when they saw that she was holding Joey. It had been one thing to plan his visit to say good-bye to his mother. To talk about the theories of whether or not it was good for him. But another to see him there, her love, her life, this angelic child who had already suffered so much. His blond hair was askew and his big blue eyes were wide as he looked down at the bed, and then buried his face in Marly's shoulder.

Last night, when they discussed the idea of his coming to the hospital, Ellen had voted against it, afraid it would traumatize the little boy forever. Rose, who at age seven had kissed her own mother good-bye in the coffin, insisted on it. Marly thought the child needed this moment because the last time he saw Jan she was being taken away bleeding into an ambulance. So she called a child psychologist who specialized in children and death. "With adequate preparation and the right to say no to the visit at any point, I think it's essential for him," the doctor told her.

Now Marly rubbed his back and held him tightly. The others could see that Maria was behind Marly, and Joey was looking out the door at her.

Marly spoke softly to the child. "Remember when I told you that Mommy won't be able to talk to you, but she can hear you?" After a moment his little head nodded in her neck. "And remember we talked about how you're allowed to touch her, though she can't touch you back?" He nodded again. "So before she goes away, maybe we can go over to the bed together and say good-bye. But only if you want to do that. It's okay if you don't. If you say you don't want to do that, Maria is standing right there and she can take you for a walk, or back to play with Jennifer and Sarah. And honey, it really is okay with all of us and with Mommy if you don't want to get any closer."

There was an eternity of silence while they waited for the little boy's reply. This brief window of time that the doctor warned them might be a matter of just a few hours was the only moment when this could take place. The frightening, noisy respirator was gone, there was no jumble of wires from hanging IV tubes, just Jan going quietly to her rest. And if the nurses' theories were true, Jan was able to hear their words.

Joey turned slowly back to look at the bed, then wiggled his way out of Marly's arms and stood on the floor, his little face just about level with the hospital bed. Slowly he walked nearer to the bed to look more closely at his dying mother. He was so tiny that the shorts he wore were wide around his skinny little legs. His T-shirt said LITTLE SLUGGER across the front. Rose and Ellen had their arms around one another's waists. Marly moved with him, and Maria stepped into the room, bowing her head sadly when she saw Jan.

He took another step, and then another, never taking his eyes from Jan, until his body leaned against the metal rail of the bed. After a minute he lifted his arm, touched Jan's hand and patted it gently and consolingly, the way the others had seen him reassure her before. His soft dimpled little-boy fingers touching her repeatedly the way he would a baby animal as he said, "It's okay, Mommy. It's okay."

Then he moved from the bed, walked to the doorway, and threw his arms around the legs of Maria, who walked him out into the hall. She was going to take him back to Marly's, and the friends would stay at the hospital with Jan.

They stood by the bed for a long, silent time.

"Aren't you glad you didn't get a face-lift?" Marly asked Jan. "How in the hell would you have explained that to St. Peter?"

Ellen shook her head and both she and Rose smiled at the black humor that had carried them through everything.

"Janny," Rose said softly, "make sure to find Allan and tell him how much I miss him, and love him and dream about him all the time." Her eyes stung with tears.

Marly leaned in and put her arms around the blanket to hug Jan's body. "Janny O'Malley, we love you so. And there will never be a Girls' Night that isn't dedicated to your memory," she said. "We're so grateful for the years we had you with us."

They stayed by the bed talking to her and one another for nearly an hour, often erupting with sentimental laughter. But soon the room got very quiet when they knew that the time had come, and that Jan's beautiful spirit was gone. And just before they left the room, Marly stopped them and turned back for one last thought. "I think I can safely speak for all of us, Janny, when I say to you, wherever you are, thanks a million, Maximilian."